THE LOST ONES

THE LOST ONES

A NOVEL

Frédérick Tristan

TRANSLATED BY ABBY POLLACK

WILLIAM MORROW AND COMPANY, INC.

New York

This is a work of fiction. The characters and situations portrayed are imaginary.

Copyright © 1983 by Balland

First published in France in 1983 as *Les égarés* by Balland

It is the policy of William Morrow and Company, Inc., and its imprints and affiliates, recognizing the importance of preserving what has been written, to print the books we publish on acid-free paper, and we exert our best efforts to that end.

Library of Congress Cataloging-in-Publication Data

Tristan, Frédérick.
  [Egarés. English]
  The lost ones : a novel / Frédérick Tristan ; translated by Abby
Pollack.
    p.   cm.
  ISBN 0-688-02336-3
  I. Title.
PQ2639.R572E313   1991
843'.912—dc20
                                                    90-25186
                                                    CIP

Printed in the United States of America

First U.S. Edition

1 2 3 4 5 6 7 8 9 10

BOOK DESIGN BY BRIAN MOLLOY CIRCA 80, INC.

to
Jean-Marie

"He walked on the path and looked at the ground soaked with the blood of victims that were strewn all around. He stared at the footsteps of infants and children who were leaving for captivity. He bent down and kissed these footsteps. Then he rejoined the prisoners and embraced them. He wept before them and they before him. He said, "My brothers, my people, all this has happened because you did not listen to my words."

PESIQTA RABBATI XXVI

IT WOULD DOUBTLESS BE APPROPRIATE for me to tell a story of my own creation, but I don't feel like it. Or rather I feel helpless in light of all the stories that enter my mind, as if a sentence of meaningless had been passed upon them in advance. I've written a good many of those things called novels, and I repudiate none of them, but the time has come to step back and put some distance between me and the imaginary, to confine myself to the real circumstances of my life and thus bring a bit of order to them.

The fact remains that if my work has had the good fortune to acquire a certain notoriety, its author has remained a mystery, even to the literati. You see, I was clever enough—if indeed it was cleverness—to have devised a singular maneuver that allowed me to keep my identity secret. Indeed, my plan was so successful that I have reached maturity as a combination of two ordinarily contradictory conditions: notoriety and anonymity. The real Gilbert Keith Chesterfield is famous, although no one has ever seen him.

I can well imagine your outrage, those of you who have reached this point in my revelations. Has the chap gone mad? you ask. Have we not seen him a hundred times at conferences, colloquia, cocktail parties? Has he not been received by His Majesty? Was it not he we all saw in Stockholm in that superb white tie and tails, accepting the Nobel Prize

from the hands of Gustav V? Have there not been millions of photographs of the author of *Beelzebub* and *The Monkey King* in newspapers,
magazines, movies, and—yes, why not—on posters?

Well, my dear and admirable public, it is time to tell the truth, not
so much to appease my conscience as out of an appreciation of the comic,
an appreciation the innumerable practical jokers in our venerable Albion will fully enjoy: He who called himself Gilbert K. Chesterfield, who
made such appropriate appearances at all those conferences and colloquia and cocktail parties, who bowed before His Royal Highness, who
spoke so movingly of his gratitude before that learned Swedish assembly, and whose photograph decorated, and continues to decorate, the
most diverse national and international publications, this man is actually Jonathan Absalom Varlet, who has never written a single line of
my works. And that's a fact.

I would point out, moreover, that neither is my name Gilbert K. Chesterfield, but Cyril N. Pumpermaker. Two precautions are worth more
than one; it's called multiplying the obstacles. I was more easily able to
give substance to the fictitious Chesterfield via the intervention of that
prodigious actor, the inestimable Varlet, who had no trouble at all assuming the role I suggested to him since, strictly speaking, he had no
identity to begin with.

Oh, how well I know the extent to which this revelation will have
disappointed some of you! What nonsense has that fool Chesterfield not
already invented to attract attention, and now he's claiming to have
concocted a fictional style with the moth-eaten characteristics of a barely
credible verisimilitude? Surely he would have done better to keep on
telling us those adult fairy tales he has so generously produced every
other year? Nay, my princelings, for sooner or later, my pretty little
drama had to cease. Varlet has left us forever. And that's the truth.

So, *fini* Varlet. *Fini* the Chesterfield you knew. Comedy or no, here I
am, compelled to tell the truth or to disappear myself. But while I choose
sincerity, there you are, all at sixes and sevens! It doesn't matter. This
new book is not a work of the imagination, but rather a stroll through
the duplicity that enabled me to write undercover while someone else
advertised himself throughout the world. For the purposes of this book,
however, I must accustom myself to behind-the-scenes revelations, to
permitting people to worm their way inside the linings, acts that I have
long found inappropriate, impudent, even vulgar. The magician may die
without disclosing his tricks, but I shall not!

I shall not because this is not simply a matter of a clever game. After all, one cannot send someone else into the flames without burning oneself. There was a curious distance—need I be explicit?—between the writer I created and my own writing. Was I trying to inspire that being in me who, for better or worse, remained Pumpermaker the shopkeeper, and from whom I was able to wring only the most insignificant stammerings, while his double, the elegant Chesterfield, plunged ahead so splendidly? Indubitably, we must credit Cyril Pumpermaker with the sneaky creation of Chesterfield first, then Varlet, and with the idea of using one in the study and the other in the drawing room. But that's a subtle distinction I shall have to clarify in the pages that follow. I did say in the beginning that I meant to bring some order to all this.

Though it's scarcely original, I am certain this split occurred during my childhood. I detested the name Pumpermaker. I knew it was a ridiculous name, and since in a manner of speaking I carried it about with me, I felt myself to be ridiculous. This was not, however, how my father felt. He was so proud of it that he inscribed it everywhere in pompous gold letters—on his office door (he was a solicitor), on personal articles like his datebook, his lighter, even the door of his car—the entire name, mind you, not just the customary initials. He was wholly and completely Pumpermaker, and when he introduced my mother, his most precious possession, he did so as "Madame" Pumpermaker. Likewise his son, his horse, even his dogs. All were products of the sublime "Maison Pumpermaker." In short, I did not like my father, although had he borne a different name I might perhaps have forgiven him his defects.

I shall not push masochism so far as to describe the suffering inflicted during my school years by this ludicrous name with its fake nobility, given the exquisite talent children have for mockery, pun, and torment. For me, it was an education in solitude, an education that reinforced my singularity and opened the door to my fantasies. Moreover, I loved games, but since I refused to play with just anyone, I simply invented partners who met my ludic requirements.

Chesterfield was born on the playground during my second year of middle school, when I was twelve, and immediately supplanted all the others. He shared my philosophical reveries. He was a brilliant thinker, far better qualified than I to rise to the summits of Milton or descend into the Shakespearean abyss. He flew with Blake's angels; he captained Arthur Gordon Pym's boat. He knew what I didn't, a convenient apologia for the snob that, detail by minute detail, I was becoming.

While I was at university, my mother and father drowned during a boating accident off the Isle of Wight. An only child, I inherited the agreeable fortune amassed by Pumpermaker, Esq., which allowed me, from that moment, to envisage a career as a writer, a career already begun in secret at Ruthford, our country home eighty miles from London. The residence had belonged to my mother, and as it hadn't been tainted with the despised patronymic, it was there that I pursued my studies, appearing in class only for examinations, and there that I slowly learned the art of writing.

My life at Ruthford verged on the sublime. Picture a young man of twenty-four, in love with fantasy and shadow, an amateur of rare and mysterious books, a young man of a reasonable nature and somewhat cynical intelligence—to compensate for my shyness—endowed with the buoyancy money seems to bestow in the eyes of others. Imagine this dreamer in a lovely Victorian country home complete with the old-fashioned comforts, the faded velvet, the polished wood, the fringes and pompons. Add to this picture an untutored garden sloping downhill to the river, where our romantic young man might wander as he liked, and you must acknowledge the presence of all the ingredients necessary to transform a pleasant abode into a magical kingdom, and an emergent Chesterfield into a sorcerer's apprentice halfway between Byron's Don Juan and a Shelleyan exaltation.

There were three servants at my disposal: the elderly Douglas, whose first name was Nelly but who belonged to Ruthford, having entered into service very young under my maternal grandparents, and thus had always been called, in the old-fashioned way, by her last name; a certain Register, jack of all trades, built like a woodcutter, more or less mute, who had attached himself to the estate like honeysuckle to an old wall, without anyone ever knowing how or why; and finally Somerset, Douglas's grandnephew, a tall boy of thirteen with a surly red-headed beauty, who lived discreetly in my shadow.

Following his grandaunt's suggestion, Somerset assumed the role of what had once been the valet. He waited table, drew the bath, made the bed, polished the boots, brushed the clothes, came and went according to my desires and needs, thus satisfying my taste for the aristocratic. Here at Ruthford, I found a discreet elegance, a light perfume, in other words quality, the quality of my mother, the delightful Mary Charmer. The solicitor had destroyed her, so proud was he to have tossed into his bed and imprisoned in his kitchens a wife from a finer world than his. I had sold his practice as well as the London apartment, and had kept none of his furniture, for each object seemed impregnated with the Pumpermaker idiom, an ugliness that strives for brilliance but that flaunts only bad taste.

Thus, under the influence of the Ruthford decor, not to mention the character of this father who had so roundly betrayed my deepest aspirations, Chesterfield began his first novel. He worked for several months in a sort of fever, like one engaged in public confession. I had just taken my degree in comparative literature and felt strong enough to allow the writer free rein. He fulfilled his task with the rigor of a surgeon, heedless of the extent to which his novel opened up singular perspectives within me.

I arose at nine o'clock. A sizable meal, prepared with devotion by Douglas, was brought by Somerset to my bedroom, which had once been my mother's. Afterward, I spent rather a long while at my toilet, not out of narcissism, but because the lavatory seemed to me the best place for the transformation from Pumpermaker to Chesterfield. I officiated at this metamorphosis like an actor in his dressing room putting on a wig and a false nose. Only here the mask was more subtle. It was necessary, in short, to erase all traits that had belonged in any way to my father's face. And I was quite successful; in fact, I should have to say that with the passage of time, all resemblance to that man vanished completely.

My toilet accomplished, I took up my cane and went out to promenade my nobility about the garden. My behavior was naïve and fatuous, to be sure, but necessary if I was to raise Chesterfield to the heights I wished him to occupy: a literary giant, no more, no less. A Shakespeare, a Dante, a Goethe. And why not? You may not like it, but at twenty I found them better masters than more recently anointed poets. And so, breathing in the air, caressing the trees, studying the reflections in the water, I prepared the author for his sovereign task, prepared him so well that after a half hour's walk, it was Chesterfield himself who returned to the house, hung his coat on the peg in the hallway, crossed the main drawing room, and sat down at his desk in the small study with the Chinese curtains.

In this manner was born my novel *Beelzebub*, whose title reflects clearly enough the sort of romanticism I have described. The main male character, Alexander, was, in fact, a mélange of those very pretentions I scorned in my father, and of those Faustian attitudes dear to the late nineteenth century, so much so that the novel would certainly not have been worth anything at all had not the affection that, beyond her death,

I felt for my mother infused the story. To keep her journal, Chesterfield had lent her his pen, and it was she herself, the dear soul I called Elsbeth, who recounted her suffering in a long threnody broken by flashes of lightning, who recounted the torment of loving passionately someone who was not worthy of that love.

The Elsbeth of the novel is the shadow of Mary Charmer, whom I still refuse to call by my father's name; and of course Beelzebub-Alexander, ferocious in his politics and his colorlessness, is none other than the solicitor decked out in a wisp of mystery. Here, however, Chesterfield was more indulgent than I should have been. I accused this man of having drowned my mother in the shipwreck off Wight, which is why, at the end of the novel, Elsbeth murders Alexander, her husband, as a kind of revenge. Yet she brings to it an immense tenderness, proof of my alter ego's budding talent, a talent I could not control so fierce was my rage.

It was now 1930 and, my manuscript completed, I abruptly found myself at loose ends. Doubtless, there were many publishers in the capital, but I had no idea how to proceed, how to inform them of my masterpiece. When I went to London, which I often did by train, I had the habit of dropping into a small bar near Euston Station where I ran no risk of compromising my solitude. Need I say how frightful I find those taverns where all one hears is the abusive grumbling of faceless drunkards? In the Three Salts, I rarely saw anyone at all, and could await my train while perusing one of the books I'd bought earlier at Spencer's.

On that particular day—it was during the month of May—I had unearthed a beautiful edition of *Le Songe de Poliphile,* a reproduction of the original French translation of Colonna by Béroalde de Verville whose style and engravings had completely seduced me. As I found the Cartesian idiom rather difficult, I was concentrating intently, when I was startled by a burst of laughter close by. One of my former colleagues perhaps, delighted to have run into "dear Pumpermaker"? I buried my nose in my book.

"I'd say you've entered a curious labyrinth!" exclaimed a childlike and rather precious voice.

I looked up and saw before me a tall thin smiling young man all in black. He was about my age but seemed to bear his years more easily. The severity of his elegance was interrupted by a red carnation in his lapel; the pale face, the dark-blue eyes, the wavy blond hair falling onto his forehead and, charmingly, the back of his neck bespoke "gentry."

He sat down at the table next to mine.

"Few Englishmen take the trouble to try Colonna. One would think that for dear old England, Italy, by which I mean the Renaissance, simply never existed. Curious, isn't it?"

I was a bit taken aback by the mixture of casualness and gentility, and as I remained speechless, he went on.

"This city gets on my nerves. Big Ben's always on time. Wouldn't it be nice to stir up the anthill? That's what the good Abbot did, Polia's friend, her lover actually, while Rome got bogged down in doctrines that scarcely concealed its lack of piety and, in a manner of speaking, its exhaustion. Wouldn't you agree?"

He stood up suddenly and seemed embarrassed. "But here I am rattling on and I haven't even had the courtesy to introduce myself! Jonathan Absalom Varlet, your servant . . ."

I rose.

"Gilbert Keith Chesterfield," I replied, immediately. It was the first time I had used the name in public.

"In fact, Italy went under shortly afterward," the young man continued, sitting down again, "passing the baton to Germany, which foundered in turn, and so on. . . . Bit by bit, the entire Western world began to founder, like an old ship, while it waited for the Orient. . . . Not terribly gay, is it? But then," he laughed, "I see no reason why it should be!"

Whence comes the seductiveness of certain human beings? From their beauty, their discourse, their gestures, a certain gleam in their eyes? Varlet was not exceptionally handsome, but he had an indefinable sort of grace that, along with the acrobatic speech, the gestures, and the blue eyes, rendered him absolutely irresistible. What made him even more charming was the fact that he seemed unaware of it.

"Are you a literature student?" I asked.

He made a face. "I have neither name nor profession, a man ripe for the plucking by whoever wants me." He spoke so easily and naturally. "Does that surprise you? I'm twenty-four years old and my only family are my books. In this mercantile world, what can I hope for? To write, perhaps? But whatever for? In any case, I don't like to write. My vice is reading. Everything else is literature!" He burst out laughing again, his childish cheeks reddening, and despite the fact that only a few moments ago I had not known he existed, I could not help admiring him.

If I look closely at the emotion that took hold of me so suddenly that

May afternoon in 1930 at the Three Salts, I can find several explanations. My solitude had begun to weigh upon me, my intellectual solitude in particular. Varlet's language and behavior betrayed the flavor of freedom, something like an ocean breeze, which could only exhilarate the orphaned shut-in. Yet it was that freedom which, on this first occasion, prompted me to cut our conversation short. I felt the edge of an abyss, overcome with vertigo. On the pretext that my train was due, I fled.

In the days that followed, I thought often of this young man. I was wrong to have aborted the conversation, and I berated myself for the timidity that prevented my knowing him better. Time passed, however, and two months later, while the countryside baked in a heat wave, I decided to go to the seaside in search of cooler climes. At least that's what I told myself. The truth was that with *Beelzebub* finished and languishing in a drawer, and with no plans to begin another novel until the first had found a buyer, I was bored. I left Ruthford in early July with two suitcases and made for Cornwall, or more precisely Glendurgan.

I don't know if you are familiar with this watering place, which appealed to me because it was no longer fashionable and thus rarely visited. Not far from Falmouth, on a claw of land digging into the ocean, Glendurgan had once been famous for its semitropical garden, its camellias, its agaves, and a sort of banyan tree a gentleman in khaki gaiters had brought back from Australia—precisely the sort of items we English love, for they seem to transform our little island into an ark that might hold all manner of species culled from the entire world—mineral, vegetable, animal, and human—something rather like a museum, or the dream of encyclopedists at the moment the millennium returns to scythe and millstone.

But back to Glendurgan. My maternal grandmother took her holidays there around the turn of the century, prosperous times for those resorts that claimed to be more or less therapeutic, where an entire society gathered to spend the winter among themselves in a world somewhat more austere than exciting, since most of them were Hampshire horse-breeders. Thus, by choosing Glendurgan, a place I'd never been, I was, in a manner of speaking, renewing a family tradition that the "Pumper-maker Betrayal" had chosen to ignore, preferring the teeming Channel beaches to the touching old-fashioned elegance of the western coast.

In a drawing-room drawer at Ruthford, I had come upon a yellowed photograph depicting a structure of the most noble proportions, a perfect image of the era when British hostelry had prided itself on its mastery of the most sacred and venerable of all arts—that of reception. Written with Victorian flourishes at the bottom of the photograph are the words *Rosemullion Hotel*, a sumptuous name that confirmed me in my decision. Yet when I arrived in Glendurgan and descended from the train with my two suitcases and a rather naïve measure of curiosity, I found a fishing port with small white one-story houses lined up all in a row along the quay, tidy little boats, and sailors with shiny-visored caps—in short, an entire community of villagers sparkling like fresh fish, the very opposite of the fusty elegant phantoms I had imagined. As for the Rosemullion Hotel, whose name derived from the spit of land that jutted out into Falmouth Bay just north of Mawgan, it was now a haven for traveling salesmen and dubious couples, a far cry from the palace I'd dreamed of!

Thus do great adventures begin—in disillusionment, boredom, and gloom. Must one always pass through a dark place and rot a bit before encountering the open sea? Since it was late when the car brought me from the station and abandoned me on the doorstep of this remnant of a hotel, I went inside; despite my repugnance I could not help appreciating the humor of the situation. To reach my bedroom, I had to negotiate a series of hallways hung with mildewed tapestries, and once there, I felt like a condemned man huddling in a lugubrious corner of his cell. The servant who led the way through this purgatory, a woman of indeterminate age, had holes large as English pennies in her stockings and ancient bedroom slippers of the most amazing shade of purple.

Vowing to make my escape the very next morning, I left my suitcases packed and followed my witch, not quite worthy of *Macbeth*, into what had once been the dining room but now served, judging by the platform, the large cash register, the microphones, and the stacks of green folding chairs, as dance hall, storage room, and, only accidentally, refectory, to use the most accurate word.

The windows must rarely have been opened, for the room was exceedingly damp, and with the dim light the high stucco-decorated walls resembled nothing so much as a murky green aquarium. All manner of objects hung about me, posters advertising liqueurs, photos of sports clubs, calendars featuring aggressive females—the sort of nonsense one finds at county fairs.

I marveled that thirty years ago, an entire society in evening clothes had sat at little tables lit by candles and crystal, sampling sweets and cakes, pinky fingers raised, and I could not help smiling at the incongruities of time that so completely reduced such pretentions to silence. After all, why had the horse-breeders come to these places created solely as showcases for themselves, if not to validate their success? So they weren't just peasants, were they! They ate the same toast and marmalade as financiers from the City, the tea served them in Japanese cups bore Her Majesty's name, and the exotic garden where they posed for photographs contained all the treasures of the Commonwealth!

The page had turned, however, and where once there had been violins, the saxophone now wailed. Sailors drained their mugs of thick dark beer where beautiful people had once raised glasses of French champagne, and where the mother of the sweet Mary Charmer had moved with that equivocal Pre-Raphaelite grace, loose hearty girls now pranced about. And I, last scion of plume and feather, ate my dried herring at a corner table covered with a paper cloth. *Sic transit gloria mundi.* After a brief depression, I nonetheless began rather to enjoy myself.

It was during dessert that the event occurred, a racket, a din, a jostling, and some oaths from the hallway. I looked up from my plate and in the half-light saw a tall young man in white, escorted by a swarm of irate little people with their fists raised. The young man towered over them, not only in size but in spirit, for while they shouted he merely smiled, a trifle maliciously, and repeated with studied constancy, "There, there, my good sirs! That is not the issue. That is not the issue at all!"— words that rendered his beraters even more hysterical.

The voice was vaguely familiar. For an instant, I thought it had come from me, from some depth of my being, a thought so troubling I wondered if I wasn't looking at my own reflection in a mirror. Then, as the group came nearer, the face of the young man in white emerged from the gloom and Jonathan Absalom Varlet stood before me once again. He saw me and stopped. Caught off guard, the others lurched to a simultaneous halt.

"Aha!" he exclaimed. "My old chum! I must beg this vociferous crowd not to spoil my happiness! And what might you be doing here, O Lover of Polia, eating cakes of sawdust and anchovy?"

He looked splendid—slender, blond, refined, amusing. His blue eyes laughed, his lips laughed, his entire body laughed at the spectacle he had created. The angry mob looked at him now with such comical confusion that I drew closer and, aping his aplomb, addressed the village players myself.

"What is this riotous mob that pursues you, Monseigneur? Have you restored such luster to this sleeping court that they wish to punish you for having awakened them?"

The good people looked at one another and shook their heads, which only intensified our amusement. Seeing our laughter, one of them exclaimed, "Do you know this man?" in a voice that clearly meant "this ghastly individual."

"Certainly," I replied. "I've known him a very long time. This gentleman is more or less a friend of the family. . . ."

The interrogator, none other than the prorietor of the establishment, frowned. God, or the devil, knew whether or not *this* peculiar fellow might not be worse than the first!

"Gilbert Keith Chesterfield, my dear innkeeper," I reassured him, in my most sonorous voice. He took a step backward.

In a perfectly normal voice, Varlet explained.

"In truth, I am culpable vis-à-vis these gentlemen and it is only natural they be angry with me. Here I am, a resident for the past month, and not one penny have I paid. My money has been delayed. Yet I must stay somewhere, mustn't I?"

I was profoundly happy. I had found the young man who had so fascinated me at the Three Salts and I was about to earn his everlasting gratitude.

"Innkeeper," I began haughtily, "I shall vouch for my excellent friend. Be so kind as to add his bill to mine, and to allay your anxieties, allow me to offer you an advance which will permit you to drink to our good health!" I took a couple of guineas from my wallet, handed them to the proprietor, and invited Varlet to join me, which he promptly did. The little band of villagers elbowed one another, laughed, and grew quite merry.

"Thank you, sir," Varlet said. "Without you, my creditors might have resorted to violence! You must pardon me this foolish spectacle. But what could I do? Away from my books, I am singularly incapacitated. . . . I'm afraid I simply cannot be without them! But public libraries are such cemeteries I cannot bear to enter them. Yet with what am I to buy books, I who have no money, no resources, no profession? But never fear, sir, I shall repay you a thousandfold. As a self-styled genealogical researcher whose degrees seem quite sufficient for my bourgeois clientele, I am able to pursue my work in private libraries by promising to find the owners of these little jewels some sort of royal ancestry to enhance their coats of arms. Everyone wants to be a nobleman. Everyone claims to be the son of kings, the cousin of emperors, the nephew of archbishops. The less one actually is, the more one wishes to be. And while I search the family archives for something which so obviously cannot be found, I earn sufficient funds to purchase my books. They are my vice, my addiction. Unfortunately, the elderly Glendurgan baronet whom I had promised a lovely ancestor in the form of a Knight Templar refuses to unzip his purse until I've found some vestige or other in his cellar, where the rats have already eaten everything!"

"A curious occupation," I replied. "In this century, that is. Are there still people gullible enough to believe this nonsense?"

"England has such a passion for royalty," Varlet replied, "that she would disguise herself as a lap dog if it would make her look like Her Majesty's pug! I doubt there's a single Englishman who does not belong to a club, or a brotherhood, or a more or less secret society that gives him the right to sport a coat of arms on his tie. Everyone considers himself an aristocrat. Or at least the son of a gentleman. That's one of the things that keeps this island anchored to the ocean floor. Without it, I'm quite sure she would float off to America."

I could not help but admire his nonchalant self-confidence, which, combined with his elegance, conferred upon his discourse the indisputable flavor of verisimilitude.

An admirable actor, I thought. *Is there really a Glendurgan baronet? Yet here he is making brilliant speeches about our foibles, while all the time he may be quite hungry!* I remember the odd phrase he'd uttered during our first encounter, in which he'd claimed to have "neither name nor profession, a man ripe for the plucking by whoever wants me."

"Forgive me," I said awkwardly, "but since here we are once again in the most improbable of circumstances, might it not be possible to see in this meeting certain omens favorable to our friendship?"

He studied me with some surprise, then leaned back in his chair. "My dear Mr. Chesterfield," he began, "I'm not certain I'm someone of whom one might make a friend. A walk-on, perhaps, but a friend? In any case, you yourself sense the extent to which our meeting partakes of a logic that in no way resembles what the ignorant call chance. Thus, I heartily advise you to beware. The long arm of intrigue, you know . . ."

"So, here at the ends of the earth and, why not, even the end of time, the good Faustus is visited by the Bad Angel! Amusing, no? I came here to get away from something or to find someone, I've no idea what or whom, and it seems to me that your ghostly apparition might at least have the decency not to distract me, but on the contrary, to interest me. As for intrigue, the trapdoor shut a long time ago."

"Excellent!" exclaimed Varlet. "Let's go a step further. Tell me, what sort of friendship is there that can withstand love?"

I was surprised, and asked him to explain himself.

"My dear fellow traveler, although we both have limited experience with the feelings which move human beings, we are nonetheless not unaware that friendship and love do not belong to the same order of things. Friendship is a reasonable exchange, while love is unreasonable warfare. The most fraternal friendship is, thus, always disrupted by love."

"Possibly," I said cautiously. "But why invoke love when we envision only friendship?"

His blue eyes stared into mine. I looked away.

"Because disruption is so interesting. You're not one of those pullulating Bank of England tea-drinkers with vapid minds, well-stuffed paunches, and yellow teeth, are you?"

So he's a socialist! I thought, but as if he'd read my mind, he exclaimed, "And whatever you do, don't think for a minute that I'm in favor of cultural revolution! Culture, after all, is merely a commodity. As for politics, that toothless sister of ambition, what good is it, given the fact that the most banal of Hölderlin's poems is more destructive than a cannon? Believe me, friendship is an illusion, a sort of lukewarm basin of water in which to soak one's feet. Only love can claim to smash dikes and push the water from the rivers back into the sea! Everything else is comfort, alibi, speculation—the distressing work of the poor and industrious."

Did I understand what he was suggesting? I'm not sure. He fascinated me by his lyricism and the power of his imagery; clearly he didn't care whether I was sufficiently lucid to grasp his meaning.

"Forgive me," I replied, sidestepping the issue, "but here we sit discussing general principles without knowing in the least who we are! To begin with, would you care to have a drink with me? In honor of the Rosemullion, perhaps?"

"A fine idea!" he exclaimed. "And we'll add a nice roast, if the cook in this excellent house has not yet gone to bed!"

He leaped up nimbly, went to the door, and called into the hallway, but it was useless to insist. No one replied.

"Let's take ourselves to the kitchen," Varlet decided. Which we promptly did. He knew the way perfectly, plunging into the labyrinth

with the ease of a ghost in a Scottish castle. The kitchen, which in by-
gone times had created banquets worthy of princes, was now an immense and funereal cavern, heaped with ancient cookware that made it
look more like an abandoned forge than a sanctuary of fine sauces. Tom
Jones himself would have refused to eat here. Gray dust covered the pots
and pans on the walls, draped with spider webs from the chandeliers.
The air of abandonment was even more poignant here than in the dining
room, for it seemed as if the very heart of the hotel had been extin-
guished and that even the memory of long-ago splendors had been thrown
out like a rotten fruit.

In a corner lit by one dim and naked bulb, a hot plate fueled by
alcohol served as a stove, a fact that clearly accounted for the paucity
of the menu. In the twinkling of an eye, Varlet lit it and began fixing us
some fried ham and eggs, shamelessly commandeering the few condi-
ments in the rustic icebox. His dexterity bordered on the magical; one
would have thought he'd never done anything else in his life.

"Dear Mr. Chesterfield," he resumed, the cooking completed, "the air
at Cornwall is highly recommended for rheumatism. Do you suffer from
rheumatism? From gout, perhaps? Ah, no. You are irremediably healthy!
Like everyone else, you are in perfect health. And yet, take note. The
kitchens of the worldly palace lie fallow. Only a tiny hot plate capable
of frying two eggs. Isn't that amazing? Watching the death throes of an
empire? To be madly in love while the house falls to pieces? What would
you call it—egocentricity? Decadence? Cruelty?"

He placed the eggs on our plates, opened a bottle of beer, and invited
me to sit down, as if he were in his own kitchen. I took my courage in
both hands.

"Who are you really, Mr. Varlet?" I asked.

For a moment, he froze, fork in the air. Then he seemed to think for
a moment, and nodded his head.

"No one, Mr. Chesterfield. And do not imagine that that is a figure of
speech. No father, no mother, no name. I was raised by the good graces
of His Majesty. Fatted in an orphanage. As for my pseudonym, I have
no idea who gave it to me, although I should wager my christener is
wandering somewhere in the byways of our destructive Anglican culture,
which so enjoys transforming royal hymns into canticles and sons from
nowhere into Jonathan Absalom Varlets. They should have chosen Nemo,
not Varlet. As a result, given this infamous name, I decided to become
a servant, to attach myself to whatever masters fate consented to give

me. Fate was good to me. I met a lord who took me in and treated me like a son."

He paused to refill our glasses.

"This man made me what I am," he continued. "His library was my true cradle. I had the privilege of a tutor, of the university! A miracle, no? And then my lord died, and his heirs, as expected, kicked me out. But let us not pursue the subject."

A shadow crossed his brow, and he shook himself like a puppy.

"They were nothing but parasites. They sniffed around my lord like a pack of wild beasts, making all sorts of noises about our relationship, as if that generous man were incapable of loving me other than for my pretty face! He'd lost his wife and he wanted a son, so he chose one. Wasn't he entitled?"

"Of course," I hastened to reply, "but didn't your benefactor think to make you his heir?"

"He did," said Varlet, "and to such a point that I would have been taken care of for the rest of my days, had not the other heirs, the nephews and cousins, succeeded in breaking the will on the pretext that I had seduced their relative, led him astray, and that he clearly hadn't been in his right mind! Of course, I might have contested, but my pride won out. I'd had the best of him. And, after all, they owed me nothing, those people."

His confession moved me. It explained both the aristocratic manner and the rebelliousness of this young man who had, by a simple turn of fate, appeared so strangely in my path, I who since childhood had also struggled with my identity. I grew bolder.

"My dear Jonathan . . . if I may call you that," I said, "your story makes me think of my own childhood, for if I had a father and a mother, I nonetheless despised the former for having debased the latter, despised him so thoroughly that I was never able to have a real conversation with either. Surely it is better never to have known one's parents at all if their only role was that of progenitor. But so it was and since both were drowned, I have at least inherited their fortune, having had no wild beasts to challenge me. In which I have a certain advantage over your situation!"

He stood up to uncork another bottle of beer. At that time of night, the hotel lay silent, the only sound the rustle of the trees in the wind. What were we both seeking in that lifeless place? He poured, then lifted his glass.

"My lord adored Italy. I traveled with him to Venice, to Florence, to Siena . . . which is why I was so startled when I saw you reading *Le Songe de Poliphile.* Who in England has read the *Hypnerotomachia?* And then you fled, pretexting your train, I believe? Without my elderly baronet and his Templarian folly, I should never have expected to find this backwater!"

"And without the summer ennui Ruthford imposes, or the yellowed photograph which deceived me as to the charm of this noble hotel, I would surely never have thought of visiting Cornwall. I've just finished writing a book, you see, a sort of novel, and once it was edited, typed, bound, and on the shelf, I'd no idea what to do. . . ."

"You're a writer?" Varlet exclaimed, leaning toward me.

"Oh," I stammered, "can one call oneself that when all I've done is write a few pages which, one way or another, make a sort of story I dare not even submit to a publisher!"

"To write and not publish makes no sense! It's like getting a girl into bed and not making love to her! So you write . . . you must tell me about it. In fact, I'm sure you've brought the manuscript with you, so you can read it to me!"

There was such childlike ardor in his request that I was loath to disappoint him, but *Beelzebub* lay in a drawer at Ruthford.

"Then we'll go to Ruthford!" he exclaimed. "I shall desert my baronet and we'll catch the train!"

His haste surprised me for a moment, but then a great flood of happiness made me blush.

"Dear Jonathan," I replied, "Ruthford is not a lord's palace and my literature will surely seem simple-minded to you. I cannot bring myself to obligate you in that way."

He laughed heartily.

"Such a roundabout way to invite your old family friend! No, truly, these old Templars bore me. And the hotel gets on my nerves. For once, I've got hold of a writer, and I mean to keep him!" He paused. "And just where is this Ruthford?"

I told him that the Charmer family residence was not far from Birmingham, about two miles from Warwick, and that a long day's train trip would be necessary to get to the home I'd left just yesterday! He seemed satisfied. It was two in the morning when we bade each other good night.

IF I'VE LINGERED SOMEWHAT OVER MY second, and decisive, encounter with Jonathan, it's because you must understand its various twists and turns. Of course, our enthusiasm can be partly explained by our youth; we were twenty-four and had little respect for convention. We seduced each other, as is common with intellectuals who have survived adolescence and reached that time of life when it seems as if the transformation of the entire world is waiting only on their appearance. In addition, although Varlet was infinitely more social than I, who was not at all, we shared the same love of reading, meaning the love of solitude inhabited by imagination and sensibility. What we had in common was those things that differentiated us from others.

Our return to Ruthford was most pleasant. It would be too difficult to reconstruct the details of our conversation, but I must describe the general outlines insofar as they resulted in the cementing of our friendship. First, as I've mentioned once before, I enjoyed Jonathan's aristocratic attitudes as well as the rather theatrical and casual way in which he laughed at himself. I also suspected his involvement in a significant inner combat, whose content and seriousness I could not yet divine, but whose quality I was certain of. A connoisseur of books as uncommon as Colonna's could not possibly house mediocre drama in his soul.

One topic of conversation, on the train between Plymouth and London, was the struggle between Jacob and the angel, and the lameness that came of it. In my opinion, Jacob was struggling with himself, the angel being the perfection he strove to attain, the limp a symbol of his imperfect success. Varlet, however, saw Jacob as struggling against God, the angel being a divine emanation who, seeing the next morning that neither one had been victorious, left his mark in the form of a limp, the symbol of alliance. Similarly Vulcan, whose role was to conjoin (hence the forge and alloyed metals), was himself fettered, symbolized by his lameness.

"No one can bind who is not himself bound," Jonathan exclaimed, loudly enough to turn heads in our compartment, surprised that two such young men should be evoking biblical episodes in a train.

"I made a pact with myself once," Jonathan said. "I swore never to let the angel get away."

"Are you so certain to have met him already?"

"Quite certain. We struggle. How we struggle! I feel his breath and his feathers. I hear him panting. If I were ever to write, God help us, I would keep a journal. No everyday facts, mind you, but a journal of the invisible. Each day, I'd write down the phases of the struggle. Except that if I wrote, the angel would most certainly take off! Adieu, my angel! That's why I'm so careful."

I must admit that my religious education had been rather spotty. The solicitor could not have cared less about God or angels. As for little Mary Charmer, perhaps she thought about them sometimes, which may have accounted for the periodic brightening of her pious face. Listening to Jonathan describe the winged flock was tantamount, for me, to poetry; I saw his interior struggle as a metaphor, even though, inadvertently, I myself was beginning to see, in the shadow of the rails, a parade of the most improbable creatures singing hosannas!

In short, Jacob and his angel pursued me for the duration of the trip, so much so that when we arrived at Warwick Station, having changed trains in London, I actually began to limp. I'd probably twisted my ankle hauling down my suitcases on the platform at Euston, but this small circumstance, added to the others, weighed on my imagination. Was I Jacob leading the angel to Ruthford, or was the angel leading me?

"Signs," declared Varlet. "Did not my lord claim that two days be-

fore meeting me he dreamed he was teaching an illiterate servant
to read?"

I had never believed such things before, but Jonathan spoke with such
easy assurance. . . . And then too, there was a return to childhood involved. The route from Warwick to Ruthford was strewn with memories
left there by little Cyril N. Pumpermaker. In the cab taking us home, I
pointed out the stream I'd fallen into, the oak tree I'd climbed, the pond
where I'd searched for salamanders that I'd collected in a glass jar, the
field where I'd ridden good Douglas's donkey. Not to mention Hangman's Tower, which I never dared enter for fear of running into the
ghost of Smyth, the miller, who'd committed suicide out of love for the
beautiful Londoner he'd once seen on the road from Stratford.

"Marvelous!" Jonathan cried, with such enthusiasm that the anxious
driver turned around to stare. "That's exactly what I meant by the ful-
gurating power of love. It's Paul on the road to Damascus in Baldung
Grien's engraving. Lightning pierces the cloud and strikes him, full force.
He falls from his horse, by which we understand a fall from the heights
of his certitude. And what a fall! The entire Western world fell
with him!"

That evening, I saw Ruthford through my guest's eyes. It was still
light when we arrived and pushed open the rusty gate to the grounds. I
had left the day before and yet it seemed as if I were returning from a
long voyage. Everything had changed. Had the banks of rhododendron
surreptitiously changed place, or had the beechwood copse decided to
move closer to the old tire pump, which seemed suddenly to have been
invaded by a mass of ivy? Had the stone bench, now covered with moss,
slipped behind the gazebo, and the headless statue of Diana been shocked
to find itself on the riverbank? The entire facade of the house itself was
covered with roses!

Somerset emerged from the kitchen and rushed to meet us, not a little upset.

"Mr. Cyril, what's happened! You've come home already? And with
a guest? Without letting us know? We must make up the blue room!
And dinner! Oh, Mr. Cyril, my goodness! I'll run and tell Douglas. . . ."
And he rushed off in the opposite direction, excited by the thought of
my return and in a dither about Jonathan, Ruthford's first guest in fifteen years.

"He's sort of my personal servant," I explained. "The affection of
those people is so deep and so naïve, it's very touching really, the more

so because it goes against all our intellectual habits. The greater the
naïveté, the more it gains in depth. Enough to give our doctors pause, I
should warrant!"

Varlet had stopped in the middle of the path. His black suit set off
the smooth face, at once radiant and grave, and the blond hair now
tinged with red by the setting sun.

"When I lived with my lord," he said, "I was just like that. I was
jealous of the dogs for loving him more than I. When he came home, I
wanted to throw myself at his feet, roll on the floor, shout for joy, wrig-
gle and jump and run around him, stare at him with lovesick eyes. Instead I stood there paralyzed, staring at the ground, overcome with
gratitude, unable to utter a word. I owed him everything."

He swallowed hard and shook his head.

"My dear Chesterfield," he said, abruptly changing the subject, "you've
inherited a marvelous countryside! How well you must write here!"

That evening, I began my reading of *Beelzebub*. We'd eaten dinner
late, in the dining room decorated with engravings of fox hunts, which
led us to speak of man's primitive instinct for tracking prey.

"Poor hunter!" Jonathan had exclaimed. "He thinks he's pursuing
his prey while really he's the one pursued."

I asked him to explain his paradox.

"Quite simple," he replied. "Would you look for me if you'd already
found me? He who goes out to conquer love is already wounded; love's
only desire is love. You must take care not to pick the wrong victim. Or
the wrong forest. Remember Actaeon. One look from Diana, a glance
like an arrow, and he's changed into the deer he's been pursuing and is
devoured by his faithful dogs!"

"Is Diana's glance not the same as the one that struck Paul on the
way to Damascus? The metamorphosis . . ."

"Probably. It's an unveiling, an uncovering, a kind of rape, nothing
cautious about it, really. Love is so brutal, so insane. Because Actaeon
violated a taboo, because he saw the secret in all its nakedness, he was
turned into a soul and devoured by faith. The stag is the emblem of the
soul, the dog of fidelity, of faith. While I was all alone in the immense
shadowy forest, unable to find the way out, searching to know the world,
I chanced upon this man, my lord. . . . Our eyes met. I had been lost;
I was found, saved. Without that look, that formidable appeal con-
densed to a flash every bit as fine and subtle as a needle, what would I
have become? A very bad boy, I should imagine."

We adjourned to the small drawing room, where Somerset brought the coffee and liqueurs with as much pomp as a liveried butler. Doubtless he wished to show our guest how distinguished the little house of Ruthford was, but was concentrating so hard that he tripped on the rug, spilled the Drambuie, and wound up taking to his heels, red as a beet.

"The modesty of love," Jonathan murmured. "The fear that paralyzes . . . How well I understand your young boy, and how I pity him! Does he at least know how to read?"

I reassured him that under the dragon-eye of his watchful aunt, Somerset went to school in Barford where he took all the first prizes, but that at the moment, he was still on holiday.

"On holiday," Varlet repeated. "Those were the times I really read. I read everything, and God knows my lord's library was well stocked! But tell me, Chesterfield, isn't this the moment to grab your devils by their horns and read me your novel?"

I had done little else but wait for this very moment, and now I was filled with embarrassment. What was this absurd book to which I'd given birth via some terrible disease of the spirit, in order to rid myself of father and mother . . . and myself as well? Yet I got up, went into the little study with the Chinese curtains, got the manuscript out of the drawer, and sat down at the table.

"It's like being in court," I murmured.

"Oh," Jonathan hastened to reply, "I know how cruel it is to bring up out of the darkness what one has fabricated for oneself alone! But the reader too is all alone. . . . So we have two solitudes that speak to each other, furtively, through the confessional torture which is the book. What have they got to say to each other, these two solitudes, which may have nothing else in common but which are brought together through the acts of writing and reading, and imprisoned in that tiny rectangular piece of white paper? Yet suddenly, there in that forest of signs and ink, Diana springs up once again. The reader is changed into a stag. Already his legs prickle because the dogs are nibbling at him!"

We laughed at the baroque metaphor, and I grew easier, then began, in a low voice, to read Elsbeth's story, the one Chesterfield had invented for her. It was the first time I'd heard that female voice in my own, and it seemed as if Mary Charmer herself was speaking, there in the small drawing room she'd loved, during those blessed days when she still knew nothing of Pumpermaker. Gradually, the music of her childlike voice deepened into the song of the cello, after she met Alexander, that smug handsome individual dressed in mourning clothes, and fell in love, with the bizarre compulsion of a passion that instantly and indissolubly binds the lover to someone she ordinarily would have ignored. And then the chamber music began, a string quartet, evoking the desperate struggle between the lover and the icy object of her love, she all tenderness, warmth, openness, he hard, cold, closed, the eternal conflict between the one who offers herself and the one who refuses.

Out of this scherzo rose Elsbeth's lament, the grave melody of a mystic pleading with her unreachable god who departs, returns, shuts himself up in scornful silence, then disappears again, ever unmindful of the desperate appeal. Was it indifference? Or wasn't Alexander a tyrant who used this strategy to imprison even more completely the slave he'd chosen for himself? When Elsbeth had languished sufficiently, the great man in black locked himself up with her in the house and ordered the blinds drawn so that no light might disturb the shadowy drama he'd decided to enact, and to inflict upon his wife. His tenor voice, the voice of authority, rose, turning Elsbeth's to ice, then bending it to his will, forcing it to give up its soul—the only appropriate word—in order to destroy her, to soil her through love itself, forcing her to turn it into hatred. It ended with Alexander's murder, through which Elsbeth believed she might free herself from her passion. Trumpet blasts, then a slow decrescendo, the only sound the wife's footsteps as she walked down the stairs to the basement. *Finis operis.*

The first reading lasted until two in the morning. We agreed to stop there, and to discuss nothing until we'd both had a good night's sleep. I searched Varlet's face for some clue to his feelings, some reaction to a tale that now seemed to me gross, inflated, gussied up in heavy leather like a woman in a bordello. But Jonathan gave no hint of his thoughts, and as I walked him to the room Somerset had prepared, I was prey to the most disquieting reflections on my pathetic little effort. I passed a nearly sleepless night, during which my imagination transformed the solicitor into Alexander and Mary Charmer into Elsbeth. He was dressed as a lion tamer, whip in hand, while she stood half naked, forced to obey the most salacious commands, her face wet with tears . . .

Douglas had set out breakfast in an appendage of the drawing room that the Charmers had called the *verrière*, a glassed-in alcove that looked out over the lawn and the banks of rosebushes. Somerset roused me from my insomnia by opening the bedroom shutters, and despite my exhaustion, I climbed out of bed with a certain satisfaction. For I had decided to apologize to Varlet and to throw *Beelzebub* in the rubbish bin. I put on my dressing gown, washed my face, ran a comb through my hair, and went down to the breakfast room where Jonathan, comfortably ensconced with a cup of tea, was buttering his toast with obvious pleasure.

He sat up when he saw me.

"My dear friend, you can't imagine how much I regret not having told you last evening how moved I was, but everything—my surprise, my happiness, the shock of discovery, my fatigue from the trip—simply devastated me! You must forgive me. But what a piece of work! What a writer you are!"

In one hand, he waved a knife, and in the other, a piece of toast. For a moment, I wondered if he wasn't making fun of me.

"I was completely stunned," he went on. "Your Elsbeth wept right next to me in my bed, or rather almost in my bed, and I confess I was unable to console her. It is the total distress of the human being that you've portrayed in that aching soul. And its dignity. Elsbeth is the very model of those saints who will never get to heaven unless they first go through hell. They need thorns and torments. Their hearts are on fire and can only burn themselves to ashes, and yet they can be ignited by an iceberg! I admire you, Chesterfield. You've freed the English novel from Dickens's tripe and Kipling's stutterings!"

"Gentlemen," Somerset interrupted, more the valet than ever, "your tea is getting cold."

"Thank you," I said to Varlet, and sat down. "Your generous opinion confounds me, however, for as I read that draft, I could not help but see its shortcomings. Alexander is as overly rigid as Elsbeth is malleable. The whole thing is sheer improbability and, I fear, so old hat that the only place for it is the dustbin."

"Have you lost your mind? Can't you see that the value of the book lies in your characters, who are the very opposite of outrageous? In fact, they're typical! What are we supposed to make of this naturalism the French have exported, which claims to give us reality by choosing the most mediocre aspects of the real? You've broken a new path, my good friend; you've made a highway, believe me!"

I was torn between the gentle cradling of his flattery and the pinpricks of my own doubt. I took a sip of tea.

"Too bad for posterity," I said, a bit too loudly. "Because *Beelzebub*'s going to stay right here in its drawer."

"Why? Are you saying you're not going to show it to Goldman, or Maldwin, or Clark and Williams?"

Those were the names of the biggest publishers in London, the ones who published the most famous novelists, philosophers, and playwrights.

"Dear Jonathan," I replied simply, and truthfully, "I've no idea if it's my timidity, my pride, my lucidity, or my laziness, but I am incapable of walking up and knocking on their doors. They look like bronze to me. Like the doors of tombs."

He laughed at my analogy and stood up, his napkin tucked in his collar and cascading down his shirtfront like a flag.

"Then I, Varlet, shall go knocking at the doors! I'll wake up the dead if I have to! You have placed me in your debt. I'll make them listen to reason, those shopkeepers dozing over their driveling fiction!"

Thus was the first step taken, and my destiny decided, on a whim, in a way, for I doubt that Varlet had quite yet decided to take my manuscript under his arm and go see Goldman or Maldwin. I was terrified, however, that he might actually do it, and this before the text was completely ready.

"God forbid you should take the book as is," I exclaimed. "I've got to work on it some more."

"Excellent," Varlet replied, without blinking an eye. "I shall wait here until you're ready. I like the house, the room is quiet, I feel quite regenerated. As for the marmalade, it's scrumptious. Did your Douglas make it?"

He helped himself to more jam, while I wondered whom to congratulate, luck or providence, for having dropped this young stranger on my doorstep. Or should I thank Varlet himself, who had the simple and convenient gift of doing the choosing for me? And so he moved into Ruthford that very morning, promising to watch over *Beelzebub* once it was in the clutches of those editors I considered such filthy monsters. (My solitary character should now be clear, as well as my distaste for transaction, in short my rejection of everything practical and my predilection for the imaginary, which ironically was the very last thing I wished to incarnate!)

Once ensconced, Jonathan Absalom Varlet took over the blue room, began leafing through the library, and in a very few days had so completely conquered Douglas, whom he never stopped complimenting, and Somerset, to whom he told fascinating stories, that we all felt we'd known him forever. Two weeks later, however, one evening after dinner, he took me aside and led me into the little study with the Chinese curtains.

"Permit me to broach a secret which I'm sure you haven't yet divulged for fear of vexing me, but I cannot help noticing that your last name is not Chesterfield, that your first name is neither Gilbert nor Keith, but Cyril, that in short you seem to be running away from your patrimony. Would I be taking advantage of your generosity if I desired a clarification of the mystery?"

I forced myself to smile. "I think an author ought not to use his real name if it lacks that minimum of elegance and power which would make it appreciated. And remembered. The truth is—and I hope this will be the last word on a distressing subject—I did not like my father. His name was grotesque. I might have taken my mother's, but I decided on Chesterfield instead."

"Quite right," Varlet replied. "Mustn't a writer use a whole gamut of identities to free him from his ego and allow him to assume the most varied, and most contrary, characters and temperaments?"

"I never could have written a word without Chesterfield's intervention, largely because my own name was a gag. My pseudonym, however, was more of a mask. The first suffocated me, forced me into silence, impotence; the other hid me and, by hiding, freed me."

Our days passed in delightful idleness. I edited my manuscript, and the closer I looked, the more I found it not so bad as I'd believed. From time to time, I asked Jonathan's advice on a word or a phrase, which led to endless discussions on all manner of subjects. I noticed, however, that Varlet always returned to the theme of love as passion, or rather as suffering, and that his other ideas had to do with the concept of ties, alliances, fetterings, and oaths. Or on the other hand, their opposites—rupture, liberation, and treason, which led me to suspect that his childhood and adolescence must indeed have been marked by severe deprivation. I saw too that his adventure with the aristocrat he called "my lord" had also marked him deeply, and that he clearly felt very much indebted to this man. But there seemed to me another reason, an even stronger one, which had inspired this obsession that so constantly invaded his conversation. I decided to find out, once and for all.

After lunch in the *verrière*, we had the habit of taking an hour's walk around the grounds if the weather was fair. That day, toward the end of July, as we crossed the wooden bridge over the river, I broached the subject.

"You know those legends about the man who signs a pact with the devil in order to build a bridge? The soul of the first creature to cross the bridge belongs to the devil? And in the end, the devil is tricked because the first one to cross is a pig?"

As I'd predicted, he leaped right in.

"The devil's bridges are Faust's ancestors," he exclaimed. "There are a great many bizarre things about these pacts between builders and the devil, but legends don't do justice to the memory of very real events. In olden times, in order to placate the spirits of the river and to receive their blessings, a man was sacrificed, walled up alive under the corner-stone, always on the left bank—the dark side, the side of shadows. Later, when animal sacrifice replaced the human, many people thought the spirits would be angry, would seek revenge, whence come the broken bridges, the devil's temper tantrums, and your pig."

"I think you know a great deal about all those myths that deal with contracts or oaths," I said. "Ever since we met, I've been amazed at how much our conversation is fed by that stream, by Vulcan, the forger of chains, by Jacob and his angel, by Paul on the road to Damascus, by Actaeon . . ."

"You are most perspicacious. You've seen that there can be no bonds without sacrifice. The contract, or the oath, is a living break in the dura-tion of things, thus it's sacred. God enters the alliance, then seals it by an infirmity, an infirmity that liberates. Vulcan and Jacob begin to limp; Paul becomes temporarily blind and a splinter of wood remains in his flesh; Actaeon becomes a stag and is torn to shreds. That's the price you have to pay. Everyone, even Christ, through whom the new alliance is forged, must suffer and die in order that His oath be fulfilled. In short, without likening my own fate to those of such august personages, I nonetheless know that if I've been lucky to have my eyes opened by an admirable man, in every respect worthy of the greatest esteem, I have not yet paid my dues."

"I don't understand you," I said carefully. "I'm sure your lord was completely unselfish in his actions toward you, and that his manna re-quired nothing in exchange!"

Jonathan gazed at me severely.

"And just what do you know about it?"

"But you . . . you should honor his memory," I stammered, upset. "Which is clearly what you're doing . . ."

He laughed, with a meanness I'd never heard before.

"Honor his memory! Erect altars to his virtue! No, he wanted something else entirely! But that's enough. This is not the time to talk about it."

And so I remained unsatisfied, my appetite, however, definitely sharpened.

Except for our walks in the garden, our meals, and our discussions of *Beelzebub*, Jonathan stayed in the library or in his room, reading. The Charmer library was filled with nineteenth-century novels and plays, in those book club editions so prized by the well-off bourgeoisie of that generation. There were few masterpieces, but many works in which feeling and duty mingled with sniveling ghosts and orphans sold to Gypsies. I have no idea what kind of pleasure my companion received from these little books, but he read them all, systematically, beginning with the lowest shelf and moving to the highest, and at a remarkable pace. He gathered up and, as his memory was prodigious, stored away countless anecdotes, documents, and ideas that, much later, he would bring forth in impressive detail.

At last, as August drew to a close, I felt my manuscript ready and I handed it over, quite solemnly, to Jonathan.

"I'll make an appointment with Goldman for tomorrow," he exclaimed, enthusiastically. "Will you give me carte blanche? I'll have to be free to do what I need to do."

"You may have as much freedom as you like," I replied. "Nothing could have made me go to a publisher myself."

"Excellent," said Varlet. "I'll be amazed if I'm not successful! My arguments and my bags are ready. Trust me."

The next day, we went to the Warwick Post Office to telephone London. Jonathan made the call.

"Hello, Mr. Goldman? What? There is no Mr. Goldman? Mr. Goldman's passed away? How very sad. Almost twenty years ago? I see. Well, would you be good enough to connect me with his successor? . . . Gilbert Keith Chesterfield. The writer. Yes, this is he. Mr. Babydoor? Who is this Mr. Babydoor? . . ." Jonathan whispered, "What a ridiculous name, Babydoor!" A moment later, "Yes. Yes, indeed. Tell me, Mr. Babydoor, would you be good enough to grant me an appointment as soon as convenient? It's about my most recent manuscript. . . . Pardon me? By mail? Certainly not, Mr. Babydoor! I've submitted the same novel to Clark and Williams, who are urging me to sign a contract, but I confess, Mr. Babydoor, that I would prefer to meet you first. . . . Your reputation, the high quality . . . Do you see?"

Babydoor saw. He suggested a meeting the next morning at eleven o'clock in the office of the president, the well-known Peter Warner.

"But really," I said, "if he checks with Clark and Williams, he'll know we haven't submitted anything at all! All these publishers know each other!"

"And they hate each other," Varlet assured me. "Anyway, if Clark and Williams say they've never heard of you, I'll say that's exactly consistent with their hypocritical way of refusing to reveal anything about their projects."

My companion's self-assurance boggled my mind, but we left on the first train for London the next morning. We'd decided that Varlet would go to the meeting alone, and that I'd wait for him somewhere close by. Both of us were convinced that if the publisher would only read the manuscript, he would love it and draw up a contract immediately. Ah, the charming euphoria of the young, even though I was far more cautious than Jonathan about this sort of thing.

"Don't we need to be recommended by someone?" I'd asked him. And "Shouldn't I have cut the last part of Chapter Five?" No matter what the question, he replied simply, "Trust me," in a peremptory manner that, without ridding me of my fears, nonetheless kept my hopes up until we arrived at Euston Station.

Goldman Publishers was in Fleet Street, a stone's throw from Ludgate Circus, which was, and still is, the neighborhood of the big newspapers. At certain times of day, a rather stilted effervescence invaded this stuffy street, an effervescence that seemed to excite Jonathan as much as it intensified my doubts. Standing there in the imposing doorway through which the greatest writers of the times had so easily passed, I felt small and worthless. Had I possessed the courage to get this far by myself, I should at this point have bolted, to despair forever of my fate. Varlet asked me to wait in front of St. Bride's Church just across the street, then he tucked my manuscript under his arm and disappeared. I watched him cross Fleet Street, slip through the crowd, and enter the building, resolute as a conquering hero. I admired his daring. Was it not written on the pediment of the facade, as on the entrance to Dante's Inferno: *Lasciate ogni speranza, voi ch'entrate*? I imagined the interior to look either like a sanctuary of polished marble in whose icy labyrinth Sir

Babydoor arranged manuscripts in huge drawers like the ones for cadavers in the morgue, or like a giant masticatory machine in whose pointed teeth manuscripts were torn to shreds, mixed together, kneaded into their original dough, then spit, at the end, from an immense funnel in the form of books, each bound in a pink ribbon!

At first, I paced up and down, but I was so nervous about the people who passed, and who seemed to be eyeing me, accusing me of something, that I sought refuge in a doorway where I huddled for a long time, staring at the monumental entrance of the publishing house. It seemed to me that behind those bristling walls, my destiny was being decided without me, that a restless mob was preparing to boo me, like a Roman circus, if the decision was thumbs down. "We do not wish to read your novel. If it is, in fact, a novel. This Elsbeth, ah! What a joke! And this Alexander, oh my! How pathetic! Buzz off, Mr. Chesterfield!"

Time passed, interminable and mocking. How I ached to flee this abominable place, to get back on the train and abandon any idea of publishing, to lock myself up in the little study at Ruthford. But I couldn't desert Jonathan, who had been kind enough to carry *Beelzebub* into the dragon's lair. . . . I looked at my watch—ten minutes had already gone by! What was he doing? What was going on? I was in a torment of panic. I could feel the cold sweat in my armpits, snaking down my spine. I turned on my heels and abruptly entered St. Bride's.

It was a wholly nondescript building, everything about it gray, cold, and artificially monumental, with a smattering of framed paintings depicting biblical scenes whose meaning I didn't care to understand. At the far end of the center aisle, toward the bleached neo-Gothic choir stalls, a private ceremony was taking place that immediately made me forget my own agony. It was a child's funeral. There was a tiny coffin balanced on two trestles, and a bouquet of flowers on top. Several women were kneeling next to the coffin, weeping softly. Standing next to them was a man, the father most likely, in a black suit undoubtedly rented as it was too big for him. He seemed to be whispering a prayer, a sort of litany that, as I drew closer, took shape, became a monologue about his son's future, the studies he would have pursued, the encounters he might have had, the marriage, the children . . . I backed away.

Outside, the crowds continued to rush past, and Goldman's giant doorway still loomed across the street. I looked again at my watch— twenty minutes! Jonathan had been discussing my book with Sir Babydoor for twenty minutes, perhaps even with the president of the company—what was his name?—Peter Warner. Or more likely, he was still sitting on a sofa in the waiting room in the midst of fifty other writers, their masterpieces wrapped up neatly in their laps. What torture! My head spun. Whatever had I been thinking of when I'd said I wanted to write? Why had I listened to Varlet? He was going to emerge in a sorry state, terribly disappointed. "They don't have time to read your manuscript. They're very important people, you understand. . . . Only famous writers can enter the temple of literature, the company of lords, ministers, academicians . . ."

"Where've you been?" asked Jonathan. "I've been looking for you for five minutes!"

I spun around, my heart icy with fear and terror.

"So?"

"Things went beautifully." He smiled. "Our child is in the hands of Warner himself!"

"You saw him?"

"Listen to me, my dear Cyril," Jonathan replied, winking and taking my arm, as we walked toward the Strand. It was the first time he's used my childhood name.

"Picture a quaint, rather antiquated office, with secretaries in glossy silk dresses and holding fountain pens. I introduce myself: 'Gilbert Keith Chesterfield!' I announce. 'Who?' croaks the deaf old lady at the desk. 'Gilbert Keith Chesterfield, the writer, Miss Augusta!' I repeat, more loudly this time. She stands up, the tiny thing, and says, 'My name is not Augusta. It's Daisy. And I'm married, Mr. Chesterfield.' And she walks away, head held high, bun in place. Amusing, no?"

"Please," I begged. "What about Warner? What did he think?"

"Just a minute. So, the office door opens part way and out comes something that looks like a beanpole topped with a pumpkin head, all stiff and tight-lipped, who asks me if I am indeed Mr. Chesterfield. 'Hmmm, I rather expected someone older,' he murmurs. 'Do come in.' Then he introduces himself, 'Harold Babydoor, editor in chief,' and he leaves me standing there while he goes and sits down behind his desk, which is overrun with files and books and statuettes and even two clocks that chimed constantly the entire time we were together. Anyway, I plunged in. 'Thank you for seeing me on such short notice, Mr. Babydoor. As I told you, Clark and Williams are interested in my most recent book. . . .' At which point he interrupts me and says, 'Enough, all right?' 'Nonetheless,' I say, 'before I commit myself to them, I need to know the terms of your contract, given your reputation, the type of book you . . .' But he interrupts me again. 'Enough,' he says, and then he leans across the desk and articulates very carefully, while he rolls his pale-blue eyes. 'You are quite an amazing young man!' Nice, no?"

"Jonathan, please, get to the point!"

"I am getting there, my dear Cyril! Truly I am! So this Babydoor made it very clear that if my writing looked as good as I did . . . in short, he's succumbed to my meager charms! Think of it, that beanpole with the pumpkin head! He was positively shivering! 'Ah,' he goes on, with a sort of groan, 'I'm sure your novel is every bit as elegant as you, and that it will be a pleasure to know you better as I read it. Quite a surprise really! A remarkable young man!' While I stand there, trying desperately not to laugh . . . So, just when that blunderhead gets up and starts to walk around the desk toward me, under the pretext of wanting to take a closer look at the manuscript, the door swings open as if there'd been a terrific gust of wind, and in walks a tiny little man, a dwarf really, but enormously fat and bald and wearing striped trousers and jacket with a rose in his lapel, and he shouts in this stentorian voice, 'Harold! My cigars!' So the aforementioned Harold clicks on like a robot, opens a drawer, pulls out a box, and struts like an automaton over to the little man who's still planted in the doorway, who looks at me with this ferocious look and says, 'Who's this?' 'Mr. Chesterfield,' Babydoor says. 'A quite pleasant young man. He's brought us a manuscript.' 'Ah,' roars Peter Warner. 'Manuscript! Manuscript! You'd do better to busy yourself with women, my friend. Or hire yourself out to a farmer. The agricultural labor force is shorthanded.' "

"He said that?" I asked, dismayed.

"I walk up to him," Varlet went on, "and hold out my hand. 'Delighted to meet you, Mr. Warner,' I say. 'I've chosen your publishing house!' He shrugs. 'I do the choosing around here,' he snaps. 'In that case, I shall take my leave,' I reply, bowing with a minimum of irony, and I start for the door. 'Just a minute,' Warner barks. 'You have guts. . . . Leave me the manuscript. I'll read it. Come back in a month. Babydoor will tell you the decision.' 'Excuse me,' I reply, 'but I must make my decision by next week.' 'Clark and Williams,' adds the beanpole. Warner's eyes light up. 'Really? Or is this a ploy? Ah, what difference does it make? All right, young man. Come back next Tuesday.' He takes the manuscript, glowers, and leaves. . . ."

"Peter Warner's going to read *Beelzebub*!" I cried, then immediately succumbed to my old demons. "He'll hate it," I murmured.

"Come," said Jonathan, taking my arm. "Let's go celebrate our first victory in the literary war! Simpson's is right over there. I'll be your guest—after all, don't I deserve it?"

"Of course you do," I replied, my courage returning. "Onward to Simpson's!"

The best-known restaurant on the Strand welcomed us with its habitual ceremony.

"Have you reserved? No? Then I'm afraid we have seating only on the second floor. I'm so sorry."

"I am Gilbert Keith Chesterfield," Varlet all but bellowed. "The writer. It's possible Peter Warner will be joining us. . . ."

The maître d'hôtel stopped short.

"Forgive me, Mr. Chesterfield," he murmured. "I didn't recognize you!" He turned to a waiter. "A table for three!" he ordered. "Number twenty-six. It's Mr. Warner's favorite, the one by the window. Right this way, gentlemen . . ."

The waiters bowed as we passed into the Sacred Temple of British Gastronomy. I didn't know whether to laugh or tremble.

"You've gone too far," I said to Jonathan when we were seated. "What if Warner walks in!"

"It will be quite funny," my companion replied with an angelic smile. "We'll ask him to join us!"

The mere thought of it made me shiver. We ordered Spanish melon and haddock.

"Listen," Jonathan began. "You should go back to Ruthford. I'll stay here. I'll need the week to get our strategy organized."

"What do you mean?"

"Allow me my secrets," he replied, with the air of one inspired.

"Now you really have gone too far!" I complained. "It's my book, after all. I can't let you act in my name without knowing what you plan to do!"

"Dear Cyril," he said, putting down his fork and looking at me with those innocent, seductive blue eyes, "whatever can you be imagining? Could I possibly do harm to a book I love, to an author for whom I have such affection? Listen, the publishing world is sticky. We have to hold all the trumps. It's your success I'm thinking of!"

I lowered my eyes. He fascinated me and yet I refused to let myself be led about by the nose.

"You can't use just any means," I protested. "And this cannot be just any success!"

"Of course not! But do I look like a prostitute? Listen, Cyril, to tell the truth, if I'm not explaining what I intend to do, it's because I don't yet know what the circumstances are. Or what they'll require of me. But you need a certain special touch in this sort of thing. . . ."

I had no idea what sort of thing he meant, and that was precisely what troubled me.

"Listen," I went on, "you have to tell me more. . . . You seem to have devised some sort of plot that surely isn't so complicated that you can't explain the basics. . . ."

"That's Cyril all over!" he laughed. "Nervous, worried, tight as a trap! All right, I'll give you the plot. But you must understand, my dear author, that Warner may be dwarfish, but he has nonetheless succeeded in siring a daughter, the remarkable Margaret."

"Where did you find that out?"

"The local paper. 'Miss Margaret Warner, only daughter of the celebrated publisher Peter Warner, attended an automobile race organized by Brompton Fertilizers and Harwood Automobile Horns yesterday.' In the photograph, the darling wore an incredible hat of the kind sported by the so-called gentry, but even with that monstrosity, she was not exactly lacking in charm. In short, I liked her, and thus intend to declare my love. Did I say love? Correction, my passion! You must agree it'll take a good week to manage that!"

I was dumbstruck. Was he dreaming, or was he making fun of me? His laughing eyes watched me carefully.

"Assuming that, despite the odds, you succeed in approaching this Margaret," I replied, "what does that have to do with the publication of my book?"

Jonathan burst out laughing.

"You are such a delicious innocent! Do you really think they publish one novel and not another because of literary merit? Publishers today don't know how to read, if they ever did. It's all run by financiers, businessmen who use publishing houses as flowers in their buttonholes. When you have an unknown writer, as is your case at present, you must find some small thing, some ingredient, that will make our *Beelzebub* an irresistible dish. Little Miss Warner certainly ought to have some influence on her father."

This seemed to me so incongruous and so unrealistic that I decided not to continue the conversation. I assumed that behind his facade of the conquering hero, Jonathan was playing out his own drama, which was, after all, nothing more than the wild imaginings of youth. We finished our meal, I paid the check, and we departed Simpson's under the suspicious eye of the maître d'hôtel, who nodded to Varlet and declared with appropriate obsequiousness, "We hope to see you soon, Mr. Chesterfield," to which I replied with a discreet gratuity. My companion left me at Paddington Station, promising to telegraph as soon as there was anything to report. He was just about to disappear into the crowd when I shouted, "Jonathan!" and rushed up to him.

"Jonathan, please let me give you some money. It's only fair, since it's my book that's keeping you in London."

"So be it," he replied, eyeing me with amusement. "It is indeed for your book, and for you, but it's also for Chesterfield, isn't it?"

I pulled several bills from my wallet. He put them in his pocket and walked away. Once alone, I had a strange feeling. What was he playing at, this boy? For a moment, I was seized with the preposterous notion that he hadn't met with anyone at all at Goldman, that he'd simply left the manuscript with a secretary. The description of his visit had been nothing but a story concocted to confuse me, an act of which I deemed him completely capable. But since I couldn't see what enjoyment or reward he might get from such a maneuver, with the exception of a free meal and a few pounds—I returned to Ruthford, reassured.

I'd scarcely stepped foot into the hallway when Douglas rushed to meet me.

"Has Mr. Cyril come back alone? Oh, thank heavens! I'm so relieved. . . . Please forgive me, Mr. Cyril, but Mr. Jonathan . . . oh, how can I tell you?"

I asked her to explain herself, but the good woman was so embarrassed, she had no idea how to go about it.

"It's not that . . . it's not that Mr. Jonathan isn't a very nice gentleman, very pleasant, but he's too . . . too nice in a way. Particularly to Somerset . . . Somerset is my nephew, you understand. I promised his poor mother to watch over him. . . ."

"Douglas," I said gently, "you must tell me what happened. Did Jonathan behave improperly toward Somerset?"

"Oh, certainly not improperly, Mr. Cyril," she cried, twisted the hem of her apron in her fingers. "But gentlemen do things different from us. They have different customs. Of course, Somerset has no complaints. At his age, they don't quite realize . . . and besides, Mr. Jonathan was so nice to him! No, I'm the one who suspected something and one thing led to another and Somerset told me everything they did in the library. It isn't Christian, Mr. Cyril. It just isn't Christian!"

I had noticed Varlet's affection for Somerset and assumed it was simply a function of the fact that he saw in him the orphan he himself had been. Hadn't he asked about his studies? Now, suddenly, a different truth was emerging.

"Are you certain of what you say?" I asked, taken aback.

"As God is my witness," Douglas replied haughtily, "nothing in the world could make me invent such things!"

I thanked her for her honesty and when she'd gone back to the kitchen, I called for Somerset.

"Hello, Mr. Cyril!" he cried, with just a hint of alarm. "Hasn't Mr. Jonathan come back with you? Is he never coming back to Ruthford?" His eyes filled with tears.

"Don't worry, Somerset," I said. "Of course Mr. Jonathan will be returning to Ruthford. He's just staying over in London for a few days. But tell me, you seem so upset. Were you so very fond of Mr. Jonathan?"

"He told me such lovely stories. . . . He told me that when he was young like me he had a dog named Garich. Why don't you have a dog, Mr. Cyril?"

His little freckled face was the image of innocence. So he too had been seduced by Varlet, like all the others, myself included, who'd encountered him. How could I reproach him for that?

"Who do you like best, Somerset? Me or Mr. Jonathan?"

It was a nasty question and I knew it. Somerset fell silent and stared at his shoes, unable to utter a word.

THE REST OF THE WEEK WAS INTERMIN-able. I'd no idea what had become of Varlet, and at times feared I'd never lay eyes on him again. Moreover, it started to rain so hard on Friday that the lawns became a swamp and I was condemned to remain inside, bored to distraction. Around eight on Saturday evening, just as I was finishing my meager repast, a car horn blared suddenly at the gate. Somerset threw on a cloak and clogs and rushed out into the rainy darkness to see who it was. I watched idly through the window, thinking it someone who'd taken a wrong turn and wanted directions to Birmingham.

Somerset returned out of breath, drenched but exhilarated.

"It's Mr. Jonathan! He's come back! With a lady . . ."

"A lady?" I echoed. Then, shaking off my torpor, "Get the umbrellas, Somerset, and go meet them!"

He hurried off, and a few moments later Jonathan appeared on the path, trying his best to shelter a young woman in white who uttered little cries each time she stepped in a puddle. They burst into the hallway and shook themselves.

"Did you get my telegram?" Varlet asked.

"Not a word of it," I replied, while Jonathan took off his streaming jacket, handed it to Somerset, and turned to the woman.

"My dear, allow me to introduce you to my friend, my brother, and more than that . . . my accomplice. His name is Cyril." He turned to me. "Dear Cyril, this is my excellent friend, Margaret Warner!"

"Oh dear, I'm so sorry to meet you in such a state," she exclaimed. "I'm just drenched. My hair's all pasted together! I must be ugly as sin!"

I stood in the hallway, paralyzed and speechless.

"Perhaps we might retire to the blue room and change for dinner," Varlet suggested.

"Of course," I replied, in a trance. "Somerset, get the luggage from the car and show them to their room."

"How odd you didn't get my telegram," Jonathan said. "It had our arrival . . ."

"No matter," I replied. "I'll ask Douglas to fix something."

"Mr. Cyril," the young woman stammered, "we don't want to bother you, do we, Gilbert?"

So now he was calling himself Gilbert? And not exactly humble in triumph either! Handsome as a god emerging from the waves, he wrapped his arm around the waist of his naiad who, although not at her best, was most certainly ravishing.

They disappeared upstairs while I went to tell Douglas, who couldn't help frowning but seemed reassured by the fact that Varlet was accompanied by a young woman. And what a woman! Peter Warner's daughter! How had Jonathan managed, in a few days, to get close enough to seduce her so completely that she'd come with him to the country and was sharing his bedroom? It was magic. Frankly, I was stunned and not a little frightened, but as I helped Somerset lay the tablecloth, I suddenly understood why Margaret Warner called him Gilbert. Varlet had become Gilbert Keith Chesterfield! He'd told me he'd used the name at Goldman, but I hadn't paid much attention. So now he was Chesterfield to both the publisher and his daughter!

When he came down half an hour later, the table was set and the fire slowly dissipating the dampness in the dining room. He wore a white cashmere sweater and a pair of brown corduroy pants I'd never seen before. We went immediately to the little study with the Chinese curtains.

"As you see," he began, "everything is going famously."

"I'm dumbfounded," I confessed. "You must have known her before?"

"Dear Cyril," he replied, amused by my incredulity, "I'm no magician. My weapons are entirely aboveboard. It's just that I seem to have the singular power to seduce anyone I want!"

"Somerset, for example?"

He studied me with an air of commiseration.

"You're not one of those shallow people who understands nothing of childish charms, are you? Or has the Judeo-Christian ethic marked you so deeply that you're afraid of carnal love?"

"That is not the point," I replied. "But let's get back to Margaret Warner."

"One would think you were displeased," he sighed. "I've done this for Chesterfield!"

"She believes you're Chesterfield?"

"Let's understand each other, Cyril. Neither you nor I is Chesterfield. Your name is Pumpermaker. Mine's Varlet. At least that's what they told me. As for Chesterfield, he may be the product of your imagination but I'm his incarnation. Would you have gone knocking at Goldman's door? Would you have seduced Warner's daughter? Not only will I get your novel published but I shall give you the confidence to write others. Many others! Chesterfield will be famous because of your talent, indeed your genius . . . and because of my seductiveness, my presence! Alone, you'd manage perhaps a mild success. But through me, you'll achieve real glory!"

I stared at him. Was he not stealing my pseudonym, proposing that I work in secret so that he might win fame and fortune?

"Listen," he said, "everyone knows it took Shakespeare for us to recognize Bacon. What would Bacon have been without Shakespeare? A thinker, perhaps. A complicated writer destined for oblivion. Shakespeare brought him energy, drama, life! And immortality! In short, Cyril, when I've brought you success, I'll disappear. It will always be easy for you to prove you're the author and not me. Your manuscripts alone . . ."

"Even so," I said, "it's still a mystification."

"And why not? What's not a lie in this world, according to you? The things men venerate most, the things they take most seriously, are nothing but a mass of boring myths and madnesses! Religion, politics, art,

morality, law! Even science is only made of hypotheses! Error rules the
world! To lie in a context of lies is to tell the truth!"

At that instant, Somerset knocked at the door and announced that
"the lady" had come down and that dinner was ready.

"We'll see about that," I murmured cautiously as we entered the dining room, where Margaret Warner awaited us. The moment I looked at
her, I was struck by her great beauty and her childlike grace. Her long
blond hair, pulled back in a chignon, framed such a perfectly oval face
that I wondered what resurrected painter could claim such perfection—
Leonardo and his *Lady with an Ermine*? Ludovico Sforza's Cecilia Gallerani? She had the same piercing look, the same thin willful lips, the
same strange and intelligent smile. She looked like a woman possessed
to the highest degree of everything necessary to bend men to her mercy.
And yet, in just a few days, Varlet had succeeded in winning her over.
The tamer had agreed to be tamed. That was no small thing, and I
envied my companion the ability to pull off such an astonishing *tour
de force.*

We began with the soup. Fortunately, I hadn't eaten much before.

"So," Margaret began, "you are the friend and confidant of our dear
Chesterfield?"

"More than you think," I replied. "But tell me"—I moved onto the
attack—"how did you two meet? Love at first sight, the *coup de foudre*,
is so rare these days. So unsettling . . ."

"Not true!" Jonathan interrupted. "True love is the child of the *coup
de foudre*. The streak of lightning. The thunderclap. Don't you remember our conversations about Paul on the road to Damascus? And Actaeon in the forest? One look. Just one look . . . and everything turns
upside down."

"He's right," Margaret said. "Until last Wednesday, I never would
have believed such madness possible. I would have laughed at anyone
who claimed to have felt that blow to the head, and to the heart. And
then this gentleman appeared, and all my beliefs collapsed!" She paused.
"He's not cruel, then, is he?"

"I was so struck by her picture, I decided right away that I had to
meet her," Varlet explained. "Those marvelous features of hers, in the
photograph, etched themselves into my memory. Well, Cupid must have
been watching out for us because when I was at Goldman, I saw some
invitations to a literary cocktail party at Margaret's father's the follow-

ing day. So I pocketed one of them and arrived at the appointed time, along with the writers and artists and politicians. And as I'd hoped, Margaret was there, standing next to a grand piano at the far end of the room. She wore a blue dress, and was more Margaret than I'd imagined."

"He came up to me," the young woman continued, shivering at the evocation of the experience, "and . . . do tell me, Cyril—is it all right if I call you Cyril?—is there a way to be married here in England without one's father and mother nipping at one's heels?"

We all laughed. Later, at dessert, Margaret turned to me.

"Have you ever read what Gilbert writes, Cyril?"

I felt a wave of discomfort.

"I know everything Gilbert's written," I stammered.

"And what do you think of this *Beelzebub*?" Margaret asked.

Varlet seemed delighted.

"I should think it was up to your father to decide on the merits of the novel. Jonathan submitted it recently and your father's promised to give him the decision this coming Tuesday."

"Jonathan? What Jonathan?"

"Oh," said Varlet. "A lot of my old friends call me Jonathan."

"It suits you better than Gilbert," the young woman said. "It's more intimate. I think I shall call you Jonathan from now on. Is that all right?"

"Absolutely," replied Varlet, without blinking an eye.

The entire meal was one endless torment for me. Margaret talked to Varlet as if she were in part addressing me and, to top it all off, kept looking to me for confirmation, referring to me as her witness. She had not read my manuscript, which her father had taken with him to the country, but Jonathan had described it to her as if he'd been the author, and in such detail that the young woman knew the novel as well as if she'd read it herself. Which was how we came to talk of Elsbeth.

"Your heroine's problem, dear Jonathan, seemed so absurd to me, so unrealistic, until you appeared at the party. I was so bored next to that ridiculous piano; I mean someone had actually put a flowerpot on it! To become infatuated with a man to the point where you can't even tell who he really is! To fall in love with someone no other woman would be seduced by! Alexander's old and argumentative and sadistic. She ought to feel instinctively how much of an abyss separates them. But it's just the contrary. It's the abyss that attracts her. And soon it's not the man she loves, it's the abyss. . . ."

"Yes," I said, "that's exactly how it should be read. Elsbeth wants to get away from her mother and, without realizing it, discovers in Alexander the image of her father. It's the little girl in her, and then the adolescent, that's seduced. And later, when the trap has snapped shut, it's the trap she idolizes, the dark place, the cave where her unconscious mind reveals itself, where her monsters run wild or are calmed, depending on the moods of her master."

"Brrr! It gives me gooseflesh!" Margaret exclaimed. "God in heaven, Jonathan, you're neither old nor argumentative nor sadistic! So where did you meet characters like that? How did you invent such blind passion?"

"Rest assured, my love," Varlet replied, leaning back casually in his chair and winking at me on the sly, somewhat ironically I thought, "the novelist invents according to laws so insane they can't be verified by anyone. The novelist is a thief. He swipes whatever appeals to him—a setting here, a gesture there, further on a feeling, over there a situation. And then off he goes on his galley ship with all his myriad pieces, and as the voyage continues they find their places, unless they turn out to be useless, in which case he pitches them overboard. The novelist has no scruples about his materials; in fact, he's freer than anyone because he doesn't know what comes from his own delirium and what from other people's fantasies."

"Nonetheless, it's you who've chosen this particular story and characters," Margaret replied, "as opposed to any others. They must respond to some compulsion, some necessity, in you. But to see you as I do, meaning with almost no distance and a pair of distorting spectacles on my nose, you don't look anything at all like those dark spirits you describe."

Dear Margaret Warner! How well her instinct guided her through Jonathan's chicanery! At that moment, I should have risen and declared, "The cause of this mystery is the fact that Varlet never thought up a single line of *Beelzebub*. The real author is none other than myself. Those abysses are mine. Elsbeth and Alexander are my children. I'm sorry they're so sick, but I too am sick, sick of all this solitude. . . ." But how was I to do such a thing? It was just this paralysis that glued me to my seat, that froze my desire and my tongue. I remained painfully silent.

Ah, how I might have mocked myself! What a ninny I was! What a weakling! Yet when I consider the events that followed, and the revelations that gradually come to me, I can scarcely blame myself. Jonathan Absalom Varlet had chosen me, as he'd chosen Margaret, as he would choose others, and we all fell victim to his charm—or rather I should say, we fell victim to his will, which we took for charm. It's either that or we shall have to restore the medieval meaning to the word *charm*— the sense of spell, of bewitchment—for I no longer doubt Jonathan's quasi-magical powers, that strange link he had with others, that *prodigious faculty of seduction.*

The rain stopped during the night and the two turtledoves left for London the following morning. Margaret drove a superb Austin her father had given her on her twenty-second birthday. They promised to let me know Goldman's decision, but in all truthfulness, I wasn't so sure I wanted this project to succeed. Varlet had created such havoc that the whole thing seemed unhealthy. *Beelzebub* seemed no longer to belong to me. Or worse, I felt as if I'd been robbed of my vocation as a writer. I began to hope Goldman would turn the book down so that I might regain my freedom. For Jonathan's presence had become a burden, and I now wanted nothing more than to turn this particular page of my life.

The famous Tuesday arrived, however, and I confess to some impatience, divided as I was between contradictory opinions and desires; in fact, given my temperament and the circumstances, I was in a state of severe febrile anxiety. As the weather was fair, I took up pick and shovel and went off with Register, the old gardener, to tackle some heavy chores and take my mind off the waiting. The Austin's horn blared at the gate around three o'clock and, covered with mud, looking like a real peasant, I greeted a radiant Margaret and Jonathan.

"The contract's signed!" Varlet cried from inside the car. He jumped out, rushed up to me, and flung his arms about me. "We've done it! Isn't it extraordinary?"

"We wanted to give you the good news right away," Margaret said, coming up to us. "My father hesitated, but in the end, he signed!"

"Margaret was magnificent!" Jonathan cried. "She explained it all to her father. He didn't understand Elsbeth's passion; he found it incongruous. Without her, we'd never have managed it!"

"Oh, I think my father was really seduced by Jonathan's publicity plan."

"What plan?" I blurted out.

"You mean you don't know?" Margaret exclaimed. "Well, Jonathan has this idea of launching Chesterfield as a fictional character. *Who is the real Gilbert Keith Chesterfield?* My father thought the idea was brilliant; that's what made up his mind."

"What . . . what are you talking about?" I stammered, staring at Varlet with astonishment.

"Always anxious, my good Cyril! Come on, I'll show you your contract!" Then, turning to Margaret, "My beautiful girl, would you be good enough to give Douglas some instructions about tonight's dinner? We must have a real celebration," and he dragged me off to the little study with the Chinese curtains.

The minute the door closed behind us, I exploded.

"Would you please explain? As far as I know, I wrote *Beelzebub*. And this Chesterfield campaign, whatever are you talking about? You're being far too casual about all of it, I think!"

"Read the contract," he replied calmly, smiling his beautiful smile and handing me the document, which I began reading at once.

"Yes," he said when I'd finished, "it is indeed a contract between Chesterfield and Peter Warner. As for the advance and the royalties, they'll be deposited to the account of Cyril Pumpermaker, who I defined as our dear author's right-hand man. As you see, the name Jonathan Absalom Varlet appears nowhere, for the simple reason that from now on, you'll be the only person who knows me by that name. On the other hand, I shall assume the identity of Chesterfield, and shall continue to advertise myself in the outside world. The money for you, the fame for me. You do the writing, I'll do the appearing. Quite fair, don't you think?"

I was in a panic. Had such a pact ever been proposed to any man?

"Of course, I'd be grateful if you gave me a bit of money from time to time, to defray expenses. But I trust you completely; I won't ask for any guarantees. Anyway, as our collaboration becomes more and more fruitful, I'm sure your generosity toward me will be increasingly impressive. I am a man of many talents, as you've guessed, although you still don't know all the services I'm capable of performing!"

I held out the contract, but he refused to take it.

"No, no, my dear friend. It's yours. Guard it carefully in your strongbox. And how that we're in the saddle, we're really going to have to gallop! When do you plan on starting your next novel? It would be good if we had it by next summer."

Suddenly, my amazement changed to hilarity; what in the devil kind of man was this? What a bizarre association we were going to form—he and I and the imaginary Chesterfield! In the midst of this whole crazy business, Jonathan seemed an honest man; he had turned himself over to me completely where money was concerned, whereas I had only to give him my manuscripts. Frankly, the substitution did not displease me. It protected me from the kind of worldly transactions I despised, and it satisfied my taste for the bizarre and the incongruous. I could follow Chesterfield's career in secret, without ever having to be personally involved in the pointless affairs and obligations of a man of letters. Jonathan was exactly the man for the job, and the job would be entirely to my profit while leaving me the time to write.

"Yes," I said, shaking Varlet's hand warmly, "it's true I had my suspicious moments, but I understand now how right you were. Our characters have pushed us both to play the Chesterfield role; he is very much like both of us. I am happiest alone and writing. And I've nothing against the kind of luxury which permits me to assure the success of our enterprise. You, on the other hand, need to shine, you need to talk, to seduce . . ."

Jonathan looked at me with curiosity, as if he hadn't expected such a quick surrender. His blue eyes shaded into purple.

"I thank you for your trust. As long as you write well, you and I will go far, you know. . . ."

Margaret tapped at the glass and I opened the study window. Her arms were filled with petunias.

"Look at all the flowers I picked! Cyril, your house is absolutely delicious! It's so simple, so rustic. . . . When we're married, Jonathan and I, we'll buy one just like it. Won't we, Mr. Chesterfield?"

"Indeed, indeed," Jonathan murmured vaguely.

As Margaret walked away, I closed the window and turned to him.

"Is that true? Do you plan to marry?"

Jonathan made a face.

"She's a spoiled child. Whatever she wants, she wants right away. Which explains the speed with which she fell into my arms. But marriage! Do I look old enough to take those kinds of vows?"

There we were again, into contracts and oaths, a fatality so strangely a part of Jonathan.

Our dinner that evening began at the pinnacle of warmth and affection. Everything seemed perfect, each of our futures blessed by the gods. We began by joking, and by counting our chickens before they were hatched, just like carefree students on a binge. Margaret, who'd led a rather stuffy life, enjoyed herself enormously. Somerset served, and at one point I noticed his eyes were full of tears. I beckoned to him discreetly and he came over to me, dragging his feet.

"What's the matter, my good Somerset? Why so unhappy?"

He sniffled and turned his head away. I understood what he felt. Jonathan was so busy with his new companion that he paid no attention to the simple but sensitive country lad who felt betrayed and forgotten. Somerset loved Varlet with the naïve and brutal passion of the adolescent, for whom no concession is possible. Suddenly he cried out, then turned on his heels and ran away. One of his clogs fell off, slid across the floor, and banged into the wall, but he kept running until he was swallowed up by the darkness of the hallway.

From that moment, the atmosphere changed. Our gaiety disappeared.

"Tell me, Jonathan," Margaret said abruptly, "what were you saying the other night about the *roman noir* and *Beelzebub*? Do you really think there's a connection between your novel and works like Shadwell's?"

"Oh," said Jonathan, "have you read *The Libertine?*"

Margaret blushed.

"I've just heard about it. Which is what worries me. Is Alexander a disciple of Don Juan's, who's really a direct descendant of that Spaniard . . . Tirso, I think he's called?"

"Marvelous!" Jonathan cried. "But in England, the great seducers, the debauchees, all have serious letters of recommendation from the nobility. Don't we believe that Charles II and John II encouraged them to get on with it, at least according to Gramont and Pepys whose memoirs I had the honor of reading in my lord's library? Listen, there was Buckingham, who killed his mistress's husband while the man stood there holding the reins of Buckingham's horse. And Buckhurst, who walked around the streets of London, drunk and stark naked. And Killigrew, who tortured those little cabaret dancers. And do you know who these people really were, my beautiful girl? Only the king's favorites! The brightest and best of the court! Next to them, Alexander is but a pale relative!"

"Goodness, Jonathan," cried Margaret, "you frighten me! Tell me those are only literary concoctions for terrifying ladies. . . . And you, Cyril? What do you think? You seem so thoughtful. . . ."

"Oh," I said cautiously, "the work of a Chesterfield is not without its dangers. It belongs to a rather somber tradition, I admit, one that exhibits an astonishing taste for the agonies of martyrdom! If you think about those poets the Preromantics, for instance . . . such descents into hell! But they paid for their crimes. Yes indeed, they paid!"

"Look at the count," said Varlet. "Three went crazy—Collins, Smart, and Cowper, although Cowper turned out to be rather mild, as a madman. Blake committed suicide. Chatterton was a sex maniac. Burns and Young became senile; Gray suffered from hereditary neurosis. Lady Winchilsea, Parnell, Shenstone, and Akenside were all neurasthenics to some degree; Thomson was a nitwit, Goldsmith a bohemian, Thomas Warton a bohemian nitwit. Not one of the remaining five could be said to possess true mental equilibrium. And out of all of them, the madmen and the sex maniac were the real poets."

"Well," said Margaret, trying to lighten the tone, "I simply dare not retire to my bedroom! It seems depravity and madness is the writer's fate! Can I still trust you, Mr. Chesterfield? Can I still confide in you without worrying about all those horrors and diseases?"

Jonathan stood up and put his arms around her.

"Dear Margaret, have I frightened you? You, the strong one? The bold one?"

Margaret was clearly frightened, and I realized Jonathan's conversation had not been pointless. She was far more intoxicated by the distress his words had provoked than by the wine she'd drunk. They left the table together, arms around each other, and were just about to climb the stairs to their bedroom when I heard, "Mr. Cyril! Mr. Cyril! Please, Mr. Cyril!" It was Douglas, shouting hysterically.

I rushed to the kitchen where I found the good woman wringing her hands, beside herself with grief, and pointing wordlessly to the saddle room. I ran inside and saw my Somerset hanging by the neck; his hands were ice cold. I returned immediately to the hallway and, without telling Varlet what had happened, asked him to take Margaret upstairs. Then, with the help of a breathless and trembling Douglas, I lowered the poor lad to the floor. This was Jonathan's first victim. Somerset had loved him with the excessive love of the pure and innocent; rejected, broken, driven mad with unhappiness, he'd climbed onto a chair and killed himself.

"It's *his* fault," Douglas wept. "It's *his* fault."

"You mustn't say that," I said, distraught. "Poor, poor Somerset. My dear little friend . . . I loved him too. . . ."

"But you didn't kill him!" shouted the poor woman, throwing herself on her nephew and covering his face with kisses. My eyes filled with tears. What kind of people were we, pathetic intellectuals, discoursing in the dining room on love and death, while in the saddle room, this marvelous child was hanging himself out of love? I was ashamed of myself, of all of us. I left this horrid scene, made my way once again into the hallway, and, head in hands, called for Jonathan.

He appeared at the top of the stairs.

"Come down here!" I called, so peremptorily that he obeyed instantly.

"What's the matter?"

When he saw my face, he followed me like an automaton to the saddle room. The moment she saw him, Douglas set up a great wail. Jonathan stood frozen at the doorway with Somerset's body spread out before him, the skin purple, eyes bulging from beneath closed lids, mouth tragically open. I looked at Varlet. He seemed calm, impassive even, although his lips quivered.

"Why?" he asked at last, and stood there silent, dry-eyed, and motionless, as if petrified, while the color drained from his cheeks.

Later, after Douglas and I had laid Somerset on the couch in the drawing room and the dear old woman had knelt beside him, I pulled Jonathan into the little study. He dropped heavily into the mauve armchair. What time was it? Three o'clock perhaps. An evening begun in gay abandon had slowly turned into tragedy, without our noticing its inexorable course. We had not known how to read the signs that presaged the storm. And now that it was too late, we fell into a heavy silence. Varlet was the first to resist, shaking his head with the fierce energy of the vanquished who refuses to accept defeat.

"The fool! The poor dear fool! And I? I who almost did the same, when my lord fell in love with a young woman and I was so jealous of her! Her name was Dorothy. I threw myself out the window, but only managed to twist my ankle. . . . Ah, my friend, I am indeed responsible. But could I have known? Could I have guessed? I made him happy, the poor child!"

He turned away to hide his tears, and when he turned back, his face had resumed its habitual haughtiness. Perhaps even a certain hardness.

"You must pay. . . ."

"What must you pay?" I asked. He shook his head and a lock of hair fell across his forehead; he did not push it back nor did he answer my question.

"And who must you pay?" I added.

"Oh please, Cyril, please," he said, getting to his feet. "Forgive me. It's been a difficult day. First the girl, then the contract, and now this! Always the ties. The ties you can't undo. The ties you can't cut. I do carry my name well, don't I? I am a valet, an ignoble valet!" He rushed out, back up the stairs to the blue room and Margaret.

He hid the truth; all he told her was that Somerset had had an accident. She appeared saddened, although she'd scarcely noticed "the poor child," and wished to stay until after the funeral. I had great difficulty dissuading her. Douglas would never have allowed her to come, and I meant to respect her pride as well as her grief, which Jonathan understood full well. They left the following morning; after all, there was much to be done before publication, and Varlet had very precise ideas on the subject of the Chesterfield campaign. It was no longer in my power to prevent him from advertising himself throughout the world, and in a way, I was beginning to be curious about the future of this rather uncommon adventure.

Signing the contract with Goldman freed me from *Beelzebub* and inspired me to go back to work. Somerset's tragic death, added to the vision I'd had at St. Bride's, led me to imagine the story of an adolescent passion, and although I didn't yet know its outlines and detours, I began to write with resolution and a certain ease. For the moment, I called my hero Somerset, in honor of my little servant, and I put him in a place that, once again, was mindful of Ruthford. He did not, however, fall in love with a man but with a young woman, the owner of the estate, who resembled Mary Charmer in certain respects, or as I imagined her before her encounter with the solicitor.

Douglas was reluctant to stay at Ruthford after Somerset's funeral, for she accused me more or less overtly of having brought Varlet into a place that had been sacred to her and that I had profaned. In a way she was right, and she felt far more clearly than I the true nature of the influence Jonathan had over us. In the end, however, she decided to remain, in part out of faithfulness to her memories and in part because she doubtless had no idea where else to go. Things grew calm once more, and rather dreary, like the weather, and the month of September 1930 passed in a great chill, a circumstance that allowed me to get a handle on my new novel, which had suddenly removed itself to sixteenth-century Germany, doubtless because of a book I'd read on the life of Jacob Boehme. The latent conflict between Catholicism and the Reformation

seemed worthy of provoking events propitious to the birth of my main
character, who acquired the name of Jacob and deserted Ruthford for
Bautzen, a little village in Silesia not far from the birthplace of the ingenious cobbler himself, the author of *De Signatura Rerum.*

In fact, what I sensed in Boehme was that overpowering cosmic vision
that had shattered the carapace of narrow dogma and the established
Church. As I've said before, I'd had no religious education, and had
always had a godly fear of clerical procedure. In my eyes, Boehme—
ostracized, suspected by the Lutheran hierarchy, denounced, pursued by
the *pastor primarius* of Görlitz, the notorious Gregory Richter—became
the paradigm of the martyr to truth persecuted by the intellectual establishment. My little Somerset-now-Jacob would incarnate innocence and
purity in its confrontation with sophists. His passion for the young woman
would become a love of knowledge, or Sophia, who from that moment I
called Rosa—not only because of the banks of rosebushes I saw from
my window in the little study with the Chinese curtains. . . .

After a few months, I learned from the local paper that the publishing
house of Goldman was about to bring out a book by one Gilbert Keith
Chesterfield, whose real identity no one knew. I took myself immediately
to Warwick and bought all the London papers. Varlet had clearly put
his plan into action. It seemed there was a mysterious writer who was,
in reality, an important personage but whom no one had ever met, not
even the publisher, who had gotten the manuscript from a third party.
People murmured about someone close to the Crown, perhaps even a
member of the royal family. And why was he hiding himself? Because,
they whispered, his novel smelled of sulfur, like hell itself, and there
would be a terrible scandal if his true identity were known. After all,
wasn't the title of the work *Beelzebub?*

I confess to being torn between outrage and hilarity at the time. This
tissue of improbabilities had been woven so cleverly that no one could
ever confirm or deny them. Yet it was easy to imagine what sort of
gossip this intriguing publicity would inspire! In fact, Buckingham Palace finally had to make a statement that no member of the royal family
was about to publish any sort of book at all, a statement that succeeded
only in fueling the most preposterous hypotheses. People murmured about
the lord mayor of London, even the archbishop of Canterbury! The whole
business got completely out of control when the rumor started that *Beelzebub* concerned the illicit relationship of its illustrious and anonymous

author with a young girl who became his slave, a rumor that reduced the book to an erotic exercise not even remotely connected to my intentions.

At last the book appeared in the bookstores, and I decided to travel to London and see Jonathan, as he'd suggested in a letter. He wanted, he said, to give me a copy of the book personally, and to bring me up to date on what he jokingly referred to as "our little affair." We agreed to meet at the Savoy Hotel on the Strand. I arrived at 11:30, half an hour early and filled with apprehension; I'd scarce entered the lobby when I ran into Margaret Warner, more beautiful and more Cecilia Gallerani than ever!

"What luck running into you!" she said.

I felt utterly intimidated.

"I was hoping to talk to you before Jonathan got here. Please come with me."

Admiring her graceful yet determined and quite regal walk, I followed her into a sumptuous room with gilded paneling and plush armchairs.

"Dear Cyril," she began, when we were seated, "since you're Jonathan's confidant and friend and in a way his business manager, I must tell you how very happy I am about the publication of his book. And how anxious about the clamor he and my father are creating about the identity of Chesterfield."

"I can well understand your concerns," I replied, "the more so since I share them."

"My father's been totally seduced by Jonathan. Really, I hardly recognize him anymore. Ordinarily, he's so suspicious of everything and everyone, but Jonathan has a way of flattering him, of making him believe he's right, and then he can make him do whatever he likes . . . and he's fascinated by Jonathan's incredible culture! What's more, Babydoor—he's the editor in chief—thinks the sun rises and sets on Jonathan. He has eyes only for him; you'd think he'd actually fallen in love with him, which is too funny! As for the secretaries, they adore him. In short, no one in the whole company can resist Mr. Chesterfield's fantabulous ideas. Frankly, I think the whole thing's gone too far."

"But Jonathan confides in you," I replied, without much conviction, "and you can give him practical advice. . . ."

She shook her head.

"Poor Cyril," she said, with a small tight smile, "do you really believe that? Jonathan does what he wants. He doesn't listen to anyone. And anyway, who am I, as far as he's concerned? I wonder. Peter Warner's daughter perhaps?''

"Don't say that!" I cried. "He's very much in love with you. . . . Who wouldn't be?''

"You're sweet, Cyril," she replied, placing her hand on mine, "too sweet. You don't realize. . . . I love him with all my heart, but does he love me? Is he capable of love? Under that fascinating and charming exterior, there's a coldness, an iciness. I can see now how he was able to create Alexander. In a way, he *is* Alexander . . . and I'm Elsbeth!"

"Aren't you planning to marry soon?" I asked. Cecilia Gallerani had collapsed into Margaret; all that remained before me was a defenseless worried woman who had no idea what to do. I instantly regretted my question.

"Oh, you know, I've come to dread the future. I just don't know what to think anymore; in fact, I don't think at all. I just wander about in the ruins of my old certainties. Who was it said that love gives you faith? I used to have both feet on the ground and now I've begun to doubt everything."

She shivered. Very carefully, I moved closer to her.

"Margaret," I said, in as friendly a tone as I possessed, "something has happened to us which we can neither understand nor control. The thing we don't understand is that Jonathan possesses an absolutely implacable power of seduction. He's talked to me about Paul on the road to Damascus, about Actaeon coming upon Diana in the forest. I didn't understand exactly what he meant, but now I think I see. The fascination Jonathan inspires is like the bolt of lightning that threw Paul from his horse, that changed the hunter into the deer. There's nothing we can do about it."

She looked at me with surprise and fear. Then she began to laugh.

"Come now, Cyril, we're losing our heads! Jonathan acts like an impatient child having a temper tantrum. We'd do better to simply tell him that's enough, don't you think?''

At that instant, a veritable tornado burst into the room, dressed all in white, except for a startling red tie, and looking every bit the dancer who invented the tango. The only thing missing was the mustache.

"Look, Cyril, look!" Jonathan cried, waving a copy of *Beelzebub*. "And this, my dear accountant, is for you!" He reached into his pocket, pulled out a check, and handed it to me. "It's our advance! Signed with the noble signature of Peter Warner himself! So we won't spend all this beautiful money on insane and ridiculous extravagances," he said, turn-ing to Margaret. "Cyril's a janissary, a veritable dragon. As long as he's sitting on our little packet, it won't evaporate. Ah, my beautiful girl, what an austere and desolate life we're going to lead!"

Margaret couldn't help laughing at his clowning. I tucked the check into my billfold and looked at the book, my book, surprised at how proud I felt. There it was, *Gilbert Keith Chesterfield*, the name I'd cho-sen, written in black letters on a white jacket. Underneath, in red, the ti-tle *BEELZEBUB* seemed to explode in a blare of trumpets, with the words *A Novel* in small black letters, and below that, the name of the publisher. I leafed through the pages, reading a sentence here and there; it was truly my book, my text, exactly as I'd written it, but now that I saw it in this form, it seemed so different I hardly recognized it.

"Who is this Chesterfield?" Varlet was saying. "The king of England himself! If not Abraham Lincoln, Isaac Newton, or perhaps even dear Jean-Théophile Désaguliers, who, I might add, is buried in the chapel. . . ."

"What chapel?" I asked.

He winked and pointed to the corridor.

"Down there, at the end of the hallway. The Savoy Chapel! How many hotels can boast of any chapel at all, much less one containing the remains of the founder of the Freemasons!"

"Jonathan," Margaret said severely, "why do you always get so ex-cited about these kinds of things . . . these dark, dirty, obscure things? Crazy people, sick people, obsessives, Freemasons! Why not vampires or ghouls?"

"And now she's angry!" Varlet exclaimed, laughing loudly. "The cra-zies, the sick, the obsessed, the Freemasons! It's so funny! Really funny! You people who call yourselves humanists! Come now, little lady, have a sense of humor!"

Margaret burst into tears and hid her face in her hands.

"Leave me alone! Don't you see how you're hurting me?"

Jonathan turned to me, faked a look of incomprehension, shrugged, and spun around.

"All right," he said angrily. "You women have such a gift for ruining the nicest moments! Good-bye, Cyril. I'll write and tell you what hap-pens in the ongoing drama of our inestimable Chesterfield. But since you're here, you must take good care of our friend. She seems to need it." He left.

"I'm so sorry to have seen what I just saw," I said. while Margaret
dried her eyes with a little handkerchief she wore tucked into the sleeve
of her dress.

"I must look hideous," she said, smiling wetly.

"You're . . . you're . . . how can I say it, I love you very much,
you know. . . ."

I must have been redder than the Chinese vase opposite me. Margaret
seemed not to have heard.

"Sometimes I try to rebel," she went on, "but instead of freeing myself, I just sink in deeper. We were supposed to have lunch together, all
three of us. And now he's gone off God only knows where, in his white
suit and his red tie!"

"Then let's have lunch, just the two of us," I suggested. "Why
pay attention to his caprices? I'll take you to Simpson's, is that all
right?"

"You're very kind, dear Cyril," she replied, shaking her head, "but
how can I go out in this condition? I'd never be able to taste a thing.
You must excuse me. And God keep you!"

She stood up, tried to smile, and then hurried off. Alone and not a
little disappointed, I walked back up the Strand to Trafalgar Square,
thence to Whitehall and the Parliament. I wasn't hungry either. I simply
wandered about London, my book under my arm, not knowing what to
do with myself. In a little while, I'd take the train to Warwick, then a
cab to Ruthford, and thus back to my story of Jacob in Germany. But
did that make any sense? How I wished a woman like Margaret would
think of me not as a friend or a confidant or, horror of horrors, an
accountant, but rather as a . . . I stopped abruptly. Was I in love with
Margaret? That would be madness, since she loved Jonathan to such a
degree that she was incapable of eating after he'd had a show of temper!
How much could I possibly weigh on a scale that had already been
rigged?

Instinctively, my feet had led me to Spencer's Bookstore, where fifty
people were queued up at the door, just like on the days the almanac
came out. As I watched, others appeared and politely took their place in
the queue. Two onlookers were conversing so loudly they appeared to
be quarreling.

"No, I'm telling you," said a woman in a purple hat, "my doctor told
me! This Chesterfield's an American!"

"And I'm telling you he's the king's chief chamberlain!"

So all these people were queued up to buy *Beelzebub*! I fled, as if to chase this hideous scene from my mind.

The same thing was happening at each bookstore I passed. It was an extraordinary event, one of those astonishing surges of public opinion inspired by Varlet's campaign, which had clearly succeeded beyond even his dreams. Later, we learned the first printing had been sold out that very first day; but at the time, I was ashamed because I knew this success had to do not with the literary quality of my work, but with the unconscionable publicity that surrounded it. The commercialism upset me, and I was angry with Jonathan for diverting the book from those whom someone of my temperament would have preferred—readers with taste, not lovers of scandal; even though, I must admit, the latter are far more numerous. I returned to Ruthford in such a state of depression that Douglas feared I'd caught the flu and made me keep to my bed for three days.

At the end of November, the literary critics on the big newspapers woke up, beginning with George Hitchcock of *The Times*, whom the public considered the most discerning connoisseur in matter of fiction and who had made and unmade countless reputations. Margaret sent me his review, and a letter that left me chilled to the bone.

"My dear friend," it began, "I'm sending you *Beelzebub*'s first review. And what a review! I wanted you to know about it right away so that you would see what an uncommon person our Jonathan is. We must simply accept his originality, because behind that mix of seductiveness and whim lies one of today's greatest writers. Of this I'm absolutely certain! Everyone who's anyone speaks of nothing but his novel. My father is convinced he's got hold of one of the most amazing publishing phenomena of our time. Nobody seems very concerned about the rather offensive publicity. I think Jonathan plans a press conference three weeks from now, just before Christmas, in order to stop the now-useless rumors. Affectionately, Margaret Warner."

Hitchcock's review took up half a page in the *Literary Supplement*. It was entitled simply "A Writer." Allow me to cite just a few of the more memorable parts: "The novel of the rather mysterious newcomer who calls himself G. K. Chesterfield is surely one of the major events of the season. This book ought to influence the course of English literature, which now appears to be making a sensational comeback. G. K. Chesterfield descends into the shadows of the conscious mind with cool lucidity, the mark of a master of his craft, a surgeon of the soul. . . . It would amaze me if this theater of passion, so far beyond criticism, were not recognized as one of the most startling pictures of our emerging epoch."

How can I describe what I felt as I read this article, which flattered my writerly gifts, and this letter, which fanned the flames of my anguish at seeing myself ravaged in Margaret's heart? For was it not I too whom she loved unknowingly in Chesterfield? And did I not have the best part of it, the deepest part? The Chesterfield Margaret appreciated most she'd found in me and in my book, but the difficult constrictive love she felt came through Varlet and his whole way of being. Thus I saw that even had I revealed myself as *Beelzebub*'s author, Margaret would still not have loved me. And I would have destroyed her illusions about Jonathan's talent, because from then on, he would have been nothing more than an actor for her, albeit an actor she would have gone on loving.

All the other papers, from the *Daily Express* to *The Guardian*, joined the chorus, praising Chesterfield as the man of the hour, his novel as the book of the year. Goldman kept printing new editions; it was a real triumph, and no one had yet discovered the real author! Finally, it was decided to remedy this unfortunate deficiency on December 22, in the main lecture hall of the university, a stone's throw from the British Museum, in Bloomsbury. A message came from Varlet inviting me to attend the conference, and although at first I decided not to go, my curiosity finally got the better of me.

A large crowd was waiting on the sidewalk; I joined the throng and finally, at four o'clock, we all jostled each other into the amphitheater. Half an hour later, it was full. I was fortunate enough to find a seat just opposite the dais; the audience was composed of various significant personages—professors, socialites, reporters armed with cameras, and a hodgepodge of the simply curious, many of whom were students. A dozen microphones bristled on the long green-baize table facing the audience. Clearly, every resource had been mobilized to lend luster to the event.

At six-thirty, the president of the university and his associates arrived. Everyone rose in silence while they settled themselves, with just a hint of ceremoniousness, to the right of the dais. After them came Peter Warner and Babydoor, distinguishable by their respective sizes; they proceeded to occupy the left-hand side. This was the first time I'd seen my publishers, and the fact that they had no idea their author was in the audience amused me no end. Last to appear was an extremely dignified individual, dressed in formal attire like a funeral director, who walked slowly and deliberately to the center of the dais. He adjusted several microphones, cleared his throat, and began to speak, articulating each syllable clearly, his voice filled with emotion.

"Mr. President, honorable rectors, professors and associates, respected publisher, editor in chief, ladies and gentlemen . . ." It was ridiculous. "We have the honor and the pleasure, I should say the joy, to welcome today in the bosom of this venerable royal university someone whom the literary press has designated novelist of the year—Gilbert Keith Chesterfield!" Applause. "It is true, certainly, that all sorts of suppositions—I should say hypotheses, some of which are rather daring—have been bruited about by a public eager to know who is concealed behind the now-famous name of Chesterfield. Well, today—I should say, right this moment—you will see Mr. Chesterfield himself for the first time, and you are at liberty to question him as you will, both about himself and about his work, although it is understood, of course, that questions concerning Mr. Chesterfield's private life are not to be considered, as is only proper—I should say, as is customary. . . ."

The academic master of ceremonies paused to gauge the effects of his oratory, then suddenly announced in his bombastic voice: "I give you the writer Mr. Gilbert Keith Chesterfield!" At which point Jonathan appeared at the rear of the amphitheater, forcing the audience to turn around and enjoy him while he walked calmly down the aisle toward the dais in a suit of anthracite blue, amid thunderous applause and enough bravos to turn the Stratford players pale with envy. He took the three stairs in a single bound, then turned to face his public, who uttered a great "Ah!" of surprise and admiration, surprise at finding him so young, admiration at finding him so charming. The applause began again, louder this time. Jonathan bowed deeply, then bowed again. I was clearly the only one not seized with frenzy, for even the rotund, dignified, serious president of the university was clapping his hands frenetically, as were his colleagues. In the end, it took Varlet himself to end the grotesque frenzy.

He was a consummate actor, speaking softly so as to impose a more complete silence. And he spoke with simplicity and bonhomie, asking forgiveness for having disarranged so many schedules, describing his embarrassment at such a generous welcome, for really all he had done in this small novel, *Beelzebub*, he said, was to do his job as a writer. And he hoped to do better next time, a sportsmanlike expression that amused the gallery and provoked a new wave of hearty applause. I thought I was dreaming until a reporter stood up and began the questioning.

"Mr. Chesterfield, when did you begin to write?"

"I believe it was in my mother's belly," Jonathan shot back. Laughter and applause.

"Mr. Chesterfield," asked another reporter, "is your Elsbeth an imaginary character or are you describing a real passion?"

"Elsbeth? But Elsbeth is myself, Mr. Brompton!" he replied, instantly once again. I was amazed; he even knew the journalist's name!

"Mr. Chesterfield, is Alexander an avatar of Don Juan?"

"An excellent question," replied Varlet. "Do you realize that Western literature has only two choices—Don Juan and Faust—with Hamlet, or insignificance, in the middle? Don Quixote is a Don Juan without a country. Do you suppose that means we are condemned to Utopia?"

A thoughtful silence followed this response, rather more malicious than intelligent, but which each person felt to be the pinnacle of pertinence.

Clearly, Jonathan Varlet was as dexterous at seducing the masses as he was at seducing individuals. It was amazing, and rather frightening, to see these urbane people, so accustomed to the world's trickery and lies, fall into the simple trap set by this young man. And incredible as it may seem, I was quite unable to rid myself of an admiration for this amazing *tour de force*. Jonathan's self-assurance only added to my fascination, I who would only have stammered and stuttered before such a crowd, which I would have seen as hostile—and which certainly would have been! In fact, I completely forgot that I was the author of the book all these people so admired!

After the magic show ended, I did not remain in London but returned once again to my burrow, filled this time with bitterness about the true nature of human creatures and their society. How much more excited I was by my association with Jacob Boehme than by all this fanfare and playacting. I was made for silence and work, for imagining and writing. By assuming the burden of the public Chesterfield, Jonathan had left me the better part.

IF THIS DESCRIPTION OF THE EARLY stages of my relationship with Jonathan Absalom Varlet is so exhaustive, it's because I find it necessary that my reader understand the logic, or the aberration, behind my signing a pact that would bind us to each other until the end of our days. Of course, I cannot continue with such a luxury of detail, and so shall restrict myself to the essential moments that marked Gilbert K. Chesterfield's exceptional career. Through these moments, the particulars of my relationship with Varlet will certainly come clear.

First—and I hasten to confess immediately—*Beelzebub*'s prodigious success brought me a fortune. My parents' legacy had already made my life quite comfortable, but now I suddenly found myself the master of a rather considerable sum. Not only did the book sell increasingly well in Great Britain, but also throughout the Commonwealth, Australia, and the United States. Translations popped up all over Europe; myriad adaptations were made for radio and theater. All we lacked was a movie, and that was to come out two years later with the advent of talking films. In short, my bank account forced me to consider investing, which I proceeded to do in certain buildings in the Cannon Street area of London.

The contract stipulated that all royalties were to be deposited to my name, and from these sums I allotted ten percent to Varlet. We'd agreed on this figure during a brief conversation that, at the time, seemed not to interest him much. To be sure, it gave him quite enough income to live the good life, something he *was* very much interested in. I doubt there's a finer example of our contrasting temperaments—I saved, he spent. While I quietly invested in Cannon Street, he hopped from one hotel to the next, departed on junkets at the drop of a hat, and bestowed his presence on any group that wished to admire him.

During the year 1931, Varlet went to Scotland, Ireland, New York, Los Angeles, and Sydney; then on to Germany and France by way of Spain and Portugal, sometimes with dear Margaret in tow. The more glittering his wordly exploits, the more difficult her passion for him. In her eyes, it was all the same, the great international hotels so curiously interchangeable, the spectacle itself unchanging. Moreover, she reproached Chesterfield for not locking himself away to write the second book, unaware of how energetically I was proceeding at Ruthford with *The Fabulous Adventures of Jacob Stern*.

At last, in early September of that year, Jonathan came to visit. He came alone, and seemed tired. I hadn't seen him for many months, and he looked to me to have matured, to have come of age, as if he bore the dust of the road. Although the papers had kept me up to date on his travels and successes, he was different from what I'd expected; he did not seem anymore the facile, brilliant young man who'd given such a dashing press conference at the university.

It must have been around eleven in the morning when his car, a white Rolls-Royce driven by a chauffeur in a braided cap, pulled up at the gate. The fog had been heavy for the past eight days, and his apparition, like a sort of milky ghost floating up the main path to the front steps, had all the earmarks of the unreal.

"Well," I exclaimed, "a true revenant! If it weren't for newspapers and contracts, I should have thought you dead and buried! Is it truly you, Chesterfield?"

"Yes, my dear Chesterfield," he replied, giving me a hug, "it's truly me. The prodigal son, I suppose!"

We both laughed and retired into the house.

"You must forgive my silence," he began, when we'd seated ourselves in the drawing room, "but I do hate to write, as you know so well! So many things have happened, so many new friends, so much language,

I'm positively saturated. But before I get ahead of myself, I shall give you an accounting. Varlet the salesman shall submit his report—summary and bottom line—and I trust you'll be satisfied with his services. . . ."

"On the contrary," I said, amused, albeit somewhat surprised by the bitterness in his voice, "I should think you'd be delighted with all your junkets, all that glory and notoriety. I'm sure you were absolutely magnificent."

"You mustn't think I care about glory and notoriety," he said, shaking his head. "But the success of our enterprise depends on them, so if I smile, you must understand it as a function of my professional consciousness. Do you really think it's amusing repeating the same polite nonsense over and over to people you've never seen before, who welcome you with the same speeches as the previous day's people, none of whom you'll ever see again? What a gallery of rogues—academics, teachers, writers, poets, reporters—bald, bearded, thin, fat, handicapped, even women! And all of them swarming and simpering and bragging and quibbling! What a farce!"

"But I thought you liked all that, the whirlwind and drama, the constant commotion . . . At least you seemed so pleased with the public performance aspect of the press conference at the university. . . . Anyway, everything I've heard of your wanderings about the world suggests how comfortable you are with the fanfare, in fact with all of that farce you seem to decry so heartily!"

"Aha, so you're angry at me for being what you yourself have absolutely no desire to be! Well, that's too bad; I'm playing my part, and my part has consequences, and frankly, it's a terrible burden. But you must allow me to get on with my report. I really shall try to stick to the essentials, mind you, but it does mean taking all this mush and distilling it to a few people and situations that might merit your attention."

He spoke precisely and for a long time about my foreign publishers and translators, and the agreements he'd signed that I'd received by post.

"Whence cometh your tidy little fortune, dear Cyril, which I must say you've earned!"

"I feel like a slave driver." I shrugged. "I may have written *Beelzebub,* but your sales have obviously increased its value! Do you really think ten percent's enough, given what you do?"

"No complaints, my friend. I'm perfectly content. But I must tell you

some of my adventures, beginning with a German musician named David
Goethman. It's worth its weight in gold! Picture this. I arrive in Berlin
on March twenty-second, at the Metropol in Bergenstrasse. They've reserved a suite for me, with a grand piano, double chest of drawers,
drawing room, bedroom, marble bathroom—all of it in that heavy
pompous style so beloved of the Germans. A very dignified secretary
comes to see me to plan my week; after all, everything must be organized so I'll know exactly who I'm seeing from one moment to the next,
or what gathering I'll be attending, and all of it in the most ritualistic
detail—in short, a more rigorous schedule than you'd find in prison. You
can imagine how happy that made me."

He took a sip of whiskey.

"So this secretary has a great long list of the various personalities I'm
expected to meet, including a certain number of government officials.
But just as he gives me the list, the telephone rings and the aide assigned
to me says that a Maestro David Goethman is waiting in the lobby and
desires the honor of a brief visit. Panic. The secretary consults his list,
finds no mention of a Goethman, and orders me not to see him since he
has no appointment! I go to the phone and hear an anguished voice
repeating his request in a most perfectly refined English. Believe me,
Cyril, when I say an anguished voice I do not exaggerate. It sounded as
if he was on the verge of death. So I brush aside the secretary's objec-
tions and invite the man up.

" 'You shouldn't have,' the secretary keeps repeating, 'he's not on the
list. And anyway, he's a terrible musician!'

" 'Ah,' I say, 'you know who he is!'

" 'He's a Jew,' the secretary says, with a great deal of scorn, and then
walks out the door, doubtless so as not to be seen in the same place with
Mr. Goethman."

We sat down at the table, where Douglas served us with an obvious
lack of grace.

"Goethman's a heavyset man," Varlet continued, "with curly black
hair and a wrinkled face. The moment the door opens, he rushes up to
me, takes my hand, lifts it to his lips, and cries, 'What a good man you
are, Excellency! I had to meet you. I had to meet the author of the
marvelous *Beelzebub*, the premonitory *Beelzebub*, the masterpiece that
announces the coming of the Antichrist!'

" 'A madman,' I say to myself.

" 'Germany is headed for horror,' he rages. 'What can the Weimar

Republic do? We're completely paralyzed economically. Five million unemployed. One hundred eighty-seven deputies from the National Socialist Party have been elected to the Reichstag, and people believe they are the ones who will raise the country from its ashes, who will bring work to the entire nation! But, Excellency, you must understand who they are. They're fanatics. Rabble-rousers. And no one realizes this because everyone's deaf! The whole world is deaf! But I'm telling you the truth, the horrible truth. They're fanatics and rabble-rousers. I'm only a musician, but I hear the ghastly sound of their boots on the pavement! Excellency, they are anti-Semites, and nothing good can come from those who do not respect the children of Zion!' "

Jonathan served himself another helping of veal stew.

"Goethman's just coming to the end, and still with that terribly anguished voice, when the door flies open again and two men in gray raincoats, black felt hats, dark glasses, and leather gloves—obviously some sort of police—burst in. One of them yells, 'Hey, you there! Who gave you permission to come up here?' And he rushes over to the musician, who tries to shield himself. He's absolutely terrified. 'Now just a minute,' I say. I was livid. 'This gentleman is my guest. What gives you the right to burst in here without knocking? Explain this intrusion!' 'This individual is suspect, sir,' one of them says, in a voice like an automaton's. 'He is forbidden to establish contact with anyone whatsoever without special government authorization. Does he have that authorization? Well, does he?' Goethman is painful to look at. He's shaking all over. Beads of sweat on his forehead. 'Listen,' I say, as forcefully as I can, 'I've no idea what you've got against this man, but I need to talk with him about a purely artistic matter which does not in the least concern you. And now, please be good enough to leave us alone.' But they just stand there. They don't move. They don't say a word. So I go into the study to call the manager, but he's not in his office and neither is his assistant. When I go back into the drawing room, the two agents are gone and so is the musician. I dash out into the hallway, where a third man has blocked the door, and I distinctly hear Goethman's voice from the stairwell crying, 'Fanatics! Rabble-rousers!' What can I do? I go back into my suite, utterly stupefied."

We'd reached the dessert, but Varlet carried on.

"First thing the next day, I make inquiries about Goethman. I ask the man in the cultural affairs office, the one who's in charge of organizing the receptions I'm supposed to attend, but I'm met with a solid wall of silence. He even suggests I might be suffering from delusions. Was it not perhaps just some starstruck fan who'd used that strategy to get to me and pique my interest? I insist, but am requested to drop the subject and told that if I don't my visit will be cut quite short." Varlet raised his voice. "Can you imagine, Cyril? Cut short? Now the Germans are beginning to seriously annoy me, so I take myself to the British Embassy and explain the whole thing to our ambassador, a charming, rather old-fashioned gentleman by the name of Davies. Positively blinding in his dignity, I might say. 'Ah yes,' he says to me, 'your story confirms what we've already detected here and there, a sort of witch-hunt really, an as yet vague and latent hostility toward foreigners and Jews. Your David Goethman is right to fear the worst. I've already warned London about it, but you try and understand our politicians and their arcane *modus operandi*. They seem to be playing some role well outside the theater itself.' 'But what can we do for my musician?' I ask him. 'Nothing,' Davies says. 'If we try to help him, we'll destroy him. They'll accuse him of espionage. Of collusion with a foreign power. Are you perhaps familiar with self-locking handcuffs? The more you try to free yourself, the tighter they squeeze your wrists.' So I left, and I can tell you I was very alarmed."

I watched him as he spoke, surprised at his concern about the fate of a Jewish musician he didn't know. It seemed so out of character for Jonathan.

"My good friend," I said, unable to stop myself, "could it be that you've learned goodness?"

"It's true that Goethe's Faust changed at the end of his life," Jonathan replied, not a little amused by my question, "turning into the architect of a canal in Missolonghi, the very canal in which Byron would drown. Frankly, that always seemed to me a lot of trite twaddle. But today's Germany is different, Cyril. They're not proposing to restore order to the world out of some foolish romantic humanism, but in the name of an insane abstraction called race! The German race! Aryanism!"

"But why should that shock you?" I asked. "The Germans only wish to become German."

"It shocks me because the whole notion of Germany itself is so recent. And so fabricated. And it's this notion that's joined itself to the idea of Aryanism in order to give the nation a past, a memory. But what is Aryanism? Is it Wagner? Nietzsche? Or Wotan, Siegfried, Parsifal?

It's all a joke, but a deadly joke, my friend. A joke that stinks of lies and death!"

"Haven't you perhaps simply developed an interest in myth?" I asked, not quite sure exactly what he was talking about.

"Myth is fascinating, yes, but only for individual people. For whole nations, no! The integrity of a country is already based on myth, so if you add to it, you're giving it a dynamic that the country will be unable to control! But wait, let me tell you the rest of my musician story. . . ."

We went into the small drawing room, and Jonathan resumed his narrative.

"So there I am in Berlin for the entire week, feted with a rather chilly and rigid solemnity I find most distasteful. I meet a few writers but no one really interesting. No Thomas Mann. Not even his brother, Heinrich. A great many hollow speeches. And then, the night before my departure, just as I'm leaving an enormous banquet where two hundred glittering personalities have applauded my presence among them, I run into a demonstration at the door. Twenty or so young people waving signs. My interpreter assures me it's only a student meeting, but I can clearly see that something quite different is going on. They're hustling me toward the car when all of a sudden, a young girl in a black shawl with long black fringes throws herself at me and seizes my arm. My escorts swear at her, but she cries, in perfect English I might add, 'I am Maestro Goethman's daughter! I beg you, listen to me!' I hug her to me and, half carrying her, push her ahead of me into the car."

Jonathan's face reddened with the memory.

"The minute the doors shut," Jonathan went on, "I order the driver to take us to the Metropol. The people with me are still outside, banging on the car, and the driver pretends he doesn't hear me. Finally, my interpreter yanks the door open and shouts, 'This is an outrage! Throw the girl out!' 'I'm a British citizen,' I tell him, 'and this is my fiancée. I demand that you let us return to the hotel. If not, I shall call my embassy!' It's the first thing that came to mind and everyone hesitates a moment while the interpreter translates. Someone gives an order. The door slams. The car starts up and we go to the hotel."

"This is positively incredible!" I said. "And then what?"

"We finally get to the room and lock the door. The girl's hysterical, shivering, her teeth are chattering. I sit her down in one of the armchairs and take a good look at her. She's much younger than I thought, sixteen perhaps, which doesn't exactly help the situation. She's got the beauty of a wild thing—the face of a Jewish angel and the body of a cat. 'Thank you, oh thank you,' she stammers. 'My father made me promise to contact you if anything terrible happened!' 'And did something happen?' I ask. She bursts into tears. 'They found him on the sidewalk in front of our apartment. He'd thrown himself out of the window. Or at least that's what the police said. . . . But my father was a practicing Jew, Mr. Chesterfield! He would never have taken his own life, I swear it!' Her distress was painful to watch. 'Have you brothers or sisters?' I ask. 'And your mother?' She tells me her mother died several years ago and since she has no brothers or sisters, she's alone in the world. 'Well,' I tell her, 'you've got to get out of the country. There's nothing holding you here, is there?' She says she has a few friends and a cat. I advise her to leave her friends and bring the cat. Which is precisely what she did."

"What are you saying? You left Germany with this adolescent and her cat?"

"But of course, my dear Cyril!" he laughed. "And you mustn't upset yourself over such a small thing. At the moment, Sarah Goethman has been studying in London since April. Margaret's delighted. As for me, well, I do believe I've grown quite attached to her."

"That's all very well and good, but would you mind telling me how you managed to get this child out of Germany?"

"It was a snap," Jonathan replied. "As soon as Sarah told me what had happened, I called a taxi on the pretext that I was accompanying her to her home. At which point, I left all my luggage in the room and told the driver to take us to Potsdam, where we caught the first train for Geneva, an excellent overnight train which crossed the border the following morning. The conductor had read *Beelzebub*, and when he found out who I was, he took me for Alexander and Sarah for Elsbeth! I told him the most prosaic, and the most dramatic, truth, which fired up his fervor for the neutrality of Switzerland and the Red Cross. At customs, he swore that I was alone in the compartment and that no one could disturb the sleep of the brilliant Chesterfield! One of the pluses of fame, my friend."

"I can just imagine the good Germans when they discovered their prize guest missing," I said, delighted with the story.

"Quite a scandal indeed. Davies, the ambassador, was called in to see the minister. The police chief was fired. I've no idea what happened to

my hosts, particularly my interpreter, but I warrant their careers have
been seriously compromised. But the main thing is the musician's daughter
was saved."

"Well, that makes you a hero. It suits you, you know. Just one more
reason for people to admire you, no?"

He didn't seem to understand my allusion.

"Yes indeed," he said, draining his Drambuie, "little Sarah seems to
adore me. . . . I've nicknamed her the Jewish Angel. She's no idea how
to thank me, and you know, she's very much like me when I lived with
my lord—that same timid devotion, that same desire to learn so as to
be worthy of her benefactor. She's like my pupil, in a way. . . . And
now, if you'll permit me, I think I'll tell you another story, somewhat
less spectacular, but which ends with a phrase I heard and that I promised myself I'd remember for you. This one happened in France.
Shall I?"

"Do carry on!" I replied.

"The French are a strange breed. They promise you cathedrals, they
give you circus booths, but just when you think they've nothing to offer,
they show you Versailles! Doubtless, it's all held together with sticking
plaster, but well enough so it doesn't collapse on your head. Likewise,
to hear them talk, you'd think there was no worse government and country
than theirs, but should you have the impudence to denigrate what they've
just critized, they shut you up with consummate vulgarity. In short, I
was welcomed in Paris in April by a delegation of nabobs, wretched
gastronomes, fancy literati incapable of uttering a single English syllable
but terribly proud of their talents for quoting Greek and Latin. Every
one of these fancy gentlemen was a president; there didn't seem to be
any members at all. Anyway, their first gesture of goodwill was to give
me a medal, after which we were blessed with a series of long-winded
speeches which no one listened to since everyone was totally absorbed
in food and drink and the ladies' décolleté."

"Did you try the frogs' legs?"

"Snails, which was far worse. Rather like fried rubber . . . You ate
one of the creatures, then drank a glass of wine, then another creature
and another glass of wine, and so on! I absolutely defy you to get through
the dozen without becoming perfectly drunk. Anyway, during one of
those interminable dinners given by the Société des Gens de Lettres, I
sat next to a young woman who kept glancing at me sideways. Quite
frightened, actually. Never opened her mouth. The fat lady chattering

away to my left explained that she was 'the wife of that sweet little Duvalier who'd written *Le Précipice des Dieux* and gotten himself the Femina Prize the year before. . . .' So I leaned toward my timid neighbor and asked her in what passed for French if she wrote too, at which point her eyes became quite anxious and her eyelids fluttered like the wings of a terrified bird. 'I'd never dare,' she murmured. 'And why not?' I asked, trying not to scare her away. She seemed so fragile, like a piece of porcelain. She gave a little gasp and glanced at me furtively. 'Probably because I'm too romantic. . . .' "

"Uh oh, I beg you, spare me your romantic escapades! Leave your piece of porcelain on the table and tell me instead about Margaret."

"But you don't understand a word I'm saying, Cyril! Nothing to do with romance, I promise you! It's that the fragile little wife of Monsieur Duvalier thought she was Elsbeth. Can you imagine? She confessed to me between two careful silences. The trouble was, her Duvalier wasn't Alexander! More like a shopkeeper, it seems. So my Madame Bovary fantasized. She told herself the story of *Beelzebub;* and finally she admitted that I'd disappointed her. I was too blond, too young, and anyway she'd once been in love with an artillery man who hunted wild animals in Africa. My delicious little woman became quite animated, lost her shyness in fact, the minute she started talking about blood and claws, and in the end, she looked at me really quite feverishly and said, 'Elsbeth kills Alexander because she changes from the hunted to the hunter.' Fantastic, isn't it?"

"Indeed," I replied. "It took a timid and probably slightly intoxicated woman to see what no critic has figured out yet! Your Madame Duvalier is very perceptive. And then what happened?"

"Just listen to yourself!" Varlet replied, amused by my sudden excitement. "Just what would you expect to happen? You would doubtless have seduced her, but not me! In any case, I was so smothered in speeches I had no time to do anything else. If I bother to tell you about this little encounter, it's only because I thought you'd appreciate the phrase: *'Elsbeth de gibier est devenue chasseresse.'* Once the hunted, Elsbeth becomes the huntress. Apparently, that's what Alexander wanted. Everything he says is aimed at elevating his young wife to precisely that role, that measure of dignity."

"Magnificent! Your piece of porcelain has opened my eyes to the hidden workings of my hero in a way that I never quite suspected. How strange to realize one hasn't understood the basic thing about a character one's carried within oneself, and described, and thought so much about. No, that's not it. I'm lying to myself. . . . When I write, do I think at all? But tell me, is this Madame Duvalier happy at least?"

"Certainly not," Jonathan replied. "She sat there like a wounded bird and then, all of a sudden, she's a tigress. One moment she's moaning about her insignificance, the next she's despairing because she has only a Duvalier to dismember! Romantic she was, and I must confess that were I Chesterfield, I'd make her a character immediately, a mélange of Ophelia and Phaedra. Although it's true that Ophelia's simply Gertrude's lost purity, just like Elsbeth's your soul in search of its liberty."

"What do you mean?" I was stunned.

"I mean that Elsbeth is your soul, imprisoned in this house from which you can't escape except by killing Alexander, your father's image, the all-too-encumbering Pumpermaker."

"What do you know about it?" I snapped, getting to my feet.

"Please forgive me," Jonathan said softly. "I thought you'd figured all that out."

I sat down heavily.

"Yes, of course, quite right, I had indeed supposed that to be true, in a way, but not quite so obvious, you know. Not quite so lucid. I see it as my mother, little Mary Charmer, freeing herself from the monster. But now, yes, I see it's really me. But could the solicitor incite me to so much hatred?"

"Madame Duvalier has offered you a more grandiloquent explanation," Varlet said. "You started with a banal reckoning of accounts and have arrived at the highest dimensions of tragedy. Which is what accounts for *Beelzebub*'s success. Everyone finds in it what they've brought to it." Jonathan paused. "And now, you must tell me about your new novel!"

"Always a difficult frontier, the second book."

"When will you finish?"

"Next year, probably."

Varlet seemed upset.

"Peter Warner's getting impatient. He's pushing me. And his daughter's found every conceivable way of making me feel guilty. Whichever, I'm going to have to disappear, under the pretext of writing my book. There's no choice. But we'll talk about that later. Would you like me to tell you about New York?"

I'd received several different proposals from America, particularly for dramatic adaptations of *Beelzebub*, a subject that interested me enormously. "Onward to New York!" I exclaimed.

"No speeches, no fancy receptions," Varlet said, draining his third glass of Drambuie. "Nothing like that in New York. Simply a mob of businessmen, many of them with the manners of illiterates and all of them simply agog with the moneymaking possibilities of your dear Chesterfield! Money. The only concern, the only horizon, the limit of all thought! Of course, the Depression is at its lowest point and doing business with the pound remains one of the only sectors where something's happening. Everything else is stagnating or falling apart outright. Bankruptcies everywhere. Unemployment. No more the great and gorgeous United States, the conquering giant of five years ago. Anyway, this chap named Bradyson, an impresario in the theater, wants to do *Beelzebub* on Broadway next year. 'How much?' he asks me. I was caught short. 'Tell you tomorrow,' I say. Everyone talks with such a penury of words, believe me. So he leaves, but then two minutes later, he's back. 'How much?' he asks me again. I was even more surprised. 'Tomorrow . . .' I say. He disappears, but fifteen minutes later, there he is again. 'How much?' I was starting to get angry. 'Tomorrow at three o'clock!' I bark at him. After he leaves, Bromfield, the publisher who was with me, says, 'You were very tough with him. Hard to resist, Bradyson.' I dared not tell him that if I hadn't given an answer, it was only because I had no idea how much subsidiary rights were worth!"

Jonathan smiled.

"So I asked Bromfield how much *Rosemary* had sold for. That was the big attraction at the moment, very fashionable. Adapted from a novel Bromfield had published. 'Two hundred thousand,' he says, quite proud of himself. Next day, Bradyson arrives at three on the dot. 'So?' I light a cigar and reply, sort of off the cuff, 'Three hundred thousand.' He gasped. 'Can we negotiate?' I blew a cloud of smoke toward the ceiling and replied laconically, 'No.' He scratched his head with remarkable energy, then rushed over to me, hand outstretched. 'It's a deal, Chesterfield. Twenty percent tomorrow, twenty in September, the rest in three payments, December, January, February, okay?' Incredible, isn't it?'"

"You are an unbelievable manager," I said sincerely, for in fact the promised amounts had been deposited in full in my account in the Bank of England.

"I also met Fath Martin, the writer in charge of the adaptation, a large round-faced fellow with a checkered handkerchief for mopping the

constant perspiration from his forehead. Neurotic perspiration, of course.
Chap thinks he's suffocating all the time. Believes someone's going to
lock him up somewhere. Wherever he goes, claustrophobia lurks; he
spends all his time opening windows and refusing to use elevators. And
he's the one who's going to shut himself into your cloister with Alexander and Elsbeth! Know what he said to me? 'Bradyson's a bastard. He's
doing it on purpose!' "

"But what are they going to do to *Beelzebub*?"

"Make it a musical comedy," Varlet replied calmly. "They're all the
rage. Even the intellectuals pay attention to them. Imagine Elsbeth sung
by a Negress! And why not? Americans will do anything. Nothing shocks
them. The only thing that matters is perfection. They've got a sort of
cult of professionalism. Other than that, they'd put Queen Victoria
onstage and send her up singing 'I'm the Queen of *Angleterre*, and I
adore all *pommes de terre*' in a hot-air balloon! Nothing puts them off."

"Even so," I replied, "the idea of Elsbeth as a show girl quite revolts
me. The critics will have a field day."

"On the contrary. American reviews—they don't have critics—are only
concerned about successes. And with Bradyson, it's a sure thing."

"I dare not think what the publicity will be like," I murmured.

Douglas appeared suddenly, to inform me she was retiring. It was
midnight already.

"You haven't said much about Margaret."

"Oh, she goes with me from time to time, ever ready to criticize, I
might add. She thinks I'm too available, too extroverted—that's her word.
But I don't see how I can do otherwise. It's true she thinks I'm a writer
and, as such, haven't got the solitary temperament of one. Which is why
I'm going to retire for a time so everyone will believe I'm writing."

"Where will you go?"

"To Venice. I haven't been to Italy since I went there with my lord.
Know who I'm taking with me?"

"Margaret," I replied immediately.

"Certainly not." He shrugged. "I'm taking my little Jewish Angel, the
delightful Sarah . . . and I'm taking you too!"

"Why do you make Margaret suffer like that?" I asked angrily.

"I have no intention of making her suffer," he snapped back. "I'm
no Alexander. She's the one that makes me suffer, with her incessant
recriminations. Sarah, on the other hand, is the perfect adolescent. Desperately grateful. She'll be a great comfort to me."

"Sarah . . . and you . . . ?"

"Naturally," he replied, amused at what must have struck him as a quite ridiculous prudery. "Even in the sleeper that brought us from Germany. After all, we were in the same compartment, the same couchette even, and she was so small, all curled up against me. . . ."

"Please . . . !" I interrupted.

"Quite right. But it didn't keep her from quite fascinating the surrealists, you know. All that freedom in grief, that wildness in innocence! Compared to her, Margaret's just a pretentious, fancy woman."

I was outraged. The "fancy woman" was too much.

"Listen, there's no question of my going with you. It would be a terrible betrayal of Margaret, who happens to be a woman for whom I have enormous respect. What's more, I have no desire to play the sycophant."

"But I need you!"

"Whatever for?"

He seemed not to understand. "Aren't we friends? Hasn't our collaboration brought us even closer?" His blue eyes studied me with a sort of surprise.

"I'd be happy to come with you if Margaret comes too," I replied firmly.

He thought for a moment.

"Right. So be it. We'll take both Margaret and Sarah. After all, you might wind up seducing the first while I continue the second's education!" After which, with just a hint of irritation, he went upstairs to bed.

Jonathan Absalom Varlet had changed indeed. Added to his casualness, there was a certain gravity now, which in no way detracted from his charm but gave him the sort of maturity conducive to his role as writer. His youth had surprised everyone at the press conference, but during his travels across the world, he'd acquired a *savoir-faire* that gave him the flavor of an old hand, even though he was only twenty-six. True, he had a prodigious capacity for adaptation, and his remarkable memory allowed him to learn languages with disconcerting ease. Also, he found it easy to slip inside the skin of whatever character he was incarnating; he could fool anyone, and could even show the craftiest of old dogs new tricks, especially in the domain of deception. Thus, and from this moment on, I did not quite trust him.

He slept in the next day, coming down only at eleven o'clock.

"You can't imagine what a joy it is to be back at Ruthford!" he exclaimed. "I feel as if I lived my childhood here. Each corner has a memory for me. Strange, isn't it? To remember things one's never known?"

When Jonathan left, I plunged back into Jacob Stern's Germany, for my young hero's journeys interested me far more than Jonathan's. To me, they had meaning, whereas Jonathan's travels seemed animated by a kind of Brownian movement wholly devoid of signification. In quest of his soul, Jacob endured fanaticism, religious wars, hypocrisy. He was thrown into prison, abused, scorned. But how much richer were these abysses than the molehills on which perched the factitious glory of our pseudo-Chesterfield, who had perhaps no soul at all?

Two days after Jonathan's visit, I received a letter from Margaret Warner:

Dear Cyril,

It seems we're all going to Venice together. Our great leader told me yesterday. He wants to work on his next novel, which pleases me, but in his painful solitude, I suppose he needs a court. That would be you and me, and a young girl he's rescued from the German police, an absolute peach whom I'm quite fond of and whom I rather suspect Jonathan's in love with. And why not? For months now, my relationship with Chesterfield has made no sense. I'm counting on our stay in the royal city of Venice to clarify my thoughts and resolve my future. I shall be delighted to take advantage, quite egotistically, of your friendship while our hero dedicates himself to his work. Our departure is scheduled for eight in the morning next Thursday, from Victoria Station. We go via Dover, Le Havre, Paris, Lyon, Turin, and Milan, arriving in Venice on the eighteenth. We've reserved rooms at the Danieli. Isn't it marvelous?

Affectionately,
Margaret

And so the project was under way. We really were going to Venice! And while Varlet busied himself with Sarah, I would be alone with Miss Warner, which stirred me up a bit. I'd forced myself not to think of her and now we were going to be thrown together; what's more, we'd be in the most romantic city in Europe! Suddenly, I regretted my proposal, but it was too late to go back on my decision, the more so since Margaret's letter alluded to our friendship in terms that did not quite conceal a sort of appeal. So I packed my bags, not knowing how long I'd be away.

I met the rest of the party on September 16 at Dover Station. Margaret introduced me to Sarah, whom I found skinny, swarthy, and unattractive—in sum, nothing to rave about, except for her eyes, which were immense, intense, and black as night. On the other hand, I was struck once again by Miss Warner's serene beauty, by the impeccable elegance of her dress and her discreet charm. Sarah was nothing but a half-baked child, while Margaret had all the seductiveness of the young English aristocrat for whom the word *fair* must surely have been invented, a word that meant beautiful, noble, blond, and loyal. And once again, I was amazed at Varlet's reluctance to accept the marriage offered him, and at the little idyll developing between the young Gretchen and himself, an idyll that could in no way compare to the quality of a union with Margaret!

Varlet was quite loquacious. He wore a houndstooth suit and explained in great detail the trouble he had with his Regent Street tailor, "a rascally idiot with such hairy ears a toad could have lived in them." Sarah was delighted, obviously thrilled to be part of the team.

"So," I said, teasing, "how's the novel going, my dear Chesterfield?"

"He's not written a word yet!" Margaret replied.

"I beg to differ," Varlet said, "it's all up here," and he tapped his forehead with the palm of his hand.

"Can't you tell us what it's about?" Margaret went on.

"Listen, Margaret Warner," Jonathan replied, "I did not agree to bring you on this trip for you to turn it into a courtroom!" Upon which he opened his book and sulked in the corner until the train began to move.

By way of dissipating the tension, I asked Sarah what she thought of England; she replied that Margaret and Jonathan had been so good to her that she would spend the rest of her life thanking them, that London was a gayer city than Berlin, that she felt so free, that her classmates had accepted her immediately and with such kindness, whereas in Germany she was regarded as "some sort of animal." She then told us about her father, who'd raised her and whom she'd loved so deeply that when he died, she thought she too would die, but Jonathan had snatched her from the dragon's claws so quickly that she seemed to be starting a completely new life. It was a sort of resurrection, a word she insisted upon.

Visibly, the child moved Margaret deeply. She watched her, eyes filled with compassion and affection. I noticed that Sarah's dress had once belonged to Margaret; clearly, they'd needed only to take it in a bit, for the child was thinner and smaller.

"Our poor old world is quite ill," Margaret said. "Given what's happening in Germany and Russia, and the whole economic crisis, don't you feel we're heading for war? My father says that the era of heroic wars ended at Verdun in a ghastly butchery. Now we're going to have a filthier kind of war where civilians and soldiers will both be involved in the horror. And why? For strictly economic reasons! Isn't that frightful?"

"There's never been any such thing as a heroic war," Varlet said, breaking his silence and peering over the top of his book. "All wars are filthy because murder is filthy. It dirties death." He dove back into his book, and the clackety-clack of the wheels on the rails.

At Dover, the train proceeded onto a ferryboat, which amazed Sarah until she turned her attention to the sea gulls. Jonathan continued to read and sulk in his corner. It was then that Margaret began to tell me the story of her childhood.

"Do you realize our great leader has no idea where I was born?" she began. "Well, it was in Harrogate, not far from York. Harlow-Car Gardens, to be precise, the horticultural center of the region. Nothing but flowers and plants and bushes wherever you go. My mother insisted on giving birth in her mother's house, as women did in those days, but as soon as I was a few weeks old, they brought me back to London. Years before, my father had started his own newspaper, a weekly, in Liverpool, where he grew up. It was a Conservative paper, so when he was still a bachelor, he was invited to the homes of all the local bankers and shipowners, the textile and rubber merchants, even the politicians and administrators. That's where he met George Goldman, the grandson of John Goldman, who founded the publishing business. Of course, George Goldman had nothing to do with books, being a manufacturer of tinned beef. The two men admired each other. My father left Liverpool for London, and when Goldman died, my father bought up his publishing house. Or so the story goes. 'From Journalist to Publisher, or: The Sensational Success of Peter Warner'! But it wasn't that simple."

"Tell me about it," I said, for I sensed Margaret wished to confide in me.

"My father was born in difficult circumstances," she continued. "He was a cripple, a dwarf, but with a brilliant mind. That's why he's spent his whole life struggling to make a place for himself, to win out over the powerful and famous. He has such a strong will that no one can stand up to him when he decides what he's going to do. His weekly was a kind of springboard. People feared his moods, his criticism. He made and unmade the careers of local politicians. But his secret garden was his love of the arts. Every year, he added new Dutch and Flemish canvases to his collection of paintings. And without anyone noticing, he kept a vigilant eye on English publishing. In his newspaper, he'd already published several short stories by authors who would later be part of his stable, people like Peepward, Gascoyne, Claydon. And then one day, he heard that George Goldman had no interest whatsoever in books, so he asked him to come round."

We left the ferry at Le Havre and continued on to Paris, Varlet still reading and sulking, Sarah sleeping. Margaret and I spoke in whispers.

"Goldman cared only about the financial aspects of the business, so the books he published dealt only with hunting, fishing, miniature models, and cricket. My father called them 'almanac literature.' As soon as my father entered the business, he turned the house upside down, bringing in literary novelists and breaking off relations with the almanac writers, a move which dangerously lowered sales figures for three years. George Goldman panicked. Which was when my father began buying shares in the company. At the same time, another event occurred: Goldman's young wife fell madly in love with my father, who was certainly not handsome, but who had vastly more intelligence and culture than your typical gussied-up illiterate Conservative. When he found out, Goldman refused to sell the stock my father needed to become the majority shareowner. And then what happens? They find Goldman dead, murdered in his country home in Harlington."

"My god!" I murmured. "I had no idea. . . ."

"Because of my father's position in the newspaper world, the papers said nothing. But that didn't keep suspicions from falling on him and on Goldman's wife, Clara, the more so since they found a passionate letter addressed to her and written by Peter Warner in the trunk of George's car! However, at the time of death, my father and Clara were both at a reception in London where a hundred well-known personalities could swear to having seen them. The police thought they might have hired a gunman but no one could prove it. The case was closed, and after the appropriate delay, Clara Goldman married Peter Warner."

"That must have set tongues wagging," I remarked.

"Not so much," Margaret replied quickly. "People feared my father, to be sure, but more than that, they admired him. No one really believed he could actually have desired his associate's death. There was a formidable series of coincidences in the chain of events, but that was all. In any case, my father continued to be invited everywhere just as before, more so in fact, because, thanks to the fine writers he published, the business became increasingly respected. Clara had inherited her husband's stock, and when she in turn died, in a stupid fall from a horse, my father found himself the owner of all the shares and thus the sole owner of the house."

"Incredible."

"Yes. That's exactly what a young police commissioner thought at the time. He reopened the case."

"What year was this?"

"Nineteen twenty. During the war, the house became really famous because of Henry Frazer's *Mud and War*, which sold almost as many copies as *Beelzebub*. Frazer had a daughter, Diana, who married my father a year after Clara's death. I'm their daughter. As for the young commissioner, he moved heaven and earth but couldn't find anything that would warrant a new inquiry. Still, the whole episode really upset my father, who suspected the Labourites of having set the whole thing up in order to ruin his reputation. The issue came up often during my childhood, but only in veiled terms which, helped along by my youthful imagination, surrounded the affair with even more mystery."

"You must have been quite marked by all this," I hazarded cautiously. Margaret lowered her voice even further.

"Once, when I was very young, a nasty child took me aside in the school playground and started singing in a shrill voice, like she was chanting a nursery rhyme, 'Her father killed her mother! Her father killed her mother!'—which was not only mean but untrue, since Clara wasn't my mother, and she died because she fell off a horse. But it made me realize suddenly that because my father was deformed and because he was so successful, he was the target of a lot of spiteful people. This drew me closer to him. Besides, my mother, Diana, understood exactly how upset I was and was clever enough to make me understand, despite my youth, that if my father was physically different from everyone else, that didn't mean he was evil. She told me a story, the one about the elves in the forest, and my father became the king of the elves, the defender of widows and orphans against all the evil people, especially the red-haired girl with the braids on the playground who dared sing such odious songs. A while later, I was taken out of school and my education handed over to a tutor."

I was flattered that Margaret had told me her secret, for it was thus that I became her confidant. My happiness doubtless showed quite clearly on my face, for Varlet suddenly shut his book and emerged from his silence.

"What are you two plotting? Such a lot of muttering!"

"We didn't want to waken Sarah," Margaret said.

"What an interminable voyage," Jonathan sighed. "I'm dying to get to Venice and start work."

We were, however, stopping off in Paris for two days, to rest, see a few sights, and attend a performance at the opera house.

"While you're escorting the two ladies about, Cyril," Varlet continued, "I shall go see Gallimard, my publisher. And my translator. France is the last European country to translate *Beelzebub*. And they think they're in the literary vanguard! The vanguard! What in heaven's name does that mean?"

Clearly, Varlet was still in a foul mood, but we arrived at last, at eight in the evening, at the Gare du Nord, where a surprise awaited us.

W HILE THE PORTERS RUSHED ABOUT removing our luggage from the compartment and loading it onto a cart, a stylish young woman in a cloche hat, straight skirt, and gray fox stole rushed up to Jonathan as he climbed, grumbling, down from the train.

"Monsieur Chesterfield!"

Surprised, he looked up, searched his memory, found nothing.

"Pardon me," he replied in French, "but whom have I the honor of addressing?"

"Dear Monsieur Chesterfield," the woman said, cocking her head, "we sat next to each other at the dinner, the Société des Gens de Lettres dinner, the last time you came to Paris! I am Madame Duvalier!"

"Ah yes, of course. And what brings you here, *chère madame?*"

"I've been waiting for you," she laughed.

At that moment, Margaret appeared on the top stair. I took her arm. Sarah followed, struggling with a large hatbox.

"But how did you know I'd arrive today? And on this train?"

"But the newspapers, of course! Just look!"

We looked. A crowd was rushing toward us along the platform, led by a dozen photographers, cameras in hand.

"My god!" Margaret exclaimed. "What's all this?"

Frightened, Sarah backed up into the train.

"Messieurs," I declared, confronting the multitude, "this is a purely private visit!"

Barely able to decelerate, the tide turned only a few inches from us. Our eyes smarted with magnesium flashes; our ears were deafened by cries of "Smile! Smile!" There must have been two hundred people clapping their hands and shouting, "Chesterfield! Chesterfield!" I was quite alarmed.

"Dear friends and old companions!" Jonathan cried, hoisting himself onto the carriage steps. "Thank you for your most fraternal welcome! The French have the genial gift of being first, everywhere and in everything. For that reason, I'm delighted to find myself among you once again!" (Cries of "Bravo!")

A reporter held out a microphone. "Monsieur Chesterfield, your novel is an international success. But it has not yet appeared in French. Can you tell us why?"

"Because the French publisher wants it to be translated better than anywhere else!" (Laughter.)

"Is it true you're going to marry Marie Pinorge?" (A French movie actress.)

"She'll need to get divorced first. And then I'd have to consent to marry a divorced woman!" (Laughter.)

"What about the economic crisis, Monsieur Chesterfield?"

An imposing figure, none other than Jonathan's French publisher, Gaston Gallimard, burst through the crowd.

"Leave the man alone, please! I'm so sorry, Monsieur Chesterfield. Our house is not in the habit of greeting its authors in quite this way. It's all the fault of the press."

Varlet shook hands, then introduced Margaret, Sarah, and finally me. "My friend and secretary," he declared, "Cyril Ruthford!"

I stared at him in amazement, but he'd already gone on.

"What a pleasure to see you again! The publisher of Gide! Of Larbaud! It's a pity French writers are so impossible to translate."

Once again, Varlet had regained that casualness, volubility, and extraordinary cultural finesse so dazzling to even the most erudite. Taking Madame Duvalier's arm, he plunged into the crowd, which parted respectfully. The rest of his little troupe followed behind.

"My father knew this Monsieur Gide," Margaret told me. "He published his *Lafcadio's Adventures*, that horrid story where a man throws one of his friends from the door of a train, out of a kind of intellectual pleasure. A 'gratuitous act,' they call it, although I daresay it's not very gratuitous for the chap who gets run over!"

We both laughed. Two cars stood waiting for us at the curb. Varlet, Gallimard, and Madame Duvalier got into the first; Margaret, Sarah, the hatbox, and I occupied the second. The suitcases and trunks had been piled onto the roof, where they formed a rather unstable pyramid held in place by straps and string. (Oh, the French!) And so off we went to the Ritz on the Place Vendôme, a location highly prized by post-Fitzgerald writers. Fortunately, we were Gallimard's guests, for otherwise I should have felt badly about the expense, since the hotel was exactly the sort of place that bored me to extremes and where I should have been unhappy indeed if I'd had to stay there too often. Too many people, too much coquetry, too many idle affected gestures. Jonathan, of course, adored it. The moment we arrived, he took us on a tour from the cellars stocked with rare wines to the top floor, which had been turned into an art gallery. He seemed every bit as comfortable as if he'd been in his own home.

We had agreed I was to play the secretary, and thus handle all the invitations extended the illustrious Chesterfield. But the telephone never stopped ringing, and since I had every intention of strolling about the city with Margaret, and eventually Sarah, I arranged for the concierge to take our messages, after which I went down to the lobby to meet the ladies. And whom should I chance upon the moment I entered but Madame Duvalier, in a chic black Chanel suit! Clearly she'd decided to lay siege.

"Isn't Coco an absolute dream!" she cried when she saw me. She whirled around so that I might admire her, then resumed her habitual timidity, a pose, surely, but a most attractive one.

"Chesterfield has spoken to me of you," I said. "In fact, he quoted me something you said during the banquet. About *Beelzebub.* You said, 'Once the hunted, Elsbeth becomes the huntress.' I must confess I'd never thought of that reversal."

She smiled condescendingly, as if to say, What can a secretary understand of all that? Jonathan had described her as a china doll, a shy and fragile woman with hidden claws, and inside, throbbing with passion. I myself found her rather frivolous. Clever, mind you, but lacking in real intelligence. Fortunately Margaret appeared, followed by Sarah looking more than ever like a stray cat. The women nodded to each other, after which we left Madame Duvalier in the lobby and went out to see the city.

The following day, I learned that Duvalier—first name, Olympe—had managed to get up to the third floor, knock at Varlet's door, and offer herself to him straightaway. Another victim turned huntress! It seems she'd gone to all that trouble in order to get her novelist husband translated into English and published by Goldman. Did it disappoint Jonathan not to be loved solely for his good looks and presumed genius? The fact is, he was vexed; when he realized the lovely Olympe's game, he congratulated her on her charms, and her ardor, and sent her home with the message that he would never help someone so spineless as to resort to such a strategy. There was rather a scandal, with Madame Duvalier rushing to Gallimard in her Chanel and demanding that he break all relations with that "ignoble Englishman," that "impotent Chesterfield," and other gallant remarks of a similar persuasion.

Of course, Gallimard paid no attention to her tears, and Olympe and her husband simply disappeared from the celestial galaxy of Parisian luminaries. On the other hand, Margaret pointed out rather sharply to Jonathan that he clearly hadn't wasted any time cheating on her with that "hussy"—actually, she used the French word, *gourgandine*—which provoked a painful scene. It was obviously not the first time Varlet had indulged in this sort of philandering nor the first time Margaret had reprimanded him, but it was the first time I'd been present, however unwillingly, at either. The scene occurred after a rather lugubrious dinner at a charming restaurant called La Closerie des Lilas, where we'd had to endure the philosophical prating of a necrophiliac academician who took himself for Schopenhauer. Under his aegis, the crayfish seemed mummified, the leg of lamb cadaverous, and the deep-dish *tarte des demoiselles Tatin* composed of moribund pears. In short, the atmosphere wasn't congenial, and when we'd taken leave of the philosopher and found ourselves safely back out on the sidewalks of Montparnasse, Jonathan cried, "My God, what a ghastly profession! Verdier is just too sinister!"

"If you stuck to writing, my dear," Margaret interrupted, tight-lipped, "instead of staging dramatic performances, you wouldn't have time for little trysts with charming china dolls like Olympe Duvalier!"

"You have a rather bourgeois conception of such things, darling; they commit no one to anything. She was a turkey, that little Frenchwoman; my error that I mistook her for a swan. And anyway, what does it matter to you?"

We'd reached the Café Dome, where local artists, known and unknown, congregated amidst pipe smoke, peals of female laughter, and accordion music.

"I knew I never should have gone with you on this trip. In fact, I shouldn't go with you anywhere anymore! After all, we're not married!"

"Quite right," Jonathan snapped.

"All right then!" Margaret exclaimed. "Good-bye! Come, Cyril. Let's leave the sublime Chesterfield to his girls!"

She dragged me into the café, where her appearance provoked the applause of several students. Through the glass, I saw Sarah hesitate, but Varlet took her firmly by the arm and they walked off together.

"I can't take it anymore," Margaret said tonelessly, sitting down on a banquette. "It was the whole evening! And Jonathan's haughtiness! Forgive me, Cyril, for making such a scene. . . ."

"But Jonathan shows you no sense of decorum," I reassured her. "You're quite right not to tolerate his attitudes. There's nothing to forgive you for."

We ordered two Buchanans; the waiter looked at us with some surprise and suggested Napoleon instead, a name that amused us and made us forget about Varlet for a moment.

"After all, what right do I have to keep our great leader from sleeping with whomever he wants?"

"It's my fault, really. I'm the one who insisted that Jonathan invite you to come along when he'd planned to bring only Sarah. I told him if you didn't come, I wouldn't either."

"I suspected as much," she sighed. "I'm nothing but his publisher's daughter. He used me to convince my father, and now I'm of no further help to him."

"When one is not in love, certain situations are indeed absurd," I agreed. "But you love him, and your love takes the place of logic. I wonder, however, just what it is in him that you love? The way he looks? His ineffable charm? His erudition?"

She sipped at her brandy.

"In the beginning, I suppose I was seduced by his style. Afterward it was his book, the surprise of it, the character of Elsbeth, the atmosphere. It seemed to me a soul was dying and calling for help and I thought the soul was Jonathan's. So I decided to save him, even if it meant saving him from himself."

So that was it.

"You see, Cyril, I'm really very religious. Mystical, actually . . . Don't laugh at me. . . . I believe in the redemption of souls. I believe one can save souls that have gone astray, heal souls that have been hurt. Do you see what I mean . . . ?"

"I wasn't raised to believe in those things, but I certainly understand people who feel the need to help those who appear to be in danger. Only I'm less sure than you about the dangers Jonathan is courting. On the contrary, he seems in excellent shape to me. And as for his soul, are you quite sure he has one?"

"But everyone has a soul!"

"That's what they say, but when you see what people are like and the way this century's going, I wonder! However, I'm not going to argue metaphysics with you. Tonight I'd much prefer a bit of mindless inebriation, and to inebriate you right along with me! The dinner was a crashing bore. I, therefore, order Schopenhauer to the devil and happily abandon Chesterfield to his Jewish Angel! Shall we throw caution to the winds and take advantage of Paris, which is reputed to be so gay, so alive, so luminous? It is the City of Light, isn't it?"

Margaret looked at me with consternation.

"Cyril . . . I'm talking to you about souls, you answer me with electricity!"

"Yes, I suppose I am awfully ordinary, but given the difficulties of mere existence, humor's the only recourse I can think of. The world's such a farce, you know!"

She emptied her glass with one gulp and made a face. Around us, the café was growing livelier. There was laughter everywhere. An enormously fat painter dressed like a sailor was telling jokes. A girl, painted like a streetwalker, was allowing herself to be outrageously caressed by a sort of androgyne with close-cropped hair, poured into a red dress printed all over with the word *Mouramouramouram.*

"Come, Margaret," I said, getting to my feet, "let's walk a bit."

She stood up and an appreciative murmur accompanied us to the door. I too admired her; she was so slender, so elegant and simple, so lacking in smugness about her beauty. But what could I offer her? Who was I in her eyes? His Majesty Chesterfield's companion, the discreet supernumerary of the great man she'd resolved to redeem. It was laughable.

We walked in silence to Montparnasse Station.

"I wish he'd fall in love with Sarah!" she said, stopping abruptly.

"But why?" I asked, surprised.

"Because it would settle him down, give him a focus, make him less distracted by other women. He has to write his novel. Sarah is a devoted little creature; she's charming and uncomplicated. The opposite of what he thinks I am! She leaves him his freedom while my love imprisons him. And to write, he must be free. That's why he didn't want me to come to Venice, didn't you see that?"

"No," I replied truthfully. "No, I didn't."

What, in fact, should I have seen? I knew Varlet would never write a single line in Venice, and if he had to shut himself up in his room to throw everyone off the scent, he'd spend his time reading or playing with our little *Fräulein!*

"Let's go back to the hotel," Margaret said. "I need a bath. I need to wash away all these horrors, take a couple of sleeping pills, and by tomorrow, I promise you, I'll have forgotten most of it. The pain of love is rather like a toothache. It's unbearable, but sometimes it subsides and you can breathe. In fact, you're almost happy. Until it comes back again, throbbing and wild and stupid! Absolutely stupid. Tomorrow, we'll take advantage of the calm, all right?"

We hailed a cab in front of the station and drove to the Place Vendôme. I shook her hand, with some constraint, at the bottom of the staircase.

"Oh, Cyril, don't look so much like a beaten dog! I'm the unhappy one, not you!" And with a bow from the red-uniformed elevator boy, she walked off.

"Once the hunted, Elsbeth becomes the huntress." Madame Duvalier's phrase rang in my ears. *Who's hunting whom?* I wondered, as I made for the bar. Jonathan or Margaret? In the end, wasn't I the only one who wasn't tracking anybody, but whom everyone seemed to be looking to trap? Wasn't I the one Varlet had robbed of *Beelzebub?* The one Margaret treated as a confidant, which so exacerbated my hidden feelings for her? I must confess I had rather a lot to drink that night.

The next day, the great Chesterfield left to discourse on his masterpiece with his translator Henri Fontenelle, taking care not to invite me to join him even though the conversation was clearly of crucial importance to me. After all, shouldn't I be the best judge when it came to interpretation? Varlet, however, had clearly decided otherwise.

"I say," he'd exclaimed, "did Dante return from the dead to lecture his translators on how to do it?"

"Perhaps it's too bad he didn't. You know as well as I how treacherous translators are. I'm not saying they do it on purpose, in fact I do believe they're quite honest, but the internal music of the sentence, the different levels of meaning—how can you expect them to interpret without adding their own little melody, their pleasant or unpleasant thoughts, right down to the domestic quarrel of the previous evening?"

"Tsk, tsk! Don't worry, I'll handle it. Aren't your German and Italian and Spanish translations excellent?"

"I wouldn't know. I don't read those languages."

"The publishers and critics are delighted," said Varlet. "The public is beside itself. What more do you want?"

And so I found myself once again with Margaret and Sarah, the latter having spent half the night touring Paris with Jonathan and the other half satisfying her benefactor's desires.

"You should have stayed in bed," Margaret said to Sarah, for our Jewish Angel looked exhausted—her little wings collapsed, her eyes ringed in dark circles, her thoughts confused.

"It's amazing," Sarah said admiringly. "Jonathan hardly slept but he was up at six and had this huge meal sent up—chicken and sausages and champagne and all sorts of other things. And then he went out."

"You'll get used to it," Margaret said. "The man's inexhaustible." Then, turning to me, "Where are we going? The Champs-Élysées? Montmartre? Notre Dame?"

We spent the day hurrying from one tourist attraction to the next, dragging Sarah with us, until we finally sent her back to the hotel after lunch. Once she'd left, our travels provided Margaret with an opportunity to explain what she'd meant by the word *mystical.*

"From the time I was very young, I always thought of my father as a powerful giant hidden behind the mask of a gnome. And I thought that if he looked the opposite of what he was, it was because he needed to disguise himself. And so I learned that even the ugliest people hide inside themselves a sort of beauty that surpasses all the other kinds, and that what's most valuable is always what's hidden. I mean, if I was out walking and saw a cripple, I'd think he was an angel, just like whenever I saw cats and dogs I really saw fairies and magicians. For me, the world wasn't at all the way people thought. The real reality, the real truth, was in the invisible. My mother, who was a true Christian, taught me

Bible stories, and everything became all mixed up in my head; I'd see
an old man and immediately he was Moses, or some little pastry cook
would turn into the young David. I remember John the Baptist was
the milkman, and Jesus our maid's son. Of course, I wasn't yet five
years old. . . .

"Later, when it started to get dark, I'd see faces close to mine; they
were like shadows but their eyes shone. I was very frightened and cried
out so loudly my mother had to come and comfort me, but she never
understood where my tears came from. And yet they weren't horrible
faces, you see. There was one, always the same one, who was absolutely
beautiful. He moved his lips as if he were talking to me, but no sounds
came out. It was like some desperate call for help. Which made me think
that these shadows were errant souls coming to ask for help, to beg me
to do something to set them free. I once told all this to a pastor, the
Reverend Mr. Cummings, who was a friend of my grandfather Frazer's.
He was such a saint; he explained to me about heaven and hell and
purgatory, where dead souls waited to be purified before entering paradise. In short, I understood that I had to pray very hard for all these
poor souls who came to me so they could find rest. So I prayed and I
prayed. You can't imagine how much I prayed! Sometimes I got terrible
headaches. I think I was around twelve when all this happened.

"And then one day the visions stopped, but I still had that feeling of
responsibility to others, especially the souls of people I'd more or less
known. Don't worry, I wasn't psychotic! Nothing ever had any effect on
my health. I was a perfectly normal little girl, and a perfectly normal
adolescent. Until that episode with the nasty girl at school who accused
my father of having killed my mother. I didn't believe a word of it, but
the suspicion that seemed to surround our family reinforced my feeling
that the world was quite the opposite of what we believed and that the
only reality was of a higher sort, invisible, and that we could communicate with it only if we were worthy.

"And then I met Hourray. He was the leader of a group called the
Eye of Shiva, an occult society more or less under the aegis of the theos-
ophist Annie Besant. My mother sometimes attended their sessions, and
when I was nineteen I was shocked to find out that other people had
had experiences like mine. What's more, it seemed my case was quite
common, that lots of other people had seen all sorts of ghosts and phantoms. Even visions of famous people like Isaac Newton and Shakespeare
and Attila sitting on his horse announcing the end of the Western world!

All this made a tremendous impression on me, even though once I'd joined the group, Hourray began to seem more like a charlatan than a magus and his flock more like a bunch of hysterics than saints. But the atmosphere was right; there were seances and the dead replied, which only confirmed my faith in the beyond.

"One night, I was seized with the ridiculous and quite neurotic desire to call upon my father's first wife, the poor Clara who'd been married to Goldman and then been killed in a fall from a horse. Really, I've no idea where the thought came from, but there we were sitting at the round table when Hourray suddenly said, 'And who shall we convoke now?' I can still hear my voice blurt out, 'Clara Warner, please.' The seance began. . . . Dear Cyril, I've no idea what you think of this sort of thing, I suppose you find it amusing, but you must believe me. . . . There was a knocking, the table began to move. 'Are you Clara Warner?' Hourray asked. One knock—yes! The table was shifting all over the place, as if it were crazy. Involuntarily, we broke the circle, dropped our hands, and everything grew calm, but the minute we joined hands again, the knocking started up, quite violently. Angrily it seemed. Hourray translated—and you must believe me—'My assassin's daughter is here.' Those were his exact words."

We were having tea on the second floor of the Eiffel Tower, in a very Art Deco sort of restaurant. Margaret saw the astonishment on my face.

"Of course you can't believe me!" she hastened to add. "Anyway, you're the first person I've dared tell this ridiculous story, even if it *is* true."

"Dear Margaret," I replied calmly, putting down my cup, "there are only three explanations: Either you take me for a real innocent, which I don't believe; or your mind was somewhat disturbed by the mysterious aspects of George and Clara Goldman's deaths and this caused you to hallucinate during the seance; or this Hourray is a phony, which I can imagine only too well. He knew your family drama and he abused it unscrupulously to lure you into the group."

"That's what I thought," Margaret replied. "So I never went back. Neither did my mother. But you must admit the story served as a kind of warning. Put me on my guard, so to speak."

"Against human evil, absolutely. As for the beyond, I'm still not convinced."

In the cab taking us back to the hotel, Margaret resumed her story.

"Still, that doesn't mean there haven't been certain incidents, certain upsetting coincidences. . . . Do you know that on the night of the cock-tail party where I first met Jonathan, when I felt I'd been struck by a bolt of lightning, well, that evening one of our maids, a young girl from the country, came to me sobbing her heart out. She was pregnant and terrified about what was to become of her. I asked her if she at least knew who the father was. 'Just a boy, you know,' she said. 'I don't know his name. It was at a party. We'd been drinking. But I know he lives in Chesterfield, in Derbyshire! I even know he's a beadle at All Saints Church!' So a few hours later, when I was standing next to the piano and this tall, blond, blue-eyed boy appeared so suddenly before me and introduced himself as Chesterfield, you can imagine the shock. . . ."

I paid the driver and we walked into the lobby.

"Shakespeare once wrote, quite rightly you know," I said, "that there are more bottomless pits in the heart of man than in infinite space. You're amazed by such a coincidence, but I'd amaze you even more if I told you certain things I know. They would make your experiences pale in comparison. But I must say, dear Margaret, how much your con-fession—for it really was a confession—has moved me, for it shows how much trust you are good enough to have in me. Shall I confess how little of Paris I've seen, consumed as I've been by my attention to your story?"

"Which you must sorely regret!" she laughed.

"Absolutely not! You seem so different to me now. But then you seem like a different person every day. It's quite marvelous. . . ."

I hesitated, but she looked at me so simply and kindly that I plunged ahead.

"And I have to say, dear Margaret, that if this trip continues as it has done, I shall know you in so many ways that . . ."

I stopped again. She smiled and placed her fingers on my lips.

"We're dining with Jonathan, I believe. We're meeting at the bar at eight. I must get Sarah up, unless of course our genius has already taken care of it. See you shortly, my friend!" She winked, turned around, and went upstairs.

The next morning, we boarded the train for Venice. It was an unre-markable trip.

We arrived at Mestre, then the Venice railway station, around eight in the morning. Our night in the sleeping car had worn me out and my first encounter with the Serene City was marred by my foul mood. The minute we set foot into the motorboat sent by the hotel Danieli to fetch us, we were enveloped in a dense fog and could see nothing at all as we crossed the city on the Grand Canal.

Despite this, Varlet was positively lyrical. He started talking at the dock and stopped only when we'd reached the hotel. We were so taken aback by his volubility that we listened, in a sort of trance.

"In his 'Meditation on the Fiftieth Psalm,' Jean de Sponde says, 'I cannot glue this glass together again! I cannot stop waterfalls! Man is the wind that comes and goes, that twists one way and then the other, that becomes a whirlwind, that intoxicates his mind, carries him away, transports him!' And he asks himself, 'With what ties can I bind this Proteus? In what form shall I capture him?' In a universe of water clocks and watches and hourglasses and sundials, Don Juan chose time over eternity. In the movement of time, God is in danger. Man may go on groping blindly, but he does not shrink from confronting his destiny. In disguising himself, he disguises it. And sometimes he blasphemes! That, is fact, is the lesson of the Renaissance. The beautiful fountains, symbols of time, harbor fearsome horses that stink of death, like the horses of Salzburg. Horses carry the souls of the dead. They cross a time which leads nowhere, but where, I ask you, where do they go? Where do the horses go?"

Had he been drinking? He leaned his arm on my shoulder.

"To create a work, a Tower of Babel, is perhaps an attempt to embrace the labyrinth. Mysticism and poetry are fed by that asceticism, that passion. For a long time, in the form of a circle, the labyrinth was God. And then it appeared that the creation itself was another labyrinth that palpitated first in the human being. The ancient myth of Destiny— in caps, Your Excellencies!—resurfaced as the ineluctable essence of things!"

Signor Sforza, the owner of the Danieli, stood with inpeccable dignity at the main entrance, flanked by his staff of servants, valets, and chambermaids in full dress. There must have been thirty of them, each more brightly polished than the next. As Varlet approached, they bowed in unison.

"Ah, maestro!" Sforza exclaimed, rushing to Jonathan, open-armed. "Maestro! What an honor for our home to welcome the creator of such a monumental, such a magistral work! After Byron and Shelley and Chopin and Musset and Wagner, there is Signor Chesterfield! And the *signora*, I presume . . . ? And the *fanciulla*! And the secretary! *Bravissimo!*" He clapped his hands. "Hey, *pollastrelli! Su! Avanti!*"

The bellhops, dressed in red and gold, rushed to claim the luggage, everyone turned in parade fashion, and we all entered the pretentious lobby decorated *"in cortiletto stile veneziano,"* as our host explained, clearly overcome with happiness although he'd doubtless never read a single Chesterfield line.

The first thing one does in Venice is to get lost. Given the fog, this was not in the least difficult. Margaret and Sarah opted to stay behind and unpack, and as the automatons in the clock tower rang out ten o'clock, Jonathan and I found ourselves on the almost deserted Piazza San Marco.

"I wanted very much to return to Venice with you," Jonathan said. "But I'm sorry you insisted on Margaret's coming with us. Her presence here is unnecessary; in fact, she is, in a way, an altogether unnecessary person. How much happier we should have been, you and I, alone, with Sarah. After all, she's scarcely more than a little ghost, a sort of spare, really, that you bring along just in case, who follows you about docilely and never claims to be anything more than she is. I want to try to find the Venice I once knew and loved, the Venice that led me to know and love my lord. But my memory is like a glass house, and in order not to break anything I must proceed carefully. I must approach things and people with infinite precaution. If I don't, everything will smash into smithereens, another reality will take over, and the miracle of return shall disappear."

For a long moment, we were silent. The basilica spread its domes before us, reminding us that this sacred and quite Eastern city was still the symbol of both the permanence and the decay of the Western world. I thought not of Byzantium, however, but of this lord whose goodness Varlet so often evoked but who remained a hazy shadow. Who was this man? What had his life been like? I knew nothing about him, despite the fact that not a day passed without Varlet's speaking of him.

"Sweet is the great intelligence, for it comes from the heart," Varlet continued. "That was my Sarastro. While I, as you can see, am only a man who thinks and feels. Nothing very extraordinary about that, now is there? Where I emote, he expressed himself by remaining silent. And so this return to Venice, his Venice, shall take place in silence. . . . I shall enter as the worker enters his home in the evening, silent and ready for sleep. You, my friend Cyril, you can help me in my journey into the past, into my real childhood. . . ."

"And how might I do that?"

"Listen to me and walk with me. I'll tell you what happened here and what happened there, and you'll keep all of it in your memory. One day you'll make a novel of it perhaps. Who knows?"

We were crossing the Piazza diagonally, walking toward the Correr Museum, a backdrop in this theater for doves.

"We arrived at ten o'clock at night. It was very dark. The boat dropped us at the quay next to the Doges' Palace. My lord took me by the hand and said, 'Open your eyes! Look!' And I looked, and I saw the basilica and the clock tower and the archways and the campanile, all lit by gaslight, the kind you no longer see today. The dull bluish light gave the monuments a strange luminescent halo; it felt as if we were moving in a dream. We turned left into a narrow alleyway, the Libreria Vecchia, and came to the Florian Café where two gentlemen sat waiting for us ever so gravely, drinking scalding hot tea at a little round marble table.

"My lord embraced both men and introduced me to them as his son. They were Venetian. One was an organist, the other an antique dealer. They both had gentle faces, like the faces of the Magi in the Nativity. I was twelve and didn't really understand what they were talking about. All I knew was that it was a serious and spiritual conversation, and of such brilliance that I vowed at that moment to become like them. And so I sat quietly, like a good child, on the red velvet seat, and listened to them talk. I think it was that night that I really understood what true aristocracy was, that it lived in secrets and by secrets, in the midst of the world and yet apart. It wasn't that the three men looked like conspirators, but their discretion, their serenity, and their humility were such that everything about them testified to their difference from other men. And to the fact that they themselves were unaware of it. Later, my lord took me to the church of San Moisè. . . ."

Jonathan paused. I looked up and the facade of San Moisè rose up before us from the fog, baroque and funereal, with its statues of skeletons and skulls and tibia.

" 'Look, my son!' " Jonathan said. " 'That is the picture of death!' My hand was still in his; he felt me trembling. 'Not the kind of death that frightens, but the death one must die to become a hero!' I didn't understand what he meant. 'There are two kinds of deaths,' he told me. 'Most people only know one, the bad kind, the kind that kills, the kind that paralyzes, the kind that transforms a young and vibrant human being into something horrible, something cold and still that has to be thrown away. But there's another kind of death, a good kind, necessary,

energizing, a kind that brings things to life, that transforms our twilight
world into a clear and marvelous dawn! That is the death one must
learn to experience.'

"Of course, I was too young to understand what those words meant,
but they've remained so deeply engraved in me that I can recite them
for you today. And that's also why I've insisted on dragging you here,
to this church—so that together we might try to understand what my
lord meant."

"But you must know, of course," I replied. "He was talking about
death and resurrection. An old religious notion, that belief in the after-
life. . . ."

"I think it's something else. You see, when I thought about it I remembered that my lord belonged to a society made up of carefully selected individuals who were privy to important secrets about the way to
live and to die and to think . . . a society to which the two men we met
at the Florian also belonged."

"Yes, of course those sorts of societies exist, but they're frightfully
disappointing. Boring, actually. And rather perverse. In any case, they're
filled with the bourgeoisie who've brought along their own abortive morality, their mercantile goodwill, and their thirst for power. Nothing very
special, believe me!"

"Who knows, dear Cyril," Varlet replied, shaking his head, "who
knows if those little societies you speak of aren't in fact a sort of well-
spring from which our larger world draws its best qualities?"

I didn't push the issue, but took advantage of the circumstances to
ask my friend how it was that with his passion for the aristocracy, he
seemed not to have any penchant at all for Margaret Warner, and why
he treated her with such nonchalance it bordered on provocation.

His response left me open-mouthed.

"I've told you already, Margaret's a spoiled child. Physically, I don't
doubt she's quite attractive. Unusually so, in fact. People in the street
turn around to stare. But she's content with that impression. I've tried
to make a dent in that enamel, but to no avail. You can't teach her
anything. And she's got nothing to give. Not even her body, I might add.
She's as frigid as an ice cube. What's more, I think she's a mythomaniac. Has she told you the story about the assassination and the seance?
I don't think any of those things ever happened. . . ."

We retraced our steps and sat down at a table at the Florian.

"And now that that's out of the way," Jonathan continued, "I'd appreciate your turning your attention to my lord and making an effort to understand his significance a bit more accurately. And in coming with me back into my past."

"I say," I replied, "aren't you perhaps mistaking me for some kind of detective?"

He smiled. "Isn't a novelist a sort of investigator?"

"At the moment, the investigation concerns sixteenth-century Germany!"

"Then allow me to express my surprise at your lack of eagerness to find out about the societies I spoke of. Wasn't the sixteenth century known for its passion for utopias? And as for Jacob Boehme, did you know that the Sparrow and Law translation of his works was one of my lord's favorite books? He saw the shoemaker from Görlitz as a bridge between the Jewish *Cabala* and Greek and Arab alchemy, as the precursor of all of Western hermetic philosophy. It wouldn't surprise me if the society I mentioned wasn't significantly influenced by Boehme."

I took a sip of my mulled wine.

"Dear Jonathan, who exactly is this lord you always talk about in such mysterious terms? You want me to study his past but I don't even know his name!"

"I don't like to say his name. Just as I evoke his memory only with the greatest respect. But it's perfectly understandable that you should ask, of course, and so I'll tell you the name he used, on the condition that you say nothing about it to anyone. You do understand, I must insist upon total discretion where these intimacies are concerned . . . ?"

"Of course. I promise not to breathe a word."

We touched glasses with a certain ceremony, and drank our wine in silence. Then he leaned across the table and murmured in my ear, "His name was Lord Ambergris."

I'd heard that name before, but where? I thanked Varlet for his trust in me while I vainly searched my memory.

"When I've finished the story of Jacob Stern," I said, "perhaps I'll tackle your lord. The little you've told me stimulates my novelist's imagination. Where did he live?"

"He owned many castles. Two in Scotland and one in England. His heirs would have lost nothing by giving me just one, you know! But they couldn't possibly have liked me. I was the stranger, the foreigner, the parasite, a kind of thief. And I might well have proven dangerous. In short, Varlet I was and Varlet I had to remain. Although thanks to you,

I've got a choice between Chester or Field! Ah, my dear Cyril, what a madhouse this world of ours! Doubtless, one day, I shall tell you the whole story. But not now, all right? Let's just keep things as they are, yes?"

He paid the bill and we walked down the Piazzetta to the hotel, where Sarah was waiting.

"Where've you been?" she demanded the minute Jonathan entered the lobby. "I was worried."

"Has Margaret come down yet?" I asked.

"She's gone out. She wanted to go for a walk by herself."

"Fine," said Varlet. "Well, my dear child, and you, Cyril, both of you come with me. I'm taking you to a restaurant where my lord used to take me. La Colomba. It's not far from here, and even though I haven't been back to Venice in over ten years, I remember exactly how to get there. Who was it who claimed that our memory for directions is better than our memory for places? Sarah, answer the question! You don't know? It was Professor Clipper, the one who turned all those mice loose in mazes in order to study their reactions. Which makes us the mice. The mice in Venice. Will we find La Colomba?"

Sarah was delighted. He took her arm and led the way. I followed.

It was a marvelous lunch. Varlet told a thousand stories to amuse his companion, and I enjoyed myself immensely. I've no recollection at all of what was said, but it makes no difference. The important thing was that by the end of the meal, Jonathan had convinced me I'd been wrong to insist that Margaret come with us!

"But since she did," he concluded, "you'll have to handle it on your own."

After lunch, Jonathan insisted on visiting the Accademia to show Sarah the series of paintings by Carpaccio on the life of Saint Ursula. I left them and returned to the hotel. At least I tried to return, but instead of turning right toward San Marco, I went left and wound up in a maze of tiny streets. I wandered through them blindly, and with some amusement, until I arrived at the Campo Santa Maria Formosa, in the middle of which rose a church of the same name. I looked about, then went inside.

It seemed deserted, but in the shadows I could just make out the form of a woman on her knees, praying. I tried to look at the paintings on the walls but there wasn't enough light. Disappointed, I went back outside. Suddenly, the image of the woman praying came to me once again.

Was I dreaming? I went back into the church. Could chance have brought me here, here out of all the hundreds of churches in Venice, just to run into Margaret? For it was indeed she. I recognized her black coat. Her blond hair, pulled back into a chignon, had come slightly undone. She held her head in her hands. What an enigmatic woman she was. "A mythomaniac," Varlet had said. Poor Cecilia Gallerani!

And then I had an absurd idea that I made no effort to resist. I would follow Margaret without her knowing. Why? Did I want to penetrate her secret self? I don't know. The fact is that when she'd finished her prayers and left the church, I followed her. *It's just an innocent game,* I told myself. *She's going to stroll about a bit and then go back to the hotel. It would serve me right if I wound up knowing nothing but how many shop windows she looked into!*

Margaret left the Campo with an air of not caring where she went. Indeed, she looked like any other Venetian woman returning home. At the Piazza San Zanipòlo, she walked by the equestrian statue of Colleoni without so much as a glance, then crossed the bridge opposite the Scuola di San Marco and walked rapidly down the Rio dei Mendicanti to the Fondamenta Nuove, just across from the island of San Michele. The fog was heavy, and I followed without being seen. She seemed to know exactly where she was going.

At the waterfront, she turned left toward the Church of the Jesuits, then stopped and, hands in her pockets, slowly retraced her steps. I slipped under a porchway, where I could watch unnoticed. She was pacing back and forth, obviously waiting for someone. But whom, given the fact that we'd only just arrived? Had she previously been to Venice? Considering her lack of hesitation as she wound her way through the city, there was no doubt about it. And then, all of a sudden, a form materialized beside her. A man, rather short, with a cap. Working class. They talked for a moment, then he walked away. *An importunate,* I said to myself, but my heart quickened. Fifteen minutes went by. From time to time, a passerby approached her, then hurried away. She'd turned up the collar of her coat and continued to pace slowly back and forth along the quay. I watched, hypnotized. Finally a man appeared, whistling, crossed the quay deliberately, and stopped in front of her. They talked briefly, then walked off together toward the Calle del Fumo. They walked quickly, without speaking. Night was falling and it had gotten chilly. I was ashamed to be tracking her, drawn after her like a magnet, but I kept on with my improbable stalking, not knowing what was happening, whom I was pursuing, who I thought I was. What could this matter to me? And yet I felt as if I was following my destiny. Until the corner of the Calle del Pistor, that is, where I lost them.

I ask you now to imagine my return to the Danieli! Everything suggested that Margaret Warner had been streetwalking on the Fondamenta Nuove, but how could that be when only moments before, she'd shown such piety in the church of Santa Maria Formosa? Then too, I could not imagine an Englishwoman with such a distinguished pedigree engaging in prostitution on the quay in Venice! Something was completely out of whack, so much so that I began to think it had been a case of mistaken identity. Hadn't the fog obscured my vision, not to mention the mulled wine and the fatigue of the trip? Hadn't I simply imagined it? Concocted a fantasy by following a Venetian woman who resembled in certain aspects my friend? I inquired at the desk if Miss Warner was in her room, but her key was hanging from the board. She had gone out, they said. Maestro Chesterfield, on the other hand, had returned and was asking for me, so I went up to his suite.

He was sitting reading in an armchair in his dressing gown, with Sarah curled up at his feet.

"Ah, my dear secretary, just the person I need! Where've you been hiding?"

I replied that I'd gotten lost in the maze outside.

"Doesn't surprise me in the least," he laughed. "But let me tell you why I wanted to see you. While we were touring the Accademia, we were struck by the look in the eyes of a little dog in the lower left of a painting by Titian called *Tobias and the Angel.* The angel is holding the child by the hand and pointing to the horizon with the other. The look that passes between them suggests the complicity that's just been established between them and between, in a manner of speaking, the invisible and the visible. They're walking in unison, one leading the other. As for the dog, why is he looking at them like that? Who is he? I should say he was fidelity. Faith. Titian painted him in that spot to make us understand that the alliance between the angel and Tobias is the fruit of fidelity. Whose fidelity? The fidelity of God himself! The look of the white dog, a rather hairless white dog, is the look of God on the world. Isn't that a wonder?"

"Indeed it is," I replied, "but is that why you were looking for me? To tell me that?"

"Absolutely! There must be a dog like that in *The Fabulous Adventures of Jacob Stern*!"

"Bravo, Mr. Chesterfield!" I laughed. "I see you've made progress in the art of writing!"

Sarah looked at me severely.

"I'm sorry," I apologized. "Losing myself so stupidly in this fog has made me quite upset. So did you like Carpaccio?" I asked her.

"What I liked best," she said, leaping to her feet like a young goat, "was the bedroom. With the bed and the slippers and the little vase . . . and the angel . . . It's called *Saint Ursula's Dream*, isn't it?"

She'd obviously learned her lesson well.

"There's also a dog," Varlet added. "Stretched out at the foot of the bed and looking at us. It's as if he were saying, 'You see, I'm not sleeping. While Ursula sleeps, I'm keeping watch!' And it's because fidelity never sleeps that the angel can appear and can wake Ursula and take her by the hand and lead her out into the countryside."

Sarah clapped her hands, then lay down again at Jonathan's feet.

"I'm your dog," she said simply

"No, no, my little girl," he replied, delighted. "You're my angel, as you well know. . . ."

We all met for dinner in the main dining room of the Danieli. Margaret was late. She hadn't had time to go to her room, and still wore the black coat I'd followed the whole afternoon. So it had indeed been she! There was no doubt about it. Deeply disturbed, I stood up and held out the chair next to me.

"I'm absolutely destroyed," she said. "All that walking all over the city . . . You start out and you never know when you'll get back."

"I hope you didn't have too many nasty encounters?" Jonathan said, looking up from his dinner. "As we know, Italians adore blondes!"

Margaret shrugged.

"After encountering you, what have I got to fear?"

"True, true. However you slice it, I'm the very model of a naughty boy."

"That's not so," Sarah protested. "You're very good. You're the best of men!"

"Out of the mouths of babes . . ." Margaret replied, helping herself to soup from the silver tureen.

"Have you been to Venice before?" I asked, as casually as I could.

"Many times. The first was with my father. We stayed in the Giudecca."

"And you probably have friends here?" I went on.

"Lots of them," she replied, not at all surprised by my curiosity. "Gasperi, the painter, the one who paints horses . . . My father was very close to the Volpis, the ones who own the Ca' Pesaro next to the Frari. And with the Manins, the descendants of the famous doge. I can't even remember them all. That's my father for you. . . . Who doesn't he know? There's also the American writer Ezra Pound, who lives in the Lido. We're going to publish his *Cantos.* I know Venice well, you see. . . ."

"You never mentioned it to me," Jonathan said.

"We all have our secret gardens," Margaret replied, attacking her soup.

What had I imagined? Wasn't it perfectly natural that a publisher as famous as Peter Warner would know the best people all over the world, and that his daughter would quite naturally take advantage of his relationships to establish entrées here and there? She'd arranged to meet Gasperi, for example, on the Fondamenta Nuove. Or some writer she had absolutely no reason to tell us about. After all, Varlet had pretty much abandoned her to her own devices. It was only natural that instead of crying in her room she would go see her friends. And yet a small voice kept whispering in my ear, "A young woman of the upper classes does not make dates with Venetian friends on the quay of the Fondamenta Nuove in the middle of a working-class neighborhood."

That night, I slept badly indeed.

C H A P T E R   S I X

O UR SOJOURN IN VENICE LASTED TWO
months. I remember it as shadow theater, spectral characters drifting
fogbound amid sumptuous buildings, coming and going through a maze
of narrow streets. As a novelist, I was overwhelmed, but first I owe my
reader the remainder of the cruel exposé on the subject of Margaret
Warner. Only then can I speak of the wanderings of Jonathan Absalom
Varlet as he pursued his quest for his lord. Such is the limitation of
narrative—the successive description of events that occurred simulta-
neously—but it remains the only way to bring some order to this strange
conjunction.

I had my suspicions about the blond and majestic Margaret, but at
the same time, I suspected myself of having transformed my own desire
for this inaccessible woman into a vulgar fantasy. It was true that she
knew a number of Venetians from the best society; in fact, she introduced me to several of the most aristocratic, although they tended to
live in dilapidated mansions with such high humidity that most of them
suffered from rheumatism, arthritis, or asthma, conditions that gave them
a curiously limp and dusty nobility.

Never have I seen such antiquated and unusual creatures as occupied
these rooms hung with moldy tapestries and fake paintings (the origi-

nals having been sold). I remember in particular Countess Ambrozani, easily a hundred years old and paralyzed in her wheelchair, transmogrified by the dust that lay upon her into a piece of furniture, but whose eagle eye seized hold of you the minute you entered the drawing room where her degenerate, hunchbacked, drooling grandson placed her every morning like a reliquary studded with barbarous jewels. There was also the great-grandnephew of Pope Leo XIII, a sort of fifty-year-old baby one could easily see playing with a bucket and shovel, who was so passionately in love with Margaret he read her poems of an impressive scatological tanginess in Venetian dialect. And there was the mayor's cousin, a poor child so crippled by polio she could walk only by encasing herself in an amazing wooden contraption, which creaked so dramatically with every step she took that we all feared it would collapse and take the little girl with it.

Margaret walked among these phantoms with a naturalness that amazed me. When I asked her how it was that she felt no revulsion for all this decrepitude, she replied, "But Cyril, this is my world, the world I know," an answer that helped me to understand her personal saga, the stories about her father and the presumptive murder and the seances and so forth.

"When I come to Venice," she said, as we strolled along the Grand Canal opposite the Giudecca, "it's to see these people. They fascinate me."

"I quite understand their fascination, but it seems to me they're just debris, leftovers from a world long gone. Isn't your presence among them just a form of charity?"

"So Jonathan spoke the truth," she laughed. "You're really quite a timid creature, aren't you, dear Cyril? But you know, when you have a father like mine, monsters are natural companions. Anyway, these are good monsters. It's just you with your cloudy spectacles who cannot see beyond their appearance."

Perhaps she was right. In any case, since it was my first trip to Venice, she took me to see everything she loved best—the Scuola Grande di San Rocco with its famous Tintorettos, the Church of the Jesuits, and *The Martyrdom of Saint Lawrence*, and, not far from the hotel, the Scuola di San Giorgio degli Schiavoni with its *Saint George and the Dragon*. She loved the dragons and I loved Saint George. We crisscrossed the city, taking in madhouses and baroque churches, and I was struck by what seemed a sort of dialogue between the paintings and the city itself, a confiding, as if Countess Ambrozani communicated directly with the Virgin in Giorgione's *The Adoration of the Shepherds*, and the little cripple in her wooden carcass walked beside Titian's *Tobias and the Angel*. Sometimes I passed the same people—a young man wearing gloves, a girl with an earthenware jug, even the Good Samaritan or Charles V—but they were really just visions inspired by the combination of Venice and the fog. Between the Rialto and the Campo San Polo, one was always accompanied by a carnival of silent shadows.

"Once upon a time they used to make women and children and even animals wear masks," Margaret said.

"Yes, there's a painting, by Guardi I think, of a monkey taking off his mask. I've often wondered if it really is a monkey, you know, as opposed to a man."

We were having lunch at Montin's, a restaurant frequented by artists behind the Terra San Stin. At three o'clock, Margaret rose, as she did every day at the same hour.

"It's time," she said simply. "See you this evening, Cyril."

And once again, I followed her across the city, stopping first at the church of Santa Maria Formosa to pray, retracing our steps across the Piazza di Colleoni, then down the Rio dei Mendicanti. But today, instead of heading for the Fondamenta Nuove, Miss Warner abruptly turned right into a tiny alleyway and I lost her.

The morning finally arrived when I decided to find out the truth, once and for all. I made sure she was at Countess Ambrozani's and then ran without stopping to the Calle del Ca. A dozen doors opened onto the street, including one that revealed an interior garden when I looked through the judas-hole. A bellpull with a boar's head handle strengthened my resolve, and I rang. There was a bit of commotion inside, then a round head appeared in the judas. Someone spoke to me in Italian and as I understood nothing, I replied in English. The young woman on the other side proved no more bilingual than I; she went for help, and a moment later the door opened a crack to reveal the face of what could only have been a madame.

"You English?"

She was so gaudily made up, with red hair that appeared to have the consistency of straw, she looked like a madwoman. I suppose what she saw pleased her, for she allowed me to enter. There was, in fact, a little garden, with a two-story, rather rustic house behind it, the whole surrounded by high walls.

"So my little man, we've come to see Mama Caratini? Good Mama Caratini?" The combination of English and childish Italianisms was grotesque, but there was no mistaking the address. Filled with what I'm sure you can imagine to be the greatest anxiety, I was hustled into a tiny drawing room filled with plaster statuettes and offered a seat on a purple sofa.

"Hee, hee, we *are* early aren't we, little man?" she croaked. "But good men don't bother about time, do they? So tell me, little man, this is the first time you come here . . . ? And who gave you Mama Caratini's address, hmmm?"

She smiled her most ingratiating smile, her black lips stretching quite out to her earrings. Her eyes, rimmed in blue, sparkled salaciously.

I explained that I was a British citizen, that one of my friends had met a beautiful young Englishwoman here whom he'd described to me and whom I too was most desirous of meeting.

"Ah," she replied, shaking her impressive bosom bespangled with necklaces and brooches and religious medals. "Yes, yes, our little man has good taste. He must be talking about Bettie, the blonde with long hair like this, no? And tall? Very, very tall? Hee, hee, my little man, I fear you must wait until the afternoon. Bettie only comes in the afternoons."

I took out my billfold and placed several notes on the table. Caratini scooped them up immediately with one hand, rolled them with alarming dexterity into a ball, slipped them into her bosom, and stared at me with heavy-lidded eyes.

"And now, *finita la commedia*! You are police, yes?"

"No. Rest assured, no. I simply want to know what the Englishwoman does here."

"And what do you think she does here?" she cackled. "She comes here to get fucked, that's what."

She noticed my panic, then, and tried to calm me.

"I am sorry, my little prince, but things are what they are, no? At least you're not her husband or her brother?"

"No," I whispered. "Just a friend. I must ask you, please, don't tell her I came here."

She laughed again, shaking the trinkets hung about her person into tinkles and chimes.

"Pay up"—she winked—"and I'll tell you."

For a moment, I hesitated. It was too late to back out. Revolted and fascinated, I put more bills on the table.

"Come now, can't we be more generous! What you are about to hear, little man, is worth a fortune. Ah, so you're disgusted? You're like her. An aristocrat like her. I knew it right away. I know aristocrats. They're all vicious. And voyeurs. Come on, more pretty little lira, little man. You will love what Mama Caratini has to offer!"

From that moment, I was no longer my own master, victimized as I was by a combination of my own timidity and neurotic curiosity. This huge woman dominated me as much by the violence of her vulgarity as by the quasi-sacred mystery of her functions. I ought to have fled. Instead, I remained where I was and paid.

"Pretty Bettie was sent to me by my sister, the beautiful Flaminia, who runs a business in London. Oh yes, my handsome prince, she started in London, your little filly. And she is not the only one from your nice proper society. All pure and white up front, my little man, and black as dirt behind. Little saints and happy scum, and that's the truth. Well, two years ago, your Bettie appears, all blond and lofty and correct. The best the market has to offer, you understand. Men get tired of easy girls. They want originals. Let me tell you, your Bettie with her snotty manners drives my sailors crazy! I tell them she's the cousin of the king of England. And you know something? The more they cover her with slime, the more she wants. I think she'd even pay for it, you know. It comes over her, like an attack. Sometimes I don't see her for six months. And then all of a sudden, she's back, with her snotty little aristocratic mug. But she's a tigress, I can tell you!"

"That's enough!" I cried finally, extricating myself from the purple sofa. My hands were shaking; I could feel the sweat running down my temples. The madame had enjoyed spilling the beans, thrilled to have the opportunity to befoul not only one aristocrat but the entire nobility through the person of poor Margaret. Well, I'd wanted to know, and now I knew. My action horrified me, particularly since I knew I'd done it only because I was certain of the outcome. I'd acted out of perversity, and the monstrous face of Madame Caratini leered at me like the image of my conscience. She continued to vomit her horrors, exaggerating them to good effect with her vicious words, her lecherous laughter, her conspiratorial winks, a caricature of everything female hell-bent on besmirching all of womankind. In my haste, I reeled and stumbled across the garden as if a fierce wind were blasting me back out into the street. As I crossed the Campo San Zanipòlo, Caratini's laughter echoed so loudly in my ear I imagined it was the Colleoni.

Burning with shame, I crept back to the hotel and hid myself in my room, but the madame's vile words stuck to me like greasy paper. I took a shower and doused myself with eau de cologne, all to no avail. The stink was coming from the inside. I had dared to raise the forbidden rock and had found, underneath, the proverbial nest of worms. But it was inside me, this nest of worms. Inside me and nowhere else. I lay in bed the entire day with a sort of fever, my body utterly drained. At last I understood what Varlet had meant when he spoke of the myth of Actaeon. I had transgressed. I had profaned Margaret's inner self, her most intimate self, and what I saw had changed me into a deer. The dinner hour arrived but I dared not go down to the dining room where my sin would be visible to everyone. For Margaret was not the guilty party. I was. I'd had no business braving the unknown. At last I fell into a troubled sleep beset with nightmares and an insidious nausea.

Suddenly, I heard a knocking. What time was it? Nine o'clock already? Half awake, I stumbled to the door and opened it. Margaret stood there before me. My torpor vanished instantly, as if someone had doused me with a bucket of ice water.

"What is it?" I asked.

"I'm the one who should be asking you. . . . We were worried when you didn't come down to dinner. Are you ill?"

She stepped into the room. It was indeed Margaret Warner. Not knowing where to look, I sat down on the edge of the bed.

"It's nothing," I stammered.

"A little fever perhaps," she replied, putting a hand on my forehead.

Such nonchalance. Such serenity. Such regal beauty. And it was all a mask.

"Leave me alone . . ." I murmured.

"Of course I shan't leave you alone. You need taking care of." She stepped back and studied me. "You're not exactly a delight to behold, my dear Cyril."

I raised my eyes and looked at her, entreatingly probably. . . . I suppose I imagined she might unbutton her coat and emerge all blond and stark naked, with black stockings!

She sat down next to me. I felt like an adolescent at the mercy of his first woman. Suddenly, I had the mad desire to throw myself at her, throw her down on the bed and shout, "I know what you do at Madame Caratini's! You're a whore! And I . . . I too have the right to you!" But I didn't move; in fact, I scarcely drew breath, paralyzed as I was by conflicting feelings that came and went in ever more rapid waves.

"Now, now Cyril," she murmured, as if to a child, "I can see something's not right." And then, suddenly, she took hold of my face and forced me to look at her. "Did you go to my brothel this morning?" she asked softly.

I pulled away, and the shame that had so tormented me throughout this interminable day exploded at last.

"Margaret!" I cried, leaping up like a madman. "Please, I beg you, you must forgive me! I've been so stupid. So disloyal. It's only reasonable that you should despise me!"

It was clear she'd expected something utterly different. For a moment, she was stunned, then she burst into laughter.

"Is it possible you've grown attached to me, my poor Cyril?"

The "poor Cyril" pierced me like a sword, but I gathered up what was left of my dignity and faced her. "How can you claim to love Jonathan and yet . . ."

I couldn't go on. She too stood up, then turned around so I couldn't see her face.

"I claim to love Jonathan and yet I'm a prostitute," she finished for me. "Is that what you wished to say?"

"Please, I beg you, don't talk like that!"

"You wanted to know"—she shrugged, her back still turned to me—"and now you do. So let's discuss it, shall we?" She turned to face me. "I suppose you want to understand why."

"I don't want to know anything," I replied, utterly devastated.

"I did it because Jonathan asked me to do it."

I sank into the armchair.

"You have no idea who Jonathan is. What he demands of others. I simply obey."

"No," I said softly. "That's not Jonathan. You don't know him yet, and already . . ."

She shook her head.

"I'm sure Caratini treated you to the whole story. Must have cost you a pretty penny. . . ."

I was silent.

"I hope she wasn't stingy with the details."

"Listen, Margaret, I was wrong to follow you. I was wrong to go see that horrendous woman. I was wrong to want to know about your life, to worry about your fate. It's none of my business. What difference can it possibly make to me if you've fallen into the clutches of people who might be out to blackmail you?"

"Is that what you think?"

It was an awfully weak alibi, but I strained to hold on to it just for a moment or two.

"What else could I think? That you were actually out there soliciting?"

"My poor Cyril," she said, sinking down onto the bed. "How can I ever explain it to you?"

Suddenly, her haughtiness was gone and she looked near to tears. For a moment, she seemed to struggle with herself, and then her will triumphed.

"I lied to you. Jonathan didn't tell me to do it. I did. Just me. I must have been about sixteen when the idea came to me that I had to pay for the others, that I had to pay to save souls. Year after year, the conviction grew, fed by my fear that my father really had killed George Goldman. And perhaps even Clara. Do you understand? I thought that through me, everything would be purified. That through me all the horror would be washed away! I wanted to take on all those sins. And that's when I met Hourray. He encouraged me. 'Your body must become a pasture for the beasts of the field,' he told me. And then he introduced me to Madame Flaminia, who ran the London house I sometimes went to."

"Hourray is a criminal! How could he have betrayed a child's trust that way!"

"But I'm no longer a child. And yet I keep on." She raised her head. "You must believe, Cyril, that there is no pleasure involved."

I tried to be brave as I gazed on the face of this beautiful woman who was at once so desirable and yet so repugnant, so complicated and yet so obvious, so clever but so stupid.

"Don't you think it best to try and rid yourself of these fantasies?"

"That's what I tried to do with Jonathan. You see yourself what the results have been. It would have been better if I'd met him on the Calle del Ca! Then he wouldn't have stuck with me like a hope that's constantly disappointed."

"Have you told him about . . . Flaminia? And Caratini?"

"He wouldn't believe me. He thinks I make things up to impress him. Or provoke him, maybe."

Suddenly everything made sense, Varlet's behavior with Margaret included. "A mythomaniac," he'd said. I had misjudged him. Of course he preferred Sarah's simplicity and love to the tangle of feelings and fantasies and instincts that made up Margaret's strange passion.

Margaret stayed on in Venice until the end of October. During that time we never mentioned our secret, and I managed at last to forget it, for the love I'd felt faded once I understood the confused desire on which it was based. My reason had not heeded the call that my instincts had so immediately responded to. And then one day, Varlet confided to me his feelings on the subject.

"All she dreams about are whips and chains. And in the dreams, it's always her father who beats her. What she feels is the adoration of the slave for its god, who in this case happens to be an impressive dwarf. That's what she means by her mysticism. She feels pleasure only in shame and tears."

When at last Margaret left the Serene City for London, we were all immensely relieved, for now we were able to begin the real search for the imposing phantom Jonathan Absalom Varlet called Lord Ambergris. Since he'd often visited Venice, my companion thought we'd be able to find witnesses who might help us pick up his trail. For we had no guiding light and no markers; we could only trust to circumstance. I suggested Jonathan meet Countess Ambrozani, thinking that perhaps she'd known his lord, so we sought her out in the center of the palace where she reigned like a pagan mummy. An ancient servant received us with great ceremony and, limping, led us into the room where the Medusa awaited, flanked by her hump-backed grandnephew. As we crossed the room, she watched us with the intensity of a bird of prey, but her thin and bloodless lips trembled slightly when Varlet explained the purpose of our visit.

"Ambergris . . ." she murmured. "What sort of man was he?"

"Very tall, very generous, with beautiful white hair," Jonathan replied. "He spoke elegant English, German, French, and Italian. I think he also knew Hebrew and Arabic."

The old woman's wizened face brightened for a moment.

"I have known only one man who fits that description," she began slowly, in a toneless voice. "He was not called Ambergris. I do not re-

member his name. My husband, the count, used to know him forty
years ago."

"This man adopted me," Varlet cried, excitedly. He moved closer to
the old woman. "I want to know him, rediscover him, his memory. When
he died, I was too young. And too stupid."

"At my age, everyone has died."

"But you must remember something! Some detail? Did he like art?
Literature? Politics? I don't think he ever actually sat in the House of
Lords. For a child, a father is someone who comes home. But where did
he come home from? Perhaps he spent his time managing his fortune?
It was a very large fortune. When he died, I discovered he owned mills
in Lancashire and a printing business in Manchester. But I don't care
about these sorts of things. The superficial facts. The externals. I want
to know who he was. Because he was someone whose every action expressed profundity, quality, discernment, and nobility."

The countess had fixed her eye on Varlet and watched him with obvious curiosity. Her body may have been paralyzed but her mind was
quite intact.

"I remember quite well this person you speak of. The count admired
him greatly. I believe they belonged to the same circle. A club of some
sort. An imposing man. One who impressed, who dominated. He must
have been at the palace two or three times. Perhaps more. He always
wore a white suit."

"Yes! Always a white suit! What did he say? What did he do?"

The countess seemed to smile, although perhaps it was only a
grimace.

"I do not exactly know, young man. All that was forty years ago. I
am so very, very old."

"When my lord came to Venice, he met with other people besides
your husband. Do you remember who?"

She made a great effort to think; for a moment, one of her hawk's
eyes closed.

"The Pizzi. Definitely the Pizzi. Alberto especially. But he is dead
now. . . . How old would he be? I do not know. There was Faliero.
Also a remarkable man. And a friend of the count too. They were all
part of the same world, you see. Some sort of sect. Something like that.
I do not remember this Faliero's first name. He was very handsome."
She laughed, her voice cracking. "Perhaps I was a little in love with that

one! When we were twenty . . . And then everything changed. And now they are all dead. But I am still here. Ridiculous, is it not?"

She appeared to doze off but perhaps she was only thinking, for she suddenly barked a sharp command at the hunchback, who was busy picking his nose.

"*Cretino! Avanti!* Who dumped such a moron on me! My grand-nephew, that one! Can you imagine?"

The nephew leaped to his feet, rushed to the wheelchair, and began pushing it to the back of the room.

"We are arranging the furniture," cried the countess, sitting up straight in her chair. "If you still need me, come back another time!"

We made our way back out onto the street through a maze of corridors that reeked of mildew and cat pee.

"*Avanti* to the Pizzi!" Varlet cried.

"But they're all dead."

"There must be someone left. The generation the countess talked about corresponds to my lord's youth. The ones that met him ten years ago may still be alive."

We returned to the hotel, where Varlet went to the front desk and asked for Signor Sforza.

"Maestro! I hope you have found everything satisfactory? I would be so unhappy if you and the *madamina* were dissatisfied!"

Jonathan reassured him, then took hold of his arm.

"Signor Sforza, would you happen to know the Pizzi family?"

Sforza was short, but he drew himself up to his full height.

"I have had the honor, maestro."

"And do you know where we might find them?"

"But, my most excellent sir," Sforza laughed, "everyone knows most of the Pizzi live in Rome! The only one here is the older brother, Marcello Edoardo. Larger than life, that one! But I can tell you nothing more, as I've never met him. In fact, no one's ever met him. . . . I mean, he sees only the very best society. A little like the pope, you understand . . . ?"

Thus we learned that Marcello Edoardo Pizzi had been Cardinal Gasparri's personal counsel for the Lateran Pact, that the following year, during the visit of Pius XI to Venice, the sovereign pontiff had visited Pizzi in his palace—had, in fact, spent the night—and so had persuaded everyone that Pizzi's personal stamp was on the *Casti Connubii* encyclical. In short, we were indeed dealing with someone very much "larger than life!"

I know nothing of the content of the note Jonathan sent to the Pizzi Palace, but it must have been persuasive, for a week later, we received an invitation signed by his secretary stating that His Excellency would be pleased to grant an interview to the *"gentile signor scrittore* Chesterfield." At the bottom of the card were the words "Dark Suit Required."

"Such a lot of ceremony," Jonathan sighed, "but we're getting closer to my lord. Will you go with me?"

I was dying of curiosity, of course, and promptly accepted. At four o'clock on a Thursday afternoon in October, in black from head to toe, we set out to see the counselor. When we told the boatman our destination, he was so impressed he maintained a respectful silence during the entire trip.

The Pizzi Palace was located on the right bank of the Grand Canal, between the palaces of the Foscari and Rezzonico, a vast eighteenth-century edifice whose facade had been redone in white marble. A handsome staircase descended to the canal so that when the boat arrived, we had only to walk up the steps to reach the main entrance, which opened before us automatically. Two blue-liveried servants received us in a hallway lined with ancient statues. Everything suggested wealth rather than luxuriousness, severity more than simplicity, intelligence rather than culture; in other words, the desired effect was more Roman than Venetian. Only the elaborate Murano chandeliers suspended from the coffered ceilings, and the heavy curtains that covered the vast windows and depicted scenes of combat between stags and dogs, added a baroque note to the prevailing austerity. We crossed two enormous rooms painted by Tiepolo before reaching Pizzi's study. As soon as he saw us, he stopped writing, replaced the pen in his writing case, and came over to us, smiling.

"So, Mr. Chesterfield, the writer! Today one writes a book and presto, one is famous! Bravo, my good friend! And who is this young man you've brought with you? Ah yes, your secretary. You have a secretary, of course. . . . Well, gentlemen, please sit down."

His English was close to perfect, but how to describe the man? Medium height, a trifle stocky, dressed in a morning coat, clean-shaven, round headed, bald, but with such bushy eyebrows they almost hid his eyes. We seated ourselves in tapestried armchairs, while he settled into a corner of the vast sofa opposite.

"Your Excellency," Varlet began, "as I wrote to you, I took the liberty of requesting this meeting in order to learn certain things about my benefactor, a man you knew well and who went by the name of Lord Ambergris."

His Excellency folded his hands across his vest and remained silent.

"When my lord died, I was still very young and thus I do not know precisely the sort of man he really was. I mean, in his innermost, his most secret, self. You see, I'm convinced that this remarkable and generous man had within him some sort of mystery that it will be to my everlasting moral benefit to know."

"Forgive me," Counselor Pizzi interrupted, "but you must have found certain documents in your guardian's archives. Did they not teach you something?"

"I inherited nothing from my lord. I left his home before I was quite sixteen."

"Ah yes, I see."

The silence that followed was interrupted only by the cooing of two doves in a cage behind the desk next to a bust of Socrates.

"May I speak openly in front of your secretary?"

"I think you may. . . ."

I stood up.

"No, no, please sit down. . . ."

I did so.

"Well," Marcello Edoardo Pizzi began, "I believe I know the man you speak of. The name you used, Ambergris, was a pseudonym. A remarkable man indeed. He came here several times a year. And I can assure you, it was an honor to be chosen as his friend. He was a very great man, you know . . . and it is true he had a secret, an indefinable something, as if he belonged to a different order of things. How can I put it? There were certain subjects no one dared ask him about. As for his name, he told me he used Ambergris so as not to be bothered by importunate attentions. In England, he was famous under his real name, of course. But I'm afraid there's nothing extraordinary about all that."

"Please forgive my indiscretion," Varlet said, "but when my lord lived in Venice, what did he do?"

"He came to Venice because he loved the city. He came to be here. To see his friends. I don't believe he ever engaged in what in our day we called an 'activity.' "

"I think he belonged to a secret society of some kind. A society made up of unusual men. Men chosen for their unique value."

The counselor seemed surprised, then amused.

"A sort of elite, yes? Well, you know, it's not necessary to establish a formal society when one wishes to meet occasionally with people one admires!"

In the end, we learned nothing else from our diplomat, although he surely knew far more than the few bits and pieces he was good enough to offer for our contemplation. I learned later, however, that he had been reluctant to talk in my presence, and that he'd sent for Jonathan a second time without my knowing it. During that second meeting, he'd apparently told him everything he knew about Ambergris, against the promise that Jonathan would never reveal a word of it to anyone, a promise Jonathan kept until 1935 when, out of circumstantial necessity, he told me what Pizzi had said.

"Onward to Faliero!" Jonathan cried, as we left the Pizzi Palace. Faliero was the "handsome man" Countess Ambrozani had been a trifle in love with in her youth some eighty years ago.

"Faliero?" I exclaimed. "Good heavens, if the name still exists it must be his grandsons!"

"To be sure. And they're the ones I want to see. When Ambrozani was ogling Grandfather Faliero, I wasn't even born. So it must have been his sons, or grandsons, who knew my lord."

I agreed to accompany him, although I felt somewhat lost in the respective pasts of all these people whose genealogy seemed to me as complex as the labyrinth of little streets in the Venetian fog.

The Falieri had once been a powerful Venetian family; indeed, Marino Faliero had been the model for Byron's drama that Jonathan and I had so often discussed. He was the third doge in the family, and had conspired, along with Isciarello the boatman and Calendario the mason, against the patrician government of Venice. In the end, the three were decapitated. All this happened in the fourteenth century, and ever since that distant era, the Faliero family had endured its prestige and its rebelliousness by exploring myriad industries and commercial businesses that had alternately enriched and ruined it. Now, in 1931, it was once again on the edge of the abyss.

Thanks to Sforza's contacts, we'd learned that the last Faliero lived in modest circumstances in a small house on the island of Giudecca.

Calling himself an inventor, he'd run through the small fortune his father had left him from his shipping business and, still in search of the perpetual motion machine, had transformed his home into a sort of cave that served as laboratory, forge, and rubbish bin. He was fifty years old, enormously tall, and cadaverously thin. He also laughed a great deal, and moved like a robot that had come unhinged. If he had not lost his mind entirely, he nonetheless fell far short of full lucidity. On his nose sat a pair of spectacles attached to a system of miniature pulleys that allowed him to raise them automatically to his forehead by pulling on a tiny cord that hung down along his cheek. We settled in as best we could between an empty case of biscuits and a bicycle frame.

"Well now, good sirs," he stammered, removing a green felt hat several sizes too small, "how can the starving Ignazio Faliero be of assistance to such fine gentlemen?"

"My dear Signor Faliero," Jonathan began, "we come in search of a remarkable man whom your father, or your uncle, or perhaps even you yourself once knew. His name was Lord Ambergris."

The madman pulled at his little cord, and the spectacles leaped from his nose to perch upon his forehead.

"Ah yes! Ah yes, indeed! Lord Ambergris. My father's time, that. A sort of goose liver pâté, yes?" He carefully replaced his hat, which caused his spectacles to fall back onto his nose.

"Goose liver pâté? Ah yes, yes. I see. Ambergris? An Englishman. Always wore white. He used to say to me, 'Ignazio, you are such a nice man. Here are two hundred lira. Go get yourself something to eat. A bit of goose liver pâté, yes?"

"Did he come here often?" Jonathan asked.

"Here?" Faliero laughed hollowly. "Never! We lived in the Sestiere Sant' Aponal then. They used to make me wear dresses. Like a girl. That's when I thought up the wind mirror. Do you know wind mirrors? They reflect the wind. You build these enormous mirrors at the seashore . . ." Suddenly, an idea came to what was left of his mind. He stopped, raised his spectacles to his forehead with a sharp pull on the cord, and declared, "The letters! I have all the Englishman's letters in a box!"

"Where?" Jonathan leaped to his feet, but Ignazio was already grubbing in one corner, then the next. Objects tumbled everywhere, and the room filled with a fine dust. Suddenly he pointed to a cardboard box on a shelf. Varlet stepped over the obstacles, climbed onto a wobbly chair, and removed the precious package, which proved to contain numerous envelopes, most of them with British stamps.

"It's my lord's handwriting!" he cried, visibly shaken.

All were addressed to Signor Bartolomeo Faliero, Ignazio's father. The postmarks indicated they'd been sent between 1908 and 1914. The first letter began thus, in Italian, "My dear Brother, I've just finished translating the Apocalypse of Baruch, the Prayer of Manasseh . . ." Another, dated 1910, began, "Dear Brother, the comparison between *Paralipomena Jeremiae* and Abimelech's dream narrative . . ." A third began, "Friend and Brother of the Spirit, the abomination of desolation is described in the Mishna (Taanith IV, 6): 'On the seventeenth of Tammuz, the Ten Commandments were smashed, the Talmud broken, the city violated. Apostmos burned the Torah and set up an idol in the Temple.' "

Varlet's face had gone the color of ash. His hands trembled. The discovery of his lord's letters was as momentous to him as the opening of Tutankhamen's tomb to Lord Carnarvon and Howard Carter. For here it was, a hitherto secret side of his benefactor's life.

"Have you read these letters?" he asked.

Ignazio snorted, which caused the spectacles to fall back onto his nose. "Goose liver pâté! With white wine! So let me explain. You put the wind mirrors all along the Adriatic coast . . ."

We pretended to listen, while we surreptitiously filled our pockets with the contents of the cardboard box, after which Varlet climbed back onto the chair and replaced the empty box on the shelf.

"Excellent!" Jonathan exclaimed. "And what if you put some of those wind mirrors on the moon?"

"On the moon? Are you crazy? There's no air on the moon. No air, no wind."

We returned to the hotel in a state of high excitement.

I wonder if my reader has ever experienced those moments of intense intellectual satisfaction where all that counts is that the object of one's quest has been found and remains only to be deciphered. Under Sarah's curious eye, we ensconced ourselves in Jonathan's study on the second floor and arranged the letters chronologically, then began to read aloud this amazing correspondence. Bartolomeo Faliero, the inventor's father, had also been a scholar. We did not have his letters, but Ambergris's responses proved that he was writing not as an amateur on the origins of Christianity, but as an expert, a specialist. It appeared that the two scholars had been fascinated by the early years of our era, and it was in this correspondence that they pursued their study of the Jewish influence on ancient Christian texts.

Of course, I did not experience these discoveries with quite the same sentiments as my companion. He had found the object of his admiration and love, and in the beginning, his excitement and gratitude overwhelmed all else. As we read on, however, the notion that his lord had belonged to a utopian society grew stronger. To Jonathan, Lord Ambergris was Sarastro of *The Magic Flute*, although he might seem to have had more in common with Tamino. I was touched by the letters, but not because of their content. What moved me was their testimony to the journey on which they were based. When I sent Jacob Stern off on the roads of sixteenth-century Germany, it was not to end his voyage with some sort of revelation, but to show that his wanderings were a pilgrimage in themselves. It was not the arrival that signified, but the journey. For is not the act of arrival equivalent to the desire to construct a temple, to give substance to an idol, to deny the infinite? As my reader knows, I had no solid Christian foundations, but it seemed obvious to me that the Golden Calf might well be Christ, to the extent that its adoration produced a singular stagnation of the spirit.

We left Venice on November 22, 1931. Two months previously, I'd departed Ruthford feeling that Jonathan Absalom Varlet was a worldly being, wholly wrapped up in his fame, his women, his travels. I left the Serene City wondering if he was not in fact a man of great depth. In addition, I'd accused him of toying with Margaret Warner, and on that point also I'd had to abandon my illusions. As for little Sarah Goethman, whom I'd found so insignificant, I now saw her as a convenience, another perception that proved grossly wide of the mark. Verily, my entire life sometimes seems little more than a series of errors and missteps. Perhaps I'm simply a rather good illustration of what people mean by a true innocent—a complicated innocent, of course, but an innocent nonetheless.

Once back at Ruthford, I resumed work on *The Fabulous Adventures of Jacob Stern*. I'd decided to send the manuscript to Clark and Williams under a name other than Chesterfield, as a way of ascertaining the real value of my writings. Perhaps I even entertained the secret hope of regaining control of the fate of my work, which I'd so cavalierly turned over to Varlet. Yet I cannot be sure that ultimately, even if circumstances had permitted, I should have acted on that decision, for the

Chesterfield imago was beginning to please me. Chesterfield was the novelist incarnate in the real world; it was like a highly sophisticated marionette whose mechanism I alone understood, even though I did not really know the puppet master himself, if only because I too was a marionette! I wondered too if life itself was not like Venice—a theater of shadows.

In April of 1932, I finished my German novel. It seemed to belong to the picaresque, although I hadn't meant it to. I wrapped it in a neat little package and sent it off to Clark and Williams; as a pseudonym, I'd chosen my mother's surname and Jonathan's first name, and thus had become Jonathan Charmer. While I waited, I worked like a demon on the grounds alongside my rough-hewn and faithful Register. Jonathan, meanwhile, was taking the Americas by storm, at least according to the magazines that came my way. As for Margaret, I'd no idea where she was. Somewhere perhaps between a seance and a creaking brothel bed? Unless she was doling out smiles and sweets at one of her father's cocktail parties. In any case, I attributed her silence to shame, and once again, of course, I was mistaken. I always am.

GILBERT KEITH CHESTERFIELD'S TWO
great American years were 1932 and 1933. *Beelzebub* was to make its
Broadway debut as a musical comedy. The producer, Ralph Bradyson,
had entrusted the novel to Fath Martin, the claustrophobic scriptwriter
who, of course, turned out to be a true professional; he understood the
dramatic possibilities perfectly and managed in a very few months to
produce a sensational script. The new title, *The Devil's Delirium*, burned
brightly on billboards from the Bronx to Battery Park.

I protested the title change, of course, but the contract Varlet had
signed gave the producer the right to baptize the work however he wished,
so I did not insist. On the other hand, the enormous sums predicted by
this same contract were indeed deposited in my bank account, which
went a long way toward easing the pain. The whole thing still felt like
a fairy tale. Or rather, a burlesque show. I knew that without Jonathan,
the book would have merely been a critical success, a verdict confirmed
by the editor at Clark and Williams to whom I'd sent *The Fabulous
Adventures of Jacob Stern.*

"Dear Mr. Charmer," the letter read, "we are sorry to have to return
your manuscript. Its quality is undeniable, but given the current crisis
in the publishing industry, we can accept only those works with mass-

market possibilities. By virtue of the very quality of your manuscript, it cannot hope to appeal to more than an elite. We are very sorry. . . ." And so on.

The letter reassured me about the value of my work, but it also forced me to recognize how much I owed Varlet for having parlayed it into an international phenomenon. And so I silently agreed to continue our collaboration and resolved to be content with it, for the inconveniences were generously offset by the enormous popular interest it received. I began to accept every proposition Jonathan transmitted to me, requiring only that the fundamentals—i.e., the book itself in its original form—remain intact. The musical comedy, a smashing success, was followed by Matthew Tennyson's talking film, then by comic strips, radio adaptations, Elsbeth dolls—in short, everything the United States had to offer a mercantile imagination already stimulated by so much success. The money poured in, and Chesterfield's notoriety verged on the delirious.

Varlet had settled himself into a sumptuous residence in Manhattan, not far from Barnard where he enrolled Sarah. The Colonial-style mansion surrounded by lawns had once belonged to Joe Stratford, hero of the silents, who'd committed suicide with the advent of the talkies. Bradyson had bought "Paradisio" and then rented it to Jonathan; my first encounter with it was in October of 1932, when I arrived in New York for the opening of *The Devil's Delirium.* A white Cadillac picked me up at the airport—yes, I dared take a plane!—and took me directly to what the Italian chauffeur called the *palazzo.* I arrived around nine in the evening; lights played through the trees on the lawns and swept down the pathways where statues of nymphs and goddesses disported. Sprays of water sparkled in illuminated fountains, and every window in the house was ablaze in light. I was stunned; it was just the way I imagined Florentine palaces must have looked in the seventeenth century, although here there was only Varlet, standing on the porch, to welcome me.

"My dear Cyril!" he cried. "Why has it taken you so long? Have you been buried in Ruthford ever since Venice?"

"Out of necessity," I replied. "Our *Jacob Stern* is finished at last."

"Wonderful! I trust you've brought it with you?"

I had.

"And now, you must enter Paradisio!" he declared, while the chauffeur unloaded my bags. "You'll see how different America is from life in dear old England!"

He wore a brightly checked tweed suit, and looked rather like a Texan in his Sunday best.

"Ah!" he exclaimed. "You don't like my outfit? I have to wear it to the advance premiere for the press. Everything here is planned as a function of the impression one desires to produce on one's public. They call it impact. Bradyson has a whole team that specializes in psychological conditioning. Nobody does anything without consulting them."

"Even your suits?"

"We've agreed Chesterfield must present a clearly defined image. But I'll tell you all about that later. Come in, come in!"

The decor was so fantastic I hesitated to step inside. Imagine a foyer the size of a movie theater, with a sixty-foot ceiling, stippled with bushes and rocks and birds and a waterfall, all of it bathed in a rosy light and soft Haitian music. There were marble floors, pure wool carpets, and in the middle of this covered garden a swimming pool lit by statues of Aphrodite in green marble, holding candelabra!

"Goodness!" I exclaimed. "Is this the set for *The Devil's Delirium*? Is your Paradisio *Beelzebub*'s insanity? Now there's a theological notion that gives one pause!"

We both laughed.

"Dear Cyril, I'm so awfully glad to see you! The plane wasn't too upsetting?"

"Perhaps I've indeed died of fright and am now in Allah's paradise!"

A woman swam up to the side of the pool and took off her bathing cap, shaking her head rapidly back and forth and loosening a mass of dark hair. Then she sprang up the steps and, streaming with water, put on a bathrobe that lay on the floor and came over to greet us. The face was vaguely familiar.

"Hello! Is this your English secretary, Chester darling?"

"The man himself," Varlet laughed. "Complete with umbrella, striped trousers, and rose in lapel! Have you forgotten your hat, dear Cyril?"

"If you told me I'd just landed on the moon I'd believe you!" I smiled, a bit embarrassed.

"A Londoner," the gorgeous young woman exclaimed, eyeing me with obvious interest, "a true Londoner! At last, someone with culture and charm!" She pretended to lick her chops.

"Doubtless you recognize the great Patricia Steele?" Varlet said. "Our sublime Elsbeth?"

I held my breath. Was it possible? Patricia Steele in Jonathan's swimming pool? The star of *Clarabell*, of *Missouri*, of *The Grand Château*? I knew she was to play the role of my heroine, but to see her thus, in a bathrobe, standing before me . . .

"Hello," she said simply, holding out her hand.

"I wanted to get a few people together," Jonathan went on, "in honor of your arrival. We have here our Alexander, the ineffable Victorian Colrave. Our producer, Ralph Bradyson, and his wife, Marilyn. The remarkable scriptwriter, our own Fath Martin. Patrick Brifford, the composer, the one who set it all to music. Sally Gurney, the director. For starters. In short, a little family gathering to welcome you and—need I add—to bolster our courage before the opening! Frankly, we're all frightened to death."

Patricia Steele vanished behind a rock while Jonathan ushered me into an adjoining room, almost as large as the first but furnished as a drawing room. There were several people present, all standing, glass in hand. A murmur of satisfaction passed among them as Varlet entered. Everyone turned to examine me.

"My secretary from London," Jonathan repeated, as he ushered me from group to group. "Not just a friend, but an intimate associate."

"Aha!" said Fath Martin, mopping his brow with an immense checkered handkerchief. "At last, a human being! I'm positively suffocating to death in this hallucinogenic monstrosity. I knew the previous owner, Joe Stratford, very well. He had the place done by some crooked Hollywood decorator. Poor boy. He stuttered, you know. The talkies did him in. Bang. First bullet went right through God only knows which lobe, but he stopped stuttering. Blew half his face off. Second bullet, no more Stratford. Interesting, isn't it? And here's another thing. The same Stratford owned a horse. Didn't know how to ride, but he liked having something in his stable. So to make sure the horse got enough exercise, he hired a Negro. Every morning, the Negro arrives, opens the stable door, unties the horse, and walks it around, holding it by the bridle. Because he didn't know how to ride either. . . ."

"Dear Cyril," Varlet interrupted, "if you start listening to Fath's nonsense, we'll never see you again. Especially when he's talking about poor old Stratford and his horse! I think it best that you have a bite of dinner."

He led me to a lavish buffet that leaned heavily toward roasts and fresh fruit. After pouring me something to drink, he turned and studied his guests.

"Do you realize who these people are?" he whispered. "And what they represent? They're not visiting my home. Or yours. They're visiting Chesterfield! Amazing, no?"

"Yes. You can be proud of your success. Two years ago, you couldn't even pay your bill at the Rosemullion!"

"True. I'd no idea you were a writer, of course, but something about you forced me to make overtures. You must win his friendship, I thought."

"You're quite a seducer." I smiled. "No one can resist you. I just fell into your net like everyone else. One fish after another, right?"

Fath Martin reappeared suddenly. Clearly, he'd had a fair bit to drink, which I gathered was perfectly appropriate to this sort of gathering.

"This Stratford with his Negro . . . I haven't finished my story yet, Chester, do you mind? So the Negro Stratford hires can't ride either, so every morning the two of them have a little stroll around the grounds, out on the lawn, right there in back of the house. One day, must have been in winter, the horse gets frightened by a dog, shies away, breaks out of the Negro's hands, and takes off. Can't you just see it? A horse galloping all over the lawn and a Negro dashing around after it! A riot, don't you think?"

He was just taking a deep breath before plunging on when Patricia Steele slipped between us, dressed now in a long crimson gown. Viewed from the front, it seemed quite proper, stuffy even, but when she turned around, a décolletage plunged to the limits of the reasonable, if one can indeed refer in that way to female hindquarters so grandiose Titian could not have failed to use them for his *Venus with a Mirror*, or Michelangelo for the Ignudi in the Sistine Chapel.

"Hey, wait a minute!" Fath protested. "What about my story?"

"Drop it," said Patricia. "No one's ever heard the end anyway. So, my handsome friend, speak to me of London. . . ."

She had that instinctive self-assurance actresses have when they combine a healthy dose of irony with their habitual performances. She played great madwomen but was able to laugh at herself at the same time.

I screwed my courage to the sticking point and stammered out a reply.

"London's just an idea people have . . . people have about London, you know. . . ."

"Marvelous! Perhaps we can say that the whole world's nothing but an idea people have about the world? So, Mr. Intellectual, what do you make of me? Would you say I was a little fool? Or a clever bitch? And don't tell me how gorgeous I am. Beauty's only an idea people have about beauty. So . . . ?"

"I'm trying to imagine you playing Elsbeth. Tell me, would you have been capable of loving Alexander?"

"The one in the book? Maybe. Even though he is awfully cold and distant. On the other hand, it's his pride that makes him attractive. He fascinates people. Like a snake. As for the musical Alex, our dear Colrave, he should stick to his Valentino bit. A wet dishrag, that one. But onstage, he straightens up. Spreads his little wings. As long as he doesn't fly away on opening night!"

"That's me she's talking about," Colrave said, coming up to us. "Nastily, as usual."

"My Alexander!" Patricia cried, throwing her arms around him. "The light of my life! You know perfectly well I'm a wonderful friend and that I couldn't possibly utter a nasty word about anyone—except, of course, for that scrooge of a Bradyson. And that impossible Sally Gurney! But you, my darling, how could I dare? You're so sensitive."

"She's a viper," Colrave laughed. "If you keep on listening to her, your veins will fill with venom!"

"You're disgusting," Patricia said, making a face. "I hate you!" and she sailed off majestically to sample the pastries.

"What a woman!" Colrave said. "An amazing actress, you know. The play wouldn't stand a chance without her."

"Is it as bad as all that?" I asked in despair.

"Don't worry, Englishman!" He laughed in that typical way Americans have, with their heads thrown back. "Script by Fath Martin. Music by Patrick Brifford. Guaranteed success. Anyway, the sillier it is, the better it sells. Must be the same in London, no?"

The evening was interminable. The trip had exhausted me, but the nonsense I heard all around me made my fatigue unbearable. I felt as if I'd plunged into a world that had exploded, as if I were surrounded by myriad fragments racing in every direction, as if an army of ants had grabbed hold of all the pieces of a puzzle and were swarming about so frenetically no one would ever again succeed in putting the original picture together again. How far we'd come from that invisible society described by Counselor Pizzi and Jacob Boehme! Perhaps the hour for the destruction of the temple had struck? Where had I read that? "Now the just are dead, the prophets asleep, and we too have abandoned the earth.

Zion has been taken from us. We have nothing left but the Almighty and his Law." I wondered what the Almighty thought of all this madness, this indifference to the Law. I remembered his Hebrew name, the one I'd read in Lord Ambergris's letters—El Shaddai, about whom Jonathan's benefactor had written, "the one who says 'Enough!' " And I, in the midst of these important people—so rich, so silly, and perhaps so unhappy—I who knew nothing of these things began to tremble.

"What's the matter?" Varlet asked. "You're tired, aren't you? The party's bored you to death? But I wanted to tell you . . . A little while ago, when we were talking about that evening at the Rosemullion, I told you the truth, you know. I wanted to please you because you pleased me. Because I felt a mysterious connection between us. I didn't know you wrote. And after that, I loved your book. You must believe me when I say I loved it. I'd never have done what I've done for anyone else. Or for any other book. I just wanted you to know."

The Devil's Delirium opened at the Starlight, the Holy Citadel of musical comedy, on October 20, 1932. I confess to knowing nothing at all about this new form of theater. I considered it simply a piece of fluff, another vapid American fad, so it was with a mixture of curiosity and apprehension that I attended the final dress rehearsals with Brifford, the composer, and Sally Gurney, the director. It was rather a surprise to hear the opening numbers sung to a jazz rhythm; Patricia Steele had a gorgeous soprano, and she did famously in what seemed to me a Negro spiritual—a slave weeping on the banks of the Mississippi River, a slave who was really my Elsbeth at the mercy of her passion for Alexander, herein known as Alex! But then, was there such a great difference between a Negro lamenting his lost homeland and my heroine crying for her god? Was it not the same appeal from the depths of the same abyss?

"What do you think?" Jonathan asked nervously, sitting down beside me.

"Well, it's certainly different from the novel, but it respects the basics. In any case, it certainly points up the difference between the old world and the new. We're still prisoners of our conventions, our psychologies, our language. While here, everything's simply exploded. New forms emerge, more primitive and yet more sophisticated. Goodness, my dear Jonathan, we *are* far from Lord Ambergris, aren't we!"

"Why do you say that?" he asked sternly, unable to mask his surprise.

"Because it seemed to me you were attracted by the rigor of his thought. And I wondered how you managed to put that together with the drama we see before us."

"I understand the difficulties I present for you," he replied, turning toward me resolutely. "It's only natural. I'd think the same, were I in your shoes. But there are too many things you're simply unaware of. How can I tell you, just like that, why I'm forced to do as I do? You couldn't listen. You wouldn't believe me. So let's just say I'm a sort of opportunist who's using your work to achieve fame. Only I beg you not to misconstrue that opportunism. We need it, you and I. For our project."

"Do you see this notoriety of yours as a springboard for your own self-expression? Even though the work expresses nothing but itself, really?"

"Of course. But you must understand that all is simply not for the best in this best of all possible worlds! Listen, Cyril, we're on the verge of events so tragic your mind could not possibly conceive of even the smallest particle. The earth is close to returning to its original chaos."

"Surely you exaggerate. I'll admit, the economic crisis is serious, but we're finally emerging from the tunnel. At least that's what they keep telling us."

"My poor friend," he murmured sadly. "You are so wrapped up in your dreams. Don't you see it's all a trap? The whole world is mined and we, innocent children, continue to advance. . . . Listen, Cyril, do you remember what I told you about my first trip to Germany three years ago? The impressions I had? Things are happening there now, thick and fast, and no one seems to notice. Outside of Italy, which is preparing a real *tragedia dell'arte*, all of Europe is paralyzed by its democracies. Everyone's simply humming along—England, France, the Netherlands, Spain. People still think they're in a postwar period. But they're not. Not anymore. It's prewar now."

Brifford ordered Colrave to sing through one number again. "Elsbeth," his tenor voice rang out, "who allowed you to love me? No one can love someone engulfed in solitude, someone whose greatest happiness lies in indifference and peace."

"Jonathan," I said, "I think I understand. Are you really looking to go into politics?"

"Politics! What a ghastly thought! Politics is the purview of that swill that's incapable of running anything or foreseeing anything. No, my voice must be heard above all these moral and political and religious conflicts. Literature is my platform, my microphone. And it guarantees me an audience. You see, I must be loved and admired. Only then will my words be loud enough to be heard."

"Isn't all that rather utopian?" I asked, surprised. "What can one man do, even a famous man, against the madness of an entire world?"

"Only someone truly impoverished can confront the insanity of the world, if only because his insanity is greater! But that's enough. We'll adjust to the movies and the microphones and the newspapers and all those unclean vehicles that peddle what people today call the news. It's not much fun, I grant you, but that's the way it is. Utopia would mean rejecting the means our century offers, don't you think?"

I was silent. Jonathan's ambition seemed excessive. And useless. Had the American passion for giganticism gone to his head?

A few days before October 20, I was treated to a demonstration of those famous "means" Jonathan had mentioned. He and Sarah and I were all at Paradisio; during the week Sarah lived at Barnard, sharing a room with another student, and she returned home only on weekends. Jonathan had told me that Sarah's education was of the utmost importance to him, and besides he didn't want her involved in the pretentiousness of his professional life. She was nineteen now, and bore the deceptive appearance of a good little girl. Given the circumstances, I was quite amused. We were all comfortably ensconced in a small drawing room discussing the next performance of *The Devil's Delirium* when I noticed her sullen silence. She seemed to be sulking, and avoided meeting our eyes. I wondered aloud.

"Yes," Jonathan agreed, "and so she is. What's the matter, Sarah?"

"You know what's the matter."

"No, really, I don't. Is something wrong at school?"

She shrugged, got to her feet, stomped over to the table, picked up a newspaper, threw it down on the carpet, then threw herself back into her armchair and burst into tears. The newspaper lay open at a two-page spread whose headlines blared, THE PASSIONATE AFFAIR OF PATRICIA STEELE AND GILBERT K. CHESTERFIELD.

"Come now, my child," Jonathan said, "I've already told you, those are just foolish unimportant stupidities. We can't keep the papers from publishing whatever they want."

"And the photos?"

I looked. There was indeed a photograph of Patricia and Jonathan

touching glasses and gazing into each other's eyes, and another of the
actress with her head on the writer's shoulder. Varlet knelt by the armchair and stroked Sarah's hair.

"You know perfectly well those are posed photos," he said tenderly.
"They were taken deliberately so we could use them for publicity for
the play. Patricia's married, and what's more she has two lovers, one of
whom she adores. Aside from our work, she and I have nothing in common. You hurt me badly when you believe the opposite."

Sarah relaxed like a spring, and threw herself into Jonathan's
arms.

"I believe you! I believe you! You couldn't love a fat woman like that!
She's so ugly. And so vile. And she squints. And she sings off-key. It's
just that you're all I have in the world, Jonathan!"

For a moment they remained that way, their arms around each other,
and fleeting as it was, the scene moved me. Sarah's affection, the obvious purity of her feelings, contrasted so sharply with the artificiality
that surrounded her that I could not help but empathize with her suffering. What would become of her in all this frenzy? It seemed to me
Varlet had assumed an enormous responsibility here, although had it
not been for him she would still be trapped, alone, in a hostile country.
But could they ever become a couple? More and more, he saw her as his
daughter, and I wondered if she was still, in fact, his mistress.

"Look," Jonathan began, once Sarah had subsided, "all this Chesterfield publicity—or rather Chester, as they say here—is orchestrated by
the head of Bradyson's team, Michael Howard. His job is to make stars
and launch careers."

"Do you think this magician can make just anybody?" I asked.

"Anybody and anything. All he needs to know is what one wants from
such and such a person or situation. Then he creates a product to match
the demand."

"If I understand correctly, he creates both demand and supply? He
conditions the public to accept the product he wants to sell . . . ?"

"Precisely. Which requires a very precise knowledge of mass psychology. That's why his first order of business is to listen. To probe. He
never defies public opinion. He just deflects it, aborts the reactions, works
it around to what he wants by manipulating people's unconscious needs
and desires. The main thing is not to antagonize the public by any action that might clash with its sensibilities or its morals. If his subject's
rape, for instance, it has to be a gentle one."

"A remarkable process," I said. "Rather similar to that of current German propaganda, wouldn't you say?"

"Related, perhaps. But the ends are not the same."

I didn't understand what he meant. After all, if Dr. Goebbels, the publicist of National Socialism, galvanized his public with slogans, it didn't seem any more deceitful to me than duping them with fairy tales about actresses! In both cases, wasn't it a question of usurping reality? Then again, what exactly was this reality if all you needed was the power, even just monetary power, to change it whenever you liked, like a puppeteer? An awfully irresponsible attitude that, exploiting people who were quite unaware of just how much they were being manipulated.

"I despise strategies," I replied simply.

Opening night arrived at last and the white Cadillac delivered us to the Starlight. The size of the crowd straining at the barriers amazed us. Given the black-tie requirement, Sarah wore a long golden evening gown and a little tiara. Frankly she looked absolutely charming, and seemed quite delighted with the whole affair. Limousines followed one after the other, stopping before the brightly lit lobby to deposit their cargo of personalities. The crowd applauded as it recognized a star or a politician walking the red carpet to the entrance; flashes of magnesium flared constantly while movie cameras rolled and crackled. Sarah slipped her arm through mine as we approached the lobby where Ralph Bradyson greeted us in full dress.

"Hello!" he shouted. "The mayor's accepted our invitation! And Paperday's coming as the president's rep!" The man was clearly beside himself.

Inside, the theater was bursting with the most illustrious names the United States could muster in the realm of entertainment and the arts. There was a massive accumulation of furs and jewels, a true debauchery of elegance, a visual feast. Clearly everyone was bent on paying homage to what Michael Howard had trumpeted as the premiere theatrical event of the season. Two seats had been reserved for us in the first row, directly opposite an enormous portrait of Jonathan that had been painted on the curtain.

"It doesn't look anything like him," Sarah giggled, trying to keep from breaking into uncontrollable laughter.

"Now there's a young lady who's having a good time!" said a gentleman next to me. "Is that Chesterfield's daughter? He looks too young for that."

"Yes, indeed," I replied prudently.

"Kenneth Right," the gentleman continued, rising to introduce himself, his countenance sere as an Irish priest's. "I own the place. But I have to tell you right away, I hate musicals. Popular taste is terrible. But is that a reason I should change mine one iota? 'My people have forgotten me, they have burned incense to vanity.' Jeremiah eighteen, verse fifteen. And if all of them want to stagger off to their destruction, do I have to follow along after them? I rent the Starlight to these madmen, but my heart remains intact. Yes sir, absolutely intact!"

At which point Sarah doubled over with laughter. The Irish priest frowned.

I shall not expose myself to ridicule by analyzing this particular musical comedy, universally acknowledged as "the model of a new genre and thus, by definition, a masterpiece." I know absolutely nothing of musical matters, and almost nothing about modern theater. But as the smashing success of the play had precious little to do with me, I shall hazard a reflection on my surprise when I discovered how misplaced my intellectual fears had been. While the audience applauded Brifford and the director and the cast and finally Chesterfield himself, in the person of Jonathan, I felt like the Shakespearean ghost attending a musical adaptation of *Hamlet* in Festival Hall. Oddly, however, although the play betrayed my own work from start to finish, I rather liked it. I hadn't been inordinately upset when Elsbeth bellowed, "I shall love you unto death," a line that in another context would have been intolerable. I even failed to shudder when Alexander cried, "One kiss, and the devil's saved!" Brifford's music, alternately sprightly and deeply moving, carried everything along, the bad and the good. In fact, when the last chord sounded at Alexander's death, my puritan neighbor popped up like a jack-in-the-box and gave forth such a stentorian "Bravo!" that the conductor turned around to stare. "Terrific!" he cried. "Just like I said. A great success! That's why I only rent my theater to real artists. The art of drama must progress! 'Awake, psaltery and harp!' Psalm one-oh-eight." And he left to congratulate the actors.

Sarah and I returned alone to Paradisio, in the white Cadillac. We had no desire to go along with everyone else to the Carlton, New York's poshest hotel, where Bradyson was giving a monumental buffet supper. And so we sat pleasantly conversing over two glasses of beer that Sarah herself served, the servants having been given the night off.

"How do you like my dress?" she asked, snuggling into the sofa. "Jonathan picked it out."

"It suits you beautifully," I answered sincerely. "You're not a little girl any longer. . . ."

"I should hope not! Anyway, even when you thought I was, I wasn't. My father's death and leaving Germany made me grow up, you know."

"Those were awful moments," I commiserated. "You must forgive me. I don't want to bring back your pain, but I'd like to know . . . Those men who killed your father, who exactly were they?"

"Germans. They were Germans. My father warned me. 'They'll kill us!' he kept saying. 'But we're German too! Just like them,' I used to answer. My maternal grandfather, he was a soldier, and he was wounded during the war. He lost an eye. He got a lot of medals. We really were German."

She grew silent, lost in thought. I too was silent.

"You're strange, you know," she said suddenly. "You've never tried to flirt with me or anything. . . ."

"Dear Sarah," I laughed, "how you do go on! I know you love Jonathan, so why should I ever dream of making myself look so ridiculous?"

"Ridiculous? What an English attitude, ridiculous. Can't people be nice to a young woman without being ridiculous? Or without betraying their friends?"

"Are you saying I was unpleasant?"

"No, not unpleasant exactly. But in Venice, for instance, you acted as if I didn't exist. You treated me like some boring adolescent. It's true. Of course, you *would* prefer Margaret!"

"Come now, you were with Jonathan. Wasn't it only natural I should see the sights with Margaret?"

"You're not going to tell me you weren't her lover! Because if you weren't, I can't imagine why she came with us."

"Believe me or not, as you wish, but Miss Warner and I have never been anything other than friends."

"Your mistake." She shrugged. "Anyway, it's none of my business."

There was a long moment of silence.

"Cyril?"

"Yes, Sarah?"

"You're not a homosexual, are you?"

For a moment, I was speechless.

"What a strange idea," I replied.

"So why aren't you married?" She smiled, amused by my confusion. "Or engaged? You must have a woman!"

"You're very curious, my dear, but I shall be glad to clear up the mystery. I have the soul of a bachelor. I wouldn't like being tied down to one woman. I prefer brief encounters. As for your phrase, 'have a woman,' I'm not sure that's quite the right word!"

She frowned, then changed the subject once again.

"Cyril, do you think Jonathan still loves me?"

"He certainly seems to. Look at your studies, your new dress."

"I liked him better when he didn't give me anything. He saved my life. He made love to me. It was all marvelous. Now he checks my grades and wants me to become a proper little woman. My hero's become my father. He doesn't even dare come into my room anymore!"

"His love for you has matured, that's all. He's an egoist, and right now he's thinking of your future. I'd say that was quite reasonable, wouldn't you?"

"Oh, do shut up, Cyril!" She smacked both fists into the cushions. "You're just making it worse. Why doesn't he marry me? There's only eleven years difference between us. Wouldn't I make an appropriate wife?"

"Have you asked him?" I replied prudently.

She lowered her eyes.

"I know. He's given me everything. He's so good to me. What have I done to deserve such generosity? He hardly knew me when he got me out of Germany."

"Doubtless he was reminded of the time when someone else saved him from misfortune."

"Yes, his lord! Jonathan talks about him with such devotion. He must have been an extraordinary man, don't you think? But tell me, Cyril, why doesn't he marry me? Why doesn't he tell me he loves my anymore?"

She fell silent for an instant.

"You've seen the newspapers," she said suddenly. "They're all full of this romance between the great Chesterfield and the voluptuous Patricia Steele. Do you think they're going to get married?"

"Come now, you know that's just part of the publicity campaign. It's not serious."

She got up and came toward me, shaking her finger.

"How do you know? I know he deceives me. I know he's playing around with that fat singer. And with others too. I know it!"

Her anguish was obvious, divided as she was between gratitude and jealousy. For one long painful hour, she continued to hop from one square to another in her personal hopscotch, hoping secretly to reach the end zone. But was there an end zone in her game? Hadn't the suffering she'd endured marked her indelibly? Could she ever forget she'd always be in exile, everywhere she went? At last, around three in the morning, she fell into a deep sleep. I carried her to her room and put her to bed, then went back to the drawing room to turn out the lights.

Suddenly Patricia Steele appeared, moderately drunk and in the company of Fath Martin, also clearly in the same condition.

"Where's Chester?"

"He's not back yet," I said. "Wasn't he with you?"

They dropped onto the sofa.

"I was pretty terrific, wasn't I, Londoner?" Patricia said, her words slurring.

"Admirable," I replied sincerely.

"He thinks I'm talking about that idiot Elsbeth!" she hicccuped to Martin. "No, no, Londoner. I'm talking about Chester, back there, at the Carlton. . . . You should have seen the expression on his face! Everybody was there, all the reporters and reviewers and critics and gossip columnists. So I grabbed the microphone and I said, 'Listen to me, kids! Chester and I are getting married next week! I'm getting a divorce! I'm sure poor Allen won't hold it against me. . . .' Ah Londoner, you would have admired the anthill. The chaos. All the pencil pushers dashing for the telephone to call their editors! And Chester . . . he was pale as a ghost! He couldn't get over it. Brilliant, don't you think?"

"But . . . but," I stammered, "it's not . . . it's not true, is it?"

"Of course it's not true!" Patricia laughed. "I just wanted to pull a few of those idiots' legs."

She got to her feet and began to sing the overture to *The Devil's Delirium*, accompanied by Martin, who sang so off-key one would think he was making fun of it. At first the duo just played about, but then they began their satire in earnest, attacking the first-act dialogue between Elsbeth and Alexander.

"I've been searching for you since my childhood, as the night searches for the dawn, as the deer for the stream. . . . But there is no morning, and no water pure enough to quench my thirst." This was perhaps one of the most significant moments in the play, where Fath Martin seemed touched by grace, and now they were parodying it grotesquely. Dirtying it.

"Hey," panted Fath, wiping his forehead with his checkered handkerchief, "can you open the window? It's suffocating in here. Feels like an aquarium. The fish are dying right and left. Whew! Speaking of which, Londoner, you never heard the end of my horse story, did you?"

I crossed the room and threw open the bay window. The night air was cool, the trees, lit by floodlights, enticing. I walked outside, leaving the duo to fall asleep on the couch. Of course, this was a fabricated nature, artfully created by clever gardeners, but the plants themselves were real. Each followed its own law, indifferent to human folly. I remembered Lord Ambergris's letter about Cain and Abel: "Cain, who built civilization by human hands, and Abel, who cultivated it with blood and sacrifice. On one side, construction; on the other, growth." I wondered if mankind was doomed either to construct only Babels or to sacrifice itself, to become a martyr.

I wandered about the grounds until dawn; it was chilly but the cold felt more real than the warmth inside the house. Jonathan arrived around five o'clock, alone. Through the window, I watched him go directly upstairs without so much as a pause at the sight of Patricia and Fath, spread out on the sofa. The upstairs shutters were still open; I watched him remove his tie and jacket, then think for a moment and go back down to the second floor and into Sarah's room. She was sleeping, lying fully clothed exactly as I'd left her. He undressed her, tucked her in, and kissed her forehead, then went back up to his own room and turned out the light. At which point, I too went to bed.

A little before noon the following day, we all gathered in the breakfast room where the servants, now back at their posts, served us the sort of meal designed to remedy the excesses of the night before. Patricia and Fath had disappeared.

"A huge success," Varlet reported. "The mayor liked it so well he invited me to his country house next week! As for Paperday, he asked if I'd mind dedicating a performance to the president. But here's the biggest surprise—three different companies asked for the film rights! Do you realize what that means?"

We were all delighted, especially because we were together again, just the three of us. Sarah babbled gaily, buttered Jonathan's toast, and poured the orange juice. Outside, an October sun bathed the grounds in a warm golden light.

A servant brought in the morning papers on a tray. Varlet opened one and began looking for the theater reviews; as he searched, Sarah and I could not help seeing the front-page headline: AFTER THE DEVIL'S DELIRIUM, STEELE AND CHESTERFIELD TO MARRY. Sarah choked down a sob, then rushed to look at the other papers. On every front page, without exception, the same headline screamed out more or less dramatically, depending on the quality of the paper; the more mediocre, the more suggestive the photographs and montages. Livid with rage, Sarah threw down the papers and stormed out of the room.

"What's going on?" Jonathan asked, absorbed in the review pages.

"Look for yourself," I replied, pointing to the front page.

"What nonsense," he said with a shrug, but I was already out the door and running across the lawn. At the far end, I could see Sarah climbing into a red convertible. She gunned the motor and took off at top speed.

"Sarah!" I cried, but she didn't hear me. I ran back to tell Varlet.

"But she barely knows how to drive!" he cried, rushing to the telephone to call the police. "My God, this is horrible! Patricia's insane! And I didn't do anything to deny it! I should have taken the microphone and said, 'A good joke, isn't it? But don't believe a word of it. Patricia has no intention of divorcing and I am absolutely committed to remaining a bachelor.' Everyone would have laughed and thought it was just a gag we'd thought up for their amusement. But Michael Howard was sitting next to me. He put his hand on my shoulder and said, 'No, let her do it. It's great! Brilliant! All those idiots will throw themselves on the news like a pack of hounds on a deer!' And so I let them take their pictures. With Patricia hanging on my arm!"

We waited all day for Sarah; the phone rang constantly but it was only Chesterfield's innumerable acquaintances calling to congratulate him. Messengers delivered telegrams, but Varlet refused to read them. Every so often, he walked to the end of the lawn and stared at the road outside the gate. He was in a state of extreme agitation.

"I must speak with you, Jonathan," I said, walking out to join him.

"I know what you're going to say," he replied, looking at me, his eyes filled with sadness. "And you're right. The life I'm leading is absurd. There's no substance to it. No reality. I've built an upside-down pyramid, starting with the tip. And the fakery goes on spreading, like a cancer."

"It's what you wanted," I replied sternly.

He leaned against a tree and looked at me.

"My goal, my intention, is to use this celebrity. I've already explained all that to you. To use it so that my voice is heard on a higher and more serious plane."

"That's what you keep telling me," I cried, with a sort of exaltation, "but do you really think this spurious marriage announcement furthers those intentions? The graver your message, the more the speaker must be worthy of that gravity."

"You're right, Cyril. And I thank you for speaking to me that way. But you must believe me when I say that fame is no more interesting to me than money. The machine's simply moving too fast. It's gone out of control. I see now the time has come to take it in hand once again; I must regain my control so that it cannot control me. Because it will throw me into the abyss . . ." He looked again at the gate. "My god, where is she? Where's she gone?"

We ate a late lunch in silence, barely touching our food. At last the telephone rang and a policeman on the other end inquired about the owner of a red convertible that seemed to be registered to one Chesterfield. Apparently, this automobile had had an accident.

"And the girl?" Jonathan murmured.

"She's in Trenton Hospital."

Jonathan hung up and dialed the hospital, but no one there had heard of a Sarah Goethman, although someone did say that an unidentified young woman had indeed been brought in two hours earlier after an automobile accident. And how was she? No one could say.

"My name is Gilbert K. Chesterfield, the writer," Jonathan said. "I want to speak to the director."

An anonymous voice replied that were he President Roosevelt himself, no one was permitted to give out that sort of information over the telephone. It was against the rules.

The white Cadillac covered the distance to Trenton in two hours, a miraculous feat given the heavy traffic. I tried to calm Jonathan's anxieties, but the truth is I was in no better shape than he. My conversation with Sarah the previous evening had brought us closer together, and I fully understood her reaction to the outrageous headlines. She believed Jonathan had deceived her, and she wanted to flee Paradisio, which had become for her a living hell. We arrived at the hospital at three, but spent another half hour trying to find Sarah. "Is it serious? Is it serious?" Jonathan kept asking, but none of the nurses seemed to know. Finally, someone suggested we try Emergency Surgery, where we were given exactly nothing save directions to the waiting room. The whole process was an unbearable disgrace.

"If anything's happened to her, I'll never forgive Patricia!" Jonathan cried. "And I'll never forgive myself either for having let the reporters peddle all those lies!"

"We had a long conversation last night, Sarah and I," I said, in an effort to distract him. "She wanted to marry you. Did you know that?"

He shook his head violently. I thought he was going to cry.

"Dear Sarah," he said at last, "I was touched by her youth, you understand. Her fear. That's why I took her away with me. And then she became the little sister I never had, a little sister I could initiate into the joys of love. Not a mistress, you understand. I had too much respect for her. She was like a dream I could touch. When we got back from Venice, I made her go back to school. I wanted to get her away from the maelstrom I lived in. I wanted her to be free to choose her own future."

"She thought you'd stopped loving her. The way one loves a woman, that is . . . She was afraid you'd taken your fatherly role too much to heart, at the expense of your role as lover. Or as husband, perhaps . . ."

"I didn't want to force myself on her. . . . My god, we're talking about her in the past tense, Cyril! It's horrible!" A tear rolled down his cheek, which he furtively wiped away.

At last a nurse, a large red-faced woman with a wart on her chin, appeared with a sheaf of papers. We stood up.

"You Gilbert K. Chesterfield? Yeah, I recognized you. I saw your photo in the magazines. I'm real interested in musical comedy, you know. . . ."

"Madam," Jonathan interrupted brusquely, "where's Sarah? The girl in the car accident? Is she hurt? Is it serious?"

"She a friend of yours, Mr. Chesterfield?"

"Please, she's my fiancée!"

She searched through the papers.

"A Triumph. License plate number 77842 B. That right?"

"Yes! Yes!" Varlet cried, taking hold of her arm and shaking her. "Tell me, please, tell me!"

"Take it easy, Mr. Chesterfield. They're operating on her now. I

wouldn't say it was *really* serious. But it's serious. The pelvis, the legs
. . . Dr. Percy's doing the operation."

We tried to learn more but in vain. The woman seemed not to know
exactly what the problem was. The pelvis and the legs. For the moment,
we felt somewhat reassured. At least she was alive! Filled with anxiety,
we waited. At some point the police arrived and asked a great many
questions about who she was, but the officer seemed more interested in
the fact that Chesterfield was famous than in the circumstances of the
accident. All we could glean was that the car had gone off the road for
no apparent reason and smashed up against a telephone pole. "There
were no papers, no identification, no license," the officer kept repeating,
shaking his head. And then, much later, someone came to tell us that
Dr. Percy was waiting for us in his office.

He was still in his operating gown, a tall thin man in his sixties. With
a stern face, he invited us to sit down, then studied us, one after the
other, with a sort of tired interest.

"A lumbar lesion. Fracture of the pedicule and transverse process of
the fifth lumbar vertebra. Double fracture of the ilium without visceral
involvement. Fracture of the right femur. With patience and physical
therapy, your friend will be able to return to her fantasies in about
eighteen months. Unless there's a deterioration of the nervous system
via the spinal cord, in which case we may have partial or total paralysis
of the lower limbs."

Jonathan's hands trembled. He crammed them into his jacket
pockets.

"It's her bones. Just her bones, right? But paralysis?"

The surgeon frowned. "It will be three weeks before we can tell anything at all. Right now, there's nothing to do but immobilize the subject.
And wait."

What more can I say? We were devastated. What we didn't know was
that this unfortunate accident was to determine both our destinies. As
Varlet remarked several years later, "Something or someone was waiting for us," as if the labyrinth of past circumstances had been nothing
more than a dry run to prepare us for the place we were destined to go.
In any case, after Somerset, Sarah was Jonathan's second victim. She'd
escaped death by a miracle, and if Dr. Percy's fears became realities,
Sarah would be condemned forever to a wheelchair. It was this possibility that pushed Varlet to a decisive move.

I also suspect that his discovery of Lord Ambergris's letters had prepared him for a new direction, a path that was to become both his and mine. And this despite the fact that from the moment I arrived in New York, he had not ceased to tell me that his fame was not an end, but a means to accomplishing some grand design whose significance I did not understand. The American artifice had at last become outrageous, Jonathan's illusory reality invaded by a kind of suspicious tension. In the end, it had collapsed under the strain, breaking down at its most fragile point. Sarah's accident was the fracture, the break. At that instant, Jonathan was freed from the constraints imposed upon him by the lies he lived with. The birth had been painful, for he saw at last how important Sarah had become for him. Up until then, he had refused to recognize the influence of his "Jewish Angel," but now that all pretense had been swept away, Sarah emerged as the most innocent and most precious part of his consciousness.

As the white Cadillac crossed Manhattan on our way back to Paradisio, Jonathan finally spoke.

"I went to Germany to find my soul, to rescue it from the clutches of insanity. We loved each other in Venice, in so many joyous moments. And then we came here, and I exposed her to another kind of madness. A madness that hurt her. And yet I had to do what I did! I had to assume the burden of that hateful notoriety. Up until now, I had to! And once again, we must pay for it. . . . We must always pay for it!"

They were the same words he'd used in the little study in Ruthford, after Somerset's suicide.

"One would think you were ordered by heaven only knows who to assume some sort of mission, and that this mission was going to exact a heavy price but that you insisted on obeying anyway. What is it?"

He turned abruptly to face me. He was white as a sheet. His blue eyes gazed at me with a combination of surprise and gratitude.

"So you finally understand . . ." he murmured. "A strange *modus vivendi*, mine, I suppose. You can't know how much I'd love to cast off these chains." Once again, he fell into a deep silence.

At last we arrived at the entrance to Paradisio. Varlet ordered the driver to leave us, but as I reached for the door handle, he stopped me.

"Let's sit here a moment. Just you and I. I want to tell you my new plans. I've been thinking about them all the way home. I'm going to need money. A lot of money. If I'm to be successful, that is. I'm asking you to be my partner. My percentage has been perfectly sufficient, but now it's derisory, given the enormous needs I must now fulfill. Understand me—I don't want a raise. That's not what I'm talking about. I want your full participation in Chesterfield's work. Our Chesterfield."

"Just what do you have in mind?" I asked, intrigued.

"We're going to negotiate the film rights for *Beelzebub.*" Jonathan smiled. "And we're going to publish your *Jacob Stern.* These two things will set the machine in motion once again. The bottom line is you'll triple your assets. You'll make a fortune. But, my dear Cyril, instead of buying more buildings in Cannon Street, I propose that you invest all your earnings in a hospital in Africa."

"A hospital?" I echoed dumbly.

"A leprosarium," he replied, and got out of the car.

I RETURNED TO ENGLAND AT THE END OF January 1933, my American experience having had a profound if contradictory effect on me. The fundamentally conservative Englishman I have always been was shocked by the frenzied affectation of the people around me, and by the remarkable energy in the realms of business and art, at least as far as my limited exposure had permitted me to observe. Sarah's accident, however, seemed to ring down the curtain on this period of dementia. As for Jonathan Absalom Varlet, his plans struck me as both generous and utopian, but I had no doubts about his ability to accomplish even the most impossible projects.

Sarah's recovery was slow, and no one could predict whether or not she would recover the use of her legs. The numerous doctors Jonathan consulted were uncertain about the results of their own treatments, which only increased my fear that our friend would remain a cripple. We took care not to let her see our apprehension, but as so often happens, she proved more courageous than either of us. Patricia Steele had dissolved in tears at her bedside, begged for forgiveness, and then rushed back to Broadway, where the intensity of her performance that evening surpassed anything she had yet delivered. Sarah found Patricia's bedside production—dropping to her knees, swearing that she'd never loved

Chesterfield and had never dreamed of marrying him, describing for an hour her passion for her lover, a certain baseball player named Drosby— rather amusing. But her greatest consolation, the one that compensated the most for her moral and physical wounds, was Jonathan's obvious tenderness, and the promise he made, in my presence, to marry her as soon as the necessary formalities could be arranged. She was German and a minor; he was English. A lawyer was engaged to find out where in America such a marriage could legally take place, but he came up empty-handed. Sarah petitioned the embassy in Washington to be naturalized as a British subject, but it replied that she would first have to reach her majority. In the end, both resigned themselves to an indeterminate delay.

Jonathan sold the movie rights to *Beelzebub* to Matthew Tennyson, the producer of *The Centurions, Judith,* and his own masterful adaptation of *Macbeth.* Thus my novel became *The Right to Love,* starring Rosanna Andrews as Elsbeth and Henry Cushing as Alexander. The film was a success worldwide, its popularity boosting once again the sales of the novel. This time, however, Jonathan refused to participate in the filming or in the numerous publicity stunts that accompanied production. He left Paradisio and moved into a smaller, less spectacular house that Sarah described, in her letters to me, as "romantic, with ivy on the walls and a tangle of weeds in the garden." Jonathan devoted all his time to his African project, rushing from investment banks to the League of Nations, arranging his financial backing with the tenacity and cleverness of a military strategist. Of course I'd agreed to his request, and had decided, not without some reluctance, to donate ten percent of my revenues to the new company. The rest went into the construction of a three-hundred-room luxury hotel in Regent Street, not far from Piccadilly. The thoroughly modern design created quite a stir, but I remained at Ruthford, my tranquillity assured by the benevolent shadow of Mary Charmer.

I'd read *The Fabulous Adventures of Jacob Stern* to Jonathan at Sarah's bedside in Trenton Hospital, on the pretext of wanting him to hear what his final draft sounded like. It pained me to deceive Sarah in this way, and I think Varlet too was uncomfortable, but we had no choice. Sarah was quite struck with the story of my little penniless stutterer Jacob riding his donkey through Germany, searching for a man whom he'd met only once and who had promised to initiate him into the secrets of the ultimate science. Arriving in Venice at the end of the story, he had still not found the sage, but had rediscovered a young girl named Rosa whom, without knowing it, he had once loved. Curiously, his stuttering ceased.

"True science is something you learn in your heart," Sarah said. "Your story seems so full of ours, dear Jonathan. Am I your Rosa, a little bit?"

"Of course," he replied softly. "In a way, Rosa is the image of wisdom."

"Oh, I'm not so wise!" Sarah exclaimed. "If I'd trusted you as you deserved, I'd never have had this accident."

Varlet seemed pleased with my book; we sent it directly from New York to Goldman, after which I decided to see Niagara Falls and to return to England by steamship. It was on that voyage that I met Mary Stretton, whose name piqued my interest, as did the fact that she resembled my mother—the same ash-blond hair, the same finely chiseled profile, the same patience and discretion. We spoke only three times during the crossing, but I nonetheless managed to learn that she was a widow, that her husband had died in India two years before during an expedition decimated by fever. She lived in a small flat near Victoria Station, and gave private art lessons to young girls. I liked her reserve, as well as her love of small animals, her fidelity to the memory of her dead parents, and her scrupulous commitment to doing the best she could at whatever project she undertook. During our very first meeting on deck, I was struck by the idea of marrying her, but a year would pass before I made a formal demand.

Back at Ruthford, I began work on a novel inspired by a Chinese tale called *The Pilgrim Monkey*, a work I would eventually entitle *The Monkey King*. And then, on a February morning, I received a letter from Goldman:

"Dear sir, I am in receipt of Mr. Gilbert K. Chesterfield's new manuscript. Since he currently resides in the United States, I would be grateful if you would come to my office as soon as possible. Perhaps on the twelfth at eleven o'clock? Thank you very much," and so on. It was signed "Peter Warner." I was quite confused. At first, I feared he hadn't liked *Jacob Stern*. Then, the idea of meeting this famous man, who also happened to be Margaret's father, paralyzed me to such an extent I had to cable Jonathan for advice. His answer arrived immediately: GO MEET WARNER STOP HAVE CONFIDENCE IN YOU STOP CABLE ME AFTERWARD. And so the next morning I arrived in Fleet Street at the appointed hour and, for the first time, crossed my publisher's impressive threshold, an entrance

I'd described three years earlier as resembling the bronze doors of a tomb. Once inside, I recognized the stairway to the second floor, the waiting room, and the information desk, as Varlet had described them. I introduced myself as "the private secretary of Mr. Chesterfield," a magical name that propelled the receptionist out of her seat and into the chief editor's office.

Harold Babydoor emerged in a state of extreme agitation. He did indeed resemble a beanpole with a pumpkin head, rather like the sort of costume children wear at carnival time.

"A pleasure to meet you, sir!" he trilled. "A pleasure to meet our dear Chesterfield's friend! And how is our great writer? Such a marvelous success, America! I've heard so much about that fabulous musical. And the film . . . Isn't it just a fabulous adventure?" He ushered me into his office. "Mr. Warner will join us in just a moment. Do forgive me for the wait, but he's involved with a quite difficult author. A politician, you understand . . . But tell me, since you've been in New York, how *is* our divine young gentleman?"

"Life in America is quite different from—" I began.

"Oh, yes, indeed! I could simply never get used to all that speed and confusion. I'm really quite Old England, you know. In fact, I'm not quite sure I'd have liked the musical. I'm very fond of opera. . . ."

At that moment the door opened, and Peter Warner appeared in a black frock coat with a carnation in his lapel. He looked even smaller and fatter than I remembered. Quite monstrous, in fact.

"Babydoor!" he barked. "My cigars!" Then, turning to me with a look that seemed to strip me naked, he said, with a raised eyebrow, "Mr. Pumpermaker?"

I crossed the room, with a certain timidity, I must confess.

"Come in, my dear sir. My daughter, Margaret, has told me a fair bit about you. Quite an impressive secretary, I gather. As well as a friend and partner . . . In short, I have been most anxious to meet you. Do sit down."

He sat opposite me in an armchair clearly designed to his specifications. In no time at all, the keen intelligence so visible in his face made me forget his deformity.

"It was indeed you on the trip to Venice with Margaret? Excellent. Well, I want to tell you how remarkable I found *Jacob Stern.* I'm sure it will be every bit as successful as the first book. The description of Germany during the Counter-Reformation, this innocent child with supernatural powers, Cammershulze, the alchemist and Cabalist—all of it is really quite brilliant. Of course Jacob won't find Papagallo, the one who initiates him into the Brotherhood of the Galopins, but isn't Cammershulze Papagallo in disguise? The man he's searching for and the man who accompanies him on his quest, are they not one and the same? A stunning idea. Makes me think of all the mystery surrounding Chesterfield's early years. The orphaned child they name Varlet and who's taken in by a famous lord, a young man graced with intelligence and charm, a true aristocrat but also a born businessman! An awful lot that, for a foundling! I've done a bit of research, you see. . . ."

I listened carefully, most intrigued.

"I hired an agency that specializes in this sort of work. They told me straightaway that the lord Jonathan speaks of so frequently is none other than Lord Sheffield. Ambergris was a pseudonym. Sheffield was a biblical scholar, and the leader of a, shall we say, a very discreet society known as the Brothers of the Apocalypse. Quite widespread on the Continent, actually. He had no children of his own and apparently grew quite attached to our Varlet. Gave him a prince's education. But he never legally adopted him, which meant that when he died his heirs had his will confiscated and declared unbinding. If Ambergris had wished Jonathan to inherit, he had only to adopt him, which he did not. And so Varlet found himself Varlet once again."

"Your information agrees with what our friend has told me himself," I replied. "But have you discovered who his father and mother really were?"

"The agency can find no hint whatsoever of the orphanage in which Ambergris found Jonathan. You must admit, however, that the orphaned Jacob Stern traveling through Germany bears an uncanny resemblance to our orphan Varlet. Not to mention the alchemist Cammershulze and the earl of Sheffield. All this searching for fathers seems quite significant, doesn't it?"

"I'm sure," I replied, prudently.

Warner settled himself more securely in his armchair.

"And now, my dear sir," he continued somewhat abruptly, "if I've requested your presence here today, it's because the mystery does not end there. The fact is I'm sure Jonathan Varlet did not write *Beelzebub*. Nor this second manuscript either."

He was watching me carefully as he spoke, and must have noticed my confusion.

"Does that really astonish you so much? Margaret's told me she's never seen Jonathan write a single sentence. Moreover, he couldn't possibly have had the time to write *Jacob Stern* in Venice. So, Mr. Pumpermaker, perhaps you would be kind enough to tell me what's up?"

"But . . . but Jonathan is perfectly capable of writing those books!" I stammered.

"Of course he's quite capable of it. He has immense culture and an indisputable artistic sense. Nonetheless, he did not write them. Someone else did."

"Do you really think so?" I asked, feigning shock.

"Not only do I think so," Warner replied, smiling broadly, "but I'm going to tell you who did. I'm going to give you Chesterfield's real name!"

I shivered under his gaze. Was I going to be forced to confess that I was *Beelzebub*'s author?

"And what is that, Mr. Warner?"

He removed a cigar from the humidor and bit off the end.

"Lord Ambergris himself," he replied.

I had to struggle not to burst out laughing.

"Lord Ambergris was an aesthete. He was intensely involved in the activities of his circle, to the detriment of his mills, his castles, and his farms. His heirs got only ruins or objects that belonged in museums. Varlet, on the other hand, made off with the earl's manuscripts, which the earl himself never dreamed of publishing. And now, what do you think?"

"An interesting theory, Mr. Warner. Quite astonishing really. As far as I'm concerned, however, Jonathan is the author of Chesterfield's novels. You see, I saw him write. In Venice."

"Really? You actually saw him put pen to paper?"

"Yes," I lied unabashedly.

Warner stroked his chin in silence.

"How is it, then, that my daughter never noticed?"

"Margaret was not with him very much."

"How could that be!" he exclaimed, startled. "I thought they were—excuse the vulgarity, but it does have the merit of being instantly understood—I thought they were lovers!"

"Not in Venice."

He looked at me suspiciously, then fell silent. I began to relax and look around. The office was an exact replica of its occupant—elegant, intelligent, and curiously deformed. It was neither round nor square, but

composed of numerous curves and corners that the bookcases endeavored to espouse, suggesting the possibility of a hidden labyrinth of
mysterious corridors behind the furniture, just as my host's graciousness
seemed to hide more than one secret.

"May I inquire why you're smiling?"

Had I been? I'd no idea.

"I don't know if you're playing games with me, Mr. Pumpermaker,
or if you yourself are a victim of this remarkable hoax. It makes no
difference. I've no intention of lifting the veil, believe me. Whoever or
whatever he is, Chesterfield remains the most phenomenal coup any
publisher has pulled off in a very long time. I shall keep my suspicions
to myself. But remember—when we published *Beelzebub*, Varlet hinted
that Chesterfield was the pseudonym of a very important individual.
Remember that Buckingham Palace had to file a protest. Was this not
perhaps Varlet's moment of truth?"

"It seems to me," I said, "that Jonathan was deeply marked by his
solitary childhood. And then by his benefactor's generosity. Which is
what led him to create two characters—Jonathan Absalom Varlet, the
foundling, and Gilbert Keith Chesterfield, the child who is found. What
bothers us, I think, is that neither Varlet nor Chesterfield is his real
name. But then, has he ever had one? No one has ever discovered who
his parents were."

"Forgive me, but there's a difference. Varlet is a name that was given
to him. Chesterfield was a name he chose."

"True, but the main theme seems to me to be this dispossession that
has pursued him all his life. Dispossessed first of his family, and thus
his name. Dispossessed of the name of his benefactor, of his fortune,
and especially of his library. Thus, Varlet's effort to store all the knowledge of the world in his memory. Did he not confess to me that he once
desired to memorize the whole of *The Divine Comedy* in case one day
he found himself in prison or on a desert island, deprived of books? And
then, the moment the opportunity presented itself, did he not strive to
replace the fortune his lord's heirs robbed him of by an extraordinary
commercial and financial maneuver—the publication of *Beelzebub*? Would
you not say these were all a sort of taking-back or reconquest of his lost
powers?"

Warner looked at me with obvious satisfaction.

"An interesting hypothesis. It does not, however, prove that Varlet
wrote Chesterfield's books. I can understand how a young man may

desire to make an impression on a world that has rejected him twice over. He may mobilize his vast knowledge and seductive powers, but he could not possibly write *Beelzebub* at the same time! It contradicts his whole strategy. What does this Elsbeth and her passion for the frigid Alexander have to do with any of this?"

"But Jacob Stern searching for Papagallo . . . The name itself is quite significant, Papagallo, the father-cock. You noticed that yourself, I believe."

"Strange," he sighed, "and if my theory about Ambergris the writer turns out to be true, the travels of little Jacob through Germany can be seen quite simply as the search for the ultimate science, a search Lord Sheffield pursued his entire life. A curious idea indeed. But then, if such sweet follies give birth to great works, who am I to quibble?"

At that moment, I realized how strong an influence Jonathan had had on me. Warner was right. *Beelzebub* was my book; its conflicts were those of the son of Pumpermaker and Mary Charmer. Whereas the idea for *Jacob Stern* clearly came from Varlet's life. In a way, then, the book was clearly not mine alone. In addition, via Jacob Boehme, did it not allude to Lord Ambergris's research, even though when I'd written it I did not know the particulars of his quest?

"Chesterfield's next book is based on a Chinese fable," I said.

"Explain."

"Chesterfield wants to expand Jacob Stern's wanderings. He wants to go beyond mere signs; he wants to give them a meaning."

"Then it's no longer a wandering, but a pilgrimage."

"Exactly. The Chinese have a great store of these legends, about which the Western world knows little. *The Monkey King* is about a monkey who has a series of adventures and evolves from the condition of primate to that of Buddha. An image of human history, if you will."

"An ambitious undertaking! But the Chinese are not the only ones to have that idea. After all, man is neither an ape nor a Buddha!"

"Yet it's the two tendencies that constitute a human being," I replied. Warner shrugged.

"Ah, literature," he sighed. "An odd vice. One is interested in people and events that one would never want to associate with in real life. We are fascinated by mirrors, even if they reflect the unknown. Or perhaps because they do."

At the end of our conversation, Warner walked me to the door.

"You know both Margaret and Jonathan," he said, stopping for a moment. "Do you think she went astray in desiring to love him?"

"Does she love him?"

He raised his arms.

"Ever since Varlet left for America, her health has deteriorated. She thought she'd be marrying him, you know. . . . I should have blessed the union, even though I now have serious doubts. Who is Varlet? No one knows, really. He's even tried to get me involved in building a hospital in Africa! Africa, mind you. Why not the North Pole?"

"Did you agree?"

He coughed.

"Out of sheer necessity. If I hadn't, he wouldn't have signed the *Jacob Stern* contract. Didn't you know that?"

"No. I'd no idea he'd asked you. It's an extremely philanthropic project, you know. Lepers . . ."

"Lepers! Lepers! What do I care about lepers? But Mr. Varlet decides and I, his poor publisher, I must go along with these impossible whims! Lepers! Good-bye, Mr. Pumpermaker."

"Please, call me Cyril. I despise the name Pumpermaker."

"I can see why Chesterfield chose you for his secretary." He nodded. "I'm quite fond of you, my dear Cyril. Margaret is too, by the way. Don't you think it would be nice to pay her a visit?"

"Of course," I replied, promising myself in the same breath to do nothing of the sort. I'd no idea what feelings the young woman could possibly still have for me.

After this brief visit to London, I locked myself away at Ruthford. It had begun to snow, creating an atmosphere reminiscent of childhood that proved most conducive to writing. The good Douglas took care of me with the discretion and tenderness so often conferred upon old servants by their faithfulness and deference. From time to time, I thought of my conversations with Mary on the boat, but for the time being bachelorhood suited me quite well. When I wrote, I felt as if I were wrapped in a warm cocoon, fed with cinnamon punch and gingerbread by a silent comforting shadow, rocked by the ticking of the glossy clock my maternal grandfather had brought back from China fifty years ago. It was a strange object, decorated with ferocious dragons and comic potbellied figures, which I was told shocked my grandmother but which she tolerated out of conjugal duty, although she steadfastly refused to wind it.

This was my grandfather's task, which he performed faithfully every Sunday morning. To me, the clock was an old and familiar genie; as it ticked away the silence, it seemed to be bringing me information from the ancient Sacred City, information that translated itself into my new book.

Where had I got the idea of resuscitating that legend? I no longer remember. A translation of *Hsi-yu Chi*, the book by Wu Ch'eng-en, was already in the Ruthford library when I moved in after my parents' death. I borrowed liberally from that sixteenth-century string of anecdotes about the voyage of a Chinese monk to India in search of the sacred writings of Buddha. What interested me most, however, was not the monk but his servant, a monkey named Souen, whose mischievousness and generosity seemed to echo my ideas about the ways in which the world appears to us, which was a theme vital to my story. Clearly, my time in New York had given me much food for thought about the illusory aspects of this world, a reflection to which Varlet's and my conspiracy obviously contributed!

During this time, I had many letters from Sarah Goethman; for me her voice shall always be an intimate echo of that humility which is the privilege of true greatness. I had treated her like a little girl, and now she seemed suddenly to have become an absolute, a symbol of suffering overcome, of despair routed by grace and by a rare kind of joy, or of serenity. . . . Had not Varlet told me that night, on our way back to Paradisio from the hospital, "I went to Germany to find my soul"? It was this soul who wrote me news of Jonathan—his trips, his thoughts, his work. I should like to quote the reader certain excerpts from these letters.

February 18, 1933. Four months have gone by since I entered the hospital. Progress is slow, probably because I'm so lazy. Happily, Jonathan is so close to me that even when he's not here, I seem to see and hear him. I have constant silent conversations with him. He helps me more than all the injections and potions and massages they connive to give me but which do not, I fear, awaken that part of me which remains asleep. It's an odd feeling, being cut in two! Above the waist, everything lives and breathes; below, it's a sort of vacuum. So here I am, transformed into a mermaid . . . what a fairy tale!

Jonathan asks me to tell you that interest in his project continues to grow, and that great sums have been invested. Even his publisher has agreed to buy shares in the company. He still hasn't chosen which country in Africa will get the hospital. It seems there's a great deal of competition, particularly between the British and French colonies. India also wants it. In short, it's easier to get the money than to decide on the location. Philanthropic ideas seem to create such delicate problems. Why indeed choose Rhodesia over Gabon? There is leprosy everywhere, as well as a lot of other diseases and sufferings!

Jonathan confesses he's been trying for months to figure out the best way to take advantage of all that ridiculous publicity he gets. It was right here, in the hospital waiting room while he was waiting for the end of my operation, that he had the vision of what he had to do—to relieve suffering through his writing and with all the money his work brings in, to build hospitals, help young doctors, sponsor scientific research, and set up new laboratories. And most important, thanks to his celebrity, to force governments and international organizations to help. Isn't all that wonderful?

I've read and reread the story of little Jacob in the manuscript copy Jonathan gave me. I've cried over the dear little boy's tribulations and laughed at the crazy adventures where the outlaws are punished! What a dark abyss the human mind can become! Why do all those Christians fight each other? Is it true they were still burning people at the stake as late as 1600? I can't believe it, and I wonder if Jonathan hasn't painted a blacker picture than he should. As for the chaste love between Jacob and the little girl who can't speak, I see it as a kind of allegory. The girl is Jacob's consciousness, in a way. But then, why does she die? So he can find Rosa again? I asked Jonathan what he meant by it but he didn't answer me. "You have to figure it out yourself" was all he said!

March 27, 1933. I had to tell you our marvelous news right away! Jonathan's found a lot of my father's work! He surprised me with it just this morning. Right there, in a big leather briefcase, there were two concertos, some suites for orchestra, the *Job* oratorio, some Polish dances, and, the most exciting, his opera *The Glass Flute*, which he dedicated to me! All of it was rescued and it's as if my father has come to life! I feel the presence of these notes on paper as intensely as if they were a human being. They are human, in

fact! They're the very best part of my father. I thought everything
had been burned by the Nazis, and now here I am humming his
melodies! A musician is coming soon to interpret all these little
signs that are so full of memories. And they're going to give a concert where my father can speak at last through the musicians! That
is truly the resurrection and the joy! It's like a message he left
behind as testimony to life, which is more real than death, to a
spirit victorious over the forces of hatred.

Jonathan told me that my father had sent copies of most of his
scores to an Italian musician named Gasperini, from Milan. He wrote
to this Gasperini, but the man had died. His widow had no idea
where he might have put the music. That's when Jonathan thought
of sending her a young American harpsichordist he knew who was
giving a series of concerts in Italy. So the harpsichordist went to
see Gasperini's widow and was surprised to find a charming woman
who knew nothing whatsoever about music, but who got along very
well with him in other respects, and gave him permission to search
through her husband's papers and so to find my father's composi-
tions. Except that the witch wouldn't let him take them away, even
though she couldn't do anything with them herself. She smelled a
good deal, I guess. Anyway, Jonathan bought all the scores from
her via the harpsichordist, but only one at a time and at a very
high price. "Ah," the widow sighed to justify her position, "it's just
that Jewish music, you know . . . with Mussolini, I mean . . . It's
very risky, you understand. . . ." When the harpsichordist finally
bought the last piece, he gave her a hearty slap, and although I
can't bear violence, I think he did the right thing.

April 4, 1933. The air is so mild I can write to you from the
terrace of our new house. Jonathan rented it two weeks before I left
the hospital. It's very romantic, with ivy on the walls and wild
grasses tangled in the garden paths. I'm glad I didn't have to go
back to Paradisio. Everything here is calm, distant, but somehow
close. It's not America but it's not Europe either. It's somewhere
else, someplace where it's easy for memory to snuggle in. The only
place I can compare to the Cedars is your Ruthford, which I've
never been to but which Jonathan has so often described as a special place where childhood can keep beginning all over again. We
have two nice young girls to help with the housework; all I can do

really is give them advice. The hardest part is waiting for Jonathan to come back from traveling around for his project, but I console myself by saying that nothing bad can happen to someone on a crusade for good. But just let him be the least bit late and I'm terrified!

The hospital's going to be built in Uganda, near the capital, Kampala. It'll be called the Inter-African Center for the Treatment of Leprosy. There'll be fifteen doctors and they'll take care of anyone who comes. Since it's a British colony, the government will give some money. The king has asked Jonathan to come see him when he's next in London, but I'm afraid that won't be for a while. The work must start as soon as possible and Jonathan's decided to oversee it himself, which means long absences. But it's only right that I contribute my share to this humane and important enterprise.

We can't wait until *Jacob Stern* comes out! The American reporters try to sneak in to see us, but we're protected behind high walls and a lot of electrified wire. Oh yes! Without it we'd be invaded, and last year's madness would start all over again, especially since articles are starting to appear in magazines about the hospital. If one didn't know that Jonathan is doing this out of charity and a concern for justice, one might wonder if it wasn't just another way to become more famous. Alas, not all the articles are in the best of taste. A few papers have got wind of my illness and make suppositions about my return to health and quote a lot of fake documents! All they want is to make people cry. It's the same for our marriage; some papers wreak absolute havoc with it. I'll let you judge for yourself. Here's the most recent headline: CHESTER AND HIS INVALID WIFE—A KAMPALA HONEYMOON?

My father used to tell me to read and read again the story of Job. I'm rereading it now and it's a wonderful consolation. I have neither the honor nor the misfortune to be one of God's elect, but prayer helps me. It's a dialogue with the invisible. I remember all the old prayers from my father, who got them from his father, who . . . It makes me happy to know that my lips are reciting the same prayers as the ones that came from the lips of Moses. We were a very old Polish family. My grandfather took the name Goethman when he moved to Berlin. If I had a son, I'd call him Yehudi, which means Jew. It was the name of Rabbi Yaakov Yitzhak of Pjyzha,

whom our family always revered. I'm telling you this because if I
were to have a son, my present physical condition would probably
not permit me to know him. At least that's what the doctors say,
although they're so often wrong!

In fact, as I learned later, Sarah was already pregnant at the time she
wrote this letter. The doctors had told her she must never have a child,
but she preferred to run the risk rather than give up, as she explained
in a letter dated July 15, 1933: "Jonathan's love makes it impossible for
me to think of myself. I must give him a son, and he shall have one. My
body may no longer be fit to give birth, but if Jonathan has honored it
as he has, then he must find it worthy of this marvelous mystery. And
that's enough for me."

I wondered if Varlet was fully aware of the dangers. In her letter of
November 23, 1933, Sarah wrote: "It shall be a winter's child. Jonathan
didn't want it to be born because he was afraid for me. But I insisted,
for without this child my life will have lost its primary meaning. I owe
Jonathan this child, I owe it to our love, and if I have the misfortune
not to survive its birth, well, the gift will be that much more precious."

The first draft of *The Monkey King* was completed in early December
but I wasn't happy with it, so I decided to take a short holiday and pay
them a visit. The truth is I feared the worst, and thought it my duty to
be with them during the birth. When I arrived, I found Sarah filled with
confidence and Jonathan a nervous wreck, even though everything, including three specialists, was mobilized and at the ready. Sarah checked
into Abraham Lincoln Hospital in Manhattan two weeks before the due
date, just in case, and so began the interminable wait. The newspapers
took full advantage of the situation to indulge themselves in a myriad
of impossible speculations. All of puritan America had apparently awakened; since, due to administrative obstacles, Sarah and Jonathan had
not been able to marry, the conservative press had a field day with the
ethics of our time. It was considered in the worst possible taste to wish
to cure leprosy if, at the same time, one was bringing into the world a
child conceived in adultery! Other papers took offense and argued the
contrary; the result was quite a scandal. In the end, even the Royal
Family took notice.

Three days before the due date, on December 10 to be precise, the
British ambassador, Davies, received permission to give Sarah her nat-

uralization papers and to marry the couple in her hospital room. The intensity of the moment is something I shall remember for the rest of my life. Davies had been ambassador to Germany and thus knew about Sarah's sufferings. In a short speech, he explained why His Majesty had urged the administration to expedite the formalities: "Exceptional circumstances require exceptional decisions," he declared. "In the name of Great Britain, Gilbert Keith Chesterfield has already done so much for culture and for humanity, it is only fitting Great Britain accord his fiancée the benefits of British nationality." Aside from Davies and myself, the only others present were Matthew Tennyson, the director of *The Right to Love*, and a rabbi who had consented to marry a mixed couple, Varlet having been raised by his lord in the Anglican persuasion.

A nurse broke the news to the press, which effectively gagged the puritan papers and paved the way for an onslaught of questions, of the genre "Will Mrs. Chesterfield survive?" In one day, every ounce of print was squeezed from this question by media great and small; it was said that as a result of her accident, Sarah could not give birth without sacrificing her own life, that she was acting in full consciousness of the risks, that she was in a sense a "martyr to love." The entire country seemed to be holding its breath.

On the morning of December 13, I was resting at the Cedars, having been unable to sleep due to my nervousness and to the outrageous publicity surrounding Sarah's condition. Around six o'clock, the phone rang. It was Tennyson.

"The surgery's begun," he said simply.

I got dressed and took a cab to the hospital. No birth had ever signified for me so clearly the mysteries of life and death. I found Tennyson in the cafeteria. He was a man of careful gesture, with a mane of white hair and the sort of grave nonchalance common to men accustomed to power. To take our minds off the situation, we talked about the film.

"I used only one set," he said, "Alexander's home. A Victorian built by a rather unusual character near Los Angeles. Trapped inside, Elsbeth . . ." What had he said? I'd lost track.

If only Souen the monkey had been there! In the legend, he could move mountains, fight all manner of dragons, even flatten Yama, the Master of Death! How easy it would have been for him to deliver Sarah's baby!

". . . and so Elsbeth behaves according to the floor she occupies.

Each floor is a level of consciousness. There's the kitchen downstairs, where the most secret thoughts are exchanged; the living room on the ground floor, where . . ."

One day, Souen decided to take on the dread toad that balanced the universe on its shoulders, an episode that doesn't exist in the legend but that I invented myself. I wanted to make my monkey a complete hero who confronted all kinds of appearances and who, in the end, had to confront himself.

What was happening? The nurse was saying something. A baby boy had been born!

"And the mother?" I asked.

"We'll save her." She smiled. "Dr. Choukroun is a real miracle worker. . . ."

Tennyson and I literally fell into each other's arms; we laughed and cried so much one would have thought we were the fathers! Outside, the reporters pressed forward, shouting for information, as we rejoined Varlet in Sarah's room. He was clearly exhausted; there were dark circles under his eyes and he looked as if he hadn't slept for days.

"The operation lasted seven hours," he said. "She won't be awake until tonight. We'll name him Yehudi. I promised her." Then he turned over and, fully clothed, fell sound asleep.

The entire country seemed to heave a great sigh of relief, followed by a wave of extraordinary enthusiasm. In this way are myths created. Because of Varlet's personality, Sarah's accident, and Chesterfield's success, the birth of an English child was greeted in the United States by more fervor than in England, where the blessed event was acknowledged by a more seemly discretion. Then too, the American press was better versed in the business of stars, English newspapers confining themselves ever so cautiously to general topics, and the comings and goings of the Royal Family. Should we want to examine further the reasons behind the American delirium, we must remember that the country was undergoing an unprecedented economic crisis that Roosevelt and his team were trying to sort out through the New Deal. Like Sarah, America had been on the verge of catastrophe, but it had survived. The child was superb—and thus America too would triumph over her misfortune!

Sarah spent the greater part of a year recovering; she could neither be picked up nor even sat in a chair, as before. An invalid, she began to gain weight, which rendered her even more immobile. Varlet had the

bedroom at the Cedars completely redone; it was filled with light, and
with a mass of equipment that allowed Sarah a certain independence.
By pushing a button, she could turn on the radio, or the phonograph,
or the electric teapot. The baby was put into the care of a nurse in an
adjoining bedroom, so that when she called, the baby could be brought
to her immediately. Despite her condition, she was extraordinarily happy.

I returned to England in February 1934, as soon as the situation
seemed stabilized. The publication of *Jacob Stern* was imminent, and in
Jonathan's absence, it was indispensable that I be there to take care of
things. Our friend had, in fact, decided not to join the party, preoccupied as he was with preparations for the hospital in Kampala. In any
case, his fame was such that his presence was unnecessary to the book's
success.

On the day of my departure, I went to say good-bye to Sarah. She
promised to write. Varlet insisted upon coming with me to the boat. As
we drove to the pier, he tried to explain, but his preoccupations were so
alien to me I'm not sure he succeeded.

"I, who cared only for books, now find myself some sort of businessman," he began, "an entertainment and a construction entrepreneur!
But there's no fooling ourselves; building a hospital is no more interesting or remarkable than building your Regent Street hotel. My lord used
to say to me, 'Find the right lever and you can lift the world. Just remember that the lever is only an instrument. Never confuse it with a
goal.' I've used literature, your literature, Cyril, as a lever. It's brought
me fame and money. And now I'm going to use that fame and money
as another lever—to try to alleviate suffering. The hospital is only a
beginning, however, because what I really want is to make the world see
that if it does not get hold of itself, it will come to a terrible end."

"What do you mean by that?"

"Oh, don't worry, that wasn't one of your almanac predictions, like
the ones hawked about by occult religious sects. No, this concerns the
true condition of every nation. You know as well as I that the world is
sick, that there's another war in the making. I saw it when I was in
Berlin and Paris, and since then my fears have become certainties. I've
even spoken to Ambassador Davies about them and he knows exactly
what I'm talking about. 'Nothing can stop Germany's will to expand,'
he told me. As for our democracies, what can they do against a dictatorship? I'm telling you, England herself will be German!'"

I must confess that Jonathan's words seemed to me utterly without foundation. He must have noticed, for he stopped and then began all over again.

"Hitler became chancellor last year, backed by Hindenburg and even more by the army and big business. Special forces were created to spread terror among all those who oppose the new regime in any way. Is the Reichstag burning? Must be the Communists. Thousands of them were arrested, along with socialists, democrats, Catholics, Jews—and all without a trial! Europe does nothing. America is silent. Hitler is free to continue his master plan. And I can assure you, he won't fail. But what Varlet and Pumpermaker can't do, Chesterfield can. Because he's famous and popular. He's going to raise his voice, denounce the horror, call to reason not only the Germans but all the other nations as well. He's going to try to persuade other voices to join him, people of all kinds from all over the world, so that their combined authority will awaken the public. What do you say to that?"

"Heavens, what can I say! I've no idea what's happening in Germany; what you've told me is a complete surprise. Is this Hitler really that dangerous? Aren't the Communists more pernicious than he? Don't they want to force Germany into revolution in order to take power for themselves? Isn't Hitler merely trying to stop them, which means he has to put the terrorists and conspirators in jail?"

"Most of the Western press is just as blind!" Jonathan cried. "When it's a question of my marriage or Sarah's childbirth, they all jump up and down like madmen, but when the issue concerns the future of the human race, nobody cares. What's more, I think the owners of the biggest papers are manipulating opinion by throwing the people a lot of nonsense while the real stakes are being played for behind closed doors. I also think there's a close connection between the exhaustion of our intellectuals and the treachery of big business."

"But who are they betraying?" I asked, feeling somehow that Jonathan was referring to me.

"My dear Cyril"—he smiled—"you'll never change. But the world does. And it keeps changing. How nice it would be to lock oneself up in a charming country house like you're about to do at Ruthford and to write and read and raise children! But instead I'm going to rush about shaking people up and wondering if anyone will listen to me!"

"Don't you think your project, humanitarian as it may be, and perhaps precisely for that reason, is doomed to failure? Building a hospital depends on a certain number of instantly verifiable givens—leprosy, famine, illiteracy, who knows what else? And it requires the coordination of many different professions—bankers, architects, bricklayers, electricians, doctors, nurses . . . All that is anchored in the real. But what exactly is your fear of this Hitler, or these rumors about what he's doing? If the press listens to you, it's only because they're dying as usual for something sensational to write about. Believe me, prophecy simply does not pay!"

"Doubtless you're quite right," he said, looking at me sadly. "And when the world wakes up, it will be in the midst of a nightmare. Then your famous reality will be all too present, in the form of cannons and planes and tanks! There'll be something in it for *all* your professionals then, far more than just the ones on your hospital list. And they won't need Chesterfield around to raise money!"

"Don't you think Sarah will be awfully lonely?" I asked, changing the subject.

"She'll watch over me."

We talked about the publication of *The Fabulous Adventures of Jacob Stern*, and about my new novel.

"It's funny," he said, "your monkey is a little like me. A kind of Impossible Warrior, no?"

When we parted at the gangplank, I wondered if Jonathan was really of sound mind or if he wasn't playing a bit on my credulity.

I thought a lot about that last conversation during the crossing, rather suspiciously in fact, for I thought his frenzy wasted on a lost cause. Or else it was just another tactic for increasing his notoriety. Perhaps literary celebrity wasn't enough anymore. Perhaps now he needed the kind of glory reserved for those who wish to leave their mark on an era. Was he going into politics? If so, which politics? Some sort of socialism, I feared. It was currently quite fashionable among intellectuals, perhaps only as an expression of their guilt at being well off while so many others weren't. As far as I was concerned, the only values that merited respect were the traditional ones, those on which the Western world, and most especially Great Britain, were founded. Revolution seemed to me every bit as monstrous as the plague and the Fire of London. Jonathan's ideas, in other words, seemed dangerous, and I was not happy to see the name of Chesterfield connected to them. Hadn't I been a good sport to put up with all the fuss that had surrounded Varlet? The further we got from America, the less I understood Jonathan's ideas and the more uneasy they made me.

But what could I say? I knew he'd do just as he liked. He was taking off like a shot in a direction he claimed to understand but that seemed frightfully foggy to me. Wasn't he going to destroy Chesterfield by dragging him into an adventure that would mark him forever? For a moment, I thought of announcing that he was not the writer people thought him to be, thus discrediting his enterprise. But it wasn't in me to do such a thing, if only out of respect for Sarah, who would surely be destroyed by such a disaster. Besides, who would believe me? I could just imagine the scene in Peter Warner's office: "Ah, how very droll! You, Pumpermaker? You a writer of Chesterfield's caliber?" He'd look at me as if I'd been changed into a giraffe or a possum! "In any case, my young friend, even were you to announce such a thing to the press, no one would believe you. Varlet is impervious to harm. An obscure Englishman claims to be the author of the illustrious Chesterfield's novels? They'll laugh you quite out of existence. There's far too much at stake for the truth—if it is the truth—to be heard! Anyway, I'd be the first to swear on a stack of Bibles that you're an imposter. You'll end up in prison, believe me. . . ."

There was a chill wind on deck the night before we docked, and I resolved to sweep away my worries, concentrate on myself, and try to succeed in my own way. Varlet's odd ideas and crazy ventures had taken up all my time and attention, and I despised myself for allowing him to drag me along in his wake. Was I not a good-humored sort? Was my work not read, admired, respected? My finances quite ample? What difference did my anonymity make? In fact, didn't it ensure my repose while my double shouted himself hoarse all around the world? Without having wanted to, hadn't I found the writer's ideal solution? At that thought, I felt better and began to pity Varlet and his schemes.

Moreover, there was Mary Stretton, whom I'd met on just this sort of boat and to whom I'd written several letters during my stay in New York. I'd hidden neither my feelings nor my intentions. And she'd replied in kind, albeit somewhat more modestly. She was a bit concerned about ending her widowhood, but thought that if we desired to have children, it would not be practical to wait. An intelligent thought, that. As soon as we docked, I dashed to the post office to cable my arrival and to invite her to lunch in London at a restaurant of her choosing. Then I returned to Ruthford, where the good Douglas welcomed me with such affection that it warmed the rest of my heart.

Two days later, I received a copy of *Jacob Stern* from Goldman and a reply from Mary, by the same post. On the jacket, the publisher had reproduced Bosch's painting of the Prodigal Son as peddler, a design that evoked little Jacob's travels throughout Germany. It was quite stunning; this novel seemed to me far better than the last, which had been rather too psychological for my taste. As for Mary's letter, she thanked me for my invitation, but since she was not used to going to lunch in restaurants, she preferred we meet for tea at the Caddie Club in Belgrave Road, whence I took myself on Tuesday at five o'clock, accompanied by a box of Swiss chocolates.

The moment I entered, I realized the Caddie was a women's club. A charming elderly lady invited me to have a seat in a little drawing room off the foyer; as soon as I entered I had the feeling that I'd already been here, in this room filled with statuettes and religious pictures, although I couldn't imagine where or how. Like an obedient child, I sat quietly on a mauve sofa with fringes until Mary appeared, in the company of a woman about twenty years her senior. Both wore pink, and both had identical blue ribbons from which dangled identical large medallions.

"On my dear, dear Cyril!" Mary exclaimed, then stopped in the doorway, blushing with embarrassment.

"I am Miss Andrews," her companion said, extending her hand. "Welcome to the Caddie Club and the Sisters of the Mountain. The Sacred Mountain, of course!"

"It's a great pleasure to see you again, after such a long trip," I said to Mary, shaking the hand of the Sister of the Mountain.

"Your letters gave her great pleasure," said the Sister.

"Well," I replied, somewhat at a loss for words, "perhaps we oughtn't to disturb your friends any longer. Shall we have a stroll in the park?"

"Absolutely not!" cried the dragon lady. "We've prepared a little celebration. After all, it's not every day that one of our Sisters receives her fiancé here! Do come, dear friend!"

"Oh yes, please come," said Mary, her voice quivering like a wounded bird. "They're so nice. You'll see. . . ."

As we entered the room, we were greeted by great applause from about twenty women of all ages. The walls had been decorated in paper garlands, and the table in multicolored silk flowers. Large cakes with icing sat enthroned amid the cups and teapots. Everyone wore pink, except for one—a tall spare white-haired woman in a blue dress with a bright red collar.

"Dear Brother," she said, in a loud voice clearly accustomed to canticles and sermons, "the community of the Sisters of the Mountain is happy to welcome our dear Mary's fiancé. We are an assembly of souls dedicated to prayer and good works. It was on the Mountain that Noah's Ark appeared after the flood; it was on the Mountain that Moses received the Ten Commandments; it was on the Mountain that Jerusalem . . ."

Suddenly I remembered where I'd seen the little drawing room before; it was exactly like the room filled with plaster statuettes where Madame Caratini had received me on the Calle del Ca in Venice! The memory burst upon me so blindingly and so unexpectedly that I almost burst out laughing, in one of those hysterical irrepressible laughs that only grows worse the more one tries to stop it and ends up completely dominating the sufferer. Thus, while the dear Sister continued her enumeration of mountains, I ascended my own Golgotha, so great was my torment, until the moment when the inevitable explosion occurred. I feigned a colossal sneeze and blew my nose under the reproving eye of the entire cenacle, an act that did nothing to further my cause. At last the sermon ended and everyone sat down, which gave me the opportunity to stammer I'm not quite sure what, while accepting a slice of tea cake. I felt that the Sisters of the Mountain judged me a perfect cretin or, worse yet, an iconoclast! Mary didn't seem to know what to think.

At one point, from the back of the room, an artful little Sister of about seventy quavered, "My dear Sisters, your mountain stories don't excite our lovers, but they do seem to amuse them. I suppose that should be quite enough for us! I shall drink to the new fiancés!" And she raised her teacup in a toast. The others followed, and we all relaxed.

"Dear friends," I replied, having got control of myself, "in fact, if I may, dear Sisters, you see before you someone profoundly chagrined at having succumbed to what is commonly called these days hysterics. It was most impudent of me to have wished to hide it. It's just that your warm welcome and your kind familiar words reminded me of my childhood, and at that moment I felt again in my deepest self such complete peace, such happiness as I knew as a child when my mother brought me bread and jam at teatime." Not very impressive, I grant you, but I was lucky enough to get away with it. The sea of broad smiles proved to me that I had been forgiven.

They let us go around six. Mary took my arm and we walked side by side, she in her raincoat with its gray fox collar, me in my black wool overcoat.

"Well," I said cheerfully, after we'd gone a few steps in silence, "here we are together again, my dear."

"I loved your letters," Mary replied, bowing her head. "But I was so frightened. America is ghastly, isn't it?"

"More than you can imagine. Everyone is quite mad, really." I stopped and looked at her. "Is it true you were afraid for me?"

"Oh yes!" she exclaimed. "George . . ." She blushed. "Forgive me. It's just that that was how I learned of my husband's death. All voyages terrify me."

We continued to walk.

"I understand that George's death must have marked you deeply. I have infinite respect for his memory, but as he himself would have told you—the will to life is stronger."

"You're right, of course, dear Cryil," she said, nodding, "but do you think I'm worthy of you? I'm not a young girl any longer."

"I beg you never to mention that again," I replied, stopping.

She moved just a bit closer.

"Thank you," she sighed. "You are so good. And so generous." As she spoke, her voice grew more confident. "You are . . . how can I say it . . . ?"

"All that is in the eye of the beholder," I replied, taking her gloved hand and kissing her fingertips.

"This new hotel in Regent Street," she asked timidly, a few steps further along, "the one they're just finishing . . . . is it true it belongs to you?"

"You mustn't bother your head about those things, my dear. I've invested a bit of money in the building, that's all."

"But that's enormous! You must be quite wealthy, mustn't you?"

"Let's just say my business is rather successful. I'm also lucky enough to own some property in Cannon Street. And a marvelous family home at Ruthford, not far from Birmingham. How I'd love you to see the house! It belonged to my mother's family, the Charmers."

"I should never dare to marry someone so important," Mary said, shaking her head, a hint of nervousness in her eyes. "But what do you do that you've been able to save so much? I'm only an art teacher, and if I had to buy a studio in the worst street in London, I'd never manage it!"

"Didn't you have some money after George's death?"

"Barely enough to cover the return of his body and the funeral expenses."

"I'm so sorry," I replied sincerely. "I just manage the family fortune and—this will amuse you—I'm the secretary of quite a famous man!"

"A famous man!" she exclaimed, coming to a stop. "Who? An actor? A politician?"

"No," I replied, anxious to keep walking. "A writer."

Mary seemed delighted.

"A writer! How amusing! And who is it? Not Lawrence, I hope?"

"Lawrence has been dead for four years, my dear Mary."

"Huxley? Morgan?" she laughed. "Ah, I know! It's Eliot!"

"None of them. Do you swear never to tell? All right, then, it's Chesterfield."

"The one who wrote *Beelzebub*?" she asked, stopping for a moment.

"Himself."

"My god!" she murmured. "What he writes is ghastly! That poor dear Elsbeth! You can't imagine how much I hated Chesterfield; he seemed to enjoy torturing the poor woman! Oh, Cyril, how can you be the secretary to someone so . . . so . . . how can I say it? So depraved . . ."

"Perhaps you exaggerate Elsbeth's misfortunes?" I replied, trying to keep things light. "In any case, one mustn't read novels as if they were confessions. Chesterfield is most generous. And most humane. Right now he's building a hospital for lepers in Africa."

"By way of atonement, I should imagine," Mary said, pouting. "But what does that mean, being a writer's secretary?"

"I take care of business matters. His dealings with publishers. He's completely overburdened, you know. Besides, he lives in New York with his wife and son. They have all suffered a great deal."

I told Mary how Jonathan had saved Sarah from the Nazis, how he'd married her even though she'd become an invalid. In short, I drew a most heroic picture of Varlet, and with such fervor that Mary exclaimed, "You must forgive me! I didn't know. Perhaps Chesterfield isn't a very good writer, but rather a man of great heart?"

For once, I preferred to drop the subject right there.

THE YEAR WAS 1934. I'D BEGUN SEVERAL drafts of *The Monkey King*, all of them unsatisfactory, until suddenly one day I seemed to find the right voice, and finished the book in two months of straight writing. During that time, my hotel in Regent Street was completed, and on a whim, I christened it the Chester. I had entrusted all the plans, the work, and the direction to a well-known architect and a group of entrepreneurs; my only responsibility was to check on their progress from time to time and, assisted by an accountant, verify the finances. Given my revulsion for business, I stayed as far away from the work site as possible; I preferred to be honestly duped than to waste time and imagination with these trivial issues.

In short, 1934 was a year of work and study, and would not deserve a full chapter had it not been for two major events—the unexpected reappearance of Margaret Warner, and Jonathan Absalom Varlet's passage through London. In the interests of clarity, I shall describe these episodes one after the other, although they occurred at more or less the same time. As a preamble, however, I shall return to my relationship with Mary, which grew increasingly comfortable the more we saw each other. Sometimes we met at the Caddie Club, sometimes outside her flat. Our usual pastime was a walk in Hyde Park, for I was encountering great resistance in persuading her to fulfill my deepest desire and come to Ruthford. It was not seemly, she felt, to visit a bachelor's residence, and I found myself obliged to resort to all manner of tactics to convince her otherwise. Once our wedding date had been set for October 29, however, she finally agreed to let me meet her train at Warwick Station at eleven o'clock on September 22, after which we would lunch at Ruthford, and she would take the five o'clock train back to London. I gave her my word that I would follow her wishes exactly.

The weather was perfect, one of those days when autumn bathes the countryside in a joyful blond sunlight. I myself was every bit as joyful, for Mary Charmer's home was at last going to receive my Mary, who was soon to be my wife. To top it off, I'd heard a few days before that my petition to change my name from Pumpermaker to Charmer-Maker had been granted by a London court. It had cost an absolute fortune, but I'd succeeded. Mary's last name, therefore, would be Charmer, exactly like my mother's, and our children would not have to be burdened by their grandfather's ridiculous patronymic. I'd rented a car and driver for the day, having promised myself to show my fiancée all my childhood places—the stream I'd fallen into, the oak tree I'd climbed, the pond where I'd hunted for salamanders, the meadow where I'd ridden the good Douglas's donkey, and the Hangman's Tower I had been so afraid to enter.

At 11:10—English trains are always late—the London-Birmingham local pulled into the station. An old woman got out with her dog, followed by two small boys. There was no Mary. I ran the full length of the platform, jumping up to see into the windows to make sure she hadn't fallen asleep in her compartment. When the train left the station, I was not only perplexed but disappointed and worried. As I walked back to the car, not at all sure what to do, a red sports car suddenly veered full-tilt off the London road and screeched to a stop in a cloud of dust not far from me. Both doors opened; Mary emerged from one, neat and tidy, and from the other—I almost fainted, so overcome was I with surprise and incomprehension—it was Margaret Warner, as absurdly out of place as a racehorse in a china factory. I hadn't seen her since her departure from Venice three years before, but now as then she wore a chic black coat and looked every bit the elegant, shining blond Scandinavian princess—the very emblem of purity! I stood there openmouthed, as if her sudden appearance had blinded me to Mary's.

"But . . . you know each other?" I stammered at last.

"Amusing, isn't it?" Margaret replied.

"I must explain," Mary said, coming toward me. "I can understand your surprise. . . . It's all my fault, really. Please do forgive me, Cyril, but it's only natural that I do some research on you, isn't it? And since you're Chesterfield's secretary, I thought the wisest thing would be to consult his publisher. Mr. Warner was too busy to see me, but he referred me to his daughter. And that's how I met Margaret, who was kind enough to drive me here."

I swallowed hard. It was bad enough that Mary had spied on me, but that her research should have led her to Miss Warner . . .

"Well," I replied, tight-lipped, "so now you know exactly who I am. I'm sure there's no one better suited than your new friend here to provide you with a detailed report!"

"Oh yes!" Mary exclaimed, apparently unaware of my sarcasm. "Margaret and I have become such good friends. She's told me such lovely things about you!"

"Indeed. What lovely things?"

"Are you angry with me, Cyril?" she asked, beginning to worry. "Isn't it normal that I would want to know who you really are? That enormous fortune, the Chester Hotel, the buildings in Cannon Street, your Ruthford—that's an awful lot, you know. . . . And I didn't really understand how all that went with being a writer's secretary. Why should he do that, I wondered, if he has all that money?"

"And Miss Warner explained everything to you?"

"Oh yes! She told me who you are and who Chesterfield is and Sarah and your trip to Venice . . . everything!"

"Thank you so much," I said with polite outrage, turning to Margaret, who was obviously enjoying herself immensely.

"You're quite welcome," she replied casually. "Your dear Mary was just a trifle uneasy about you. You're too rich, my dear Cyril! But we do love you and your fortune won't be an obstacle, I promise."

"How lovely. And now, instead of standing here talking, perhaps we should go on to Ruthford? Douglas will lay an extra place."

As Margaret's car was a two-seater, I went ahead in the rented car while the two women followed along behind. Frankly, I'd no idea what to make of all this.

"Oh, what a lovely house!" Mary cried, clapping her hands once we'd arrived. "Do you mind if I just have a run in the garden?" And she skipped off toward the river like a baby goat. Margaret and I entered the foyer; with her hair pulled high into a bun, she looked more the vestal virgin than ever.

"I've missed you, Cyril," she said, removing her gloves.

"Well, I must say I wasn't exactly expecting this."

"I wouldn't have missed it for the world," she replied, looking around, sniffing the air. "Thank God," she sighed, in the voice of one who returns home after a long absence, "nothing's changed. The coat rack with the bear, the mildew on the mirror, the fox hunt . . . You can't imagine how often I've thought of this place. I remember it was raining, and Jonathan and I were absolutely soaked, and you welcomed us so kindly."

I helped her off with her coat; she wore a red tweed suit that set off her skin and hair quite nicely.

"You've seen my father, haven't you? But what about me? Have you forgotten me?"

"Not exactly. It's just that we parted on such an ambiguous note . . ."

"Oh, Cyril," she replied in a hoarse voice, tossing her head, "such grand phrases you come up with!"

At that moment, Mary reappeared.

"Marvelous!" she exclaimed. "There's even a river and a wooden bridge!"

"I'm glad you like my house," I said sincerely, as we walked into the small drawing room.

"Do you realize that if Jonathan had agreed to marry me, I would have wanted to live in a place exactly like this?" Margaret said, settling into in an armchair opposite the fire. "But Sarah won, didn't she?"

"You can't really envy her?" Mary said gently. "She's so ill. And her husband's always traveling."

"You think that because she's paralyzed," Margaret said. "But out of love, she had Jonathan's son. I read all about it in the papers. She might have died, mightn't she? What a selfless gift!"

"It was a beautiful thing," Mary admitted. She seemed to consider everything Margaret said with great understanding.

"I can see how the event might titillate your taste for the mystical, as you're wont to put it," I said to Margaret. "But I can assure you it wasn't terribly romantic."

"Do you know that Margaret and I have the same vocation for mysticism? I've told her about the Sisters of the Mountain. Don't you think she'd fit right in, Cyril?"

"Your new friend has already belonged to an occult sect, the Friends of Brahma, if I remember correctly . . . ?" I could just imagine Margaret in the Calle del Ca, dressed all in pink with a blue ribbon!

"You don't!" Margaret laughed. "It was Shiva, not Brahma. And we held seances, which is quite different from occultism. It's known as spiritualism. And anyway, I wasn't a member for very long. The invisible has no need of machinery, really."

"Quite right," Mary said, with conviction. "One of our Sisters was once involved in this spiritualism. She was a spinster and believed she'd met the spirit of the son she'd never had. In the end, we had to put her in an asylum. She's dead now."

"If you're ready . . ." Douglas interrupted from the doorway.

"My dear Douglas, do come in. I want you to meet my fiancée."

"Excuse me," she said, drying her hands on her apron, "my hands are wet."

"Cyril has told me so much about you," Mary replied. "I'm sure we'll get along quite well together."

"This house has needed a woman for a long time," Douglas said, blushing with pleasure and embarrassment. Then, recognizing Margaret, she blurted out, "Oh! It's the young lady who . . ." Her unfinished sentence hung in the air as she remembered the night Somerset died, then she turned around and murmured, "It *is* lunchtime, sir. . . ."

"I love Burrough's china," Mary said, once we'd sat down. "They're such lovely puzzles. I wonder what these represent? I can never figure them out but they amuse me so. Like when I was a child."

"You're still a child," Margaret said.

"Do you really think so? Do you think I could run such a beautiful house? Oh, and Cyril, I must tell you, I go to the Caddie Club once a week, on Wednesdays. Even when I'm married, I shan't abandon my friends, you know."

"Of course. Perhaps I'll take one of the Cannon Street apartments so we'll have a place in London where you can stay."

"You can always go to the Chester!" Margaret added.

Mary laughed, then remarked on the marvels of the pâté.

"Douglas makes about thirty of them every year," I said.

"Then you hunt?" Mary asked, uneasily.

"Good heavens, no! I have a horror of guns."

"I love to hunt," said Margaret. "Those lovely hot little bodies in the palm of the hand . . ."

"Ugh!" cried Mary. "You disappoint me. . . ."

"On the contrary," Margaret replied, "there's something sacred in reaching the inaccessible. Birds fly so high and so far away, and you, just by lifting a sort of long arm, you can reach them."

"You reach nothing at all," I said. "The beauty of birds is in their flight. And you destroy that. What an odd idea—to want to embrace life by killing it."

"It's a necessary sacrifice," Margaret replied. "The Latin root of the word *sacrifice* means to accomplish the sacred. Through his holocaust, his violation of the profane, the victim becomes sacred."

"Sounds like your mysticism speaking," I said. Margaret lowered her eyes.

As Douglas served the haddock and soft-boiled eggs with wild mint sauce, our conversation returned to Chesterfield, or rather to Jonathan and his Kampala project.

"Whatever's happened to him?" Margaret asked. "He didn't seem much taken with that sort of thing in Venice. Somehow I can't quite see him as the great philanthropist."

"Make no mistake," I replied, "Jonathan was preoccupied by his lord in Venice. He was grateful to him for having rescued him from the gutter and for giving him such a superb education. Via Sarah and the leprosarium, he wants to repay that debt."

"Well, I like that Chesterfield better than I like the writer," said Mary. "The writer seems nasty and confused. Perhaps he's frightened of women, and that's why he's so belligerent about them."

"You haven't read *Jacob Stern* yet. Women are treated with great sensitivity in that book. Jacob, who is lame, loves the little girl who can't speak. They spend whole days in a gazebo in a garden just looking at each other."

"I've no desire to read a second book," said Mary. "*Beelzebub* was enough. One must not encourage those sorts of writers, even if their loves are mute! Don't you agree, Margaret?"

I confess that I asked myself several times during the course of that afternoon if I was doing the right thing by marrying, but since events have a tendency to move more quickly than we do I could no longer turn back without causing a scandal, and without scandalizing myself as well. After dessert, we went back into the drawing room and began to write out the wedding invitations. We chose a small and quite ancient town named Faversham, in Kent, not because of the story of poor Thomas

Arden who was assassinated there by his wife and her lover, but because that happened to be where Mary's mother lived. Her father had disappeared before she was five, and it was not considered in good taste to inquire into his whereabouts. As for Mary's mother, she was not quite compos mentis, if ever she had been. Mary had been raised by an aunt, her father's sister, but the good woman had left England and gone with her merchant husband to Hong Kong, where he was involved in trade— wool, cotton, and silk, to be precise. Since the Stretton family was reduced to Mary and her aged mother, while my own was confined exclusively to myself, our invitations went only to Peter Warner, who we were quite sure would decline; my architect and my banker, to whom we suggested we'd understand if they were too busy to join us; to the family in Hong Kong, who were too far away even to reply; to Sarah and Jonathan, who, we were also quite sure, would content themselves with sending a congratulatory telegram; and to the Sisters of the Mountain, all of whom we could be certain would accept!

"But you must come too!" Mary said to Margaret, who had been poking at the embers in the fireplace while we wrote. "In fact, what do you think Cyril? Why not have Margaret be one of our witnesses?"

"I've no idea if Miss Warner is free that day," I replied, glancing desperately at Margaret.

"But of course I am!" she cried, putting down the poker. "What a marvelous idea! I shall indeed by your witness, Mary. But who'll be Cyril's?"

"I've no idea," I muttered, in a foul temper. "We'll find someone at church. The beadle perhaps."

"Out of the question," Mary declared. "It's simply not done." Her naïveté was making her increasingly unbearable, much to Margaret's delight.

Once the invitations were completed, I asked my fiancée if she would care to see the house. She was delighted, so I offered our excuses to Miss Warner and left her by the hearth in the drawing room.

"I adore a fire," she said. "I could sit here for hours just watching it."

"Take care you don't burn yourself," I replied, on my way out.

"Burning is nothing. What we need is to consume ourselves. . . ."

"She's a remarkable woman, isn't she?" Mary said as we reached the second floor.

"Remarkable indeed."

"I'm so awfully lucky you didn't fall in love with her! She's so fresh and beautiful and elegant."

"Not quite so fresh as all that, you know."

"What do you mean, Cyril?" she replied, looking at me with some astonishment.

"Nothing. Or perhaps, how can I put it? She's just not my type."

Mary took my arm and we stepped into the blue room, the one re-served for guests.

"I must be dreaming. How could I ever have expected to meet . . . on a boat, after a few days' vacation in New York . . ."

"Nonsense. You mustn't think that way. Just look. This isn't our room, actually, it's the guest room."

"Our room? But aren't we to have separate rooms?"

I turned her around to look at me, and took both her hands in mine.

"My dearest, you must accustom yourself to the idea that in a mar-riage, the husband makes the decisions. I have no rights over you today, but once we're married, I'll have them all. And you mustn't forget that."

She took a step back, as if frightened; her breath came in short gasps and all the color seemed to drain from her face.

"Oh! You . . . you . . ."

Then suddenly, she blushed violently, and we were in each other's arms. For the first time, her body seemed to be responding to an ardor, a passion, that came from the depths of her being. Her knees buckled, her hair came loose, and she abandoned herself to me. Finally, I stepped back and looked at her. She was trembling, and her eyes sparkled with a new light.

"I must tell you something . . . here. Now. I lied to you." She hid her face on my shoulder. "George and I . . . we never . . . I've never . . . he couldn't, do you understand?" She burst into tears and a strange happiness flooded through me. I gently stroked her hair.

"Well," Margaret exclaimed when we reappeared, "the house is cer-tainly far larger than I'd thought! My dear Mary, it's five o'clock. Time to go back. I promised you."

"Already? Then I shall go say good-bye to Douglas," and she rushed off to the kitchens.

"She's quite amazing, isn't she?" Margaret remarked.

"How so?"

"I wonder if she's an idiot or if this is simply the height of cleverness," she replied with a positively radiant smile.

"Not everyone leads a double life," I replied.

"Like me, for instance? Well, let me tell you something, my dear Cyril, I think they do. The whole world is a fake. The trick is to figure out how to walk the tightrope. That's Jonathan's strong point."

"You still love him, don't you?"

"Chesterfield, the new philanthropist? No indeed. It's all quite ridiculous."

"Rest assured, the lepers are only a pretext."

"Your old kitchens are absolutely adorable!" Mary cried, bursting into the room.

And so we parted, Margaret holding my hand just a fraction of an instant longer than appropriate.

Once the women had left, things calmed down considerably. Every Saturday and Wednesday, I checked on the Chester, and then met Mary outside the Caddie Club. We awaited October 29 with the kind of patience proper to well-brought-up people, but ever since I'd learned that my fiancée had not know carnal love with her George, my desire for her had burned the more brightly. And then, during the first week of the blessed month, I learned that Varlet was coming to London! As she'd promised, Sarah wrote me once or twice a month; her letters were rather like an American chronicle fast becoming African as she detailed the progress in the construction of the Kampala hospital. Little Yehudi was flourishing. David Goethman's work was being recorded by major orchestras. Our musical comedy had extended its run. Tennyson's film had opened to rave reviews. *The Fabulous Adventures of Jacob Stern* had been translated into twenty-three languages. In short, from the sound of it, everything was proceeding swimmingly.

And yet, between the lines, behind the accumulation of these sensational stories, lurked something else, something stifled, suppressed. Doubtless poor Sarah, confined to her bedroom, had a rather fragmented idea of the universe the ingenious Varlet was building; one can well imagine how incomprehensible the maelstrom outside must have seemed to someone as sensitive and nervous as she. Certain circumstances, however, had begun to rear their ugly heads, and to intrigue me no small amount. Sarah wrote:

May 7, 1943. Jonathan showed me the blueprints for his Madison Avenue offices. His two companies are planning to move in next month; the first company handles all the merchandizing of his works, the second the construction and administration of the African hospitals, for there are to be several of them, Kampala being a sort of trial run! Apparently, there's going to be a third company too. For advertising. Jonathan's spent the last month interviewing people; he's going to need a lot of personnel. He's already hired someone to be the coordinating director of all three companies, a Texan named Simon Partner, a sort of cowboy with lots of gold rings and teeth, but he seems to be a wonderful specialist in this sort of work. Until recently, he was one of the vice-presidents at Ford Motor Company.

All this costs a great lot of money, which comes from royalties, and from some sort of subsidy or special fund given to countries by the League of Nations. Jonathan's hired at least ten accountants to manage it all. I think there'll be three hundred employees altogether, "for starters!" as he says. How far we've come from Venice and those happy moments looking at Carpaccio's *Saint Ursula*! I can't imagine how he plans to write the next book, as he doesn't even have a minute to sit down and think about it! And yet he's been talking here and there about a book that's to be called *The Monkey King*, about the history of mankind "from the ape to Buddha." (Those are his exact words.) Sometimes I wonder if perhaps he hasn't hired someone else to write the book using his ideas, his characters, and his plot. I'm not sure, really, but I don't see how it could be otherwise, given all the work he has to do. It seems it's a perfectly acceptable practice, even though it quite amazes me.

Yehudi's starting to walk and babble. The girl who takes care of him is really quite charming and conscientious, but it's sad that I can't bathe him and dress him and take him for walks myself, all those simple and essential things mothers do that I can't because I'm so tied to this bed! You know, Cyril, sometimes I think it would be better if I'd died. A paralyzed mother isn't good for a child. And I'm so useless! I'm just in the way, really. And so I pray, to the God of Isaac and Jacob. I'm studying Hebrew with a Polish rabbi. Sometimes we speak Yiddish, bits of which come back to me like little remnants of my childhood. At home, we used to speak German, English, and Yiddish, but when my mother died, we more or less stopped speaking the last. My rabbi is quite funny, and tries to make me laugh by telling me old Hassidic stories. It's my only entertainment, my only real pleasure. When Jonathan comes, it's like a tornado rushing through.

Sarah's information about the new offices and the three companies left me openmouthed. Varlet had warned me he was becoming a businessman, but I'd no idea he meant to organize things quite this way. It's true—as I was to learn later—that the merchandizing of the Elsbeth doll alone required separate subsidiary-rights contracts with a manufacturer of rubber toys and a manufacturer of miniature clothing, contracts involving quite impressive sums, given the fact that in the state of New York alone, twenty-five thousand dolls were sold each day! Elsbeth had a substantial wardrobe, a house with miniature furniture, a husband called Alex, and a few friends, not to mention some up-and-coming pets, a car that would necessitate a garage that would necessitate an entire city complete with railway station and electric train, a prospect that convinced Varlet to invite Dumbee Toys to join his group of companies and that prompted him, a year later, to become its major stockholder.

As for the hospital in Kampala, Jonathan flew down once a month, and despite various obstacles it was scheduled to open in March of 1935. Apparently, certain political factions led by a revolutionary tribal chieftain named Mwanda had sworn to keep the project from being completed, protesting that it was simply another colonialist enterprise designed to depopulate the villages and increase the labor force in the capital's factories, factories that barely existed, of course. The contractors had enormous trouble finding enough labor and ended up having to import workers from neighboring countries, which was like putting a match to a stick of dynamite. Serious battles took place between Mwanda's partisans and the British police who controlled Uganda. In the end, Mwanda, along with thirty or so of his cohorts, was arrested; the revolt left eighty dead, however, which provoked a reporter to write, "To save the lives of millions, must a few undergo a holocaust? In the Kampala affair, the subversive action of the rebels sacrificed many of their African brothers to a bloodthirsty Moloch who, appeased tomorrow, will allow leprosy to be defeated, perhaps even wiped out of Africa altogether, as it has been for so long in Europe." I wondered what Varlet thought of all this, but as Sarah wrote, "The devil, who desires only men's misfortune, appoints certain evil people to try to destroy the efforts of those who are fighting for their welfare. The world is a permanent battleground between the powers of darkness and the forces of light."

Had I been forced, at that time, to put Jonathan into one category or the other, I should not have known which to choose. Doubtless, there was nothing in his doings that went against the common good, but I could not rid myself of the notion that there was an odor of sulfur about these enterprises, if only by virtue of the disconcerting ease with which they were accomplished. Varlet's seductiveness seemed to work as well with commercial undertakings as with individual people. It was thanks to him that my own business affairs had come to such unexpected fruition; I never ceased to be astonished at the permanent miracle of his, and consequently my, financial success. In fact, I'd been mulling all this over when the telegram arrived: MEET ME LONDON, OCTOBER 20, ELEVEN O'CLOCK, RUBENS HOTEL STOP JONATHAN.

At eleven o'clock on the twentieth, I stepped into the lobby of the Rubens, a small discreet hotel a mere stone's throw from Buckingham Palace. In order to dodge the press, Jonathan had registered under the name of Varlet. He asked me up to his room where he welcomed me with his habitual warmth and affection; the various prejudices I'd been entertaining about him melted away instantly. His eyes and smile seemed to change the hotel room into a kind of palace from *The Thousand and One Nights.* I had been in a lugubrious mood until I crossed the threshold, when my drear humor vanished. Whereas the weather outside was gloomy indeed, here the light seemed to bounce off the curtains and the furniture. Jonathan gave me a great hug.

"I can't tell you how marvelous it is to be back in London and to see you again!" he said in a husky voice. "America wears me out. I plan to move back here as soon as I'm able. Not here exactly, but in some small out-of-the-way piece of Old England. Glendurgan, for instance!"

We both laughed heartily, surprising the gentleman in a bright green suit using the telephone at the far end of the room, with a cigar in his mouth and a Yankee accent so thick I had trouble understanding him.

"That's Simon Partner, the head of my holding company," Jonathan whispered, winking at me. "Quite an amusing character, but a real steamroller." Then, in a louder voice, "Sarah sends you her love. I pity her so . . . that accident, you know. I just can't seem to forget it. It was so stupid, wasn't it?"

"And Yehudi?"

"A jewel, Cyril," he replied, his whole face lighting up. "An absolute jewel. Dark like his mother, but with his father's blue eyes. In fact, it doesn't take much imagination to see he's got my lord's profile!"

Jonathan was without pretense—simple, vivacious, and touching, not at all as I'd feared, nothing of the businessman about him really. Partner's presence, on the other hand, hovered over us; Sarah's description, the cowboy with lots of gold rings and teeth, was quite perfect. He slammed down the receiver and, chewing the end of his cigar, rolled across the room like an old sailor.

"Hello!" he boomed, with the sort of smile one sees on campaign posters. His head was square and his hair stood straight up in a crew cut of the same shape. He grabbed my hand in his enormous paw and shook it heartily.

"This is my old friend, Cyril," said Jonathan.

"Hiya, Cyril!" Partner drawled, breaking into a laugh that exposed his several gold teeth. "My God, talk to me about England! You seen the phone? And the bathtub? And the bed with all that fancy molding? Feels like we're in some exhibit from 1900. You think the English know electricity's been invented?"

"So you've found yourself a wife, I see," Jonathan interrupted. "I'm coming to the wedding, and that's a promise."

"But you're so busy! Anyway, it's an awfully simple ceremony really. In the country, you know . . ."

"I should hope so! Your Mary must be one marvelous girl!" He noticed my surprise. "Oh yes, Sarah reads me your letters. Gives me a sense of the old country. I even know you now go by the name of Charmer-Maker! My congratulations, Mr. Charmer! Your mother's name, I believe . . . ?"

"You seem frightfully well," I replied. "I gather all this action suits you."

"Thank you. I'm only hoping dear Simon will relieve me of the burden."

"Burden, humpf!" Partner echoed. "Ten million dollars in 1934. Triple in 1935. Guaranteed!" He rolled to the bed, opened a suitcase, and pulled out Elsbeth, which he waved above his head while thick bursts of acrid cigar smoke came from his mouth and nose and probably his ears as well. "You see this piece of disgusting rubber with a rag around it?" Guess what it costs us. Including taxes and packaging and all the rest of it. Huh, whaddaya think? Not even a dollar, my friend. No, sir. But you know how much we sell it to the wholesalers for? Three dollars! Can't do much better than that, huh?"

The "huh" that punctuated his sentences sounded more like the bark of a dog than anything else; the man was a living monument to vulgarity.

"Will you come with us to the opening of *The Right to Love?*" Varlet asked, cutting Partner's peroration short. "You and Mary are our guests, of course. You'll see how Tennyson managed the adaptation. It has the seriousness of tragedy . . . but then, all human acts are tragic, don't you think? Since our dose of happiness is measured out so carefully?"

Jonathan had to attend a luncheon with the stars of the film, so I decided to take my leave around noon, promising to be at the press conference on the twenty-fourth, for which he'd already given me a press card.

"May I ask you to do me a favor?" he said. "I'd very much like to see Ruthford again. Just the two of us. We could talk the way we used to. Do you think Douglas is still not on speaking terms with me?"

We decided he should come out for dinner on the twenty-fifth.

"That makes me very happy," he cried, seizing both my hands in his. "Afterward I'll take three days' rest and go to Scotland. Incognito. I can be back in London by the twenty-eighth, and then to Faversham for the wedding. I'm leaving for New York the morning of the thirtieth. Some schedule . . ."

"With His Majesty himself as a reward!" I added, amused and yet admiring.

"Having been unable to do what I've done, the princes hope a little honor will rub off on them if they're nice to me. And why not? Frankly, however, this particular prince has something more to tell me. . . ."

I dared not ask what he meant, and so took my leave.

The following evening at nine o'clock, Mary and I were seated in the Coliseum Theatre. My fiancée had hesitated, of course. Was it wise for a young woman to ruin herself in an American stupor with this fellow Chesterfield of whose works she decidedly did not approve?

"Don't worry," I said. "Matthew Tennyson has an excellent mind. We met in New York while we were waiting for Yehudi to be born. I'd be very surprised if his film contained even a suspicion of the trivial."

"Unfortunately, I can well imagine what a man of improper thoughts might do with such a sadistic story!" she said with dignity.

"Great Heavens! I forbid you to imagine those things. Have you by chance read de Sade, my dear?"

Mary blushed and turned her head. "Anyway, I don't have a long dress. I don't go to this sort of gala, you know."

"I know. You need a dress for this, and one for the twenty-ninth. I insist on paying for them. In fact, I think Strenton's in the Burlington Arcade would be best."

"You're an absolute angel, my darling Cyril." She smiled. "But I have my wedding dress already. I made it myself, and it's to be a surprise. As for tomorrow night, do you really think it's reasonable to go to Strenton's?" Her eyes sparkled at the very thought of it.

"Only Strenton can make you the right sort of dress in such a short time. He's a true artist. I'm certain you'll turn out ravishingly."

"But if I'm to wear such a beautiful dress, I'll have to go to the hairdresser . . . and I'll have to buy shoes and gloves and a bag and a hat! It's quite impossible."

In the end, we entered the Coliseum that evening with Mary dressed, shod, gloved, and hatted in the latest style. Strenton had taken care of everything, so well in fact that I felt I was not taking my fiancée to the opening but a fashion model pretending to be just the slightest bit gauche.

Given the amount of tragic apparatus, Tennyson's film resembled Sophocles more than Chesterfield. The smallest gesture had the value of a sign, and the play of light and shadow was so powerful it felt like a Rembrandt. Little by little, the characters seemed to sink into the night, leaving only bodies brushing against each other, whisperings, silence. With his gaunt face, Henry Cushing's Alexander looked like a monk from the Spanish Inquisition, while Rosanna Andrews's pure profile gave her the air of Bernini's Saint Teresa. Finally, one had no idea which lovers or which shades were passing each other in the hallways or the unmade beds. "We are no longer on this earth, but in limbo," the *Times* reviewer wrote. "If it's true that all great art is one of appearances, then Tennyson has brought the art of film to perfection."

Mary was disturbed but entranced. At the end of the film, there was a long silence, followed by an explosion of frenzied applause. The ladies' eyes were red, for many who had taken Elsbeth's side during the film swung back at the end and wept over Alexander's death. When Tennyson and the two stars appeared, they were given a well-deserved ovation, after which the audience began to chant, "Chesterfield!," who was finally forced to join his colleagues onstage. Everyone stood up, and the great swell of their enthusiasm swept through the theater to break at Jonathan's feet as he stood there in his tuxedo—tall and dignified and showing signs of great suffering.

"He's so young!" Mary exclaimed. "And so handsome! Look at those eyes! My goodness, Cyril, you didn't tell me he was so good-looking."

"He doesn't look so bad now that you've seen him, does he?" I replied, laughing.

"I shall have to reread the book," she replied firmly, and began applauding again energetically.

Varlet gave a short speech thanking his audience for being "so attentive and so generous," praising Tennyson for having "reconceived *Beelzebub* as a masterpiece," Rosanna Andrews, "whose tears we shall forever remember, for they were neither tears of sorrow nor of joy but of pure emotion in the presence of the beloved object," and Cushing, who "is neither god nor devil, but a man surrounded by a corrupt universe." He added too that the world represented by Alexander's house was none other than our own, and that modern man could no longer hear his conscience that called out to him so continuously and so heartbreakingly. "Elsbeth is that conscience knocking at the door which Western man no longer opens. Everything about him is coming apart but he neither hears nor sees it. And so he shall die, poisoned by his decomposing soul." Finally, so as not to end on such a somber note, Jonathan cried, "But as long as England, our England, remembers, she shall remain the guardian of the West!" Everyone stood up once again, applauded long and loud, and filed out at last, wholly satisfied.

The following afternoon, Chesterfield was indeed received by George V in the small drawing room reserved for visits in Buckingham Palace. I was not there myself, but according to the papers, their meeting lasted for an hour. "At five minutes to five precisely, Chesterfield arrived in the courtyard of the palace. He was ushered into His Majesty's presence by the lord high chamberlain, and emerged exactly fifty-three minutes later. To the questions shouted by waiting reporters, he replied by inviting them to his press conference on the twenty-fourth. Presumably, His Majesty congratulated. G.K.C. on his good works in Africa on behalf of our most disadvantaged children, the lepers, as well as on his literary works." It wasn't much but I was patient, knowing that Jonathan would give his conference and then come to Ruthford.

The conference took place in the vast intermission hall at Victoria Theatre, which, as of four o'clock, was jammed with reporters from every paper in the world. Varlet arrived, accompanied by Tennyson and Peter Warner. I suppose it was a historic moment; at least it seemed as if those in attendance felt that way, for their attention resembled nothing so much as a kind of meditation.

"Ladies and gentlemen, compatriots and guests from abroad," Jonathan began, his voice grave, "the reason for this meeting is doubtless not the one you have been waiting for, and have had every right to expect. I know that what I say here today will be transmitted live, and I'm quite sure my listeners think I shall comment on Matthew Tennyson's remarkable film *The Right to Love* or the appearance of my new book *The Monkey King* or the London revival of *The Devil's Delirium* or even the progress of the hospital in Uganda. Of course I shall comment on these events if such is your desire, but only in the light of a far more important issue, one of such exceptional urgency that I shan't keep you waiting any longer. The event of which I speak concerns the condition of the world. Whether film or novel or musical comedy or leprosarium, everything I mention is intended to achieve but one goal—to alert public opinion worldwide to an imminent catastrophe which, if we do not take immediate action, will ineluctably occur. I beg you not to think that I speak so dramatically out of intellectual pessimism or a taste for the sensational. But just as Alexander's home rots from within, so is the entire Western world—largely as a result of a betrayal by its elites and its bureaucracies—being led to what may be an incredible but clearly perceptible call to murder. Most of those who hear this call throw up their hands and abdicate. Others turn away or change sides. Whichever, the result is an entire era destined for barbarism."

We were all on the edge of our seats. Varlet's words, spoken in Chesterfield's name, fell upon us one after another like a series of blows dealt by a boxer to his stunned opponent.

"I'm speaking to you with the ill-concealed awareness that I'm venturing into territory which is no longer of our time and not yet of our world. At this very hour, certain bold hunters have already ensnared our old concepts of human reason, and feeling itself is defenseless before the tumultuous onslaught of fear. Thus it is that we come to the end of an era, its successor already being set in motion by a few solitary figures. On this twenty-fourth of October 1934, there is not a single human being worthy of his anxiety who is not awaiting this call, a call which some have already heard and are now, modestly but adamantly, forcing the rest of us to hear. For if we must acknowledge the injustice of our era in the fact of the most moving and the most lucid demonstrations, it is also true that no real challenge has been raised to the spirit of dispersion, of vulgarity, and of decadence with which our era is infested, and no sufficiently powerful examples have appeared that might awaken us to the truth. Instead, there is a singular attraction these days for the chaotic and the original, an attraction that reigns like a carnival queen and knows nothing of governing its people or of offering them the way to a few brief moments of eternal recognition. We believe in the vanity of human grandeur because we fear the end of the world. It is the great madness of those mesmerized by science to dream of the coincidence of the death of all civilizations, and of the infinite fall of the earth into obscurity. It is true that those periods in which nations have felt their weaknesses have always believed they were blocking the path to the future; Egyptian monks during the time of Solon searched desperately for the inspiration and salvation found in the old traditions, searched beyond a century which seemed to them humanity's final shudder. To be sure, there is no deplorable moral circumstance that does not bring forth the most detestable historical events, from the plague of the year 1000 to the diffuse anxieties of our own day, and these events appear at precisely the moment when our minds are the most apt to acknowledge their catastrophic message. The serpent of the apocalypse, who is not the fearsome dragon we all imagine but rather a small, agile, tricky viper whose bite is minuscule and slow, is coiled in the heart of each of us so that we may add to the doom of universal creation. Fed by our fear—I dare not say our cowardice—we end up prostrate and burdened, our pride reduced to the puerile courage of a child lost in the darkness of his own garden who whistles a trite little melody in the hope of convincing himself he's not the coward he feels crouching in each of his footsteps."

Was there ever such a diatribe? Had it come from anyone else, the audience would have been scandalized, but since it was from Chesterfield, they all held their breath.

"We can see the strange rot that has undermined our religions, our philosophies, and our arts, institutions in other words which ought to help us to participate in the unending birth of the universe. It's as if as inhabitants of a new planet, we had to acquire an immediate knowledge of all things without the help of any cult or culture. We call ourselves modern because conditions have changed; we forget that we possess higher and more durable human powers. To be sure, this does not mean we should run counter to history. Nor should we give dead gods a place in a regilded cosmogonic system. But to the present call, we must respond in unison. We must confront our now fragmented process with a physical and spiritual adventure ordered by universally agreed-upon reason and feeling. The world is one. The smallest happening in China eventually influences England. We must leave our provincial reflexes behind and strive to attain a cosmic dimension. And yet what do we see? At the very center of Europe, in the Germany of Goethe, a disease is spreading, a cancer that contaminates all it touches. While we, paralyzed behind our intellectual and geographical borders, we watch the tumor cheerfully, afraid that we shall be afraid, ordering the evil to disappear of its own accord. Strange medicine indeed! If we do not pay attention, the world shall be driven back, in the name of laziness and compromise, into the lap of terror!"

Varlet's speech lasted an hour. Afterward, the reporters asked their questions timidly, for the ones they'd prepared had nothing to do with Jonathan's words. "Mr. Chesterfield," began the representative from the *Herald Tribune*, "I'd intended to ask if the character of the monkey is in any way autobiographical, but given the circumstances it seems quite irrelevant! [Laughter.] Instead, I'd like to ask if you feel writers should be politically involved at this time, and if so, how?"

"I think my introduction indicates quite sufficiently my feelings on the subject, but let me make clear that by *politics* I do mean writers should take a specific ideological position or join a specific party. Rather they should involve themselves in a consideration of the human condition, no matter what posture their individual countries maintain. In a sense, this means that the intellectual's commitment involves a responsibility inherent in each event, a responsibility to interpret each event as accurately as possible, and in complete freedom. The writer may therefore appear to hold quite a contradictory position in the eyes of militants in this or that political organization, but if the truth requires contradiction, then in all honor, the writer must contradict himself."

A tall thin individual with buckteeth and a red wig rose and asked, "What information do you have that allows you to call Germany sick—your expression—and to charge that this country is threatening all of Europe?"

"There are certain diseases which are by nature contagious," Varlet replied firmly. "They swarm and they spread, but in their early stages they do so quietly, stealthily. Germany has caught this contagious disease and at the present moment, no one seems to notice the corruption. Let us speak clearly—on the pretext of restoring order, Hitler and the National Socialist Party have forced the citizens of Germany to submit to intolerable political pressure. Democrats and liberals are suspect and thrown into prison. Communists and socialists are chased underground. Jews are shipped off to camps."

"Are you on the side of the Bolsheviks?" the redhead cried. "And who says these camps exist? Only the Communists! On the contrary, Hitler's a barrier against Soviet hegemony!"

"I'm not saying Russia is any Garden of Eden," Jonathan replied. "But don't you see how easy it is to fall into that dualism? For you, Hitler's Germany is right to fight the Communists and the socialists and the Jews because they seem to you to be the objective allies of decadence. Instantly, you create two opposing Germanys, each with good reason to detest the other. At that point, terror is inevitable. This is exactly the sort of dualism Hitler loves to encourage, for he knows that thanks to his police and his army, he will wind up master of the game whenever he likes. This is Pan-Germanism, you can be certain of it!"

The next day, the newspapers devoted several columns to the press conference. For some, the warning was salutary; for others, it was just an example of literary woolgathering. A few asked if Chesterfield was not perhaps considering turning socialist. I would remind my reader that at this time, England had just elected a coalition government in which the Conservative Stanley Baldwin had agreed to particpate, the same Baldwin who would eventually become prime minister. Nerves were raw and Varlet, a bit too accustomed to American frankness, might not have been quite aware of how his words might sound at such a delicate moment. In short, the press was not its habitually enthusiastic self. *Pink Pig*, a satirical paper, summed up the situation with its typical crudeness: "Chesterfield would do better to go play with his dolls and stop manipulating political ideas, which he seems to understand only as grandly lyrical melodies." I must confess I too had been irritated by Varlet's lyricism, and had resolved to tell him so when he came to Ruthford.

As promised, he arrived at seven o'clock at the wheel of a car Peter Warner had loaned him. The reaction to his conference had disappointed him, but he was nonetheless delighted at finding himself with me in the old familiar house once again.

"Let's not talk about it, all right? It's quite minor, really. Let this evening be devoted to friendship, to confidences. . . . I feel a real need to let my hair down, and for me, you're a kind of father-confessor, Cyril."

We settled ourselves in the study with the Chinese curtains.

"So you're getting married," he began. "To have children, I'm sure.

Well, you'll see, it's quite marvelous, a life growing right there, in the belly of the woman you love, and you've no idea of what's really happening. A truly mysterious adventure. It's in those moments that the divine presence is perhaps the most perceptible. I'm crazy about Yehudi, you know. . . ."

"And how is Sarah?"

"She's gained a great deal of weight. The doctors say it's just part of her condition, but she doesn't complain. She never complains. And yet it's so horrible, such a hideous catastrophe. Do you remember the adolescent girl that came with us to Venice. That wasn't so very long ago. . . ."

He stood up and went to the window to look out at the lawn. Then he turned back to me.

"Did you ever see Margaret again?"

I described to him the surprise Mary had concocted for me, which amused him no end.

"Her father wanted me to see her," Jonathan said. "But I didn't want to."

"Well, she'll be at the wedding."

"It doesn't matter. She turned out to be so disappointing."

"Why do you say that?"

"Because her inner and outer selves didn't match. Something about her is a lie."

I dropped the subject, as I knew far better than he what the matter was and I did not want to be indiscreet.

"I met her father, you know," I said. "A strange character, size aside . . . He thinks the author of *Beelzebub* is Lord Ambergris!"

Jonathan raised his eyebrows.

"How odd," he said finally, before sitting down again. "We do form a most amazing partnership, you know! I'm just surprised no one's figured it out yet."

"Well, since no one's come forward and claimed authorship, then you're still the author. It's as simple as that."

"Don't you feel bad about that sometimes?"

"No," I replied sincerely. "I'm the one who chose the name Chesterfield to hide behind. You loan him your appearance, talent, style, and even some of your ideas. I find that most satisfying. After all, Jonathan, you're one of my creations as well. When you appeared in the little bar next to Waterloo Station, and then again at the Rosemullion, it was my imagination you came out of, my dear friend. Sometimes I think every person I meet is one of my characters, and has no reality except through me."

"Interesting. So it was you who arranged my encounter with Sarah in Berlin, like some sort of demiurge? And her accident? And Yehudi's birth? And you concocted the success of both our businesses? And Hitler and Germany, is that you too? I must say I like the idea. I love it, in fact. It excites me. For a long time, you know, I believed that I lived only because my lord willed it. I believed I was an image he'd created for himself of the son he never had, a sort of projection of his thoughts and desires. And who can prove the contrary? Isn't he my guide? Isn't he the one who arranges circumstances in certain ways so that I'll do what he wants? Am I not a marionette in his hands? When certain great minds die, or rather abandon their bodies, I think they must simply borrow other bodies and go on with their work."

"I wonder if Lord Ambergris would have appreciated Partner and your Elsbeth dolls," I said, somewhat cruelly.

"Who knows?" he replied with a shrug.

At that moment, Douglas announced through the closed door that dinner was ready. She knew that Varlet had arrived, and wanted to avoid seeing him. For her, Somerset's shadow was still very much present. We both rose and went into the dining room.

"Dear Cyril," Jonathan continued, "have I told you how oppressive American life is and how much I'd love to return to England? It's not the artificiality that displeases me, for after all, deceit is everywhere, beginning with ourselves. No, its the horizontality that depresses me. People's horizontality. No verticality anywhere! Everyone is glued to the ground; if they could bury themselves in it, they'd be even happier! Our era has made History, with a capital *H* of course, its god and its dwelling place, and what's more horizontal than history? Our paltry philosophers have reduced everything to mere phenomena. No more reality, just phenomena. Nothing has any significance anymore. There's no direction. We're entering the Age of Fragments. We think of the world now as a broken mirror that reflects nothing more than the pieces of a puzzle. We've lost our coherence. And such a lot of carrying-on about it! God is dead because He is only absurdity and nonsense."

"You've turned into quite a pessimist, I see. Has America really gone as far as all that? Everything here is still based on force of habit. And why not? Habit is a very powerful unifier."

"Ah, yes, habit. Listen, during my last but one visit to Kampala, I was convoked by the British governer, a chap named Storch, ex-military out of India, complete with mustache, airspeed indicator, and leggings, the one who put down Mwanda's revolt and had him locked up in the main Ugandan prison in Masindi, near the Murchison Falls. I was curious about this Mwanda and asked Storch for authorization to visit him in his cell. 'Are you quite mad?' he says to me. 'The man hates you. Anyway, his English is frightful.' I kept at him, though, and finally there we were one day, on the way to Masindi—the governor, a handful of English soldiers, and me—driving across this enormous savannah filled with all manner of beasts fighting among themselves, from the zebra to an odd sort of hare with tiny ears. Storch was furious. He hates the Bantu and the Bantu feel the same about him. Finally we arrived in Masindi and went to Mwanda's cell. Surprise! The leader of the revolution was locked into a bamboo cage so small he had to remain seated. What's more, they'd tied his hands behind his back. His face was completely swollen, and a ghastly odor came from what was left of his clothing."

"Good heavens!" I cried. "Did Storch know about this?"

"That's what I asked him. He replied that it was customary for these tribes to treat prisoners this way. He tried to improve prison conditions all through Uganda but the Bantu themselves were against it. And do you know why? Because everything in that country is regulated by an ancient system of symbols no one can oppose. A man who cannot stand up becomes a woman, and by being reduced to impotence, he's considered nonexistent. He's nothing more than a sort of body without a soul; in fact, should he ever be freed, it's considered most appropriate for him to die via a ritual during which he is reinitiated by being reincorporated into the tribe. But there's worse yet. When I wanted to get closer to Mwanda to talk to him, the horrified wardens yanked me back. To talk to a body without a soul is as dangerous as talking to death. Mwanda himself was fully aware of this; he sat without moving in his filthy cage, as if he weren't really there at all, and when he saw me, he rolled back his eyes so all I could see were the whites."

"Extraordinary."

"It all comes from the conception of a coherent world," Varlet continued. "During our own Middle Ages, the Christian world understood this kind of order and lived by it. As you know, it comes from an obedience to certain rules recognized as absolutely fundamental. But now,

out of a desire for freedom, the modern world has rejected its foundations so as not to have to obey the rules. I suppose we've indeed been
liberated from our cages, but now we wander here and there, without
aim or goal. We deny God, but when we come face to face with ourselves, will we ever be able to lead ourselves anywhere? When there's
no more God, the world abounds in gods. Idolatry is atheism's ransom."

"Forgive me," I interrupted, "but you're talking like a believer. Only
one who believes can conceive of what you're saying. For the rest of us,
confronted with the absurd, or with the natural order of things, belief is
an illusion."

"Doubtless. Which is why I prefer faith, or fidelity, to belief."

"But to be faithful, one must believe!"

"To hope is enough," he replied simply.

Our conversation finally turned to *The Monkey King,* and I told him
the original anecdote. There was once a monkey named Souen who became the king of his tribe. Unhappy with Buddha, he went up to heaven
to complain about the absurdity of the world. To appease him, Buddha
offered him a place at his side, but Souen refused and, by his revolt,
caused an extraordinary war among all the celestial entities. After a series of epic battles, from all of which Souen emerged victorious, he was
struck down by Buddha himself. As punishment for his pride, Buddha
chained him to a mountain. With the passage of time, however, Buddha
desired to give his sacred writings to China. So he freed Souen and
ordered him to go to India along with a monk and to collect the three
baskets that held the holy texts. Accompanied on his voyage by a swine,
and after many fabulous adventures including confrontations with monsters, phantoms, and magicians, Souen succeeded in his mission. In the
end, having attained wisdom, he himself became a Buddha.

Jonathan was delighted with the story and asked me to read him some
excerpts, which I was only too happy to do. We read of the struggle
between the monkey and the gloomy toad, the meeting between Souen
and Kuan-Yin, the Goddess of Mercy, and finally the arrival in heaven
of Souen and his swine after their trials and tribulations. The stories
amused him enormously, and he congratulated me heartily.

"Alexander's pride combined with little Jacob's goodness seems to have
given birth to this monkey rebel who thinks only of the welfare of others. Souen is a Robin Hood, a righter of wrongs, God's warrior, in a
way. Even when he fights Buddha, it's out of love for the Buddha in
men. It will be another great success, Cyril. More so, in fact. This hero

will renew our taste for the epic, for the dialogue between the visible and the invisible that our era needs so badly. Opposite Faust and Don Juan, here comes a monkey who can reconcile them with both God and men."

"And your Partner can make Souen dolls! How ghastly."

"Souen, the hero in crisis!" Jonathan laughed. "The one who against all odds overturns the order of things. I can imagine what some good publicity will do with it. But to tell the truth, what I like best about this hairy character with the prominent jaw is his tenderness. Important, tenderness, isn't it? Sarah's taught me that."

The time for personal news had come, and we adjourned to the small drawing room where the fire burned brightly in the hearth. Varlet sat down, waited for me to pour him a Drambuie, and began.

"Dear Cyril, you must forgive me if I feel the need to tell you some rather intimate things, but I'm so unhappy for Sarah. We still love each other, and I have great respect for her, but paralyzed as she is, and so heavy, our relationship is confined to exchanges of tenderness, and our joy to watching Yehudi grow up. Every day, she sinks deeper into prayer and her Hebrew studies, but I suppose that's good, isn't it? In the beginning, I used to spend my evenings at her bedside telling her everything that happened during the day. We talked about Yehudi's education. And then, little by little, I started coming to see her every two days, then every three. I had a lot of pretexts, of course—meetings, trips . . . She was never angry with me, you know; it's just that her face grew more and more serious. She understood, I'm sure. . . . Now I visit her only once a week, and reproach myself constantly for my cowardliness. In fact, I go only for Yehudi's sake. How can I say it? It's that bedroom. Her bedroom. It fills me with horror."

He spoke in a whisper, his head bowed. I took care not to interrupt.

"You know me . . . I'm both faithful and yet somewhat scattered. My deep attachment to Sarah hasn't kept me from keeping company with other women here and there, but never seriously. They throw themselves at me, you know that. And that satisfies my need for fidelity. It doesn't feel as if I'm betraying Sarah because I never attach myself to anyone else. And then two months ago, just as they were finishing shooting *The Right to Love*, I met Rosanna Andrews at a cocktail party Tennyson gave to introduce me to the cast. You can guess the rest. I fell in love with her just like a schoolboy and, horror of horrors, she rejected me! But I was trapped; I couldn't keep myself from loving her. Her face and her body haunted my nights. The more I wanted her, the more distant she became. It was more than just physical desire; a real feeling was born, and then grew and grew, like a torrent. And I was swept away like a wisp of straw. How could my tenderness and respect for Sarah stand up against this devastating madness which had seized hold of me, forced its way into me, violated me if you will—while Rosanna remained as cold as marble?"

He emptied his glass with one swallow.

"I'm ashamed, Cyril, but I must tell you the whole truth. I've asked Rosanna to marry me."

I was speechless with shock.

"That's what she wanted. I told her about the feelings that bound me to my wife, the purity of them. I told her about Yehudi. But none of it mattered. She talked about her principles and her reputation and god only knows what else. 'If you love me the way you say you do, you must prove it' was essentially what she kept saying. But I couldn't accept the hideous bargain. It would mean the betrayal of both Sarah and Yehudi. And yet the madness continued to roil inside me; it burned like a furnace. I knew Rosanna was playing games, and in a strange way, I was pleased that she was. Nothing would have been worse than her indifference. And then a week ago, when she knew I was coming to London, she said, 'I'll give you until you leave New York to decide. After that, it'll be too late. I have to think about my own life, don't I?' And I collapsed. I gave in. I promised to ask for a divorce when I returned from England."

"The woman is abominable!" I cried.

"Yes. And doubtless it's that very cruelty that fascinates me so."

"No," I replied. "You want her because she's refused you. Your vanity exacerbates your desire. You're ready to ruin everything to have her. But she's a woman no one can ever possess, Jonathan. She'll use you, and when she's tired of you, she'll throw you away. You can't possibly compare Sarah with her!"

"Cyril," he said sadly, "you know there's no argument and no willpower that can stop this kind of passion. . . ."

"Come now, you're not a schoolboy anymore, for heaven's sake. Instead of humiliating yourself at Rosanna Andrews's feet, you'd do better to pull yourself together and run for your life. Isn't there something you need to do in Kampala?"

"I'm miserable knowing she's here in London but at another hotel.

I'm jealous of Cushing and Tennyson because they can be with her more easily than I. What would I do in Kampala?"

"Listen, you mentioned a little holiday in Scotland. Get drunk on the open air. Or on whiskey. Then sober up. And remember your lord. What would he have done in your shoes?"

"He should have strangled Rosanna, I think," he replied, looking at me with a mélange of amusement and pity.

"In any case, and no matter what her reasons, her bribery is absolutely unacceptable. Because it is bribery, isn't it? You've no right to give in. You used to tell me Sarah was your soul. Are you going to abandon her?"

"No," he replied, raising his head. "No. That's something I can't do. Half of me is horrified by Rosanna and refuses to accept her terms. The other part wants to plunge ahead. I want to negotiate, but Rosanna refuses. But listen to me, Cyril. . . . What I'm going to say is atrocious, I know, but I feel as if Sarah's room stinks of death, while Rosanna is a life-force, like being on the open sea. . . . Oh, I know, it's horrible, isn't it? But out of faithfulness, can I reject life?"

"When we arrived in Venice," I replied, "you took me to the church of San Moisè and you quoted me what your lord said about a regenerative death, the one that mustn't be confused with petrification. I don't remember your exact words anymore, but the meaning was clear—a regenerative death versus a death that petrifies. We wondered then what he meant. Wouldn't a paralyzed Sarah be the guardian of that regeneration which is passed on through faithfulness and tenderness, while Rosanna, at the height of her beauty, conceals the true death of the soul?"

"The myth of the magician," he sighed. "Yes, I know, Rosanna is nothing but an illusion."

He stood up, finally.

"Forgive me the drama, my good Cyril, but such is friendship. I'm off to Edinburgh tomorrow, where I've some marvelous memories from my childhood holidays. There's a woman there named Dorothy for whom I have the utmost respect. My lord was in love with her. With what modesty and propriety was their love woven! I'm not worthy of their memory."

He seemed so weary, so disappointed in himself and in everything. Slowly, he went upstairs to the blue room.

J ONATHAN DID NOT, IN FACT, ATTEND THE wedding, and for several months the only news I had of him was through the press. Obviously, what he'd told me of his passion for Rosanna Andrews saddened me, on Sarah's account. But time passed and Mary and I settled into Ruthford, far from Varlet's sorts of problems. *The Monkey King* had been a best seller, particularly in the United States, where my hero captured a public passionately pursuing ways of surmounting the economic crisis. In his February 1935 speech on the results of the New Deal, F.D.R. declared, "Through its zeal for new beginnings, the U.S. has at last emerged from the tunnel. I have confidence in the will of our citizens, and in their spirit of initiative, for like the monkey Souen, they will lead us to triumph over the forces which oppose our destiny." Who could imagine better publicity? In department store windows, the Souen doll replaced the Elsbeth doll; after all, had Partner not invented the slogan "Souen Against the Slump!"—thereby transforming my little monkey into a fetish? I no longer had the strength to be horrified.

On December 22, 1934, the following letter arrived from Sarah:

Dear Cyril,

How I should have loved to be at your wedding! I thought of you and your Mary in that little English town I've never seen, and

the photo you sent was so like the picture I'd imagined that I felt
I'd really been there with you. I loved the ladies you say call themselves the Sisters of the Mountain! Their faces are so clean and
fresh one would think they'd just finished bathing in a glacier. And
what happiness in your wife's eyes! Anyone can see how much she
loves you. She's the only one not looking at the photographer! She's
looking at you, or rather contemplating you. Please do give her my
best wishes. I'm sure she'll be the perfect helpmate for you. Unlike
me. I'm just a wretched thing now, of no use to anyone. Yehudi
has developed a great fondness for his governess, Peggy, a delicious
English girl Jonathan's secretary found for us. She knows just how
to talk to children; she sings and tells stories and dances and mimes,
in short she's a total theater in herself, much to the delight of our
little imp.

Jonathan is increasingly busy with his various engagements and
we see him less and less. It seems to me that the feverish way he
tackles his many affairs comes from a need to escape. A few months
ago, I imagined, stupidly, that he was fleeing me—I'm so fat and
ugly and immobile! But now it's as if he just can't sit still, as if
nothing can satisfy him. That's what worries me. He's like some
sort of compulsive eater. And everywhere he goes, so goes Partner,
the cowboy I've told you about who's always chewing or spitting. I
thought he would take some of the burden off Jonathan, but it's
just the other way around; he keeps pushing him to start something
new. What amazes me the most is how anyone can write in these
conditions; you'd think the books wrote themselves! But the monkey is so amusing and so inventive, and how much he resembles
Jonathan! I've tried to tell Yehudi the story but he's so young, and
besides, he prefers Peggy's songs and games. I'm quite alone, you
see, and your letters always bring me such pleasure. Don't forget me!

Your friend,
Sarah

The simplicity of the letter moved me deeply, but at the same time I
found it reassuring for it suggested that Varlet had not succumbed to
Rosanna's temptation, or at least had not asked for the divorce she'd
demanded. My dear Mary, to whom I read the letter, shed tears of compassion for Sarah and became rather carried away on the subject of

male egotism, although I had been careful not to divulge the secret of Jonathan's reckless romance. Sarah's letter of February 22, however, toppled Mary from her emotional ethers and dropped me into some frightful reflections. Judge for yourself.

My poor friend Cyril,

I've just discovered that Jonathan no longer loves me. There used to be much tenderness between us, but now suddenly that too has vanished. He wants to pursue love elsewhere, but as he still has a spark of feeling for me, he didn't know how to tell me that I was an obstacle. Apparently, the flame has been smoldering for several months; whoever she is (and I know nothing about her), she's insisting on marriage—which means, of course, that we must first get divorced! What could I say? How can I ask Jonathan to sacrifice his life to spare the feelings of a cripple? Doubtless I could have whined and cried about Yehudi and the fact that he binds us together more tightly than our defunct love, but that would have been only a kind of blackmail. So I held back my tears and granted him everything he wanted. Have the living dead any rights at all? Perhaps the right to suffer, as long as that too is kept hidden.

I'm twenty-two years old and am not only at the end of my life but at the bottom of an abyss which seems to have no bottom! I know I've reached it, however, because I no longer feel any pain or hope or even love. It's a kind of profound renunciation of the self; I desire neither to live nor to die. I'm still studying Hebrew with my rabbi, but without interest or disinterest. If Jonathan had left me in Berlin, I should already be dead without having experienced anything. So how can I complain?

Love,
Sarah

Twenty-two! I'd almost forgotten she was so young. On Mary's advice, I wrote inviting her to visit us at Ruthford. Her reply arrived the following week:

My dear friends,

Jonathan has finally told me everything. The woman he loves is none other than the star of the film, the famous Rosanna Andrews. I've seen her photograph in so many magazines. She's beautiful, with eyes I imagine are green as serpents'. Poor Jonathan sat on my bed, looking like he hadn't slept for days and days. I took his hand and told him not to suffer on my account, that my love was greater than my pain at losing him. I know anyway that he's been lost to me since that stupid accident. It was only by divine miracle that Yehudi was born, for between New York and Trenton I felt as if I'd been struck by lightning. Jonathan said that wasn't true. He said we were both prisoners of an illusion, that there would be new medicines, that I'd regain the use of my legs. Then he confessed to me that when he told this Andrews that he was going to divorce me to marry her, just as she'd demanded, she'd laughed and sent him away, saying she'd never marry him, that she'd only said that to gain time because she was so convinced he'd never do it. Anyway, she's leaving New York for Hollywood and has no time to spend on bemused lovers, etc., etc. You can imagine how Jonathan felt, coming back to me when he doesn't love me, when he still loves, in vain, that tigress in skirts. I would so much rather he'd been happy! He fell asleep next to me as children do, holding my hand.

When he woke up the next morning, he was very contrite and reproached himself bitterly for this passion which in his own eyes had so degraded him. I assured him that such an ordeal was surely necessary—he, the consummate seducer, had himself been seduced, and apparently for the first time! You can imagine how upset he was, not just because of that but because this failure seems to have made him doubt himself. He spent most of the morning in the bathroom, as if he wanted to wash off all the dust that had accumulated around his soul. Then, around eleven, he came back to my bedroom and said he was retiring from the presidency of his companies and turning the position over to Partner so that he could devote himself full-time to the fight against the plague, and against that other plague, anti-Semitism, particularly in Germany. He wants to establish an international association against racism. And he wants to take a trip around the world—and I'd go with him, "a lovers' voyage" he called it. He doesn't love me anymore, but in a way he wants to make amends. I let him talk. I watched him try to drown himself in projects. "We must think of Yehudi," he cried at one moment, as if this were a brand-new idea. . . . Jonathan's such a mixture of grown-up and child!

What to make of it all? I felt a glimmer of hope but refuse to pay attention to it. I feel like someone asleep who knows that if he wakes up, his toothache will begin all over again, and so remains suspended between sleep and wakefulness, barely breathing, waiting for the first twinge . . .

Love,
Sarah

The long letter comforted us somewhat, for it seemed that Varlet had got hold of himself. Moreover, he was considering taking Sarah on a trip, which was surely the first step toward rebuilding the damaged order of things. And then the notion struck me that perhaps Sarah had shut herself up in her bedroom deliberately, to punish herself for the accident, allowing herself to become obese, and so playing the invalid more than was really necessary. Her letters suggested how easily she adapted to, even took pleasure in, her role as a cripple, a martyr, *voire* a saint, and I began to understand what Jonathan felt was so unhealthy about that closed room where—height of masochism!—Sarah spent her time learning Hebrew in the company of a rabbi! I can understand, given her condition, that the young lady should have a penchant for mysticism, but I suddenly saw that she'd been using that leaning with the eerie cunning of a mind that turns into vices the purest soarings of the spirit. The windows had to be thrown wide open; she had to get out of that room where so much accumulated rancor had become a senseless holocaust. Varlet had been right. If he could just pull Sarah from that tunnel, there would be new hope.

I wrote to Jonathan, explaining what I thought of the situation. He replied immediately:

Dear Cyril,

You've made explicit what I've felt so confusedly, and I thank you. The accident which maimed Sarah so cruelly wasn't just an accident but, whether she consciously wished it or not, a suicide. She's been blaming herself for so long, and wanted to punish herself for it by giving birth to Yehudi, which she thought would kill her. But when this suicide, like the first, failed, she unconsciously decided to deprive herself of life by burying herself in her room forever, which is really just another form of suicide. That's what I've been feeling, and have been unable to articulate; it's what's made me upset to the point of nausea. I wasn't trying to escape from Sarah, but from the death that smoldered inside her. Of course, she herself had no idea what was happening; with the best will in the world, she kept making her condition worse. And do you know why? Because she was tormented by the idea that her father may have jumped from his window in Berlin. The idea has been anchoring itself more and more deeply in her mind, until it's become an obsession. In a way, his suicide had to be paid for, and suddenly there she was, paying for it, driving her car into a pole! More than all her broken bones, it was this double guilt that kept her locked up in her room.

Which is why, as you so clearly understood, I decided to force her out of herself, force her to travel, and with me. She resists me like a demon, claiming that she's not up to it, that she'll only be a burden, that she'll be prostrate with the pain, but I pay no attention. We're going to go around the world, a trip I've dreamed of for so long, and I'm sure Sarah will recover her zest for living, and that my love for her will be reborn. The blind passion I felt for Rosanna was precisely this need for fresh air, even though I deceived myself thoroughly about the woman herself, who was only playing on my naïveté. If all goes well, we leave in early April; the year 1935 will mark my return to my books, which I've sorely neglected. I intend to take quite a library with me on the boat. As for our marvelous Yehudi, we cannot bear to leave him behind, so he and Peggy will come along. He's too young for the trip to mean anything to him but at least he'll be with us, which is the most important thing. As you can gather, what's left of the bachelor has finally begun to think like the head of a household!

As for you, my happy young couple, what have you been up to? I imagine Mary amid her Sisters of the Mountain while Cyril admires the facade of his Chester Hotel! I don't think London will ever change, or Ruthford either. The winds blow across England without stopping; they may leave you a few Chinese or Indians or other dust motes from far-off lands, but look how quickly these Chinese and Indians turn British and move right into the mainstream with the same phlegm, the same concern for the status quo, as the natives! Here in America, there are so many races, and they never mingle. There's a Chinese New York, and an Italian, and a black. . . . There's really no such thing as an American, only all

kinds of people who live side by side in America. They're citizens
of a constitution, not a nation. But enough of these elegant rumi-
nations!

Love to you both,
J.A.V.

And so the storm passed. Relieved, Mary and I resumed our simple
conjugal life. We'd decided to winter in London, and so had purchased
a pleasant six-room apartment opposite Green Park. From our front
windows, we looked out on grass and trees, but at a sufficient distance
so as not to be bothered by strollers. My study was in the southernmost
part of the apartment, with a view of St. James's Palace; Mary was to
decorate the other rooms as she liked, a decision for which I must congratulate myself. The apartment soon took on the look of the inside of
a ship, with the sorts of old maritime furniture that one can still find in
antique shops and that, combined with a few Chinese pieces, created an
atmosphere of quiet comfort and tasteful exoticism. In fact, Mary dreamed
of nothing so much as voyages to distant lands. Her childhood had been
cradled in the stories of James Cook's expeditions and Stevenson's *Treasure Island*. When she learned that Sarah and Jonathan were embarking
on a trip around the world, she was feverish with an excitement that
would not abate until I'd promised her a trip to Spain, and perhaps
Italy. It wasn't Borneo, but it was good enough, and we began packing.

And then something occurred that dashed not only our plans but those
of our friends as well. Just as we thought everything had resumed its
habitual orderliness, the hideous catastrophe occurred. I shall try to explain in detail, despite the horror that fills me as I remember.

It was March 3, 1935, around eleven o'clock in the morning, when
the telephone rang in our Green Park apartment.

"Hello, Cyril?" It was a female voice, one I did not recognize.

"Cyril?" It sounded like someone shouting into the fog.

"Who is it?"

"Cyril, it's Sarah. Yehudi's disappeared!"

"Disappeared? What do you mean, disappeared?"

"He's not here. I'm in my room. Peggy's looked everywhere. He's just
disappeared!"

"Where's Jonathan?"

Silence.

"Jonathan's in Africa. He's due back in three days. I can't get hold of him. Cyril, I'm sure they've stolen Yehudi!"

"Have you called the police?"

Silence.

"They're here right now. They've looked everywhere. My baby's been stolen, I know it!"

"We'll be there as soon as we can," I said immediately. "We'll take a plane and we'll be there right away." She burst into tears and we were cut off.

On the morning of March 4 we arrived in New York, where the newspaper headlines, alas, brought us up to date abruptly. CHESTERFIELD'S SON KIDNAPPED! they shouted. So that was it!

> Yesterday, March 3, at about eight o'clock in the morning, the governess of G. K. Chesterfield's son, Yehudi, noticed that the two-year-old child had disappeared from his room. A search was organized throughout the house and grounds, but without result. Once on the scene, the police could only verify the disappearance. The wife of the celebrated writer and philanthropist was alone in their home, the Cedars, at the time. Chesterfield is currently in Kampala, where, as is commonly known, he has established a leprosarium. Now, after twenty-four hours of suspense, as we have already described in our earlier editions, the authorities are convinced that little Yehudi has indeed been kidnapped. As we go to press, the kidnappers have still made no effort to contact anyone. We can all imagine Sarah Chesterfield's agony as she waits. . . .

The radio in the cab blared all the way to the Cedars, while the cabbie kept up a running commentary. A black man with a red cap and green glasses, he spoke an almost incomprehensible argot, in which we made out the words "Chester," "kidnapping," "Jewish," and "racket." Given the fact that Chesterfield had established an association against racism, one announcer declared, it was possible that the child's disappearance was linked in some way to anti-Semitic groups. Another reporter suggested that the kidnappers were Bantu from Mwanda's Revolutionary Party, after which a woman stated with great forcefulness that the whole thing was a question of espionage, that the Germans had decided to punish Chesterfield for having dared to defy them. Finally, a policeman said that it was probably a case of blackmail and that a ransom demand was doubtless imminent, a theory that seemed to us rather more logical than the preceding hypotheses. Mary was terrified. The shadow of the Lindbergh case hung over all our heads.

A police barrier had been set up around the Cedars to keep the sightseers at bay. A mob of reporters swarmed against the gate, and as we made our way through to the inspector guarding the entrance, we were much photographed, not to mention deluged with questions such as "Are you members of the family?" and "Any ransom news?" We said nothing while the police checked our passports. The crowd too had lapsed into a heavy silence, of the sort associated with disasters and funerals. Death was present, almost tangibly so, made sticky by our fear. When he was born, Yehudi had been hailed by the press as "an American son," saved from paralysis at the very moment the New Deal was saving America from economic ruin. He became the symbol of American vitality. And now the symbol had vanished. Someone had stolen him and no one knew how far this blasphemy would go. Thus sometimes does an entire people feel in its most secret bowels events in which it recognizes its own destiny. Jonathan had been wrong to say there was no such thing as an America, for right there, before his own home, Negroes and whites, Jamaicans and Chinese had gathered, all prey to the same anguish in the face of the drama that, mythically speaking, made them one. In every state, men and women sat by their radios, and throughout the world, people waited fearfully for the outcome of this ghastly drama. For all the ingredients were present—the suffering mother, the famous philanthropist father, the symbolic son! Short of tragedy, the press had plenty of room to plunge ahead with wild abandon. As we crossed the courtyard, we felt as if we were walking on a glass bridge; the trees seemed like a setting in a dreamscape that the slightest breath would cause to collapse, revealing the dark abyss below.

The Cedars was a Colonial-style home, reminiscent of the Old South; given its lovely windows, triangular entrance, peristyle, and the veranda lined with potted orange trees, one would not have been surprised had a full contingent of black domestics in gingham and tunic appeared. Varlet had chosen the house precisely for its evocation of the South, the sun, and the flavor of joyful holidays, but in the present context it was simply grotesque. Inspector Roberts escorted us to the foyer, where we were greeted by a tall thin redhead with reddened eyes, livid cheeks, and a nervous tic in her upper lip. We understood that this was Peggy,

Yehudi's governess, although she seemed to have lost the sense of even the most elementary proprieties, for she stammered and wrung her hands and seemed incapable of uttering anything even vaguely coherent. The inspector himself took us to Sarah's room, at the far end of the corridor.

The moment we entered, the full drama of the event leaped out at us. It was not a bedroom, but a sort of cave. Sarah had gradually changed what must surely have been a cheerful room into a sepulcher where she'd buried herself alive. What had been vaguely suggested in their letters now appeared in all its painful reality. Dark curtains and tapestries had been hung on the windows and walls, and although it was late morning, the shutters were closed. A bedside lamp with a bluish shade cast a dull and parsimonious light; the bed linen was black satin. And there, leaning against a pile of mauve cushions and wrapped in a deep purple dressing gown, her hair coiled around her head, her eyes burning with fever, lay Sarah, staring at us. But was it us she saw? Her ashen lips were shut tight, as if to hold all her pain inside. I took a step toward her, but her eyes remained fixed on the door; there was no expression at all on her face. I knew the young woman lying before me was Sarah, but there seemed to have been some clever substitution; this woman with the bloated face was a caricature of the adolescent I'd known in Venice, and of the young girl I'd last seen in New York two years before.

I sat down beside her on the bed and took her hand.

"Mary's come with me," I said, my throat dry. I noticed her right hand resting on the telephone someone had placed next to her. Finally, she turned her head and seemed to acknowledge our presence.

"You shouldn't have gone to such trouble," she murmured. Then, in the voice of an automaton, "Jonathan called. He knows. He's coming back. . . . He's coming back."

Mary leaned over Sarah and kissed her.

"Would you like me to make some coffee?" she asked, as if it were the most natural thing in the world. "Or some warm milk?"

"She's under sedation," the inspector said flatly. "Carlson's given her a shot. Something with a complicated name. There're two nurses in the next room. We're very organized, you know. . . ."

The mechanical voice emerged once again from the prostrate body.

"Yehudi will never come back. They're going to kill him. I'm absolutely sure of it. They're going to kill him." There were no tears, no emotion at all on her livid face. The only things about her that seemed alive were her deep dark eyes.

"Who are these 'they' you're always talking about?" the inspector asked patiently. He was still wearing his khaki-colored raincoat and looked like a movie actor playing the role of a New York policeman. Sarah did not reply.

Suddenly, the telephone rang and, in an instant, everything changed. Sarah's face twitched violently as she picked up the receiver and brought it to her ear. A policeman sitting on a chair on the other side of the room pushed the button on a recording device. Another began scribbling in a notebook. A third picked up the receiver on another telephone. All of them seemed to have come from nowhere, like the devils in a German opera. A loudspeaker had been hooked up so that we clearly heard the caller's nasal voice; it turned out to be someone selling a twenty-volume set of encyclopedias. The receiver fell from Sarah's hand; one of the policemen replaced it on the telephone.

"Been like that all day," the inspector said. The other policemen had already vanished as abruptly as they'd appeared.

I took Inspector Roberts's arm and led him outside; I wanted to know if they had any idea at all about what had happened. With a click of his lighter, he lit a gold-tipped cigarette and blew a cloud of smoke toward the ceiling.

"Only three possible solutions with this type of thing, sir. One, the kidnapper telephones and demands a ransom, pretty common in this kind of case. Two, the kidnapper releases the child and we find him wandering around on some street. Three, we never hear anything at all. Ever. In the first case, you play it as it goes. In the second, well, it's a question of patience and good luck. As for the third, no one ever found the Burroughs girl who disappeared last year. Or the Holliday kid either. It's a long list. Once they set their price, a few of them get nervous and just want to get rid of the kid—alive in the lucky cases—but try and figure out what goes on in the heads of people like that!"

"You never found any trace of them? No prints?"

The inspector looked at me with a certain commiseration.

"This case here is the kind all policemen have nightmares about! The son of a famous person is kidnapped by nobody knows who. The press goes crazy; everybody's tense and watching and waiting; the whole police force gets involved. Even the president gets involved! You think there's any stone I've left unturned? We've taken fingerprints from the entire house, from the attic to the basement; the kid's room's been gone over with a fine-tooth comb; the grounds have been searched within an inch of their lives. The neighbors up to two miles away have been grilled, the roads blocked, questions asked in every dubious area we know about, appeals sent out over the radio, in the papers. Yehudi's photograph's plastered all over the country. The borders, the railroad stations, the airports are under surveillance. What more can I do? We have to wait."

"But how did they manage to get the child?"

"Simple as pie. He's asleep in his bed; the kidnapper comes in dressed as a milkman, leaves the bottles on the kitchen table. The maid, Claudia, goes to get some money to pay the bill, the usual end-of-the-month payment. The man slips into the hallway, gets into the child's room, picks him up, and takes off. When Claudia gets back to the kitchen, he's gone. She thinks there's been a misunderstanding and she'll pay the bill tomorrow. Half an hour later, the governess discovers the bed's empty."

"But this milkman, or rather this so-called milkman . . ."

"Just a sec. Two weeks ago, the Harold and Tennyson Dairy hires a new milkman, someone named Morrison. They give him this neighborhood. We had Claudia describe the milkman to the owners, and it was in fact Morrison who'd been delivering milk to the Cedars for the past two weeks. He's the one who got into Yehudi's room, we're sure of it. Anyway, he hasn't shown up at the dairy since then. Only problem is Morrison's got no address. It's a fake name. There is no Morrison. As for the description, he looks like any Italian—handsome, dark-haired, with a mustache! The simplicity is the mark of a real professional."

"How could he know that Yehudi's room would be so close to the kitchen? It's the third door to the right off the hallway, isn't it?"

"Also a snap, unfortunately," the inspector sighed. "A month ago, *Week* magazine did a big spread on the Cedars, home of the famous G. K. Chesterfield. And naturally, they had pictures of Yehudi in his room. They even published a little floor plan of the house! That's what gave Morrison the idea for sure. . . ."

"So it was just one person who did the whole thing, aided by certain circumstances. . . ."

Roberts lit another cigarette and frowned.

"Unlikely. There's the hand of a master here—the choice of Harold and Tennyson, the fact that the regular milkman on this route, a guy named Phillips, was sick and needed a substitute. We figured there might have been a conspiracy between Phillips and Morrison, but Phillips really was sick. In fact, he almost died from food poisoning. Mushrooms, they

think. Was he deliberately poisoned? The fact is Morrison was the first
to show up and apply for the job, even though no official ad had been
placed. But nobody paid any attention to this little detail; they figured
it was just coincidence. We're interrogating all the dairy employees right
now; so far, nothing, but it's all we've got." He paused, exhaled a col-
umn of smoke, and went on. "Unless the whole thing's a setup to throw
us off the track. Imagine, for instance, that this so-called Morrison didn't
kidnap the child. That he's just some petty crook using an alias to hide
his identity. The real kidnappers just use him without telling him anything about what they're up to. They get him hired by Harold and Tennyson. He's supposed to deliver milk to the Chesterfields every morning
at the same time. Peggy discovers the child's missing at eight-thirty.
Only one person's entered the Cedars before then—the milkman. Suspicion automatically falls on him, particularly since it's a fake name and
he's disappeared. But what proves that Yehudi wasn't kidnapped much
earlier? During the night, for instance? The governess takes him to see
his mother around eight at night, then she puts him to bed. After that,
nobody sees the child. He doesn't cry during the night; he doesn't wake
up. Mrs. Chesterfield says that's pretty common. Very calm baby, apparently. You see what I mean?"

"No," I replied.

"Okay, what if instead of putting the child to bed, Peggy handed him
through the window to some accomplice around eight o'clock? That would
suggest we're dealing with one helluva scenario. Then this Morrison's
only purpose would be to deceive us about the real time of the kidnapping. But that creates another problem: How could this supposed accomplice have gotten off the grounds, insofar as they're surrounded by
electrified wire and the gates are closed from eight at night until eight
in the morning when the milkman comes?"

"Well," I replied, "how about if Peggy brings the child to his mother
an hour earlier than usual? Sarah's so locked up in her artificial world,
she wouldn't notice the difference."

"Ah yes, Mr. Holmes!" the inspector cried, delighted. "We only know
about Yehudi's bedtime from Peggy. That would work pretty well,
wouldn't it?"

"I just saw Peggy in the hallway. Haven't you arrested her?"

"Of course not. She's not the one we're interested in. It's the others.
The ones who arranged it all. They mustn't know we're suspicious. All
we did was ask her a few questions. Anyway, she's a nervous wreck.

When the time comes, she'll spill her guts, but she couldn't know anything about where they're keeping the child or anything about the real people in charge. They probably blackmailed her. She was obviously necessary to their operation. Necessary but insignificant. The way things are now, she's got nothing we need to know."

The telephone rang again and we rushed back into the bedroom. Jonathan's voice, tense and vibrant, filled the space.

"Hello, Sarah?"

"Jonathan! Oh, Jonathan!"

"Is there any news?"

"No, nothing. Oh, Jonathan, it's awful!"

"I'm at the London airport. I'll be in New York by tomorrow morning. I've read the papers. You must keep up your spirits. I'm coming."

"Oh, come quickly, Jonathan! Come quickly!"

"I love you, Sarah! I love you!"

It was like some desperate appeal hurled across a nocturnal ocean; we all stood paralyzed by the clearly audible pain in his voice. Mary put her arms around Sarah and talked to her as if she were comforting a child. The whole scene was unbearable—majestic, miserable, and completely absurd. I began to lose control.

"That Peggy knows something. . . . She must know who's behind it, who gave her her orders. . . ."

Roberts pushed me out into the hallway.

"Mrs. Chesterfield mustn't know about our suspicions. Because they're only hypotheses. As for Peggy, I'm telling you again it's to our advantage not to push her. You can see for yourself she's on the verge of a breakdown. When the time comes, she'll talk all by herself."

"And in the meantime, the kidnappers do whatever they please!"

Roberts shrugged.

What can I say of that interminable day? Each time the telephone rang, our hearts leaped, but it was never what we were waiting for. The two nurses took turns with Sarah, and the injections kept her in a sort of waking dream. From time to time, Peggy would appear at a turning of the corridor and then hurry away, red-faced. At noon, Claudia served a light lunch in the dining room, which we ate without appetite. She was a young voluble Italian who never stopped complaining—the police had questioned her brutally, she was going to lodge a complaint with the mayor, she refused to stay any longer in a country where milkmen stole children. We had just reached dessert when Roberts returned in the company of a small man in black with a felt hat and a goatee. He wore no tie, a detail that immediately identified him as Sarah's rabbi.

"Poor, poor Mrs. Chesterfield," he said with a thick Eastern European accent. "Moshe Ivanovich," he declared, introducing himself. While Roberts returned to his post at the gate, we accompanied the rabbi to Sarah's bedroom.

"Oh, you've come!" she cried, waking up instantly. "Rabbi Moshe!" She began to speak in German, or perhaps Yiddish, I'm not certain, a flood of words she seemed unable to control. He replied in English.

"The arrows of Shaddai have struck me. My blood sucks up their venom and all the terrors of the Lord have formed ranks against me. That is Job's lament, yet Job is the one God has chosen. Happy is he who is tormented and scorned, for God is with him. We are dust, but there is no millstone that can grind us down."

He continued in what seemed to be Hebrew; we left them alone together and returned to our dessert. At that moment, Peggy entered the dining room; she must have been crying nonstop since the previous night, for any makeup had been washed from her face and her eyes were puffy. For a moment she hesitated, then threw herself at Mary's feet.

"Oh, madam, you seem so good and so kind! Everyone here looks at me as if I'd kidnapped Yehudi! I can't stand it anymore!" She burst into tears.

"No one is accusing you, my poor Peggy," Mary replied, stroking her hair.

"What time did you put Yehudi to bed?" I asked, thinking to take advantage of the opportunity.

"They've asked me that a hundred times already!" she sobbed, raising her eyes to me. "It was eight o'clock. Eight o'clock. That's the time I always put him to bed. I love that child. I love him as if he were my own son. He doesn't have a real mother, you understand. What's going to happen to him?"

The afternoon was endless. The doctor came at two, and again at five; the rabbi remained at Sarah's bedside. She'd become a poor silent thing, no longer capable of answering the telephone. Mary and I found a deck of cards and began to play, dispiritedly. The police and the nurses bantered back and forth. I felt as if we had been entrenched in a military encampment, and were just sitting around waiting for the attack to begin. Finally, at six-thirty, Roberts reappeared and took me aside.

"We've got something," he said, unfolding a piece of paper on which someone had glued letters cut out of a newspaper. "Read it yourself. Not a single fingerprint. I'm going to send it to the lab anyway. . . ."

The Chester boy is in the hands of the RDH. He will be returned only after the ransom is paid. First instruction: All police must leave the house before midnight tonight. Proof that the RDH has the child: the enclosed medallion. If instructions are not obeyed to the letter—death.

My hands trembled.

"I showed the necklace to Claudia and Peggy," Roberts said. "It's his."

"What's the RDH?"

"Nobody knows. The Fifth Avenue precinct got a call at six o'clock saying that an envelope had been stashed under a garbage can outside Book and Bell in the Bronx. And that's exactly where they found it."

"What are you going to do?"

"Exactly what they say. Get out of here by midnight. We're not going to find the kid or the kidnappers here anyway, that's for sure." With a click of his lighter, he lit another cigarette. "Here's the plan, Mr. Charmer. All our agents will leave, except for two or three who'll remain outside to watch the entrance and keep the tourists away. I'll make sure we leave with a lot of commotion. I personally will stay, however, to handle the telephone."

"But that's just what the kidnappers don't want!"

"But they won't know I'm here."

"If your theory is right and Peggy is an accomplice, surely she'll know how to warn them!"

He looked at me with obvious interest.

"Very good, Mr. Holmes! Are all Englishmen as sharp as you? If so, I feel sorry for the crooks! Well, yes, I'm afraid you're right. Our little governess will get word to them. All she needs is some agreed-upon sign that can be seen from outside. Open or shut a curtain, maybe. If that's the case, then the kidnappers will demand my departure and our hypothesis will be verified. I'll leave the house and you'll take my place. You and your wife."

"How? What do you mean?"

"Since Mrs. Chesterfield can't handle the phone, your wife will answer in her place. You'll record everything, even the most irrelevant conversations. I'll call in every half hour and see what you've got. Okay?"

With much ado and sirens screaming, the police left at midnight, much to the surprise of the reporters massed outside the gate. Roberts read a brief statement.

"On the order of the alleged kidnappers and so as not to impede the opening of any eventual negotiations, the police have decided to vacate the Chesterfield residence. No further comment." With great ceremony, he climbed into a police car, which took off, tires squealing. Half an hour later, he slipped back inside through the rear door, just as Rabbi Ivanovich was emerging from the stupor in which he appeared to have been sunk for several hours.

"You who are such a good family friend," he said to me in a deep voice accustomed to prayer, "I must tell you how deeply moved I am by this unhappy affair. I know what Mr. Chesterfield did for Sarah in Germany, how well he took care of her, even marrying her. All that should have been blessed by the Most High, and yet another ordeal is sent them as a sign of His anger. And how should we interpret that?"

"I'm sure it's just one of those passing trials," I replied. "Yehudi will be found alive, and thus the grace of God shall be manifest even more clearly."

I didn't believe a word I uttered, but what can one say to a rabbi? He raised his eyes to the heavens; his face was as wrinkled as an old apple.

"The people of Israel have endured the Law of the Most High. It is because he loves us that he has chosen us as scapegoat. All nations are sinners; they have given themselves over to the three sins of Satan— money, sex, and pride. All that can come from this is violence. The world staggers toward its end, and the Most High in His infinite mercy demands that Abel pay tribute for Cain."

"How can such a merciful God act this way with His children?" I asked.

"It is because He loved Abel that He chose him for His holocaust," the rabbi replied in his quavering voice. "Is it not our best cattle we must sacrifice?"

"But a man is neither a lamb nor a cow!" I exclaimed. "Forgive me, but if God's chosen people are chosen only to be led to the slaughterhouse, how much better it would be to be forgotten in some dark corner of the universe!"

"Alas, we have no choice. Job felt the same way. The civilization that issues from Cain has continued to proliferate. He had to kill Abel to survive. That is the primary significance of the martyr. Abel accepts his death to save Cain, and it is the one he saves who kills him."

"And is Cain then damned, since he is the murderer of his savior?"

"No, Cain is saved by the same gesture that will make him accursed. 'And Cain said unto the Lord: "My punishment is greater than I can bear. Whosoever findeth me will slay me!" And the Lord said unto him: "Therefore whosoever slayeth Cain, vengeance shall be taken on him sevenfold." And the Lord set a sign for Cain, lest any finding him should smite him.'"

"But that's all upside down! The guilty are saved and the innocents assassinated!"

"It is the innocents who hold back the arm of the Most High lest the entire world be destroyed!"

Sarah's voice emerged from the shadows like a lamentation.

"Hasn't Jonathan come yet?"

It was the twentieth time she'd asked. I sat down next to her on the bed.

"The plane is scheduled to land at eight o'clock. You must be patient just a little while longer. It's only three. . . ."

"Is it true there's no news of Yehudi?"

"Rest," said Inspector Roberts. "We're waiting for the kidnappers to give us their terms."

Sarah thrashed out feebly.

"We'll pay the ransom! We'll pay whatever they want! We must save Yehudi!"

"We will save him," Mary said, leaning over her. "They only want money. Jonathan will give it to them. Don't fret."

"He must be so frightened," she said hoarsely.

The telephone rang; Mary answered. It was the Fifth Avenue precinct.

"Inspector Roberts, please. . . . Hello, Roberts? We got another message from RDH. In the letters section of *New Magazine* this time. 'The RDH demands that the police completely evacuate the Cedars. This is your last warning.' What to do?"

"Nothing," Roberts replied. "I'm on my way out right now."

"Hypothesis confirmed," he said, turning to me and hanging up the phone. I caught up to him in the hallway.

"Aren't you going to interrogate the girl?"

"The girl, as you put it, is controlled by the kidnappers. They've blackmailed her. I've got some new information. She's got a little boy herself. And he's gone too. Happened three days ago. Peggy's sister was taking care of him, but Peggy made her keep quiet. The kidnappers told her they'd kill her son if she didn't do what they wanted. Handled the whole business by phone. She doesn't know anything about them. Can't get any more out of her. . . . She's a victim too. . . ."

I remained dumb; the magnitude of the operation was overpowering. As Roberts had said, they were professionals, and I began to think we were dealing with that remarkably well organized band otherwise known as the Mafia. Who else was capable of such a complex and terrifying strategy?

There were eight of us left—Sarah, Mary, Peggy, Claudia, the rabbi, the two nurses, and myself. At four o'clock, the phone rang again; it was Simon Partner from the west coast wanting to know if Jonathan had arrived yet. He was flying into New York himself, and was due in at noon. Afterward, we tried to get some sleep, Mary and I sprawled in two armchairs on either side of Sarah's bed. I was exhausted, but found it impossible to sleep; Mary, on the other hand, had no such trouble. I'd feared that the circumstances would upset her usual equilibrium, but she proved strong, determined to be useful, and inexhaustibly generous. She'd helped the nurses, the maid, Roberts, and of course Sarah. Worn out, she slept the sleep of the just while I tossed and turned and reconsidered my entire life. After all, it hadn't cost me much to invest ten percent of my royalties in the Uganda hospital. Varlet had gone much further than I, and I was surprised to find myself thinking that if I was doubtless descended from Cain, he was moving slowly toward becoming an Abel. Was that why my main characters—Elsbeth, Jacob Stern, Souen—were all victims? So that I might exonerate myself?

The ringing of the phone woke Mary, who stood up and answered it. I pushed the recorder button and the loudspeaker retransmitted a man's voice that seemed to come from the depths of a cavern.

"Mrs. Chester?"

"Mrs. Chesterfield cannot speak to you now. She's sleeping," Mary replied.

"Wake her up."

"Mrs. Chesterfield is under sedation. I'm her closest friend. You can talk to me."

The man hung up. Sarah had not moved; her haggard eyes stared unwaveringly at the ceiling. A nurse came and took her pulse.

"Was I wrong?" asked Mary.

"No," I replied, "he was just surprised, that's all. He'll ring back."

Half an hour later, the phone rang again. It was the same voice, although more metallic.

"Are you Mrs. Chester's friend?"

"Yes."

Sarah raised herself on her elbows and opened her mouth, but no sound came from her lips.

"Listen carefully. We won't deal with anyone but Peggy Evers. We have her son. She must do as we say. Put her on."

I called down the hallway for the governess, who arrived immediately, moving like a robot; but then, suddenly enraged, she wrenched the phone from Mary's hand and, before the caller had a chance to say anything, shouted, "My son! Give me back my son! You promised me!" There was a click; the caller had hung up.

I helped the poor girl into the next room; the situation had indeed become a nightmare, which was doubtless exactly what the kidnappers were hoping for.

"You must get hold of yourself, Peggy. I know what happened. You did what you did because you were forced to. Now you must think only of saving both children. What do they want, these people? Money? Chesterfield will give it to them, you must know that. You must be brave and do exactly as they tell you."

She wiped her eyes and found the courage to smile. Another ring. It was Roberts this time. I explained what had happened.

"Good," he said. "We've got your line tapped."

"They must be suspicious of that."

"Not necessarily. But we'll have to be careful. Nothing to do now but wait."

It was not until dawn, around seven o'clock, that Sarah finally woke up. They'd stopped giving her injections during the night so that she'd be completely lucid when Jonathan arrived. The nurses washed her face, changed her clothes, and aired the room.

"My dear friends," she said to Mary and me, "it was good of you to come so quickly." She asked us to tell her what had happened during the night, which we did, but without mentioning the role Peggy had been forced to play. The rabbi had fallen asleep in a corner of the room, his hat over his eyes. He too woke up and asked to take a shower. With daybreak, things seemed better, as if the miasmas of hatred and death had been dispersed by the sun. At seven exactly, the phone rang again. This time, Sarah answered.

"Hello." It was the metallic voice again. "Mrs. Chester?"

"Speaking."

"Glad to hear you're awake, Mrs. Chester. . . ." Sarah's face tensed as she tried to control her emotions.

"Tell me what you want and give me back Yehudi, I beg you. How is he? Is he all right?"

"Quite all right, Mrs. Chester," the voice replied magnanimously. "Please don't worry. Put Peggy Evers on, please."

The governess had been lurking behind the door; she rushed to the phone and cried, "Hello? Hello?"

"Listen to me, Peggy. You're going to explain our conditions to the Chesters. We await the return of the great man himself. As soon as he arrives, the reporters will concentrate on him. You will take advantage of this to leave the house by the back door. Turn right and walk straight down Palisades Avenue. We see even the shadow of a policeman, and bam! Finished. Do you understand, Peggy?"

"Yes, yes . . . oh yes," stammered the girl.

"You warn the police, you make the slightest mistake, we kill your kid. Get it?" He hung up abruptly.

"I don't understand," said Sarah. Finally, Mary had to explain that Peggy's son, Peter, had also been kidnapped, but she said nothing about the fact that it was Peggy herself who'd given Yehudi to the kidnappers.

"Oh, my poor Peggy!" Sarah cried. "Do these monsters need so very much money? You must tell them we'll pay whatever they want. Whatever, you understand?"

Peggy nodded, then left to get ready. Jonathan rang at eight o'clock. He'd just landed and was about to get a cab. An immense gust of hope seemed to fill the room, as if Jonathan's return would miraculously fix everything. In seconds, the house ceased to feel like a fortress under siege. At a quarter past nine, I heard a great to-do and rushed out to greet him at the gate. Like a pack of hounds, the reporters had surrounded him and were pounding him with questions. He tried to disengage himself, but to no avail.

"I have nothing to say," he kept repeating, until finally he managed to break free and join me.

"Where are we?" he asked immediately. He was unshaven, and looked thoroughly exhausted. I brought him up to date quickly, then led him into the house.

"Jonathan!" Sarah cried, as soon as he appeared in the doorway. He rushed to her side and they threw their arms around each other, remaining that way for some time while Sarah sobbed heartbreakingly.

"Has Peggy left?" I asked.

Mary replied that she'd seen her off at the back door just a few minutes before.

"Don't worry, everyone," Varlet said, standing up. "I've go idea what these people want, but we'll pay and Yehudi will come back to us, safe and sound."

He picked up the phone, called the police department, and, after some delay, was finally connected with Inspector Roberts.

"I want to find my son alive, Mr. Roberts," he said. "I don't care if the kidnappers are caught or not. I'll pay whatever ransom they want. So I trust you'll be kind enough to stay out of this and let us handle it."

"You're wrong there, sir. There's a big risk you'll pay and never see your son again."

"And why would that be?"

"Because we don't know who this RDH is. In fact, I was wondering if you had any ideas yourself."

"None whatsoever."

"Think hard, Mr. Chesterfield. We're not living in a novel here. This is reality. They're very well organized. A brilliant move, the double kidnapping. I fear we may be involved in a far more complicated situation than we'd thought. There're a lot of people who'd like to hurt you, Mr. Chesterfield. Your political positions alone . . . Germany, Uganda, and several others I'm sure."

When he'd finished talking to Roberts, Varlet turned to me.

"I'm not the one who has enemies. It's God who has them."

I understood what he meant, but did he think building a leprosarium would put God on his side? Besides, weren't lepers among the elect, like the Jews, the ones God had chosen to suffer that others might be redeemed? Wasn't wanting to take care of them equivalent to robbing God of their sufferings, and thus the healthy of their salvation? I shrugged.

The reasoning was absurd. The rabbi looked at me sorrowfully, as if he'd been reading my mind.

"Evil spirits are everywhere," Jonathan went on. "Didn't they dynamite a wing of the Kampala hospital? One of the English doctors was wounded and had to be sent home. What's happening here is only a sign of the fact that the whole world is sick. Hitler's hypnotized everyone in Europe. Put them all to sleep. Especially the English! Aren't they about to sign a naval pact with Germany? Russia grumbles, Spain squirms, Italy marches in the streets. And here in America, what's happening? No one wants to see or hear. They're convinced the League of Nations can resolve it all with words. Words! What a joke!"

He paced back and forth, carried away by the sound of his own voice.

"Stop, please!" Sarah pleaded. He walked to the bed, kissed her hand, and asked her forgiveness.

And so passed the morning of March 5. The telephone rang constantly with friends and acquaintances asking for information we couldn't give them. Jonathan and Mary took turns answering. Around one o'clock, just as we were finishing a hasty lunch in the kitchen, Simon Partner arrived. He and Varlet shut themselves into the study for half an hour, then the cowboy left. At two, the police called. They'd found Peggy wandering down a street in Manhattan but she refused to tell them anything. They were bringing her back to the Cedars, and Roberts was coming with her.

As soon as she entered the house, she rushed to Jonathan and clutched his jacket, her eyes filled with fear.

"Make the inspector leave, please, please! I won't say anything while he's here! My child's life is at stake!"

Inspector Roberts hesitated, then retired.

"Now tell me," Varlet said, "what happened?" What do they want?"

"Two million dollars," Peggy said, out of breath.

"That's my entire fortune. How am I going to get that in cash? And by when?"

"They said they didn't care about the money. They had something over their faces, like sacks with eyes cut out. There were three of them, I don't know where we were, in a room, sitting behind a table. They put a blindfold on me and took me there in a car. It was horrible!" She sank into a chair, her face twitching convulsively. " 'If you want to see your son alive again, you'll keep doing what we tell you, you got that?' they said. I said yes. I said I'd do whatever they wanted. Then the big one with the husky voice, the one sitting in the middle, he said, 'You tell Chester it's not the money we care about. It's the power. We want to take away the power his money gives him, the money he uses for things we oppose. Chester's a Communist. He's fighting against the renaissance of the German people. He belongs to a Judeo-Masonic sect that wants to pervert the Western world and make it ripe for Bolshevism.' "

"So that's it," Jonathan murmured.

"Then they told me two million dollars and said that was only the beginning. That afterward you'd have to make a public statement saying you were wrong, that you'd made a mistake. I didn't really understand what they were talking about."

"Did they tell you how the money was to be paid?" I asked. Peggy shook her head.

"Well," Varlet sighed, "now we know what we're up against. They want to destroy my projects. Only they're forgetting one thing—money's nothing. It's my name, my reputation, my notoriety that serves as my springboard. All they've done with this odious move is to reinforce that." He was silent for a moment, then exclaimed, "I'm going to make a statement to the press!"

"Wait a minute," I interrupted. "We're talking about Yehudi's life. These people are capable of anything. And they hate you."

"Don't worry about Peter," Jonathan said to Peggy. "You'll get him back. Alas, as for Yehudi, his name seals his fate."

"Listen," I said, as we walked across to the gate, "you must weigh each and every word."

"Of course," he snapped. "Yehudi's life depends on it."

The moment we walked through the gate, the reporters fell upon us. There were at least two hundred of them, armed with microphones, cameras, and fountain pens. Jonathan climbed onto a road marker next to the gatekeeper's cottage.

"I have a statement to make," he cried in a loud voice. Immediately, there was total silence, all faces straining toward him. All across America, the same silence was being transmitted live to millions of radios.

"This is Gilbert Keith Chesterfield," he began, his voice strong and clear. "As you know, my little boy, Yehudi, has been kidnapped. We now know who the kidnappers are and what they want. They're a small group of extremists who share the racist views of the German National Socialist Party and who refuse the rights of citizenship to their democratic compatriots. Liberals and socialists are thrown into prison merely for opposing the present dictatorship. Writers and famous scholars are forced to flee. Jews are systematically barred from all activities and are gradually being deported to camps. I've created an association against racism to fight this monstrousness, this cancer that is spreading throughout the world. We know now that Yehudi's kidnappers want to keep me quiet, to gag me! They fear my influence. They have offered me an ignominious deal—keep my mouth shut or lose my son! That's what those people are like! That's the totalitarianism that the United States and free Europe still refuse to recognize! I therefore propose the following, and here I speak directly to the kidnappers: I shall pay them one million dollars to be delivered to them any way they like, in exchange for Yehudi and for the son of Yehudi's governess, whom they are also holding. If they accept, I promise the police will not bother them or get in the way. I await their decision. That's all, ladies and gentlemen. No questions, please."

He stepped down and the reporters opened ranks to let him pass. We returned to the house in silence. A few moments later, the U.S. attorney general, Roy Bentley, telephoned; he'd just heard Jonathan's statement and wished to offer his help.

"We'll make some discreet inquiries in the radical sectors," he promised, but we all heard how helpless he felt. Varlet ushered me into the study.

"Firmness is the only card I've got left, Cyril. There's no way I can raise that two million. Even if I sell off everything I have, it'll take forever. It's all in the business. On the other hand, Partner tells me he can raise a million by tonight. He's got the banks to agree. It's that or nothing. I suspect the kidnappers deliberately raised the price to force me to negotiate, especially since they know that if they kill Yehudi I'll fight them even harder!"

We went up to Sarah's room, where Mary was tending to her as one would a child. Without being specific, we told her that the negotiations were proceeding satisfactorily and that therefore she must be brave. All Sarah could say in response was "But do they know how to feed a baby? If only they don't hurt him! He must be so frightened!" The unbearable waiting began all over again.

Around four o'clock, the precinct called to inform us that in a synagogue on Third Avenue a package had been found that contained the clothes Yehudi had been wearing when he was abducted. There was also a message: "Jews and Bolsheviks will be exterminated. Peggy Evers's son has been freed at 7234 Downing Street. Signed, RDH." Peter was indeed found during the course of the evening, but as he was only three years old, he was unable to tell the police anything worthwhile. And so all was silent once more. At seven o'clock, a message from Sarah to the kidnappers was recorded and carried by all the stations; the painfulness of its content I shall leave my reader to imagine. Meanwhile, a vast network of police continued searching and interrogating, but with no results. At nine o'clock, Jonathan made another statement, this time begging the kidnappers to put their respect for life and for humanity before their ideological passions. The doctor returned, and ordered Sarah tranquilized and removed to St. Andrew's Clinic close by, where she could be watched until the outcome was assured.

Alas, there was no outcome. The kidnappers gave no further signs of life, from which it was assumed that Yehudi had been assassinated. His body was never found.

WE REMAINED IN NEW YORK FOR A
month. I shall refrain from describing what happened during those
frightful empty days except to say that bit by bit our hopes vanished,
leaving in their place an absence made more acute by the fact that no
one knew for certain if the child was dead. Sarah managed for two
weeks, then slid into a kind of gentle madness, hardly recognizing anyone, believing that all of us who visited her were Jonathan, with whom
she pursued a strange and endless dialogue about Yehudi's future. Varlet moved heaven and earth to find his son, promising fortunes to anyone who could help him. In vain, the newspapers and radio echoed his
appeals until slowly, its appetite sated, the public forgot.

What had, then, actually happened? Although all hypotheses were
admissible, we agreed the kidnappers had been fanatics driven to fury
by Varlet's speech. When one thinks about it, his short statement to the
press at the gate of the Cedars was both extremely clever and extremely
dangerous. To be sure, it brought a necessary firmness to the negotiations by reducing the ransom demand to an acceptable, albeit still considerable, level. Anyone, no matter how greedy, would have been satisfied
with such a sum. Except that we were dealing with people filled with
hatred, people for whom the lure of money was nothing compared to

their destructive desires. In fact, as we later learned from the British ambassador to Germany, the order to kidnap Yehudi had come from the Chancellery itself. Apparently, Goebbels had not forgotten the humiliation of Chesterfield's abrupt departure in 1931, a humiliation kept alive by American and English papers that often referred to the romance of Jonathan saving Sarah from the Nazis' clutches. The kidnapping, then, seemed more a strategy to erase that affront and to punish the writer for having dared interfere in German affairs. Goebbels's participation also explained not only the professionalism of the abduction, the precise attention to detail, but also the outcome, which, by definition, had to be fatal.

Knowing this did not, however, prevent Varlet from feeling the terrible weight of his personal responsibility. He'd adored the child and he berated himself for having sacrificed him. His moral torment was heightened by the fact that the catastrophe claimed Sarah as its second victim. When we left New York, we also left behind us a deeply wounded man. An episode that occurred on April 5, the evening before our departure for England, may serve as a poignant example. Varlet had left the Cedars and moved into a suite in the Claridge Hotel from which, with the help of Simon Partner, he continued to run his empire, although he spent most of his time collecting signatures on his famous "Petition Against Racism," which would appear several weeks later.

We arrived, Mary and I, around six, and shook hands in silence. Jonathan had the stunned expression of someone who'd just walked away, apparently intact, from a holocaust.

"So you're leaving?" As we nodded, he said, "I've just got Thomas Mann's signature. Do you realize what that means? The real Germans are revolted by what's happening."

He led us into the drawing room, which contained an impressive concert grand.

"How is Sarah?" Mary asked.

He shook his head, gesturing vaguely.

"I went to see her yesterday. In the clinic. I don't think she understands. Or remembers. She just talks about Yehudi and smiles. . . . It's awful, and yet it's a blessing. She doesn't seem to be suffering."

"What do the police say?" Mary continued.

"Nothing. They don't know anything. We'll never hear from the kidnappers again, I suppose. Or rather I know. They've killed Yehudi because, in their eyes, he represented the little Jew. Worse than that, he was the product of a union between a Jewess and an Englishman! And on top of that—height of irony—a famous Englishman who had the temerity to oppose them! It's because of the association . . . after I founded the association . . ."

Simon Partner burst into the room with his customary rhinoceros-like grace.

"Hiya!" he bellowed in a cloud of cigar smoke. "Market's up to three twenty-seven. We sell?'

"We sell," said Jonathan absently.

Partner groaned audibly.

"All right, we don't sell. Why bother asking my opinion?"

The cowboy shrugged. "I just don't get why we're holed up in this hotel when we got offices."

"I hate offices!" Jonathan snapped, then, forcing himself to calm down, added, "Listen, Partner, do what you want. I trust you, you know that."

Partner turned and left, grumbling.

"It's true, I can't stand to be in the office anymore. And I can't stand staying here any longer either. Soon I won't be able to stand living in America at all! I'm trying to run away from everything I've done, trying to get away from myself, I suppose." He smiled wearily. "I'm just so tired."

"Why not come with us to England?" Mary said.

"I'm sure I will someday," he sighed. "Someday soon. I don't know. How can I leave Sarah all alone here?"

"Why not bring her with you?" I proposed. "You can leave the dolls to Partner and get out of all that. It isn't right for you anyway."

"Yes, I must. I've told you, the money, the fame . . ."

"Right," I replied. "So now you have the money and the fame, and it's time to focus on your real struggle. I'm going to be honest with you, Jonathan. Until I saw for myself what those monstrous individuals were really like, until I saw the intensity of their hatred, I didn't believe in what you were doing. It seemed so misguided, so futile, perhaps even dangerous. And then, suddenly, I saw that we have only one choice, a choice between Utopia and death."

He seemed to emerge from a dream.

"Ah? So you've understood at last? At night, I toss and turn and think no, it's not possible. Or no, it's just too absurd. . . . An innocent child! But I'm the one they wanted to punish. I oughtn't to have said what I said. I oughtn't to have provoked them. I ought to have pleaded with them, begged them. They wanted to see me at their feet, and out of pride, I refused. It's my own pride that killed Yehudi."

"Now hold on there," I interrupted, "you know that's not true. People like that act out of two things only—mental chaos and blind instinct."

He took my hand and held it.

"Thank you, both of you, thank you. Your friendship moves me deeply, but what can I say? What can I do while my mind is nothing but a gaping wound? I've tried to drown myself in stupid business things, but nothing takes my mind off this obsession. It prowls about inside me like a sick animal until all I really want to hear is that Yehudi is in fact dead. Can you understand that? Why is it that to bring a little order to the world I must endure such terrible chaos?"

"Other people may have acted differently, of course, but events have pushed you to do what you've done. Pushed you with disconcerting facility, I might add. After all, your incredible success can't entirely be explained by the novels!" He looked at me with the intensity of a drowning man desirous of transmitting a final message.

"I was guided, Cyril. Led and directed. Everywhere. I felt as if my lord were inside me, pulling the strings. But would he have demanded such payment? It's not possible, is it? Or perhaps he wanted to punish me for my frivolous passion for Rosanna. For the fact that I wanted to flee my own soul. And look how I've been repaid!"

"Jonathan," I said firmly, "it's good that the scope of this drama and of your suffering has a meaning for you. But you must admit that a crime like this is more absurd than horrible. Why bring your lord into it? He was your benefactor. It is other forces you should accuse, and you are right to commit yourself henceforth to destroying them."

"Thomas Mann signed!" he exclaimed. "Yesterday, I received André Gide's agreement. All these voices will be heard by governments who still don't seem to understand the kind of menace Germany poses in the hands of Hitler and his men. Ever since Hindenburg's death, the Chancellor has been free to do what he likes, backed by big business who see him as the savior of the economy. The worldwide economic crisis has engendered a monster applauded by blind people! Our embassy in Berlin confirms the existence of camps where everyone opposed to the regime is imprisoned. And all of it flies in the face of the most elementary rules of humanity."

He seemed to grow calmer as he spoke so we took our leave, although not until we'd exacted his promise to come back to England with Sarah as soon as possible. Then, as five hours remained before we were to embark, we went to St. Andrew's to visit our poor friend. The hospital was a pretty white building surrounded by lawns and flower beds; clearly the directors had wished it to be warm and welcoming and gay, which paradoxically made it rather icy and sinister, like being in a refrigerator. Or a morgue. Sarah's room had a green carpet, which made it seem like an aquarium. She was lying on a narrow wrought-iron bed supported by two inflatable rubber cushions; as soon as she saw us, her eyes brightened.

"Dear Jonathan," she exclaimed in a startlingly youthful voice, "how sweet of you to bring me daisies! I'm going to give them to Yehudi. He loves daisies. But tell me, did he get to school on time?"

"Of course he did," Mary replied, sitting down beside her. "How do you feel?"

"Like an angel," she said cheerfully. "After the ordeal comes peace. And the happiness of knowing it's turned out so well. I prayed so hard, you know. The Most High *had* to answer me!"

She'd lost a great deal of weight and now looked almost like an adolescent, like the Sarah I'd known in Venice. Was it possible she'd so transformed reality . . . ?

"Dear Jonathan," she went on, looking at Mary, "you must give a bit of money to Rabbi Moshe. He was so good to us. And I was telling Yehudi just a little while ago, my father is so happy to see us all back together again. He comes to see me sometimes. And he brings a little violin. He plays and he sings and he dances! And then all the peasants gather around and dance with him. And I too! I dance too! Oh, how I dance!" She began to laugh. "When I think that before the accident, I didn't even know how!"

A nurse entered the room.

"Oh, there's Yehudi!" Sarah cried, her face filled with joy. "He's gotten so big, hasn't he?"

"Let's have a little soup now," the nurse said, and began to feed her as one would a child. "She's always happy, you know. As if the world were one endless party. She arranges things and people to fit her desires. The doctors have never had a case quite like it."

"But doesn't she remember anything of what happened?" I asked. "Anything of her real life?"

"She talks about Berlin and Venice and London, and it's always marvelous. And why not?"

She wiped Sarah's lips with a napkin, patted her cheek, and left.

"Well," I said, "you must come to see us at Ruthford."

"Oh yes, I'd love to! Dear Jonathan, you never told me you'd bought such a big house. You remember, it was my birthday, wasn't it? We'll have a playroom for Yehudi. And a swimming pool and a forest with pine trees and behind it, a mountain covered with snow. Lots of snow! I love the snow!"

Our voyage back on the *Athenia* gave us the chance to recuperate. The recent events had profoundly distressed us both, but a week on the high seas helped to restore our spirits. Mary had proved very strong; I had often been surprised at her endurance and presence of mind. I'd never seen her cope with true misfortune, but our frightful adventure had shown me how capable she was of devotion and courage. As I've suggested before, I'd married out of a kind of duty and because Mary seemed to incarnate quite well the sort of wife that corresponded to this duty. She'd known how to do our apartment with the happiest of results. She handled her various domestic responsibilities modestly and punctually, guiding the maid firmly but gently. In short, she was going to make an excellent mother to the two or three children we both so desired. It was doubtless because we'd just had a close brush with death, but on the liner returning us to England, I discovered a lover.

On our second night out, there was a gala in the brightly lit ballroom. We'd leased our costumes from the purser in charge of stores; Mary had gone alone to choose hers, for she insisted on surprising me. As the orchestra attacked a waltz, she entered the ballroom—a stunning young woman with absolutely bare shoulders, her long dress looking like those worn by high-fashion models when they introduce the season's new styles. She moved so easily in the gown it seemed as if she'd never worn anything else. The ship's coiffeuse had composed her hair into a mass of curls that left her neck also quite bare. Everyone turned to stare; I felt quite proud. This was a Sister of the Mountain? We ordered champagne, as if by this ball we might shake off the morbid miasma that had engulfed us for so long. For hadn't we been hostage to a misfortune that, after all, did not really concern us? How egocentric we become when the sufferings of others threaten to make us part of their destiny! We commiserate, but refuse to become involved. Each of us confronts suffering alone because we cannot endure the suffering of others. That's what I thought then, and yet I had written *The Monkey King*, where Souen takes upon himself the suffering of his entire tribe. How great the distance between the writer and his heroes! It's because the writer is a coward that he creates knights, because he fears women that he invents Don Juans.

During this ball on the high seas, I felt as if the whole world were a festival and I, Cyril Charmer-Maker, a sort of deep-sea diver swimming amid unknown fauna. Through my mask, I watched the drinkers and dancers waving and fluttering, and understood little of what they were doing. On the other hand, there was Mary, a new Mary, so alive and with such exciting shoulders, like a mermaid among crabs and lobsters! One must live, finally. One must live and reject the phantasms of a Varlet, the illusions of a Chesterfield, the absurdity of an entire world! I led Mary onto the dance floor; it was the first time I'd ever danced and it seemed as if an old cardboard carcass were being ripped away from me, as if I were emerging victorious from some unknown combat that had restored me to the light. I breathed more deeply, I saw more clearly, and the Mary I held in my arms was so light, so very light. The crossing was a kind of honeymoon, a real one, a bath in the Fountain of Youth. We arrived in London with a new serenity; I was going to begin a new novel, I could feel it.

Upon our return to Green Park, we were surprised to encounter one Felicia Johnson, a Sister of the Mountain, who was comfortably installed in our apartment and welcomed us as if we were paying her a visit. Mary had in fact left a set of keys with the head of the association, "just in case," and the good woman had thought it a fine idea to loan them to this Felicia, a freckle-faced child of sixteen, with a large round nose and pigtails held by elastic, about whom we knew nothing at all. She seemed quite astonished by our astonishment.

"Mrs. Graham gave me the keys," she explained. "I've come from Liverpool to go to school here. I want to be a lawyer."

"A lawyer!" I exclaimed. "But that's quite impossible!"

"Then I guess I'll be the first," she replied with a shrug. "How do you do?" She held out her hand.

And so there entered our lives quite unexpectedly someone who, in a strange way, was to play a small but decisive role in Jonathan's existence. For the time being, we agreed to let her stay in a maid's room on the top floor. Then we resumed our ordinary London routine, driving out to Ruthford on the weekends where we were happily welcomed by our good Douglas. These were tranquil and happy weeks, during which I greatly appreciated my wife's warm and discreet presence. And it was during these weeks that I wrote the opening chapters of *The Man Without a Face*, in which a character named Tusco is reborn into different eras and encounters rather singular creatures—a medieval alchemist, an Irish magician, Emperor Rudolph of Prague, a designer of uncanny and fantastic gardens, one Ratenau who converses with angels, a coquette from Pisa with a troubled little face, a monk spreading the plague throughout Venice, a clockmaker named Nuncingen (perhaps my favorite), and Queen Christina of Sweden whose amazing destiny had always fascinated me. In short, it was really a series of stories, all attempts to render the invisible, and connected by the uncanniness of the characters' situations. I had already begun this process in *Jacob Stern*, convinced as I was that the purpose of art was not to describe what one sees but what one doesn't see, or what is hidden. Great art, I thought, is like a coat of arms; it reveals not meanings—always fragmentary and contradictory—but a meaning.

In *The Man Without a Face*, I had a bit of fun with dogmas and their myriad machineries, for as my reader knows, I did not take organized religions seriously. On the other hand, I had begun to feel inside myself some sort of appeal from another dimension, an appeal that I'd used as a novelist but that had now begun to spill over into my daily life. The sinister events in New York had at least had the merit of confirming me in my belief that the solitude that I had often taken for faintheartedness was superior to the sorts of activities and dealings of which Jonathan was guilty. I use the word *guilty* advisedly, for what had his efforts produced, except catastrophe? Where the dimension of the invisible was concerned, I felt, of course, that it must be contained within the limits of the reasonable, and that I must be on my guard against the sorts of ramblings that lead only to weakness or madness. I am not, as you will note, a disciple of William Blake, even though I admire his courage.

Margaret Warner, however, caused the ramblings to began again, more furiously than ever, and this when our lives had just returned to their habitual serenity. This odd person, who'd rushed in just after the wedding ceremony to congratulate us and had refused to stay for the dinner, had, much to my relief, never reappeared since. Mary had been vexed, however, by what she interpreted as a snub, declaring that if the publisher's daughter did not find her worthy of friendship, she had better not show her face again. In the beginning, Mary had been flattered by Margaret's attentions, and so she suffered when she no longer heard from someone she considered a friend. I had, of course, explained to my

wife that Miss Warner was perhaps not quite as socially correct as she
innocently believed, but then, had I not myself been deceived? I only
regretted not being able to tell Mary what I knew of that fiery iceberg's
private life, but did not feel I could reveal what I'd learned by indiscretion—an attitude I would soon come to regret.

Early in the month of June 1935, Goldman Publishers arranged a
lawn party at the home of Peter Warner. We had been invited as Chesterfield's representatives, and arrived at Guildford at about three o'clock.
Mary had never seen this delightful little Surrey town whose High Street
is one of the most interesting in all the south of England, so we visited
the hospital with its cupola and clock tower, and Trinity Church, all of
which greatly pleased my wife. She adored the ancient stones, and the
monuments so laden with memories. I showed her the house where Charles
Dodgson, the beloved Lewis Carroll of our childhood, had died. Afterward, we arrived at the sumptuous country house Peter Warner had
bought ten years before, after the bankruptcy of its previous owner, the
Russian poet Charlienko, who'd managed to dissipate a quite prodigious
fortune in alcohol. We parked in a driveway behind several other cars,
doubtless the finest collection of Rolls-Royces any collector could
imagine!

A butler in a black uniform greeted us at the top of the steps, verified
our invitation card, spun about sharply like a robot, took a few steps
into the entryway, and handed the card to another servant, this one in
blue, who bowed deeply, placed our card on a tray, and escorted us into
an immense drawing room already abuzz with guests. Once we were
inside, a third valet, in red, took our card from the tray, studied it like
a connoisseur of celebrities, and in a strident voice barked, "Mr. and
Mrs. Charmer-Maker!" At which point Margaret, who'd been talking
with a professor as bald as he was hirsute, swept up to us.

"My dear, dear friends!" she cried, holding out both hands. "I was
so afraid you wouldn't come! My adorable Mary, how I've missed you!
And you, Cyril, how've you been after that ghastly kidnapping? You
were in New York, weren't you? I read all about it in the papers. And
followed it on the radio. Poor Sarah! I think about her especially, because Jonathan . . . well, you know, men don't feel those sorts of things
the way we do. But come in, come in! You must have a drop of champagne. . . ."

Her frivolity was feigned, I could feel it, the gaiety an attempt to hide
the depth of her ennui, or of her anxiety perhaps.

"And what about you, Margaret?" I asked. "Have you been back to Venice?"

"I simply cannot do without the Serene City, you know," she replied, looking at me sardonically. "I still have various affairs there, every bit as crazy and chaotic as before. Dangerous, sometimes." She laughed. "Have you told Mary about my Venetian life?"

I shook my head, speechless.

"Well, that does reassure me! You haven't told her about Countess Ambrozani—dead now, poor soul—or about Calcati, the pope's great-grandnephew, or even Beatrice, the little girl in the movable chair?"

"Not really. I didn't actually know them very well. The countess, you say, is dead?"

"Her little hunchbacked relative pushed her, and her wheelchair, down the stairs. But she didn't die right away; those old people are quite indestructible. They took her to the hospital and the hunchback to an asylum. I saw her just a few days before she died, and she was very much her former self. 'When I'm all better,' she told me, 'I shall arrange for Tinto's release. I miss him terribly!' The poor woman didn't have the chance, however. During my last trip, they had just taken her to San Michele and put her in that ghastly marble Ambrozani crypt. Adieu, *signora*. . . . It was a pretty piece of Venice they buried with her, you know."

She held out two glasses of champagne.

"Oh, how I'd love to see Venice!" Mary exclaimed. "Cyril and I were supposed to go to Spain and Italy just at the moment Yehudi was kidnapped. So instead of Granada and Venice, we got New York! We lost in that transaction, I can assure you! It was a ghastly experience. And as you say, poor Sarah!"

"Is it true she's lost her mind?" Margaret asked, biting into a cake.

"Oh!" Mary replied, rather shocked by the tone of voice. "She was terribly brave, but the waiting and the outcome and the uncertainty . . . It was the grace of God that gave her a gentle madness. She believes Yehudi is with her and she's happy. Truly happy. As for Jonathan, contrary to what you may think, he suffers and blames himself."

"So he suffers, does he? He blames himself? Has he changed so much then? He the great seducer? The brave strong hero? Has he met his match at last?"

There was a certain bitterness in her voice.

"How could he not have changed after such an ordeal?" I asked.

"You're the mystic. You should be able to understand what profound transformations can occur as a result of such suffering!"

She laughed again, an odd icy little laugh more like a grimace.

"A mystic! Yes, I suppose I am one, in my own way. I see you haven't forgotten, Cyril. One must pay, you remember? One must always pay. There's an accountant in heaven. Or hell, perhaps. Do you remember what I once told you about redeeming souls? I've prayed a lot for Jonathan to become exactly what he's become. Besides, you've doubtless told Mary that I once loved him enough to lose him. But it wasn't enough, obviously. He had to have Yehudi's death. And Sarah's insanity . . ."

"Now just hold on there!" I cried. "What are you talking about? That's an abominable notion you've got of God! Unless you're talking about Satan, that is."

She was wearing an expensive orange crepe de Chine cocktail dress and looked, as usual, exquisite.

"You don't believe in anything!" she snapped back.

"I may not believe in the balderdash that comes out of churches, but I believe even less in yours, my dear," I replied, forcing a smile. "I believe that in the eternal struggle between life and death, life is always the victor. Death is an illusion, a trap. Suffering is also an illusion. They ennoble only insofar as we know how to tear away their masks and recover the life behind them."

"But wasn't it the powers of death who kidnapped Jonathan's son and didn't return him?" Mary asked. "They were the ones that won!"

"I know nothing is harder to believe, and yet weakness and fragility do triumph over strength. What is more fragile than life as it faces the powerful beast of death? And yet life goes on, it multiplies, it gains on its own losses. We're all in one way or another courted by death and yet we're on the side of life. After all, doesn't decay itself foster life?"

"My dear Cyril, at last you've managed to say what I've always believed! Decay engenders life. To be born requires one to decay, to rot!"

I looked at her with some suspicion, which made her smile and look away.

"Yes, I know, you're going to tell me those are only excuses. . . ." Then, recovering her aplomb: "What a philosophy for a party! Do you know it's my father's sixtieth birthday? You must go congratulate him. When he was an adolescent, everyone told him he'd never live past twenty. Perhaps that's one of the reasons he's been so successful!"

She turned away to speak to a young couple who'd been trying to catch her attention, and Mary and I made our way to the sumptuous buffet. We'd just begun to nibble here and there when a frightfully tall and hearty young man with a mass of unruly dark hair inquired if I was indeed the friend of the writer Chesterfield whom Miss Warner had told him so much about. He must have been about thirty, with skin as pale as a chicken breast and such a prominent Adam's apple it looked as if it might pierce his throat.

"Forgive me for bursting upon you this way," he went on, "but sooner or later we had to meet. I am Leonid Charlienko, the son of the previous owner of this estate. Margaret has told me a great deal about you, which perhaps gives me the right to approach you."

When I introduced Mary, he kissed her hand with much flourish but, as he straightened up, almost lost his balance, grabbed for the buffet table, and grimaced. "I do drink too much, of course. . . . I smoke too much too. I may be a descendant of peasants, but I bear the burden of every vice. You take a peasant's land away and what's left? The horizon. Ah yes, the horizon, right there, inside my head, alongside the crows, *caaaww, caaaww,* but a horizon minus the earth, you understand . . . Exile! And alcohol, smoke replaces the earth. Stupid, no? Or perhaps, like my father, the valiant Vassiliev Charlienko, there's a bit of poetry in there rushing for the horizon, except there's no land left so it races on the wind! Poetry! Wind! Or on sheets and sheets of paper, all piling up . . . an atticful! And so the great Vassiliev too began to drink and smoke, and you know why? Because of the crows. They're always there, the crows. You, me, everyone else, all the crows!"

Mary looked at me anxiously. He took a glass and offered it to me. "Shall we drink to this fortuitous encounter? Better I should be frank with you. I have a motive. Let's drink to that! A serious motive, actually . . . For after all, as witness to the great Vassiliev Charlienko, my father, who hoarded masses of poems in the attic and then was forced to sell the attic . . . Ha, ha! A great lesson, that was. I told myself, I said, Leonid Charlienko, son of the great Vassiliev, you shall not collect your poems in the attic. And this for a very simple and very magnificent reason—I've never written a poem in my entire life. A good reason, no? Besides, I have no attic anymore. Sold! This house, these grounds, sold! Every bit of it, sold! You must admit it's quite amusing to be able to say, as I so often have, this room, this very room in which I now have the honor of speaking to you, this room belonged to my childhood but no longer belongs to me. Look, over there, on that wall, the tapestry

. . . the little design next to the flower. I was five when I drew that. I'm the only one who knows what it means. In short, I'm a ghost come back to his old haunt. Ulysses and the Potomachus, or Telemachus, I can't remember . . ."

He downed his glass and continued.

"And so, dear madam and sir, I am a writer. No, rest assured, not a poet, a writer. Never published anything, of course, but nonetheless a real writer. The proof—that wholesaler of paper, Peter Warner, rejected *The Ungodly*. A masterpiece it was! And do you know why Peter Warner rejected my manuscript? Because Babydoor is an ass. Have you met Babydoor? Almost as ugly as I am . . . He said . . . What did he say? *'The Ungodly:* a Russian tale.' Ha, ha! A Russian tale! As if I, Leonid Charlienko, were writing Dickens! I was suckled on Tolstoy and Dostoevsky, and Sir Babydoor—what a ridiculous name—wants me to copy one hundred times, 'The sons of my mother are the nephews of her sister,' or some such artillery of mashed potatoes, genre 'Lake Country Fantasies'! Thank you very much, but I am a real writer!"

"It's true," Margaret said at my elbow. "Leonid has written a marvelous novel. You must read it, Cyril. I'm sure you'll like it."

"Hasn't your father read it?"

"When Babydoor rejects a manuscript, my father never reads it. But if you like it, as I think you will, perhaps you might tell Jonathan about it."

"Agreed."

It was decided that Margaret would bring me the masterpiece herself as soon as she could.

"A thousand thanks," Leonid said, raising his glass. "But who is that approaching, like a werewolf stalking?" He faked a look of terror and staggered off.

The werewolf was Peter Warner himself, ramrod straight in his black jacket and striped trousers, a red rose in his lapel.

"Mr. Charmer, as I believe you now call yourself, or rather my dear friend, may we be serious for a moment? I've heard nothing from Chesterfield since that ghastly business. Perhaps you would enlighten me."

I replied that I knew no more than he, since Jonathan wrote but rarely and Sarah was no longer able to do so at all.

"I confess I never took our friend's political positions seriously when he was in London," Warner went on. "I felt his press conference was quite disgraceful, actually. But now, as time has passed, I must acknowledge he was correct, not that I believe this Hitler is such a menace to the entire world—quite the opposite, really—but that the press campaign against racism has proven a remarkably effective strategy. *Beelzebub* is selling as briskly as when it was first published. People feel it was quite prophetic, that it shows us the world as a concentration camp! Quite amazing, wouldn't you say?"

"I wonder if they'll see Alexander as a model for Hitler?" Mary said, laughing.

"Why not?" Warner replied. Then, turning to me, "Would you happen to know what novel he's preparing for us at the moment?"

I explained the theme of *The Man Without a Face*. Fortunately, he seemed pleased.

"After Alexander, the antihero, comes Souen, the hero. And now Tusco, the anonymous, for a man without a name possesses all names, and a man without a face is every one of us. Chesterfield's trick is to amuse us with stories that have neither rhyme nor reason but that teach us who we are. We have no rhyme or reason either, you see."

"Forgive me," I interrupted, "but that's not quite Jonathan's way of thinking. What he describes is a world with two faces—absurd for those who wish it so, orderly for those who succeed in giving it an order. Basically, however, he's betting on order. Although not just any order! Alexander is obsessed with order. Souen struggles against an artificial order in order to create a higher and more humane one. Jacob Stern goes out into the disorder of sixteenth-century Germany so that he might discover an order hidden inside of us. . . ."

"Yes, yes," Warner interrupted, "but what does he think now, after what happened to his son? Literature is helpless before the facts. You tell me 'a higher and more humane order,' as if somewhere there's a conjunction between the human and the divine. Wouldn't that be possible only if we were all to strip ourselves bare, to became naked, destitute?"

It always came around to the same thing—the Cains had to keep killing the Abels, not only to free but to purify themselves. What an odd paradox is man that he must forever betray his savior!

A few days later, Margaret arrived at Ruthford bearing Charlienko's manuscript. We had decided to return to the country for the last lovely days of summer, and had left the London apartment to Felicia. I was hardly delighted that Margaret had found a means to intrude upon us, for I suspected that the curtain had not yet descended on her love for

Jonathan and that by visiting us she hoped to come closer to him. A curious mystic she was indeed; she must have bought at least a dress a week from the most elegant shops in London, for each time we saw her she was wearing something new. This time, it was a white outfit that perfectly matched her car.

"My dear Margaret," Mary said, "you can't imagine how I envy your chic."

My wife enjoyed telling people what they expected her to tell them. In reality, Mary never wore makeup and dressed simply, and her appearance suited her admirably. She did appreciate Margaret's elegance, however, and even I must admit Margaret's taste was perfect. She managed to wear the most eccentric things so naturally that they became quite pleasant.

"I love dressing up," she said. "It's my disguise."

"Whyever should you want a disguise?" Mary asked, as we entered the small drawing room.

"Out of modesty, I suppose. But mostly so I can play a character that bolsters my self-confidence. Sometimes, I'm afraid of myself, you know."

When we were comfortably ensconced in Mary Charmer's fringed armchairs, Margaret began to talk about Leonid Charlienko, including her shock at the way her father had got hold of the poet's Guildford estate.

"It's as if he stripped him of the last bit of dignity he had left. Ever since, he's wandered about the world absolutely penniless. As for the son, well, you'll read *The Ungodly*. I think it's a masterpiece. But even there, you can't imagine the price he had to pay for the right to reach such a summit."

"And yet he seems quite fallen," I replied with the merest suggestion of irony.

"He's returned to more primal forces," Margaret declared rather grandly.

"Aha! And are these forces situated in smoke and alcohol? You do realize your Leonid's a drug addict?"

"Yes. He's also a remarkable and most unfortunate boy. He lives his passions right to the end of his fantasies. That's where his novel comes from. It's an inimitable voice from the depths of his being. . . ."

I smiled.

"When I think that just a few years ago, right in this very house, you shrieked when Jonathan talked about the English tradition that gave us

Beckford, Chatterton, and Parnell! And now here you are, a convert to that morbid romanticism, that distillation of drunkenness, madness, and syphilis in some of our greatest writers!"

"Dear Cyril," Mary said, "I find you quite severe in your judgments. If I understand it, the young man's misfortunes were visited upon him by his father, who drank excessively long before he did. Is he responsible? Mustn't one try to encourage him to change, which surely his soul desires?"

"And he's so handsome!" Margaret smiled.

"I understand what Mary means," I replied. "It's Margaret I'm not sure about. It's certainly our duty to help the unfortunate overcome their vices, but to do so he must want to, which is not quite so certain. . . . It's a delusion to believe that alcohol and opium are the sources of genius! Does Chesterfield become inebriated? Does he drug himself?"

"Chesterfield's a good writer," Margaret said, "but he's not a genius. Just read this manuscript and you'll see we're in the presence of something that goes quite beyond other works, an overpowering book, one of those that changes everything, like an earthquake!"

I was quite taken aback by Miss Warner's exaltation. And then I began to wonder if this Charlienko wasn't perhaps her lover.

"Forgive me," I interrupted, "but where does Leonid get the money for his drugs?"

"He has friends," Margaret replied swiftly, albeit a trifle uneasily. "Friends who are passionate about his writing and who help him out."

It was mad, but such was the logic of the blond and distinguished publisher's daughter! I could easily imagine Margaret playing the prostitute and donating her ill-gotten gains to her charming friend so he could buy himself drugs! Anxious to resolve the confusion, I asked Mary if, in the absence of Douglas, she would mind getting us some tea and cake, which she was happy to do.

"That's a good little woman you have there," Margaret said the minute Mary had gone off to the kitchen.

"Don't mock me, Margaret. Talent and genius do not lie where you think they do. As for Leonid, are you the one who supports his habit?"

"Of course. And I reap certain compensations from it. Also, to spare you the task of tailing me, I'll also tell you he's sometimes my lover. Now, are you satisfied?"

I blushed, which she did not, of course, fail to notice.

"Poor little Cyril, you're so terribly bourgeois. So timid. So buried in the crabbed morality of the shopkeeper. Have you never understood anything at all about Jonathan? He's like Leonid. They're both seeking their own destruction. In a certain way, his son's death and his wife's insanity satisfy his taste for perdition. . . ."

"Shut up!" I said sharply. "What you're saying isn't only cruel, it's absurd. Jonathan loved Yehudi and he loves Sarah. And more than that, he needed them to find the real purpose of his existence. His only error was his failure to understand that. He ruined everything because of his devotion to a certain notion he had of success, which he only wanted in order to use it to fight something that went far beyond him—leprosy, Nazism . . ."

"The Archangel Michael! Saint George versus the dragon! You're raving mad, Cyril. Can't you understand that he offers himself to death like Prometheus to the vulture?"

Mary returned at just that moment, bearing the tea tray before her. Immediately the room filled with a delicious aroma, a mixture of toast, marmalade, and Darjeeling. How much more substance there was in this simplicity than in all of Margaret's elucubrations! However could I have fallen, even for a moment, into the trap laid by her frigid beauty? Was it the physical attraction of that undeniably elegant body so impossibly sired by a deformed father? Was her father's apparent monstrosity hidden in the folds of Margaret's soul, while her perfect exterior appeared in the disguise of perfect virtue? This reversal had the same disquieting charm of those gorgeous flowers that one later discovers to be venomous, or carnivorous, or foul smelling. Fearsome they may well be, but one simply cannot avoid their fascination.

"Tell me more about your Leonid," Mary said, as she poured tea.

"What more can I tell you? He plays the piano and the violin; he speaks three or four languages; he's a marvelous magician. It's so sad to see him deprived of the fame he deserves just because of Babydoor. He's really a sort of Christ, you know."

"I'll read the manuscript," I said, irritated. "But can't you give me a brief outline?"

"Of course. It's the story of a man blessed with every grace and talent. No one can resist him; he goes through life conquering and seducing, accumulating fortune and glory. Everyone he loves is struck by the fact of his success, and by the fact that his success brings him no happiness. He's a Faust without a Mephistopheles, unless of course he's his own demon. His name is Robiev and he lives in Petrograd."

"We're all our own demons," Mary said. "Anyway, your young man drinks so much you can't blame his situation entirely on other people! Is there really a time when one's own will is annihilated and thus one's responsibility vanishes? I don't think so. That would really be too easy."

"Leonid drinks and takes drugs the way other people commit suicide," Margaret replied.

"One does not desire to commit suicide out of a fear of death," I replied. "For people who despair of life, everything and everyone begins to reek of death. Nature too. It becomes just as dead as everything else. There's no place to hide, no escape, no refuge! And in this reversed world, death seems the only cure for death. Although once you're dead, do you still consider yourself dead? After all, death is an idea of the living."

Margaret seemed rather taken aback, but continued.

"Robiev ends by seeing that his powers of seduction damn everyone he touches. Leonid thought of calling the book *The Evil Eye*, but that's too trite, don't you think? And you know why everyone he touches is doomed? Because his touch changes them into objects. They go from a mode of being to a mode of possession; they become things. In the end, the great magician plays to an audience of statues."

"Does he commit suicide too?" I asked.

"No," Margaret sighed. "He's too exhausted even to think about it. He's saved by irony; the truth is life's just a parody of itself."

"Well," said Mary, after an uncomfortable silence, "that doesn't sound very amusing. Alcoholics see ugliness everywhere they look. One shouldn't be surprised by their nausea."

"Sounds like a lot of other stories to me," I said. "The only themes the Western world knows are Faust and Don Juan, antidotes for Saint Anthony. With Don Quixote and Hamlet as variations. That's the history of Utopia in a nutshell. Outside the seraglio, there's only psychology."

"Is psychology so hateful then?" Margaret asked.

"It is in life and in novels when it tries to pass for something it isn't. It's quite faddish—a serious fad, of course—to be infatuated with Dr. Freud; there's no explaining anything anymore except by breasts and sex. Psychology is quite mechanistic, but that's true of our age in general. Everything's explained by 'phenomena.' Our philosophers have become plumbers who keep attaching one concept to another like a series of pipes. Our thoughts are dominated by a vague and shapeless determinism, but contrary to what Calvin thought, we're not being determined into salvation but into the absurd, which is after all just a modern form of damnation. It's scarcely surprising there are all these aimless seducers, these Fausts who have no passion for knowledge, people like your Leonid with his drugs. With all our systems and structures fallen to pieces around him, Jonathan seems to me to be trying to manipulate the absurd in order to accommodate goodness. And if the absurd is winning, it's because goodness isn't always made for happiness, but for order."

"Dear adorable Cyril," Margaret said with a vague shrug, "whatever are you going to think up next? Jonathan's forays into literature and action were simply the reflexes of a drowning man. Whether you're telling stories or building a hospital for lepers, it's nothing but a lie. Order and goodness are alibis. In the face of chaos, isn't the self the only recourse? What are all those proper religions that assure you happiness comes from the dissolution of the self? No more than a perverted kind of suicide, that's what!"

"If I understand you," Mary said, "everything's suicide! One becomes involved in the world out of suicide. And one retires from the world out of suicide."

"Because the world itself is suicide. Haven't you ever heard of the Fall?"

"Not in quite that way," Mary replied.

"In the face of the world's permanent suicide," Margaret said, "all that's left is the self, a self ennobled by flagellation."

"And what does that mean?" I asked with obvious irony. Margaret looked at me sadly, but rose to the challenge.

"Whips and tears, my dear Cyril, whips and tears! Isn't that the way men and women seduced by God treat themselves? Remember the ecstasy of Saint Teresa, the angel that shoots her with an arrow. It's not simply the arrow of love; that's just another metaphor. No, it's really suffering transformed into sensual delight, ecstasy held in suspense at the moment of denouement, an ecstasy which is a stripping bare, a complete divestiture, a total abandonment to the abyss!"

"Another suicide," said Mary.

"On the contrary," cried our mystic. "But how did I get off into this subject?" She laughed. "Just read *The Ungodly* and you'll see. . . ."

Once back in London, I reviewed the accounts for my apartment buildings and the Chester, then went back to work on *The Man Without a Face*. In short, I forgot all about Leonid and his manuscript. And then, one evening—perhaps a month after our conversation with Miss Warner—Mary knocked at the door of my study.

"Forgive me for disturbing you," she said, "but I've just finished reading the manuscript Margaret left with us. You know, the book by that Russian who drinks so much . . . Well, you must read it. It's terrifying but quite beautiful, I think."

"Well, well, you've reminded me of my obligations, haven't you? I suppose I just lost the Russian somewhere in my memory, which as you know is an absolute muddle. Is it really as interesting as all that?"

"Listen, I know Jonathan's your friend and I know you really can't compare two different writers, especially when one's famous and the other's unknown. But I can't tell you how much I prefer Charlienko's style, and in a way his passion, to Chesterfield's, which is really too stylish for my taste."

The "stylish" was like a knife in my heart.

"Stylish!" I exclaimed. "What do you mean, stylish?"

The anger in my voice surprised her.

"Too stylish . . ." she stammered, "too literary perhaps. A little hollow . . . How can I say it? With Charlienko, you feel life and suffering and experience. . . . Jonathan's work is a little too fabricated, too contrived, don't you think?"

"Listen," I retorted, "I've no idea what you know about literature—you probably prefer Blancket to Shakespeare—but to say that Chesterfield's stylish, hollow, contrived! You can't mean it!"

Surprised by my outburst, Mary nonetheless carried on.

"If Chesterfield's stories are so popular with the public, it's because there's a facileness about them. An easiness. I admit Charlienko's novel is less accessible, but perhaps that's the price one pays for profundity?"

I fell silent, and my dear wife had no idea why I spent an entire week sulking. In the end, however, my curiosity got the better of me and in an execrable humor, as my reader can easily imagine, I opened *The Ungodly*. Was it well written? Or wasn't it? Despite my bad faith, I was quite fascinated. The main character, Robiev—a drinker, a cheat, a prof-

ligate with both sexes—manipulated reality like a puppeteer, bending it
to his will, turning everything he touched to gold. What a superb liar he
was, and how much more real his lies than the wretched reality into
which St. Petersburg was rapidly sinking! How to blame him for being
so far from the norm? His wife drowns herself, his mother is poisoned,
his two sisters are sent to Siberia. The people adore him, the aristocrats
envy him, the bureaucrats torment him. And the more people want
to force him into reality, the more he invents. He's like a display
of fireworks that lights up all of an old Russia devoured by its phantoms!

"So?" said Mary.

"Yes, indeed," I grumbled. "But what's the good of comparing two
writers as different as Chesterfield and this Charlienko?"

"You're right," said Mary. "Anyway I know, you're a faithful friend.
Well, perhaps the tragedy Jonathan's just got through will sharpen
his pen."

I wrote to Miss Warner to tell her how much I'd enjoyed her protégé's
work, promising to have Chesterfield read it when the opportunity arose—
something that seemed to me fairly unlikely. In response, it was Leonid
who paid us an unannounced visit. It was a Monday, just as I was about
to leave for the Chester to unravel a difficult carpet-sweeper problem, if
I remember correctly. The doorbell rang and Felicia, who was helping
Mary with her mending, went to answer it. To my infinite displeasure,
it was Charlienko who entered, dressed like a beggar but with a certain
irksome distinction. I was sure he'd spent long hours before the looking-
glass carefully mussing his hair, and that the sailor's sweater under his
jacket had come straight from Harrods.

"Forgive the intrusion," he said, brushing past Felicia, "but Margaret's told me how much you liked my novel and I insisted on thanking
you straightaway!" As I seemed in no haste to offer him a seat, he rushed
on. "What a super flat! Does the hotel business make that much? You
do own a hotel, don't you?"

"It's just an investment," I replied irritably.

He, on the other hand, seemed blissfully unaware of the inconve-
nience of his presence. "Wouldn't happen to have a spot to drink, would
you? Once upon a time, I had a great thirst for the infinite which I
managed to reabsorb into a quite mundane inebriation. I may stumble,
but I do not fall." He sat down without waiting for my reply. "The other
day you were with a marvelous young woman," he went on. "Is she

your wife? If so, I congratulate you. One knows the soul of a man by the kind of wife he has. And the little girl who opened the door—is she your maid or your daughter?"

"Charlienko," I began solemnly, deliberately consulting my watch, "I was just about to leave. I must ask you to be good enough to tell me the reason for your visit."

He seemed shocked.

"Good heavens, am I disturbing you, Mr. Charmer-Maker?"

"I have a meeting, that's all. What can I do for you?"

At that moment, Mary entered the foyer; Charlienko leaped to his feet, bent double, and cried, "Oh, the lovely lady! I recognize you! You were with Mr. Charmer-Maker the other day when you came to my father's former residence. Would you be his wife perchance?"

"I would indeed," Mary replied, delighted. "And I must tell you, Mr. Leonid, how extraordinary your novel is. There's just no other word for it. Extraordinary! Robiev is a fascinating character. Does he resemble you, Mr. Leonid?"

"I daresay I'm not the one to ask," he simpered. "But tell me, dear madam, are you familiar with Russia?"

"No, and I regret it, because if it's anything like your novel, it must be fascinating!"

"Oh, it is, it is," he sighed. "but now it's in the hands of those Bolsheviks and it's a mere shadow of its former self. The countryside's become every bit as lugubrious as the people. And God knows we knew how to have a good time, to drink, to sing! But now, all is silent." He turned to me. "But please, please, don't go out of your way for me, sir. You were just about to leave, you said? Well, then, off you go. I'll just keep Mrs. Charmer-Maker company."

"Mrs. Charmer-Maker, I regret, is obliged to accompany me."

He smiled and turned back to Mary.

"How nice to have a jealous husband! What better proof of love? Well then, very good. I shall be off. I thought I might stay and chat for a bit, but that's the way it is. *Au revoir*, then. And thanks!" He made his own way into the hall, found the door, and left.

"You've upset him," Mary said.

"It's he who's upset me. I was just about to leave and it really wouldn't be proper for you to stay alone with him."

"And with Felicia. Don't you trust me?"

"He's the one I don't trust. His Robiev is too lifelike not to be autobiographical. I'm afraid he'll convince you the moon's made of green cheese!"

"You're quite right," Mary laughed. "I liked his book and I liked talking to him about it. Although I wonder if one can talk reasonably about anything at all with a Charlienko."

I took up my hat and cane and left. Our flat was not even a mile from the hotel and I enjoyed covering the distance on foot when the weather was fair. I was just about to walk up Piccadilly when, like a demonic jack-in-the-box, who should leap out at me from behind a carriage entrance but Leonid Charlienko!

"You startled me!" I confessed, tight-lipped.

He laughed.

"I only wanted to know if you'd told the truth. That's why I waited for you. And indeed you have gone out, it's true. But it's not true that your wife had to go with you."

"What does it matter?" I retorted, continuing my walk.

"Ho ho! You can't get rid of me that easily! It's one thing to choose not to see a beggar with his hand out along the roadside, but I'm not a beggar."

"Indeed," I replied, still walking. "For starters, you're even a decent writer. A few trifles here and there that could stand correcting perhaps . . ."

"And how would you know that?" he asked, leaping about in front of me like a puppy dog. Then he whirled around and held out his arms, blocking my path.

"Would you mind letting me by?"

"All right, all right," he replied, shrugging. "Just because you were Chesterfield's secretary, you obviously think you've the right to go about handing out diplomas, but writing is not the same as handing out awards, Mr. Innkeeper!"

"Will you please let me pass?" I repeated firmly, taking hold of his arm. He moved aside and curtsied grotesquely while I continued on my way.

"Your wife's nicer than you are!" he continued, trotting along beside me. "Margaret warned me. You're an incorrigible bore, and I feel quite sorry really for that poor Mary!"

"What do you want?" I asked. "Fisticuffs?"

He took a step back.

"Oh, oh! The nasty man is angry! No, no, I just wanted to investigate the quality of your humor. Conclusion: You have none."

We'd reached St. James's Street. "Excuse me," I said, and turned into Parker's, where I usually bought my clothes. The head salesman recognized me immediately and greeted me with the utmost courtesy. Charlienko remained outside. For half an hour, I compared and made choices and talked, hoping my Russian would grow tired and go away. But no, he merely sat down on the curb and waited. Finally, I gave up and left the store.

"Did you buy some lovely ties?" he asked, resuming his place beside me.

"My dear young man," I replied, "there comes a moment when irritation disappears and only indifference remains. I would suggest that you not pursue your little games too far."

"And why not?"

"Because the unpleasantness you will cause me will surpass any interest I may have in your novel and thus you won't be able to count on me to help you in any way."

"My God!" he cried, with fake grandiloquence. "I've ruined my career! I've smothered the embryo in its egg! Alas, poor me!"

"Poor you indeed," I replied calmly. "Margaret was right when she claimed you were addicted to suicide, but I should prefer another word somewhat less serious and which corresponds rather more exactly to your case. You enjoy ruining everything. *Failure* is the word, I believe. An addiction to failure."

"Excellent. You are obviously a first-rate psychologist. Well, then, so be it! Let us fail! Just like our Creator, wouldn't you say? The world's not such a marvelous success either, it seems to me. And you, Mr. Charmer-Maker? Where exactly would you say your successes lie? In your hotel? Your wife? Is that a life I'd want? And your friend Chesterfield with his soporific little stories and all his money and all his fame, hmmmm, tell me? Do I want to be in his shoes?"

We arrived at Regent Street and I stopped.

"Would you please be good enough to stop following me, Mr. Charlienko."

He spread his arms wide and shrugged, as if he hadn't understood a word I'd said.

"And I thought you were going to invite me to tour your palace and treat me to dinner and—why not?—set me up in a room with a well-stocked bar! But no. You simply have no social graces, Mr. Innkeeper. What a shame. . . ." He raised an imaginary hat and left me.

The following morning, as I'd not received the things I'd ordered from Parker's, I telephoned the shop and was told that one of my servants had been around to collect them the day before. On their description, I realized it was another one of Leonid's tricks. Indeed, I received the following note:

Dear sir,

I find your concern quite touching. Moving, actually. I myself should doubtless not have chosen the purple suspenders or the argyle socks or even the long boxer shorts—I tend toward the shorter—but your homage is a comfort to me for it shows me how much you appreciated my work. I am most grateful.

Leonid Charlienko

It was laughable, but I did not find it amusing; instead I called Margaret Warner and told her exactly what I thought of her protégé. Despite her efforts to calm me down, I was not appeased. And then other issues arose that occupied my attention; for example, the news that Chesterfield had decided to return to England. Or rather, in an interview with *The Times*, he announced his intention not to remain in America. "I am a European," he told the interviewer, "and during these tense times, I feel it imperative that I return to my native land. America still does not understand that she's being deceived. When she wakes up, I fear it will be too late for the West."

In point of fact, Jonathan Absalom Varlet did not return until November 1935. Simon Partner had been delighted to assume all administrative responsibilities, and Jonathan returned to us quite naked, if you will. And in a way, purified. After having ignored him somewhat during his American sojourn, the London papers now hailed him with the lavishness of a father welcoming his prodigal son. This time, however, it was not the young successful writer, but a man who had suffered, a witness to a devastated anguished era in which, one way or another, each of us recognized ourselves. If his repeated warnings to Europe had at first been taken lightly, they were now at last being heard. No one quite knew where the real danger would come from, since Hitler's aims were not yet believable; we were all convinced that "this barking dog, this circus entertainer, this master of ceremonies," as *Punch* put it, could easily be kept at a safe distance. After all, weren't our Western democracies strong merely by dint of what they stood for?

I met Jonathan on November 10 at the Chester, where I'd reserved the best suite for him. It was a moving moment.

"Well, here I am, rid of both dolls and ledgers!" he exclaimed as I entered the lobby. "You have here before you, dear Cyril, a new man!"

"What have you done with Sarah?"

His face darkened for an instant.

"As soon as I've bought a house, I shall send for her. Her condition is stable; she lives in the happiest of illusions, with Yehudi and me beside her. There's no particular treatment, you know; she'll be better off at home than in a clinic."

"Don't they think they might cure her eventually?"

"Do you know what you're asking? To be cured means to return to a hideous reality. She'd lose Yehudi a second time."

He was dressed in black, and his blond hair, cut short in the American style, gave his face a harshness tempered only by the sadness in his eyes.

"But what about you and Mary? And the new book? How are you coming along?"

I began to tell him about our life but his mind was clearly elsewhere, his eyes looking at things without seeing them.

"Guess what's happening in Edinburgh," he interrupted suddenly.

"Edinburgh?"

"You do remember my lord?" he replied, amused by my surprise. "He owned Kells Castle between Musselburgh and Hamilton House, in the country near Edinburgh, at the seaside. I went there a few times when I was an adolescent. Well, I've just learned that the heirs have let it fall into rack and ruin, and have put it up for sale. What say you?"

"I'll go with you," I said simply.

And so, on November 13, we boarded the train for Edinburgh. Mary had declined to accompany us, claiming she had an important meeting with the Sisters of the Mountain. It was during this trip that Varlet told me, for the first time, about his birth and abandonment. I can still see him sitting in the compartment we'd reserved so as not to be bothered with strangers, the curtains drawn tight, for indeed it was just about impossible for him to go out without being recognized and besieged with condolences.

"Despite all the affection I feel around me, I can't stop thinking about the horror this world is capable of. In Uganda, Mwanda's supporters started a riot at the main prison in Masindi, then took advantage of it to rescue their chief. About ten government soldiers were killed, so the governor immediately ordered reprisals in the neighboring villages. People say hundreds were slaughtered . . . and all because of the hospital I built to care for lepers! The lepers don't come; they obey their chief. Instead, we have piles of cadavers. Innocent people. Am I responsible?"

"It's all politics," I replied. "Everything is. Now that's probably an observation very much of our time—everything's a function of everything else. Humanity's become so much more universal, I suppose. And yet the more universal we become, the more fragmented we are. Our parents' dream of universal unity is not only impossible, but absurd! There're just too many disparities—in economics, customs, ideologies . . ."

"There was a line in my lord's letters, a line that sums up the modern world quite well I think. 'As the spiritual gives way to the material, so does the psychic replace the spiritual.' The psychic is dispersive; perhaps it gives the illusion of unity but it's an equality based on the lowest common denominator, in the quagmire where humors and interests wage war with one another and where they end by destroying the very thing that should bring them together. Look at my lord's heirs, his nieces and nephews, whose frantic lust for possessions has brought them to the verge of mutual destruction. And now they've lost everything!"

"Forgive me," I interrupted, "but you've always been so very discreet about these heirs, and about everything connected with your childhood. I don't wish to be a nuisance, you know, but it's all really quite mysterious."

"And not yet completely cleared up." He smiled. "Well, I don't suppose it makes sense any longer not to tell you. Only you must promise never to reveal what I say to anyone—until after my death, that is. At which point I suppose you'll make a novel of it. . . ."

I promised.

"**W**HAT I'M ABOUT TO TELL YOU, MY dear Cyril, was told to me in fragments, and I'm still not entirely sure I understand their meaning. It's not unusual that I must wait for someone to unveil another piece of my past to clarify an episode I've grasped only superficially. Frankly, I believed I'd come from nothing and that if my lord had found me, it was only by the grace of God, or by pure chance. Were my parents working class? Peasants? Or did they belong to the bourgeoisie? I didn't know, and I thought I never would. I'd been told how cavalierly unwanted children were given to orphanages in the early years of the century. They were like turnstiles, these orphanages; you put the child in, whirled it once around, and presto—the child disappeared forever from a world that had rejected it, and reappeared on the other side in a world that, willingly or no, was obliged to receive it.

"That image haunted me for a long time. During the night, I'd have visions of strangers dropping me into revolving wooden doors and slowly turning them around and around. I'd reach out and try to hold on to the sides of the door to stop it, but my fingers would get caught and finally, terrified and in agony, I'd let go. The turnstile sounded exactly like the trapdoor that opens up underneath a hanged man. I would turn and turn in the darkness, and when I got to the other side, a big red hairy face with protruding eyes would be staring at me. It was always the same, the same hideous dream, as if I were being ripped out of myself and thrown into the jaws of a hostile world. Sometimes there'd be organ grinder's music, but more often it was the sound of bagpipes, always the same sound, like a funeral march. And I'd be sitting on a wooden horse on a merry-go-round and I'd want to get off but there was always a strap keeping me in the saddle.

"My lord took me in when I was six; before that, I lived on a farm in Dumfries. As far as I can remember, they were hardworking honest people who used me as a domestic, but who also kept a sharp eye on the semblance of education the local pastor attempted to inculcate in their other children. Basically, they allowed me to gather up the crumbs, which is how I learned to read and write while the others, who were terribly lazy, stagnated in blissful ignorance. They were called Starkley, these farmers. They had three dogs, including one called Garich who was my friend, a sort of griffon with long black hair. What else can I tell you about those years? I was neither happy nor unhappy. I just felt as if I were marking time. Waiting.

"Then one gorgeous sunny afternoon, a carriage stopped in front of the house and I was told to put on my Sunday clothes. I knew nothing of the change that had been planned, and thought I'd be coming back at night. The father, Starkley, was dressed in his Sunday best too, and he came with me, but didn't utter a single word during the ride. Two hours later, we arrived at Dalbeattie, where my lord owned an estate called Threave Castle which had been built in the fourteenth century by one Archibald, the lord of Galloway. It was a ruin, surrounded by a lake, that generations of people had tried to rebuild but that kept crumbling. At that time, they all lived in an immense and quite bourgeois house at the far end of the grounds. When I climbed down from the carriage, I'd no idea how much my life would be changed by that day— I'll never forget it—the eleventh of June, 1912.

"Afterward, everything was like a fairy tale. Lord Ambergris, whose real name was John, earl of Sheffield, treated me as if I were his son, although without legally adopting me. But you know all that. All I can add is that we mostly lived in Blenheim Palace, in Oxfordshire, just north of Woodstock, and one of the most beautiful estates in all of England. Very baroque it was, too, designed by Sir John Vanbrugh and built between 1705 and 1716. Queen Anne gave it to the first duke of Marlborough, out of gratitude for his having defeated Louis XIV; it was—

and still is—surrounded by French gardens dotted with sumptuous fountains. In short, I'd been spirited away so suddenly from a modest farm in Dumfries and deposited in the lavish elegance of Blenheim that for quite some time I couldn't believe my good fortune, although as I grew older I became very much the prince in his golden castle.

"Later, when I turned sixteen, I told my lord of my perplexity. He evaded my questions, saying only that during one of his visits to his Dumfries properties he'd been struck by my small person and, upon learning that I was an orphan, had resolved to take me in and treat me as his son. I didn't really believe him, and began to think that I really *was* his son by some illicit liaison, and that this was his way of compensating me for his negligence. When he died, I expected there'd be some sort of explanation in his will, but there wasn't. In fact, there was nothing at all in his will and, as you know, the clauses naming me among his heirs were contested—on the one hand I hadn't been legally adopted, and on the other there was no proof that I was, as they say, 'a bastard acknowledged by his father.'

"Blenheim Palace remained, then, in the hands of Marlborough's descendants, the Spencers. In fact, Harold Spencer, the former Conservative prime minister, was born there. Threave Castle, Kells, and Murgrave eventually passed to my lord's grandnephews who lived in America, which meant there was nothing left for me. I believed, then, that my lord had made his will without suspecting that my legal position would give me no rights at all. And that seemed to me passing strange. I went to see his attorney to make sure there was no other will, and asked him if he knew why my lord had never legally adopted me. 'I've no idea,' he told me. 'But I often asked the earl that very question and he always replied, 'I can't. I know who his father is, and he would never permit it!' Ah, Cyril, you can't imagine how that shocked me. My lord wasn't my father, as I'd thought, but he knew who was, and my father was clearly a very important person since the earl of Sheffield couldn't adopt me without his authorization! Imagine the wild fantasies a revelation like that can produce in an adolescent! I saw myself as the bastard son of a prince, although at the time I was homeless and struggling with problems far less lyrical and more urgent!

"Counselor Pizzi—you remember, the man we went to see in Venice—confirmed the fact that Lord Ambergris used that name when he went abroad in order to facilitate relationships with all sorts of people without anyone knowing they were dealing with the earl of Sheffield. In addition, no one had ever learned the identity of the child who used to accompany him sometimes and whom he called Jonathan. There was a rumor that I was the son of Ambergris's sister, who'd had an affair with one of the sons of Gerald Spencer, the former chancellor of the Exchequer, but Pizzi said he could never find out for certain.

"The earl of Sheffield's last visit to Venice, a few months before he died, was in June of 1929. He had a long conversation with Pizzi about their mutual research on topics like the relationship of Christ to the Essenes and the Zealots. And then the talk turned to me. Obviously, the counselor had inquired about me out of sheer politeness, but my lord, knowing perhaps his end was near, said, 'I'm so terribly worried about the child. I can't adopt him, and if something happens to me, I fear that despite my will, his inheritance will be taken away from him.' 'Why is it that you can't adopt him?' Pizzi asked. 'Because he's the heir of a most illustrious man, and if I adopt him, he'll lose his right to that title.' 'Well then,' the counselor replied, 'leave him something while you're still alive. But—and you must forgive me my curiosity—whose son is Jonathan really?' My lord apparently became upset, and Pizzi dropped the subject.

"When I became famous under the name of Chesterfield, it nonetheless took quite some time for the person who knew the secret of my birth to realize that Chesterfield was Varlet's pseudonym. This person asked me to come and see him when I arrived back from New York. During my first return visit to London, he received me most cordially. Yes, you've guessed, I'm sure. We're talking about His Majesty. I assumed he simply wanted to congratulate me for my literary works, and for the leprosarium, but no. You can imagine my shock when George V asked me to forgive him but that it was a question of state security! He made various allusions to my past, but I didn't understand them because he was careful to conceal the most essential piece of information. In any case, I left that meeting convinced I was the product of an illicit union between some illustrious personage and an inappropriate woman. After all, why else would they want to get rid of me if not to avoid the scandal?

"And now you're going to laugh. . . . After that I began collecting photographs of the males in the royal family, going back quite some time, to see if I could find a resemblance between me and my sire. Doubtless my mother's lineage was stronger because I didn't seem to belong physically to the descendants of Victoria and Edward! Of course, I might be connected by a daughter and not a son to the people who cast me aside and with whom I felt no particular affinity. But more than that, there was something grotesque about my feeling that I was an aristocrat when I was really a turnstile child! What right did I have to associate myself with princes to whom I was probably nothing more than a moment's indiscretion? And how much closer I felt to my lord, to whom, I now understood, these eminent souls had given me to appease their remorse!

"I wrote the king and told him that Chesterfield cared nothing about his past and would keep the little he knew of his lineage a secret. In the same letter, I begged His Majesty to deign to hasten Sarah's naturalization papers. Which is how we were able to marry a few days before Yehudi was born, and it was thanks to this marriage that I was at last able to break the ties that bound me to the illusory father and the improbable mother who'd conceived me in error. On the other hand, however, I'd no reason to assume it had been an error. Perhaps I was nobody's error. But then, who was I? And here, my dear Cyril, you must understand just how much your appearance in Glendurgan saved me from my predicament. I was looking for a name and you offered me not only a name but a character. I was empty and you filled me. The abandoned puppet suddenly finds a life, a soul, and a corpus of work! It was a blessing.

"And so I believed I could worm my way into someone else's life and soul. And into your work. But Chesterfield wasn't real; all I'd done was cloak myself in an illusion. My life began to get away from me; it began to ferment and multiply like flies in sugar. No, I wasn't an artist, I was a businessman, a publicist, but even that success wasn't mine. I'd usurped it by using your talent. And what was I myself capable of producing? Rubber dolls who aped your characters and who only forced me to confront my own flimsiness. Then I threw myself into good works, but that too was only another gesture, another illusion. I became the vendor of leprous phantoms, the patron of an illustrious crusade which ended in the Masindi massacre! My fame was hollow. I wanted to populate it with heroic combats against dragons, but all that appeared were a few pathetic ghosts.

"There was a price to pay, but other people were paying it for me. The more important people thought I was, the more I sank into insignificance. I was just the plaything of an idiot. And then came the hour of truth, when the game turned bitter and the Nazis took me at my word because they too thought they had the secret of an idea of man that

surpassed the human. Yehudi might have been the beginning of a new
humanity, the beginning of a tenuous reconquest of the human, but the
helmeted guardians of order spirited him away and Sarah, in whom I
saw my soul, lost her mind. Thus, here I am, much like your man without a face, more alone than ever because the hopes and beliefs that so
many had in me have faltered."

He fell silent and I wondered what we were doing in this compartment with the drawn curtains, and what we were looking for in Scotland. Withal, we arrived in Edinburgh at four o'clock and drove along
the coast through Musselburgh, then left the main road until we reached
Kells Castle. Austere and bristling with the cries of gulls, its massive
majestic flanks and square tower loomed over the sea; under a gray sky,
it was altogether formidable, this ancient fortress erected against the
invasions of barbarians, which had itself become barbarous. When Varlet first mentioned it to me, he'd called it "a jewel." That wasn't quite
the epithet I should have chosen for this rugged and rather gloomy edifice, but I was in for a surprise.

The moment the car came to a stop in the courtyard, an astonishing
personage appeared. With his beard and great shock of red hair, his kilt
and wool socks, and a tam with a pompon perched upon his enormous
height, he looked like a character straight out of folk legend. Throwing
open the car door, he snapped to attention with a click of his heels,
raised his chin, and declared, "Allan Fergusson, at your service, your
lordship!" Jonathan got out of the car and held out his hand. "Glad to
meet you, Fergusson . . ." They shook hands for a long time, the Scotsman, gaunt as an old dog, grinning from ear to ear, and Varlet not quite
knowing what to think.

"Mr. Fergusson is the sellers' agent," he explained to me. "But then,
I'm not clear as to who the sellers are exactly," he said, turning back to
Fergusson.

"The city of Edinburgh," the old dog replied in a stentorian staccato.
"As the previous owners couldna pay their taxes, the city can sell the
property as best it can. And do I have to tell your lordship that this is
the first time there's been this sort of a scandal in this honorable house?
Why, just ten years ago, it still belonged to the earl of Sheffield!"

We entered the house through an immense door topped with a coat
of arms attributed to Malcolm III, "of silver the castle with three towers
of sable, crenellated and covered and faced in silver." The interior was
a complete surprise, for while the outside was crude and dark, the inside

was exquisitely delicate. Aubusson tapestries covered the walls, the furniture was pure Renaissance Spanish, and although the ensemble might have been pretentious in another context, here each armchair, table, and objet d'art was so charmingly arranged as to convey a taste for modesty and order, echoing the Sheffield motto: "War Outside, Peace Within," inscribed over the mantelpiece in the main drawing room.

"It appears that in the masculine world of your childhood," I said, "there was also the hand of a woman."

"True." Jonathan nodded. "My lord lost his wife a few months after they were married and out of loyalty to her memory he never remarried. On the other hand, he had a close relationship with a young woman named Dorothy Temple, whom he brought here to live. This was her home, and she never left it. When she died, in 1928, she was buried on the grounds; I'll show you her tomb in a bit."

"Gentlemen," Fergusson began, with that voice particular to museum guides, "you see before you a fireplace bearing the motto of the Sheffields, who were long the owners of this estate. At the death of the last earl, who had no descendants, the estate passed to the Dumbees, an American family descended from the collateral branch of the Sheffields. The Dumbees have never been here; in fact they've never been to Scotland at all. The castle was a sort of investment for them, and finally, for a commission, the city of Edinburgh decided to sell Kells in order to remedy the absentee-landlord situation. And now, begging your permission, your lordship, I think I'll not say another word on this subject."

"As you like," Varlet replied. Then, turning to me, "I bought the toy company in New York from the Dumbee family. So that they wouldn't mortgage the castle."

"Goodness, you did pursue them with a vengeance, didn't you?"

"Let's not exaggerate. I was simply twice as powerful as they, that's all."

"Did they know who was hiding behind the name of Chesterfield?"

"Of course. Dear Peter, John, and Philip . . . At first they all hoped that the famous writer was only a look-alike of the pathetic little Jonathan Absalom Varlet . . . quite a ridiculous error, no? Very novelistic actually. The eldest, Peter, got down on his knees to me; Philip offered me his wife. Despicable people. Partner gave them their just desserts."

"And now you're going to buy Kells?"

"I sincerely hope so! . . . My dear Mr. Fergusson, please don't bother about us. I knew this house well, once. I lived here as a child."

"How is that, sir?" the old dog replied, clicking his heels. "You, your lordship? Was there a Chesterfield family here?"

"No, but there was a young boy, Lord Ambergris's favorite, who spent some wonderful holidays here."

Speechless, Fergusson shook his great mane of red hair vigorously; clearly Jonathan's statement surpassed his intellectual abilities.

"There's a spiral staircase in the rear. Back there," said Varlet.

"A spiral staircase?" the Scotsman echoed. "No, your lordship. Permit me to suggest that you're confused—but no."

"On the contrary." Jonathan crossed the room to the rear wall, which was lined floor to ceiling with bookcases. "This is where I read Shakespeare for the first time. And Milton." Instinctively, his fingers found the Oxford edition of *Paradise Lost.* "And here's the *Theatrum Chemicum,* 1602, in three volumes, with John Dee's *Monas Hieroglyphica.* The marvelous John Dee who became the confidant of Elizabeth I and Rudolph II of Prague. You can't imagine how much I dreamed about him. He was one of my favorite companions. What a lot of prestigious works fallen into the hands of riffraff who, thank God, never knew what a treasure they had!"

"There's still no spiral staircase," the Scotsman insisted.

"Fergusson," Varlet said, "you're an honorable man. A war veteran. You must swear never to tell anyone what I'm about to show you."

Fergusson nodded, clearly ready to promise whatever Varlet wished.

"Watch," Jonathan said. He reached behind the books on a certain shelf, the entire panel pivoted with a great creak, and a door appeared. Our friend felt around the lintel and suddenly, as if by magic, the door opened and there was the spiral staircase, just as he'd promised.

"I haven't been here since my lord died. Please, Cyril, do come with me." His face had grown deathly pale.

"I don't know if I can permit you to go up, your lordship," the Scotsman blurted out, petrified.

"It's all right . . ." Varlet murmured, and began slowly to climb the little staircase. I hastened to follow him.

At the top was a small room smelling of mildew and lit by a transom. The spiders had been at work, so that the few pieces of furniture were bound together with fine threads that we had to sweep away in order to get inside.

"That's Dorothy's little desk. She used to sit there and daydream and write in her diary. Sometimes my lord came up here to fetch her, but I didn't know it existed until much later, after her death. My lord made me swear never to tell anyone, but I've thought a lot about it ever since." He brushed aside a cobweb that trailed across the desk and tried to open it, but it was locked. With a sort of urgency, he began looking through the various tins and boxes in hopes of finding the key. I wondered what had given rise to this sudden feverishness; finding the key seemed to be of crucial importance to him.

"Ever since my lord's death, I keep seeing this place in my mind—the library, the staircase, the desk. And now I can't find the key!"

"You must come down, your lordship!" Fergusson's voice echoed up the staircase. "I shouldna ever have let you go up. . . ."

"My god!" Jonathan cried suddenly. "What an idiot I am! I completely missed the meaning of my lord's last words. He was sitting right there, in that armchair facing the flower beds. Night was falling on the lake, tinting it red. It felt like the earth's final hour, as if the entire universe were going to tumble into the abyss at the same moment as this wonderful man. He took my hand in his; I'll never forget the touch of his burning fingers. 'Listen,' he whispered, 'the key's in John's Revelation.'" And then he died. Naturally I thought it was some sort of spiritual advice, but he was talking about the Book of Revelation downstairs, the one in the library! He often showed it to me."

We ran down the staircase and began searching for the book while the old Scotsman looked on, openmouthed. At last, Jonathan found it, bound in black leather, and began leafing through it, but no key fell from between the pages. It was only as he closed the book that he noticed the uncommon thickness of the binding, which he examined closely and then managed to separate from the back of the book. And suddenly there it was, the hiding place, which indeed held a key. Like excited children, we rushed back up into the little room. The key fit perfectly into the desk.

Jonathan had once again turned pale. One after the other, he opened the two drawers, only to find them empty. Between them was a sort of little cubicle with a door, which he opened gingerly. Inside were three other drawers, the first containing a box that held a ring with the family seal. Varlet put it in his pocket. The second contained an envelope marked "For Jonathan." I recognized the handwriting immediately as being that of Lord Ambergris. Varlet uttered a groan, seized the envelope with a trembling hand, stared at it as if hypnotized, then slipped it into the same pocket. The third drawer was empty. He closed the desk and placed the key on top, after which we descended the stairs in silence.

My heart was pounding. So the earl's letter had remained locked in this drawer for all these many years without the one to whom it was addressed knowing anything about it! I was sure it held the answer to the enigma of my friend's birth. The library panel pivoted back into its usual place against the wall and we continued our visit, but my impatience was so great that I am unable, today, to describe the innumerable rooms we saw. Jonathan seemed in a daze, and I was surprised at how little haste he showed in opening the letter. Finally we reached the immense kitchens with their two fireplaces, full battery of copper pots and pans, and fabulous sideboards, which held magnificent collections of stoneware.

"This is where I really lived," said Varlet. "I used to stretch out on a sheepskin before the hearth and read for hours while the smell of roast meat tickled my nostrils. For me, reading will forever mean wood fires and the aroma of great roasts; my favorite books are always the ones that return me to that time."

Leaving the kitchens, we followed a lovely path bordered in boxwood to a towering oak tree at the far end, under which lay a moss-covered stone slab—the resting place of Dorothy Temple, who had loved Lord Ambergris. Fergusson had remained at a discreet distance, seeming to understand that our visit had become a sort of pilgrimage. Jonathan sat down on a stone bench and pulled the envelope from his pocket. I wandered off, desirous of leaving him alone with this significant moment. A path led me to the edge of the ocean where I stood and waited, prey to a dizziness easily explainable by the circumstances. Were the lives we led insane or reasonable? I could not have said, for our reality seemed woven with such irregularity and on such an inelastic frame.

At length, I grew worried and walked back to the tree, where I found Jonathan still seated on the bench in the same pensive posture. He'd clearly opened the envelope, which now lay on the seat beside him, and read the letter inside, but when he heard my footsteps, he raised his head and looked at me with a sort of surprise. Suddenly, he began to laugh.

"Ah, my dear Cyril, life is so comical, so incredibly comical! There's simply no other word for it. And our pretentions are so laughable!" He held out the letter to me. "See for yourself." Then he stood up and went

to pay homage to Dorothy's grave. I sat down in his place and read the
following:

Dear Jonathan,

When you find this letter, I shall have left you. I think it indispensable, however, that you know who you are, even though the
facts of your birth ought not to be revealed to anyone. In doing
what I am about to do, I perjure my oath, but I remain loyal to the
affection I have always felt for you. Here, then, is the truth I
owe you.

On May 20, 1912, I received a visit from my cousin, Harold
Spencer, who was then with the Admiralty. He told me that a son
of his had been born to a young girl he'd loved very much, a girl
named Dorothy Temple. The affair had been kept secret, particularly because Dorothy's mother, an irascible and puritanical woman,
had given the child, at birth, to the Cheltenham Orphanage, under
the name of Jonathan Absalom Varlet. Whence came this preposterous name? From Jonathan, David's friend, killed during the battle of Gilboa about which the king sang? Absalom, the son of this
same David, killed by Joab because he'd betrayed their father? *Varlet*,
an old French word one gave to young noblemen apprenticed to a
lord to learn the art of chivalry? In any case, a strange name dreamed
up by a fanatic of the Bible to atone for a sin she did not want to
pardon!

Withal, when Spencer learned that you'd been taken away from
your mother, he desired to find you out, but was unsuccessful until,
on her deathbed, this stubborn old woman, feeling some remorse
perhaps, confessed to her daughter where she had hidden you. This
was in May of 1912, the date on which my cousin begged me to
take you in and raise you, for his high office did not allow him to
divulge something that his political enemies would immediately exploit, thus ruining his career. At the same time, he asked me to
take care of Dorothy Temple, with the understanding that she was
never to tell you her secret lest you boast of it in public. I was not
supposed to allow you to meet Dorothy, and if I did so, it was only
in response to her ardent requests, for by this time a deep friendship had developed between us. Faithful to her word, she never
once betrayed who she was; it was her deepest joy merely to watch
you grow up.

Thus are you Jonathan Absalom Varlet, descended directly from the Marlboroughs. This is the reason I could never adopt you, for it would have deprived you of your real father's ultimate recognition if, one day, he should so consent. I am sure you will have the wisdom not to reveal to him what you now know, for such an avowal would ruin you forever in his eyes. A powerful statesman whose influence, God willing, will continue to grow, your father would never believe that I might have betrayed him, and will thus hold you responsible for the treason. He will deny you, which would be even more tragic than the exile in which he has been obliged to keep you.

His Majesty has been taken into your father's confidence; not so that, in the event of his death, you should assume his name, but so that his legitimate heirs may not be dispossessed of their rights should you decide to claim yours. For you are the eldest, Jonathan, and thus may claim both title and fortune! Have no doubts—His Majesty will support your father and your half brothers against you. Thus, you must be discreet so as not to attract the wrath of our sovereign, who is concerned about the career of one of his best servants. This is the most important demand I wish to make of you and from which I am certain you shall profit.

Finally, in case my legal heirs succeed in annulling the provisions in my will concerning you, I bequeath to you the sum of twenty million pounds, which you will find in your name, account number 623437, in the Bank of Geneva, a sum which will permit you to enter the world in conditions suitable to the education I have given you. May those who, because of circumstance, deny you be forgiven. May you, by your intelligence and your mercy, absolve them. And may the blessing of Our Lord Jesus Christ, risen again, be with you. Amen.

I went up to Jonathan, who stood beside his mother's tomb, seeming to pray, and remained at his side, in silence, for a long moment. His face had grown calm, as if he had found true peace at last.

"I thought that learning my father's name would change my life," he murmured, "but it's learning my mother's that has moved me. Dear Dorothy, who welcomed me here on all those holidays, as if she were only a grown-up friend who cared . . . Each of her gestures, each of her words must have overflowed with affection for me, and yet I never

noticed that her tenderness and kindness were the expressions of a mother!
When she died, so suddenly, I felt as if all the fairies had left my childhood, but I didn't come to the funeral. My lord didn't wish me to, and
now I understand why. He couldn't tell me who that woman really was,
that marvelous woman, the best woman I ever knew!" A sob caught in
his throat and he turned his head, unable to go on.

"Your lordship!" cried the old Scotsman, springing up from behind a
little copse. "I thought I'd lost you! These old grounds—so badly kept
these days, I must say—such a forest they are become. . . . Ah, you're
looking at Miss Dorothy's tomb. A remarkable woman, they tell me.
She's the one who decorated the inside of the castle. Fortunately those
American heirs never came here; they would've turned everything upside down! They have no taste, those people, do they?"

"From now on, my dear Fergusson, I guarantee you I shall take care
of everything," Jonathan Absalom Varlet exclaimed. "I would ask only
that you contact the seller, for I'd like to sign the contract tomorrow!"

Fergusson was stunned.

"But . . . but of course, your lordship. Tomorrow, yes, certainly . . .
But are you sure? I mean have you really thought about it?"

"Yes. Kells is filled with ghosts that are dear to me. For the first time
in my life, they're my ghosts and not someone else's! I've found my
home, Cyril; these are my roots and it is here that I must now plant
myself. I shall bring Sarah." He pulled out the little box he'd taken from
the desk, opened it, and placed the ring he'd taken on the little finger
of his right hand.

Some time later, we returned to Musselburgh and took rooms in an
ancient inn called the Old Salt. The restaurant windows looked out over
the sea, which at that time of year was always choppy, as if it were
angry. We began our meal in silence, served by a corpulent young man
with a bad cough. The lighting was so intimate, or rather so niggardly,
that we could not see the features of our fellow diners. When the fish
course arrived, Jonathan murmured, "Do you remember last year, when
I came here to Kells? It was at the worst moment of my passion for
Rosanna. . . . I was like a ball of yarn that a cat had tangled. I had to
find the thread, the starting point. I wandered about the area for three
days. The castle was closed but I climbed over the wall and spent hours
on the grounds. I didn't know then that Dorothy was my mother, but
now I understand why I was so attracted to that stone slab at the foot
of the old oak tree. At the time, I believed it was the library and all its

treasures that attracted me; after all, in a way the library had been my mother, and in my memory, the one at Kells was like a tender and glamorous refuge. I know I spent long hours reading and studying at Blenheim, but its vastness and grandeur made me uncomfortable. Whereas here, at Kells, I felt at home. And now I know why."

He paused, his face filled with emotion.

"What a lot of courage that woman must have had never to betray her love to me! She knew that if she ever told me the truth, I'd be taken from her forever. She'd promised my lord her silence as long as she could see me at Kells for my holidays. And when she died, she took her secret with her."

"How did she die, in fact?"

"She simply went to sleep one night and never woke up. My lord was so unhappy, he never really got over it. I'm sure my mother's death hastened his own. He's buried in the Sheffield family tomb in Chatsworth, but I'm sure he'd be happier here, next to Dorothy. And you know, since my father doesn't wish to acknowledge me, I'm not going to take the name Spencer but rather a combination of my mother's and my lord's. What do you think of Jonathan Temple Ambergris?"

"Now that suits your perfectly, Mr. Chesterfield." I smiled.

"Must we continue this comedy, Cyril? Now that I've found my real name?"

"But how will you tell the world that you've been playing a joke on it for five years? It will be your ruination . . . and the end of my books!"

He poured us both some wine and then raised his glass.

"To my rebirth!" he cried.

At that moment, a diner who'd been hidden from us in the shadows replied in a slow rasping voice.

"And to your health also, good wayfarers! English, aren't you? Saw you a while ago at the castle. I'm the caretaker, you know . . . even though those Americans haven't paid me so much as a farthing! Ah, my good sirs, the orchard and gardens at Kells, like the Garden of Eden they are, and even Miss Dorothy said that the good Lord had left this little corner of the earth to the angels!"

"You're Crispie, aren't you?" Jonathan said, rising.

"Crispie?" echoed the man in the shadows. "Of course I'm Crispie. But by the devil's horns, who told you that? People call me Cockenzie now."

Jonathan approached his table.

"I recognized your voice, my good Crispie! Don't you know me?"

"Aye, faith!" the good man exclaimed, standing up. "Now wouldn't
you be the little man . . . the earl's Jonathan? Yes, yes, of course it's
you! I didn't see that before. You'd be the only one who'd know Miss
Dorothy used to call me Crispie!"

Old Cockenzie trembled on his splindly legs; the emotion had left him
breathless and he panted as if he'd just come in from a run. He had the
purple face of a beer drinker, deformed by a nervous tic that twisted his
lips and pinched his nostrils. Jonathan held out his hand and he shook
it heartily, all the while repeating, "Can you imagine? If anyone had
told me . . . Can you imagine?"—after which he burst into laughter.

"Well now, so it's bloody Mr. Jonathan! A real fox, that one!
You remember old Gordon? You really did him a turn, all right! Did
we ever have a laugh, Mr. Jonathan! Only you could bring off tricks
like that!"

"Please, do come sit with us, my good Crispie."

"Not on your life, Mr. Jonathan. Sit at the same table as a gentleman?
Never. I'll just stand here, if you don't mind."

"Tell me, Crispie," Jonathan continued, sitting back down at the table, "aside from the fruits and vegetables, how do you manage?"

"Oh, we manage, Mr. Jonathan. It's me what does the cleaning right
here, at the Old Salt, and they give me a bowl of soup at night, and a
beer from time to time. Bah, I'm not complaining. They're good people,
you know. . . ."

Jonathan picked up a glass from the next table, filled it, and handed
it to Crispie.

"Tell me about Miss Dorothy," Varlet said.

"Eh, well . . . you're the one can talk about her better than I, Mr.
Jonathan. You're the one she liked, you know. Loved you like you were
her own. Besides, that's what they used to say in the kitchens. . . .
'Hello, this Mr. Jonathan's got no family and sure enough he's found
one a whole lot better than the louts what deserted him,' that's what
they said in the kitchens. Nobody better than the earl there wasn't, and
he never had a swelled head about it either. Just like Miss Dorothy. Now
that's two that would've made a nice couple!" he added, clucking. "It
was sad we were when Miss Dorothy left us, poor soul. . . . And the
earl, if you'd have seen him the day they buried her . . . Well, the dead
belong to the dead, now don't they? Mustn't disturb the ground, they
say around here." He drained the rest of his glass at one go.

Frédérick Tristan

"I remember Gordon," Jonathan said. "He was the shepherd, wasn't he?"

"Wasn't very smart, that one, was he, begging your pardon, Mr. Jonathan," Crispie laughed. "You told him once, 'Go find the green devil, my good Gordon. . . . That's what you told him, that was, and he, good soul, 'The green devil, Mr. Jonathan? Where's that where I'm going to find a green devil, Mr. Jonathan?' And you, just sharp as a fox, you said, 'At the end of the storm, my good Gordon!' The end of the storm, right, Mr. Jonathan? Now just where'd you find such a thing as that, Mr. Jonathan?" Crispie was laughing so hard he could scarcely breathe, clutching his glass in his hand.

"And what happened?" Jonathan asked.

"What happened? But he went! Yes sir, he just upped and went! He waited for a real good storm and off he took himself to find the end of it. And that night he comes back with his bag empty and he says to you, 'Mr. Jonathan, how do I know when I get to the end of the storm?' And you sat there, all calm and natural, and you said, 'It's not hard, my good Gordon. You look for the beginning. And when you find it, well then you know the end is at the other end!' A real piece of work that was, wasn't it, Mr. Jonathan? Down in the kitchens, we all laughed so hard we were crying. And there was Gordon waiting for another storm, and then off he runs to find the beginning of it! Of course, we were all watching out the window waiting for him to come back. And was it pouring! The rain was coming down in buckets! Anyway, he didn't come back and it was dinnertime. Miss Dorothy had rung and we started to serve and forgot all about poor Gordon. Until the clock struck nine and there he was, looking all burned to a crisp, his face black as soot and his clothes in rags. 'I did it!' he says, 'I found the end! And the devil was there!' All of us in the kitchens, well, we were impressed, I can tell you. . . . And then we finally figured it out. He'd climbed up the top of Duffle Hill and the lightning had struck him! 'I saw the devil!' the poor man kept saying. 'Only he wasn't green, but red!' Afterward, he was always just a little touched, you know. . . ."

"Poor Gordon. I was awfully cruel, I suppose, but he was so gullible. Dorothy gave me quite a scolding, and I deserved it."

"And the hangman!" Crispie said. "You remember the hangman, do you not, Mr. Jonathan?"

"That's a bad memory," Jonathan said, his face darkening. "I'd rather we not talk about it."

"Well then, I drink to your good health!" said the Scotsman, holding out his glass, which Jonathan promptly refilled.

"I wasn't a very good lad," Jonathan said simply. "What saved me was the books. Without them, I would have remained a rather nasty character. Always making fun of things. I remember one evening—I must have been about twelve—when my lord called me into his study. 'Jonathan,' he said to me, 'do you know the difference between an honest man and a good man, an *homme honnête* and an *honnête homme*?' As I didn't answer him, he said, 'An honest man is one who acts according to the law; a good man acts according to his inner spirit. But what is the law? And what is spirit? You don't know that yet, do you? Well, my friend, I'm going to entrust you with a treasure—not the kind people hide in purses, but the kind one keeps in his heart. And that treasure is a book! And in this book there are two characters—Babble and Cattle. Babble does everything properly but he remains a prisoner in his room because he's afraid to open the door. Cattle, on the other hand, opens the door and goes walking in the garden. When he comes back at night, Babble scolds him for going out, but Cattle doesn't answer him, for out in the garden he has learned how to love, to love even those who never leave their rooms. Books are gardens where one learns to understand well and to love well; they're outsides that reveal to us our insides. To read is not to leave ourselves, but rather to know ourselves.' "

"Well said, well said!" Crispie cried. "You need schooling to understand that sort of thing. Blimey, let me be swallowed whole by a whale if I ever heard anything half of a quarter as intelligent as that. He was a very great man, our earl, right, Mr. Jonathan? No sawdust in his brain, now was there?"

We enjoyed his high spirits and the local dialect, and we drank to the memories. Then we said good night to Crispie and went up to bed, exhausted by the trip and the emotions of the long day.

That night I had a strange and terrible dream whose memory has remained with me like an open wound. In the dream, I was seated in the dining room of the Rosemullion Hotel in Glendurgan. My grandmother, Mary Charmer's mother, was playing the violin while Jonathan and I ate our dinner in silence. She wore a hat with a veil that hid her face, but I knew it was she. She stood behind a chair and coaxed from her instrument a sort of lament, much like the crying of a child or the meowing of a cat. At the next table sat my mother and my wife, the two Marys, passing whiskey back and forth between them and drinking straight from the bottle. I was outraged, and wondered if Jonathan had noticed them. At that moment, an enormous bulldog raced into the room and began barking ferociously. The two Marys' table overturned, spilling both women onto the floor. The dog jumped on them, seized one of their hands in his jaws, and tore it off, after which he pranced to the door with great pride, his repulsive trophy dangling from his bloody mouth. Jonathan and I continued to dine in silence, pretending not to notice that anything was amiss. The two Marys calmly stood up, laughingly dusted each other off, and came up to our table, where they said, in unison, "Who has forced us to come back?" "What are they saying?" I asked Jonathan. "Who has forced us to come back?" they repeated. Jonathan continued eating, paying no attention either to them or to me.

Had I left the table? Suddenly I found myself in a long corridor with a stairway at the far end, but the closer I came to it, the more it receded. I felt afraid, then panicked. Both Marys were chasing me and screaming hideously. Why was I so terrified? I finally reached the staircase and began my ascent, but there were hundreds of hundred-dollar bills on the steps and I kept slipping on them, and grabbing onto the banister to keep myself from falling. The bulldog had now joined the two Marys; I could hear his hoarse panting drawing closer and closer. In one last desperate effort, I managed to haul myself up to the top step. Dorothy's room stood open before me and I hurtled inside, smashing through the spiderwebs. My face, my chest, even my hands were covered with cobwebs; I spun around, trying to free myself, but succeeded only in becoming more entangled, suffocating and shouting and endlessly falling into an abyss echoing with laughter.

I came awake and turned on the light; the sight of my humble room calmed me immediately. What had it meant, this dream? I lifted my head from the pillow; someone was knocking at the door.

"Who's there?" I called, uneasy once more.

The door opened and Jonathan entered, a brown dressing gown over his pajamas.

"Sorry to disturb you so late," he said, coming toward me. "You were doubtless fast asleep. . . ."

"It doesn't matter. I'm glad you're here. I've just had a most disagreeable dream."

"I know," he said, sitting down beside me on the bed. "The two women and the dog . . . I was standing just outside the door and heard everything. But now you know what it was all about, don't you?"

I gaped at him.

"No. I don't understand at all, really."

"Remember what the two women were saying." He smiled. "They were asking who'd forced them to come back. Isn't that so?"

"Yes. I think they were referring in some way to an ancient drama, but I don't know the story. And anyway, it has nothing to do with me."

"On the contrary, it has more to do with you than you think! For you yourself, my dear friend . . ."

I felt a vague distress.

"I myself . . ." I echoed.

"Yes, you yourself did not come here by chance. All these people we see, who are they really? Come now, try, please . . . Margaret, Mary, Sarah, Dorothy—don't you recognize them?"

"No," I answered sincerely.

"And Warner and Partner and my lord—yes, even him!—don't you recognize them either? They're all walk-ons, bit players with masks. . . ."

I thought for a moment, trying my best to hide the fear that welled up inside me once again.

"Are you suggesting it was a rehearsal?"

"Yes!" he cried, his arms spread wide. "You've got it! A rehearsal. That's the very word. You, me, the others, we're all in a full-scale rehearsal. In Venice, when you followed Margaret to the Fondamenta Nuove, or in Paradisio where Patricia Steele gamboled about, or even in the peculiar London office of our dear publisher, that exemplary dwarf, didn't you feel how much of a discrepancy there was between your reality and all other realities? Didn't you feel how untrue it rang?"

"I don't know any reality other than my own," I protested. "What exactly are you insinuating?"

"I insinuate nothing! I only affirm it. Do you think you've come here for nothing? You too have a role to play, my dear friend. I'm not saying you play it terribly well, but at least you play it."

I stared at him, speechless.

"Don't you see?" he went on.

I shook my head.

"Well then, I shall have to explain it all to you. Now listen carefully, please."

I readied myself to listen, but then I realized that although he was talking to me, I heard nothing.

"I must hear," I said to myself. "I must understand."

But no matter what I did, I couldn't hear him. I knew that what he was saying would illuminate my whole existence, and that each word lost would never be found again. Desperately, I tried to seize a word here and there by reading his lips, but all my efforts were in vain.

"Stop! Stop!" I cried, filled with anguish. "I can't hear a thing you're saying!"

He began to laugh then, and his voice echoed in the silence.

"We've both returned from our graves, my good friend!"

I shied away from him in horror.

"Yes, yes! This is just a difficult phase we must pass through, but it's such an absurd punishment, no? Condemned to live together forever, you and I! Rather a good joke, isn't it? Remember eight o'clock, March 22, 1784. Eight o'clock, March 22, 1784 . . ."

And then I remembered, I'd killed a man. I, Rudyard Cockenzie. I'd killed a writer named Malthus Ambergris in order to steal his work. My wife's name was Margaret Spencer.

"No!"

"Oh yes, yes . . ." Jonathan insisted.

I flailed against the spiderwebs that wrapped themselves about me like a shroud. I was suffocating, dying. And then I woke up, for real this time, and found Jonathan shaking me.

"You were in such a sound sleep! We'll be late for our appointment with the attorney."

I sat up.

"Do you have a fever? You're perspiring so."

"My god, what a horrible dream! Never in my entire life have I ever had anything like it. . . ."

As I dressed, I slowly regained contact with reality, yet remained fearful of falling once again into the nightmare that had so accurately exploited my terrors. It was the first time a dream had plunged me into an illusion so perfect that I'd taken it for reality, but I was careful to say nothing of it to Jonathan when we met a quarter of an hour later in front of the inn.

"I did a lot of thinking last night," he said, striding purposefully down the street. "Kells shall be the hub of my activities. You know I've turned over everything commercial to Partner, and now Sarah will come, the Sarah who's returned to her childhood. As for you, dear Cyril, you shall have to set about writing a book that coincides with my ideas. What about it?"

"Right now, I'm working on *The Man Without a Face*, with a hero who's continually reborn from century to century. He's quite a bit like you, actually. Not your ideas, of course, but you yourself. Personally, I don't think it's a novelist's job to illustrate ideas."

The air was especially cold and dry, and steam came from our mouths as we spoke. Hands deep in our pockets, we walked, shivering, with our heads drawn down into the collars of our coats. Allan Fergusson was waiting for us at the attorney's office, stamping his feet rhythmically as if dancing to the tune of an imaginary bagpipe.

"Hello there," he called. "I was afraid your lordship had changed his mind during the night. . . ."

The attorney, one Lennox, slightly stooped and wearing both spectacles and hat, received us immediately in a rather typical well-off country attorney's office where all was calm, serious, and blanketed in the appropriate layer of dust.

"It's a great honor to welcome someone as famous as you, Mr. Chesterfield!" he crowed, rubbing his hands in restrained satisfaction. "Fergusson here tells me you used to live at the castle."

"I was called Jonathan Absalom Varlet then," my friend replied, startling the old man, who immediately rose from his desk and took Jonathan's hands in his.

"But my dear Mr. Jonathan, I didn't recognize you! And yet I saw so many pictures of you in the papers. Whyever didn't I make the connection?"

Excited and shaken by his discovery, he begged us to be seated.

"Alas, I read about that terrible business of the kidnapping. So it was your son . . . ?"

"Precisely. And I need a quiet place to bring my wife, a place to shelter her and our sadness. Kells seems perfect."

Lennox immediately assumed his professional demeanor.

"But of course, Mr. Chesterfield. The earl's heirs have neglected their treasure, and it's a great joy to me that you should be in a position to take over, as in the time of Miss Dorothy whom we all remember so fondly."

He picked up a thick file from his desk, untied the ribbon, and opened it.

"The city of Edinburgh, currently the owner of the estate, will be particularly flattered to count you among its citizens," he proclaimed winningly. "What you have done to further the cause of peace has earned you the esteem of every one of us, and I'm sure that our mayor, the excellent Boddington, will want to welcome you with all the honors that are your due."

"Please," Jonathan interrupted, "I want Kells to be a place of meditation and retreat, and so would ask only that you be kind enough to request the local authorities not to publicize my arrival. I shall be particularly grateful to you for that."

Lennox stammered a few apologies, and then tackled the administrative questions. Varlet's declaration about his need for a retreat seemed to me a good omen, the sign of a real change. I imagined him settled at Kells for the rest of his natural life, but then, I do always seem to be so wrong about such things!

IN APRIL OF 1936, SARAH WAS TRANS-
ferred from the psychiatric clinic in New York to Kells Castle. Jonathan,
accompanied by a nurse, took the *Britannia* over and back, and for
Sarah, the voyage home seemed like a veritable ascension into the heavens.
I finished *The Man Without a Face*, which Goldman planned to publish
in September. During the early months of the year, however, I was in no
position to concern myself with the affairs of either Chesterfield or Varlet, for my personal worries had become a burden sufficient unto themselves.

To backtrack a bit, after Jonathan purchased Kells and we returned
from Scotland, I was surprised not to find Mary there, for we'd agreed
she would await my return in our London flat. Instead, I was greeted by
our law student, Felicia Johnson, who lived in the maid's room upstairs
and helped Mary with the housework as payment. Though she'd been
sent to us by the Sisters of the Mountain, her true loyalties lay with the
socialist youth movement, which championed the cause of the labor
unions, read the *Adelphi*, and supported the workers from Wigan and
Barnsley. I confess I wasn't overly fond of her politics, for I felt she and
her cohorts were being manipulated by the Communist party, and thus

by Moscow. Of course I understood that the metalworkers and the textile workers were unhappy with their lot, but I couldn't imagine why students would want to get involved in their business. I saw their actions as a sort of intellectual disease, a betrayal of the bourgeoisie from which they'd all come, especially the students in law and letters.

My conversations with Felicia were always limited to two parallel monologues, which a certain amount of good humor enabled us to overlap without rancor. I had, however, been dumbfounded to find a monthly magazine in my sitting room called *The Anti-Christ*, edited by someone named Ravelston—a person of some means who masochistically poured his guilt onto its pages, where the vilest and most overt attacks appeared side by side with the most obscure political reflections. At the time, I did not believe that Felicia took these ill-assorted articles seriously, but that they served her as a sort of spear carrier, or perhaps a smoke screen, when she wished to end our arguments by sprinkling about a few pithy quotations. Generally, I chose those moments to laugh, which drove her quite out of her wits, for I was, after all, nothing but "an ill-informed bourgeois," "a collaborator with social vampires!"

"My dear Felicia," I said, "here we are again, caught in the old dualism, which is a serious problem indeed. The workers are on strike; that's their right. The Conservative press is enraged, and that's their role. The official Labourites call for new elections, and suddenly, the British Union of Fascists rushes out of the closet and begins shouting, 'Death to the Jews!' Wouldn't you say there was something altogether pathetic and absurd about all that?"

"The Conservatives' role, as you put it so well, is to dilute the workers' demands by cloaking them in political jargon," Felicia would reply arrogantly. "Even the Labourites use that tactic in their campaign. We don't claim to be able to change the world just like that, you know. That would be Utopia. All we want to do is make sure the workers don't die of starvation and despair in the mines! We're simply opposed to political unrealities, that's all."

In any case, when I returned from Scotland, Felicia informed me that two hours after I'd left with Jonathan, my wife had gone out, with a suitcase.

"Don't worry," she'd said, "I'll be back on Friday."

Felicia had thought that I surely knew about it.

"Naturally . . ." I murmured, although I had no idea what this unforeseen absence meant, especially since it was already Saturday.

"Miss Warner telephoned," Felicia continued. "She wants you to ring her back as soon as you get in."

I promised myself to do nothing of the sort, and instead rang up Miss Graham, the head of the Sisters of the Mountain, who informed me that Mary had not been at their usual Thursday meeting, which had, frankly, surprised her very much. Thinking that my wife might have decided to go up to Ruthford, perhaps because Douglas was unwell, I rang up. Douglas answered and, after she'd informed me that she'd finished putting up all her jams and jellies, declared she'd had no news of Mrs. Charmer. At this point, I began to feel quite uneasy indeed.

I still hadn't decided what to do when at ten o'clock, the phone rang.

"Why haven't you rung me back the way I asked you to?" Margaret Warner said.

"I'm very concerned," I replied. "Mary's not here."

"Don't be such a baby, Cyril," she laughed. "Of course you're concerned, but it's quite simple really. Mary's here with us, in Guildford. We're among friends. That's what happens when you leave a young wife all alone. . . ."

"Glad to hear it," I replied, feigning indifference. "Would you mind if I had a word with her?"

"Just a minute," she said, after a slight hesitation. I waited for a while, then "Mary's outside," she reported. "She can't hear me. Would you like me to have her ring you back?"

It all sounded contrived to me.

"Tell her I'm coming to fetch her," I said, impatiently.

"But . . ." Margaret began, but I'd already hung up.

I arrived at Guildford an hour later to find all the lights blazing. During the trip up, I'd been reviewing, not very kindly, the various elements that had led up to this moment and I guessed we were headed for quite a drama. Why had Mary left with no explanation? Why hadn't she told me her plans if she was already on her way out the door, suitcase in hand, a mere two hours after my own departure? It all smacked of conspiracy, not to mention hypocrisy, but then why hadn't she come back before my return? Why hadn't she phoned me herself instead of having Margaret do it? I simply could not imagine Mary betraying me, and yet the facts seemed to point to that conclusion. Moreover, the closer I came to Guildford, the more ridiculous I knew I was going to look in the eyes of Miss Warner's friends. Wasn't I the living, breathing image of the jealous husband?

The moment my car pulled up, Margaret appeared on the porch. She was dressed in white and had thrown a fur-lined black cloak around her shoulders.

"How kind of you to come so quickly!" she exclaimed. "Quite a testimony to our friendship, wouldn't you say? We have Sir Oswald Mosley here with us tonight. A truly great man, don't you think?"

"Mosley? You mean the head of the British Union of Fascists?"

"The very same. We're really quite lucky. He's been holding a seminar here for the past week, along with Maxwell and Dundee." I must have looked quite alarmed, for she hastened to add, "Now Cyril, don't look like that! I know perfectly well you don't give a fig about politics, but that's no reason to deprive Mary!"

"Mary? Whatever could Mosley have to say that would interest her?"

She shrugged.

"Mary is more politically responsible than you. But come in, please!"

She led me into a large drawing room where thirty or so people sat quietly like good children, listening to a speaker who gesticulated constantly as he repeated, "And that's why . . ." each time he made a point.

I searched for Mary, then saw her seated in the first row between a corpulent man with a shiny bald pate and a skinny fellow I recognized only too well—Leonid Charlienko.

"Look how well behaved she is," Margaret whispered. I shot her a furious look and she smiled back. What sort of ambush had we fallen into, Mary and I? For I'd no doubt that Miss Warner had arranged the whole affair in order to do us some kind of harm. She knew we blamed the Nazis for Yehudi's kidnapping, and she knew the battle Jonathan was waging against the sort of racism these people advocated. By luring us here, she was compromising us in the eyes of our friend. How could Mary not have seen this odious ploy?

The speaker, who I learned later was none other than Maxwell himself, was explaining how Germany ought to serve as an example for all of Europe. Socialists and anarchists alike had been muzzled. The Jews and Masons, troublemakers capable of high treason, had been imprisoned. Vast programs had been set into motion that would revitalize not only the economy but the public's confidence. The financiers, who had once fled a "Jewified" Germany, were now returning in droves, with their capital. And thanks to whom? To Hitler, of course! "Which is why we English should think on this history lesson, especially now when certain negative influences persist in harassing our 'life projects' and attempting to make people see them as 'targets for Bolshevism.' "

Everyone applauded. The speaker—an insignificant-looking, rather jovial sort of individual, with an impeccable haircut, tie, and manner, bowed, and returned to his seat next to Charlienko. And then the all too notorious Mosley took his place and began to speak.

"We have arrived at the conclusion of our seminar, which has been devoted to the urgent question now being asked of the entire Western world, 'Shall we agree to become victims of communism?' or 'Shall we permit cowardice and treason to triumph over our most sacred duties?' And of course you have answered—you have all answered—'No! No, we shall not allow the West to be delivered into the hands of barbarians! No, we shall not allow the anarchy, chaos, and murder which must inevitably follow a policy of demagoguery or of wait and see! On the contrary, we must be the true knights of the Western world! We must see to it that truth triumphs over falsehood! We must become the purveyors of the future!' "

Everyone broke into loud applause. The moment Mosley had finished, I threaded my way between the seats until I reached Mary.

"Well, hello there!" cried Charlienko. "If it isn't the tie lover!"

I grabbed Mary's hand and pulled her to her feet.

"Cyril! What's the matter? Cyril, please!"

As soon as we reached the sidelines, I let go of her hand and gave her a look of the most intense disapproval I could muster.

"Would you please tell me what this is all about?" I almost shouted.

Stunned, she looked at me for a moment and then burst into tears.

"Come, come, crying won't change a thing. Just tell me what you're doing here."

"But . . . but you can see for yourself . . ." she stammered. "Margaret invited me. They're very interesting, really. . . ."

"You might have let me know."

She raised her eyes and looked at me rather fearfully.

"Margaret said you'd be happy if I came. I thought I'd done the right . . ."

It was pathetic.

"Listen, please, do dry your tears. Tell me, how can someone be both a friend of Chesterfield's and sit and applaud this Mosley? Do please answer me that."

At that moment, Charlienko appeared at Mary's side.

"My poor Mary, has the nasty tie lover made you cry? That's not nice at all, Mr. Pumpermaker!"

In an instant, I'd struck him across the face. His lip began to bleed, but I took my wife's arm and pulled her to the door. "Communist twerp!" Charlienko called, waving his handkerchief. Immediately, the room filled with menacing faces.

"What Communist?" Maxwell demanded, waving an enormous revolver.

"Please, please, my friends, it's all right. It's all a mistake. . . . There are no Communists in this house. Leonid, you've had too much to drink. And you, Cyril, try to control your jealousy! We've no time anymore for those outmoded sentiments!"

I shrugged and marched out to my car, followed by Mary, who was still crying.

The whole episode pained me exceedingly. I knew Margaret was capable of just about anything, but I was light years away from imagining that Mary might become one of her victims. My wife wept continuously during our return to London, but I was unable to determine the exact cause of those floods of tears. Was she filled with remorse at having failed to tell me her plans? Did she realize, belatedly, the error she'd committed by listening happily to the discourse of those Nazi insects? Had she been frightened by the sudden appearance of Maxwell's large revolver, which said a great deal about his mentality and that of his friends? Or did those tears suggest some more sentimental attachment to that boor of a Charlienko? Not a word was uttered until we'd entered the flat, but the moment the door shut behind us I cried, "For God's sake, whatever did you think you were doing there?"

"You can't possibly understand," she replied, sinking into an armchair. "You're so reasonable . . . or rather, such a rationalist. Margaret's talked to me about so many marvelous theories . . . about the stars. And magic. I feared you'd make fun of me."

So, all the time I'd thought Mary was with the Sisters of the Mountain, she'd actually been with Miss Warner—and Charlienko, as I was to learn later—engaged in strange rituals whose insignificant mysteries my wife explained to me with disconcerting naïveté. I did not know yet that these ceremonies were part of a secret society called the Golden Dawn, the pillars of which had been, during the early years of the century, characters as dubious as Mathers and Crowley, a society that, for the past ten years, had been the plaything of a handful of unscrupulous opportunists determined to use the occult to achieve their political goals. Usually quite well off, these people had selected a few illuminati and made them their front men, people like Dundee, whom I'd seen the evening Mosley gave his speech, the same Dundee who'd been decorated with the title of high priest and who had reached the level of Adeptus— all of which positively dazzled my poor Mary.

"He knows everything about the science of Hermes!" she cried. "I swear to you he's managed to join the Cabala and the sacred secrets of ancient Egypt!"

I tried my best to reason with her, to show her it was all a trap, but the truth is she *needed* to be mystified.

"Listen," I said, "no matter what you think about these absurdities, you must admit one thing—your great magus Dundee is a pawn of the British Nazis. And you know what the Nazis think about our friend Chesterfield and the Jews."

She put down her handkerchief. "The Jews stole their whole religion from the Egyptians," she replied firmly. "This is the Curse of Akhenaton!"

The inanity of her reply rendered me speechless.

"You must stop seeing these people at once," I finally managed to say. "They confuse your mind. And perhaps your heart too."

"I can't leave them," she replied haughtily. "I gave my word. I am a Zelator, and must obey my spiritual advisers!"

I went to her and forced her to look at me.

"My little girl, if you have any feeling at all left for me, you must get hold of yourself. What you're telling me is nothing but fantasies which will only lead you astray, and then exploit you. It's late now. Let's go to bed and tomorrow, if you like, we can continue our conversation."

She shrugged, and stood up.

"You've hurt me very much," she said, and walked off to her room. I was stunned.

Mary did not appear at breakfast, which we habitually ate together in the dining room. At nine o'clock, I took the liberty of knocking at her door, which she opened and then stood there without speaking, wrapped in a purple peignoir, her hair in curlpapers and her eyes swollen.

"I was worried. You didn't come down to breakfast. It's an awfully nice time of day, breakfast. Don't you agree?"

She shrugged.

"Those are strictly middle-class thoughts, Cyril. I'm a different woman now. I've been initiated into the highest spiritual mysteries, can't you understand that? And because you're still among the laity, you cannot imagine what happens to you when these secrets are revealed!"

"May I come in?"

"Absolutely not. After what you said yesterday? Casting suspicions on my friends, my brothers, while they're working to change a world that's been led into debauchery by people like your Chesterfield!"

I did not insist, but went to shave, convinced that a definitive break had occurred between us, a break clearly caused by none other than Margaret Warner and her rambling Russian!

For two days, Mary hardly spoke a word to me. And then, on Tuesday morning, after having poured the tea and carefully buttered her toast, she suddenly decided to explain herself.

"Dear Cyril, when we were living through the things that happened to Sarah and Jonathan, I felt so sorry for them. And then I thought about it. Is it really true that Yehudi's kidnappers were members of the National Socialist Party? Didn't that theory come from Chesterfield's imagination? A man who dares to write *Beelzebub*, a novel on the borderline of the most decadent pornography, and who goes abroad, to Germany, where he's received with every honor. And once there, he corrupts a young girl and, against every law and every morality, persuades her to flee her country. And then he engages, with her, in the most degrading business there is—self-publicity, self-advertisement, in order to satisfy his sadomasochistic manias and to contaminate an entire society through his book and his play and his movie and his dolls and all the rest. To be sure, his genius for drama enables him to convince everyone that all this twaddle is a result of his humanism! Think about it— the hospital in Kampala, the campaign against racism, oh what a great man he is! But none of it, alas, none of it is real! Margaret's father told her that Jonathan has never written a single line of any of his books. He's just a salesman for a Judeo-Masonic sect allied with an exhausted Catholicism and with a bunch of socialists under the control of Moscow! His marriage with that Jewess is only a pretty picture designed to dupe the masses. As for his son's disappearance—and I wonder if it really is his son—this Yehudi whose name is so aptly chosen . . . Cyril, I'm telling you—even admitting that the child is his, believe me, the kidnapping was orchestrated by the same publicists who made his novels and his operetta and all the rest of it such a success!"

I stared at her, terrified. She'd just exposed her theory—or rather her convictions—with the equanimity of someone describing a walk in the woods.

"Who's put such ideas into your head?" I cried.

She looked at me with a mocking smile.

"I see the other side of things now."

I stood up abruptly and threw my napkin onto the table.

"You've been brainwashed by Margaret Warner and that drunkard Charlienko!"

She made a face, but continued to smile sardonically.

"Leonid is just as good as you are, my friend. . . ."

"Well, that's it then. Henceforth, the only conversation you and I shall have is through our lawyers. I see no reason to continue my life with someone so alien to me!"

"I couldn't agree more. I've been aware of your insignificance for months now. You're forever on your knees adoring your Chesterfield, who is the perfect image of everything I detest. I shall be glad to leave you your freedom!" And she calmly finished her toast.

It was an interminable divorce. I retired to Ruthford, while Mary remained in the London flat. Fortunately, I'd taken the precaution of drawing up a separation-of-property agreement before signing our marriage contract, but the witch still used all sorts of blackmail to extort from me everything she could. Moreover, she was pregnant, by Charlienko, who came all the way to Ruthford one day to argue with me while amusing himself by shooting off a rifle. In short, they were a ghastly few months, which, out of an understandable sense of decency, I shall refrain from describing to my reader.

And then, one morning in May, Margaret Warner appeared in my drawing room, unannounced. I was shocked at her boldness, while she, on the contrary, sat there delighted, triumphant, and gleaming like a marble statue in the sunlight.

"Are you so surprised to see me then?" she asked, tossing her head.

"Nothing you do surprises me. You're capable of anything. And worse. You're the one who devised the whole plan to separate Mary and me. Well, it was a great success. In fact, I must confess you've done me a service. It was a great mistake, marrying her."

She arranged her dress over her knees.

"I couldn't agree with you more. But you mustn't imagine you were my primary target. It's Jonathan's head I'm after!"

I ought to have chased her out right then, but I couldn't resist hearing what she had to say.

"Are you so blind as not to see that Jonathan Absalom Varlet has made a fool out of you? That he couldn't care less about you? He's taken advantage of his undeniable seductiveness to invent a whole life for himself and to pull the wool over all our eyes. Do you think I have no right to complain? He did the whole romantic number with me so that I'd get my father to publish his book. And once he'd pulled it off, it was ta-ta, Margaret! You know you were responsible for my coming with you to Venice because, at the time, you thought you were in love with me. And I was fool enough to believe I could use the occasion to resuscitate my relationship with him. And what happens—he goes off to America with Sarah! And do you know why? Because he was already organizing his antiracism campaign, that lovely strategy to draw even more attention to himself, and raise him to the pinnacle of fame and glory, the most tainted glory ever, a glory exactly like those hideous rubber dolls, a thoroughly simian glory, that's what it was! But enough of that. Because that's not the real horror. You must realize just who it is you've chosen for a friend, Mr. Charmer. . . ."

She'd become quite animated as she spoke, and was now carried away by her hatred.

"First, you should know we've investigated the real identity of the brilliant Gilbert Keith Chesterfield! You'll die when you hear the results." She pulled some typed pages from her handbag and began to read. " 'Report by Goldfish and Gibson on the origins of one Jonathan Absalom Varlet, December 15, 1935. On the confidential request of Mr. Peter Warner, publisher, we began an investigation into the origins and identity of the aforementioned. The basis of our inquiry was the fact that the aforementioned was taken in, as a child, by Lord Ambergris, the earl of Sheffield. We proceeded to interrogate all persons likely to have known the child during the time he lived with the earl. These persons were unable to furnish us with precise information about the origins of the aforementioned, with the exception of one David Lennon, eighty years of age, former gardener at Kells Castle in Scotland, a property belonging to Lord Ambergris, bought by the city of Edinburgh from the heirs, and which is currently being transacted for by the writer Chesterfield. The aforementioned Lennon claims that young Varlet was the son of one Dorothy Temple who lived at Kells for many years and was Lord Ambergris's mistress. Lennon based his conviction on the fact that Mrs.

Temple once asked him to take a vase of flowers to "her son's room," after which she blushed and said, "to Mr. Jonathan's room." We thus began an inquiry into the origins of Dorothy Temple.' "

Margaret gave me an ironic look.

"Interesting, wouldn't you say? But wait . . . the best is yet to come!"

I was paralyzed in my armchair, as if nailed to the spot by a serpent's gaze.

" 'Dorothy Temple was born on November 16, 1883, in London, to Moses Temple and his wife, Sarah, née Laserstein, a family of immigrant Jews who had come to England several years before. . . .' " Margaret stopped suddenly, and stood up. "There it is, in black and white, your Chesterfield, alias Varlet! He's a Jew! Anyway, his mother was Jewish, and everyone knows you're Jewish through the mother!" She stood there arrogantly, proud of her discovery.

"So?" I asked simply.

"What do you mean, so? Varlet's Jewish! Chesterfield's Jewish! And you ask me, so?"

I too rose.

"Listen, Margaret, if your information is correct, Jonathan's origins only authenticate his activities. Isn't it logical that he marry Sarah? That he espouse the cause of persecuted Jews?"

"Really, Cyril," she exploded, "you don't understand anything! Don't you find it unbearable that a Jew, the natural enemy of the Western world, should continue to parade about as he does on the pretext of defending this same Western world? That's treason! And I want this scandal revealed, once and for all!"

"I know Jonathan's rejection mortified you," I replied calmly. "And that's understandable. I myself had difficulty at the time accepting his attitude, which I found careless and cruel. But since then, so much has happened! Hasn't he suffered enough, with his son's kidnapping?"

"He lost his son because he made him a symbol!" she cried, quivering with rage.

"My god," I murmured, "you're doubtless quite right. But do you understand what you're saying? And why all this hatred for Jews?"

"Because they're foreigners! Aliens! They meddle in everything, everywhere. They're like termites. They crawl right into your house and gnaw away at it from the inside. Europe is rotten! England's rotten! The termites have eaten everything! What's left of the grandeur we used to have? The socialists are Communist stooges; they've brought the class struggle right into our cities. And Marx. What was he, if not a Jew? The degradation of the West began when a Jew called Jesus spread his doctrine of renunciation all around the Mediterranean through Paul, the rabbi. Socialism is the offspring of Christianity, and Christianity is the son of Judaism! We must get rid of this cancer!"

She was reciting Mosley's bible, which was identical to Hitler's, identical to the shouts of the hysterical mobs I'd seen in the newsreels. I remembered something I'd once said to Jonathan two years ago, something like "The only choice left to us is between Utopia and death." But what Utopia? And what death? I began to understand just how the world had been sundered, but not why this division was so unavoidable.

Warner's "discovery" made headlines in the yellow press. "Chesterfield a Jew!" they cried, followed by perfidious allusions to the writer's "incredible success." And then, as suddenly as it had started, it stopped, and it was not until a few weeks later that I learned why. By then, Jonathan had settled Sarah into Kells and wanted very much to see me. My divorce had just ended with a compromise by which Mary won substantial alimony plus the flat in Green Park, where she promptly began to live with Charlienko. I was angry, but happy to have regained my freedom despite the high price. Varlet and I met at the Rubens Hotel, where he could pass unnoticed. The last time I'd met him there was in the days of Simon Partner; how everything had changed in just a few months!

"Very true," he said, begging me to sit down, "and more than you think!"

"I can't tell you how sorry I am about those newspaper attacks. The Warners planted them, as I'm sure you know."

"I've told my attorney to break the Goldman contract," he replied simply. "But listen to this—the great Harold Spencer invited me to come see him!" He was positively radiant. "And you know where? At Blenheim Palace! I went there yesterday!"

"Your father?" I replied, greatly agitated. "At last!"

"I arrived at the palace at eleven. . . . Oh Cyril, if you only knew. . . . I couldn't put one foot before the other; it was as if I were going to meet God himself . . . as if the walls were shaking and the windows vibrating so hard they'd surely break . . . And there he was, enormous, the omnipresent cigar between his fingers, and so like his photographs I was certain it was all an illusion. His eyes seemed to look right through me. By what name would he call me? I wondered. He coughed, and then in his raspy voice said, 'Gilbert Keith Chesterfield! To think that I've not met you before this!' He waggled his cigar at me. 'Please, come closer.' "

He stopped, overwhelmed with emotion.

"Forgive me, Cyril, but it was an awesome moment for me. He didn't know about my lord's letter, of course, and I was determined not to tell him I knew his secret. 'It's an honor to meet you, sir,' he said to me. 'I've read all your books. Not the kind I prefer, mind you, but I liked them. Then too, you've suffered a grave misfortune. And I wanted you to know what an English reader like myself felt about that. I promise you, we shall continue the fight against Nazism.' I stammered some sort of thanks, and he put his hand on my shoulder. 'Continue your work, my friend. You are doing a fine thing.' then he changed his tone somewhat and said, 'You grew up here, did you not?' 'Yes,' I replied. 'I too,' he said. 'In fact, we're related somehow, through the earl of Sheffield. A great honor for the Marlboroughs, that. They haven't had many writers.' 'Except for you,' I said. 'I've read *The World Crisis*, and also the first volume of your essay on your ancestor, the glorious conqueror of Louis XIV.' He gave a sort of grunt, stuck his cigar in his mouth, and said— in that tone used to giving orders—'Is it true, Mr. Chesterfield, that you've bought Kells?' 'I've taken it out of the hands of foreigners, yes,' I replied. He laughed. 'Excellent! You must keep it as a sanctuary.' And then he added, 'As for the gossip in the papers, you may count on me to take care of it. I cannot abide pedestrian humor.' "

Jonathan's eyes filled with tears.

"I think at that moment he knew I'd guessed who he was. But neither of us betrayed our oath."

I took advantage of this intimate moment to tell him what Miss Warner had told me about his mother.

"I made my own inquiries too, you know," he replied. "Dorothy Temple was in fact Jewish. Out of discretion, or perhaps a sense of propriety, my lord did not tell me the whole truth about my origins. Which makes it even easier to understand why it's impossible for my father to acknowledge me. It would simply be too great a scandal for dear old England. Just imagine a descendent of the Marlboroughs with Jewish blood! And yet, it's rather enviable, don't you think, being in exile? After all, that's where the temple is built, for God reveals Himself only in the desert."

He was in a state of exaltation and it was at that moment, in a modest

London hotel, that I finally saw him as he really was—neither Chester-field nor Spencer nor even Varlet, but exactly like my own man without a face—naked, solitary, the victim of a curse that instead of destroying him made him even more heroic.

We were interrupted by the telephone. Jonathan picked it up, mumbled a few words, and then hung up.

"We're lazy literati, Cyril," he said. "Our literature is locked into old conceptions that even we no longer quite believe. Perhaps it's a kind of alibi for us. The books you write and whose paternity I assume are merely part of that vast needlework whose charm intellectuals so enjoy complicating. Up to you to continue or not, but life, Cyril! Life!"

"What are you going to do at Kells?"

"Those are my roots"—he smiled—"but as you've guessed, I shall intensify my struggle, if only out of responsibility to Yehudi. Have you been following the news from Spain?"

"Quite. I've even got my own informer in the person of a student who lives in our Green Park flat. She was, and doubtless still is, rather a militant. Pro-minorities, you know. Comes from an alarmingly generous heart . . ."

"Why do you say that?"

"Because I find her quite naïve. Carried away by a blind and blissful idealism. Do you really think the Spanish question is that simple? One has to be English to believe that the good chaps are all on the Republican side, and the outlaws with the general. . . ."

"And that's only the beginning. Do you realize how divided the left is? Moscow has forced the revolutionaries into loggerheads with one another. What we're witnessing is a flood of mysticism no one can control, and while that's going on, the Falangists are getting organized. Sanjurjo received a promise of support from Hitler; Mussolini is delivering money and munitions. Even here in London, Juan March, the financier, has found partisans in Mosley's ranks. In short, it's fascism meddling undisguised—taking over, really—in Spain's internal affairs. Believe me, they'll wind up obeying the warlike desires of those predators, and all of it in the name of defending the Western world!"

"But surely socialism isn't as disastrous as all that? Its heart does seem to be in the right place, you know."

"Socialism is a tool! Everybody uses it. The Russians deform it to meet their own needs, the Fascists use it as a target for their accusations of Communist collusion. It's not socialism anymore; why, it's even used in business! We're betrayed on all sides, Cyril. Nothing's pure any-more—no idea or ideology—which is why there are no more righteous causes. They've even taken away our right to fight for a truth. And yet, we must choose, and we must choose the weakest and most innocent party, even if behind their humble facade lurk the most powerful hy-pocrisies. There's no time left to distinguish among nuances, for if we hesitate, we're doomed to impotence."

"But why choose between fascism and communism when both serve an abstraction that makes men into playthings? That notion of order goes quite against the very nature of humanity, you know. Particularly if you agree on a definition of freedom as everyone's right to make mis-takes, and then to make up for them and so emerge from the ordeal greater than before. Totalitarianism, no matter what kind, is just the opposite—it's an error no one has the right to correct, and which denies ever having been an error in the first place! It's based on the omnipo-tence of anonymity, which they dress up by calling it a collective."

"That's why I've become so involved—not in the sense of joining a particular political camp, but to bear witness to innocence. I don't know if it's possible to remain pure in a world that's breaking apart, but if no one tries to extricate the conflict from the contradictions that imprison it, soon no one will be able to stop it. And then, my dear friend, all of Europe will be at war."

My memory of that evening touches me deeply, for it was clear that Jonathan was going through a painful period. Everything—his meeting with his father, Sarah's arrival at Kells, the newspaper gossip—pointed to a turning point in his life. And as he'd so often remarked to me, his life had been bathed in such an uncontestable unreality that even his successes seemed a waking dream. I sensed now that he wanted to at-tach himself to real circumstances, and to attempt thereby to put down roots. I learned he'd met with certain members of the Labour party but hadn't got on with them very well. What they said didn't seem to match what they did. As for the Spanish question, no one could really get a handle on it, distorted as it was by the myriad divisions among the Republicans. I think people suspected Chesterfield of dabbling in Trot-skyism; in any case, he soon found himself quite alone with those gen-erous, albeit incongruous, ideas of his. As he told me himself, he could not help remaining a "bourgeois" and thus could not comprehend everything concealed behind all those exalted Republican proclamations.

Oddly, Felicia Johnson chose just this moment to resurface. She'd left the maid's room at Green Park at the same time I'd moved out, but I ran into her in the Comstock Bookstore near Hyde Park Corner, which I'd used to frequent as a student and where one could still find all sorts of odd things at ridiculously low prices.

"Well," she'd exclaimed, "I'd no idea you bothered with dusty old holes-in-the-wall like this!"

"On the contrary, I'm the one that should be surprised. Seems quite natural, actually, for an old reactionary like me to go in for antiques, but you, the revolutionary . . ."

She laughed and then immediately changed the subject, with that energy young people have for jumping from topic to topic.

"I was just thinking about you. Or rather about your friend Chesterfield. I know he's very famous and I'm sure it's not easy to ask him a favor, but perhaps with your help, Cyril . . ."

She explained to me that one of her friends was a reporter for the *Daily Herald* and that he wanted to meet Chesterfield to discuss the European situation. It would be a fabulous professional coup for her friend for it would give him the chance to get his political views recognized. I was fond of Felicia and so wrote to Jonathan, sending along her friend's name. Two weeks later, I received the following letter.

Dear Cyril,

You shall forever by my fairy godfather. Richard Brown, the reporter you sent me, came out to Kells yesterday and I was completely seduced by the ardor with which he spoke of defending our beleaguered Spain. For a no one like me, political commitment may be a way of forging an identity, but at what cost! I believe political commitment is synonymous with the renunciation of lucidity. Frankly, I prefer to be no one and to know it, rather than to delude myself in the name of some ideology or other. Your young reporter has the look of a man torn in two; he spoke to me of Goya, of the man in the white shirt who rejects death even in the face of the firing squad. There seem to be quite a few of these men in white shirts, and of rifles spitting nonsense and absurdity. It's not a question of the truth on one side and falsehood on the other; whatever the beliefs, it comes down to Abel against Cain. I agreed to meet the editor of the paper, however, who intends to ask me to write my impressions of the Spanish Civil War. And why not?

All the best,
Jonathan

And so Chesterfield joined the *Daily Herald*, an event seized upon gleefully by the public. People still remembered Yehudi's kidnapping and were extremely interested in Jonathan's acts and opinions concerning international events. The anti-Semitic attacks in the press had had a profound impact; moreover, this was the first time an English writer had assumed the role of reporter. It seemed to everyone that literature had at last dropped its reserve, turned its attention to daily life, and was attempting to give serious consideration to a worldwide crisis everyone felt was hopeless. Letters addressed to him inundated the paper, even though he hadn't yet written a single piece, letters that more or less said, "Tell us the truth, for we no longer know where we are and we're afraid." He answered them in his first article, where he confessed that he did not know either what was going to happen to Europe, but that he meant to try to get a clear picture by visiting those places where significant events were taking place. Which meant, first off, Spain, "because it is through Spain that all other countries confront one another, not only countries but ideas, and not only ideas but the will to power. What we are witnessing in Spain, behind the masks, is a tug-of-war between Nazi Germany, Stalinist Russia, and the chaotic aspirations of a people dramatically divided, exploited, and deceived."

A second wave of gossip aimed at sullying Chesterfield's reputation was launched by Mosley's extremists, and seconded in her rage by Margaret Warner. The campaign charged that Varlet had never written a single line of his own books, and that those same books that bore his name had been dictated to him by a group of conspirators headquartered in London, in Great Queen Street to be exact, a secret society of which Lord Ambergris had once been a grand master! By vigorously and unscrupulously manipulating various bits and pieces, certain journalists contrived a scenario suggesting that *Beelzebub* and *The Monkey King* were "subversive and decadent" works, whose purpose was to distract the West from its duties. A cartoon appeared, showing Chesterfield, blindfolded and led by a Jew wearing a Mason's uniform, holding a pen upside down and marching up a cliff from which, to all intents and purposes, he was clearly about to fall. This new attack had as little impact as the first, but testified to the ardor of his enemies and their determination to discredit him by the most blatant methods. Here too, Harold Spencer was obliged to intervene expeditiously; a week after this balderdash first appeared, not even the remotest allusion remained.

Varlet seemed untouched, however, by all the brouhaha. He had survived a far more tragic ordeal, and the vagaries of a handful of fanatics could not hurt him. I, on the other hand, felt these events profoundly, the more so since they came from a group that, via Mary, suddenly seemed uncomfortably close to me. The poor woman clearly had no idea of the madness she'd become involved with. She who dreamed of adventures like an adolescent had discovered, in the occultism and hallucinatory lyricism of Nazi promises, an outlet for her fantasies. In becoming her lover, Leonid Charlienko concretized that outrageousness she'd longed for and of which I'd clearly deprived her. In her eyes, as that Russian put it, I was merely a "tie lover," and when I paused to think about it, he was right. At first, I received the verdict with anger, and then with the lucidity of someone who has nothing left to lose but himself. I'd written novels and then hidden behind someone else. I'd taken advantage of Jonathan's luck and his genius for publicity. In just a few years, I'd become a well-fed, self-satisfied property owner. I'd taken no risks. Of course I'd contributed to the Kampala hospital, but I'd had to be coerced; I remembered how irked I'd been when Varlet had applied pressure. In short, it seemed as if events had ennobled Jonathan while scarcely touching me at all. All I'd got was a spray of mud.

There are moments in everyone's life when one's conscience feels soiled and heavy. I wasn't sure what to blame myself for, but my whole life seemed to be accusing me and I, the very image of success, surprised myself by seeing only failure in all my endeavors. What good had my novels done, except to amuse a mass of blind readers who forgot them the minute they put them down? And how did my buying blocks of flats in Cannon Street and the Chester Hotel distinguish me from my peers? Then too, just as I'd married the blandest woman I could find out of a fear of femininity, so had I engaged in life only out of boredom, literature representing for me merely a sort of rainy-day diversion. In vain I told myself over and over that the public's enthusiastic reception of my work ought surely to mean something, that my characters and the episodes in my novels reflected a sensitive part of the human animal, but I couldn't persuade myself that all this flattering commotion had any relationship whatsoever to the quality of those novels. And that was that.

My erstwhile pride had turned to gloom. It had shriveled up and no longer resembled anything so much as an old and bitter pretense that I was going to have to slough off.

It was in this state of confusion that I arrived for a visit at Kells in June of 1936. I felt I had to see Jonathan; he was the only human being with whom I could speak honestly of real issues. And I wanted to see Sarah, whose madness seemed to protect her so well from the world. Moreover, I knew Chesterfield would soon be leaving for Spain, or so the *Daily Herald* had announced, and I intended to see him before he left. I took the train to Edinburgh, then rented a car and drove to Dorothy Temple's former residence. The weather was simply glorious, the cries of the gulls harmonizing with the muted rhythms of the ocean, and it was with gentle kindness that the austere edifice welcomed me.

"By all the whales of Saint Law!" cried old Cockenzie, alias Crispie, when he saw me get out of the car. "If it isn't Mr. Cyril!" He was seated on the porch steps but rose to his feet with a grimace and limped toward me. "It's not that I have a good memory, but Mr. Jonathan said to me, he said, 'If you see a tall man with reddish hair and spectacles, it's Mr. Cyril. Come and get me.' You're pretty tall and, if I may, you're not a brunet or a blond. As for the spectacles, well, there they be on your nose, right? So you must be Mr. Cyril. It seems to me we've met before, haven't—"

"Well done," I replied. "But please, don't trouble yourself. Just tell me where Mr. Jonathan is and I'll find him."

Crispie pointed to the far end of the lawn, and as the chauffeur drove off, I headed for the spot the old gentleman had indicated.

Varlet was pruning the roses. In his shirtsleeves, with a broad-brimmed straw hat on his head, he was the very picture of the perfect gardener one sees in those magazines that encourage city dwellers to cultivate a few flowerpots. When he heard the crunch of gravel, he turned around, put down the clippers, and pulled off his gloves.

"Welcome to Kells! You can't imagine how pleased I am at your idea to come pay us a visit! I feel just like someone who doesn't know if he should laugh or cry—should I laugh at myself, or weep at the misery of being alive? . . . But look, Cyril, it's the month of June and I'm pruning roses! Parasites fill me with horror, but what do I see? Caterpillars, lice, vermin everywhere! If I'm not careful, in no time at all there'll be no roses in this garden!"

We shook hands, and I asked about Sarah.

"She's happy. She knits. She sings. Yesterday she even managed to take a few steps. But her world is no longer the same as ours. I'm very much alone, you know . . . except for all those letters!"

"What letters?" I asked, as we strolled toward the house.

"Hundreds of letters that paint pictures of all the suffering in our exhausted society. Some come from Germany, Austria, and Poland; others from Spain, France, and Italy. And all of them weep, and all of them groan. Threats and torture and murder everywhere! And in the midst of all these cries for help, our weekly crime report from New York, cold as the morgue and always the same: 'No new clues.' Oh, how I wish it would all stop!"

He stopped and drew a shaky hand across his forehead.

"And yet I must read those letters," he said softly, "and answer them. Perhaps not right away, but soon. I wanted to be famous in order to feel alive, to have a name and doubtless to serve. And now that I'm the first victim of that fame, I've no right to refuse. That would be cowardly, wouldn't it?"

My luggage had been placed in the main entrance hall.

"Chesterfield's works—your works, Cyril—are worth more than what I've done with them. It would doubtless have been better had you been known only by a select group of admirers who would have respected you. But instead of that, here I am changed into a medicine man. And your works are misunderstood."

We settled ourselves in the oversized armchairs in the drawing room. Jonathan continued his monologue, and I did not interrupt. I'd come to renew my strength through him, and here he was, every bit as helpless as I.

"I should have studied plants or insects. Little things. But instead, I took on the whole planet! Here I am, holding it in my arms, unable to rock it. Or cure it. A pretty state of affairs, isn't it? Humor, wherefore art thou?"

Around five o'clock, after raising a barrage of questions without answers, he looked at his watch and said it was time to visit Sarah. I followed him through the library and into a room that had been arranged so artfully as not to seem designed to harbor an invalid. There were flowers everywhere—on the tables, the dresser, the wardrobe, even the foot of the bed where Sarah lay. She had lost even more weight, and I saw once again the adolescent who'd come with us to Venice so many years ago. Except that her eyes seemed not to see, not as if she were blind but as if the blackest of nights had massed itself in her mind, a blackness rent from time to time by strange glimmers. Oddly, she recognized me.

"Cyril!" She turned immediately to the nurse who sat beside her counting out drops. "Please leave us," she said. "These are the gentlemen with the reports."

And so, in a room with too many flowers, we had come to the very bedside of the West. The analogy seized hold of me brusquely and would not let go as I stood mute, staring at the frozen display—Sarah imprisoned in her blissful dementia and Jonathan lost in his monologue, their words meeting in a curious fashion in some invisible sphere.

"When we've finished building the cabana, we'll send for the great Shishlaferter, the only violinist who can play *The Glass Flute*. My father insisted on the opening A-flat, because it was the floodgate. That was his very word—the floodgate! It's true. After the A-flat, the whole opera starts to pour forth. Really pour. The water rises. The houses begin to float. They bob along, adrift on the water. Adieu, ladies!"

She laughed, while Varlet pursued his monologue.

"Kampala couldn't halt the plague. All my petitions couldn't defy the war. The Souen doll was just a toy that filled our coffers. A generous magic wand, indeed! Just like Midas. Everything I touched turned to gold, and I too was stuck with donkey's ears. And then the flood was upon us! Money, oil, dollar bills, Wall Street! And who do you think Hitler is? And all his fascists? Nothing but the servants of money! The West is mired in a dictatorship of gold, and opposite us—what is there? A dictatorship of bureaucrats. On one side, animated by hysteria, the servants of industry and commerce crowned with laurels of banknotes; on the other side, paralyzed in their administrative straitjackets, the horse-headed servants of an omnipotent paper chase! And all of it in the guise of progress! Materialism everywhere! Doubtless the first time in history people aren't fighting in the name of some ideal, but in the yoke of the material."

Sarah raised her head from the pillow.

"Besides, we know who the beast is," she said firmly. "They hid it from us for a long time, but now we know. Yehudi told me. He told me! It's the grainy monkey, the Master of the Gallinaceous Fowl of Pomona! 'Ah! Ah!' he cried, flinging back his head. And the others, all the others bowing down to the ground and murmuring, 'Amen! Amen!' "

Jonathan seemed to listen attentively to her insane litany. When she fell silent, he started again.

"The beautiful universal plan has broken into a thousand pieces. Modern man is scattered, fragmented. He wanders without aim in a world without law. His works reflect his inner vacuum, which is overrun with the phantoms of solitude and anguish. Look at Picasso—balance is destroyed, monsters emerge from the very womb of the quotidian. They wanted to kill the God in us, the meaning of things, and replace it with meanings that are by definition hostile to one another. Contradictory. Our intelligence roams blindly through the labyrinth of data which pours down in continuous torrents and whose incoherence paralyzes us. Our factories are the producers of ever more numerous quantities of goods that turn inevitably to garbage. We have no more direction! Which way is our Orient?"

"It seems to me," I interrupted, "that Chesterfield's work attempts to find the traces of a direction. The anecdotes he uses are nothing more than the progress of mankind in its effort to rediscover its lost identity. Don't you see, Jonathan? You were seeking a name for yourself, and the whole of the Western world is seeking the same thing, through you as through the others. We've lost the name that identifies us to ourselves. That's why we walk and walk, in quest of our name, which is also the name of our origin. We must recover our memory, beyond the innumerable stratifications of our forgetfulness. Only we won't find the name of any particular individual; what we seek is the thing that makes us a person, which is the same as what defines all of us who gather together freely. Only then can we abandon the Other and begin to clothe ourselves in the Self."

"Dear Cyril," Jonathan said, visibly moved, "you've just said what I myself feel so strongly. But isn't it maddening to realize how far away we are, and the world is, from that point of view? Just a step away from the abyss we are. Never has the night been so black and we who are plunged into it know it will be blacker still. We've reached only the dawn of Good Friday."

"Why mention Good Friday in the midst of such a profane moment?" I asked, surprised.

"Because the holocaust is at the very center of profanation. The sacrifice is perpetuated by impious hands in the most abominable underground chambers. And the Holy One offers Himself as the redeemer to the filthiest, for in the deepest part of the vilest matter lies, concealed, the spark of the purest spirit—even if it is against all likelihood, and all hope. The lightning strikes, the spear pierces the heart, Paul falls from his horse, and grace falls upon a lost and wounded world at the most tragic moment of desolation."

That evening, we listened to some Sibelius recordings that the illustrious composer had given Chesterfield in homage and that were inscribed: "To the father of Souen, a just man, a free man, who understands the saving weight of suffering. Respectfully, Jean Sibelius." Sarah had fallen asleep like a child, curled up in the arms of the teddy bear that had once belonged to Yehudi. And over all loomed, still, the double shadow of Abel and Cain.

J ONATHAN ABSALOM VARLET ARRIVED IN
Paris in September 1936, without anyone knowing that this name masked
the famous G. K. Chesterfield. Richard Brown, the journalist Felicia
Johnson had sent via my good offices, went with him. Brown had joined
the British Communist party in 1933 and was promptly sent to Moscow,
whence he returned horrified by the endless trials. Harry Pollitt, then
the secretary-general of the party, advised him to go to Spain, where he
might acquire "a healthier attitude about the real problems." Facile
contrasts were being made at that time between the political rigidity of
Stalinism and the irresponsibility of anarchist terrorism; Brown arrived
in Madrid amid the dissolution of the Cortes and the ensuing elections.
He witnessed the "victory parades" with left-wing socialists calling for
a dictatorship of the proletariat, much to the chagrin of President Azaña,
to whom the prime minister, Largo Caballero—whom everyone called
the Spanish Lenin—paid passing little attention.

Brown had wholeheartedly espoused the May Day demands of the
Madrid socialists for a government of the working class and a "Red
Army," but the Communist party, led by José Díaz, pronounced the
position of this "left-provocateur" unrealistic. When our young journalist understood just what sort of deception was being perpetrated on the

Spanish people, he resigned from the party and began working for the *Daily Herald*. A few weeks later, he met Jonathan at Kells. During this month of September, Brown introduced Varlet to a variety of people in Paris who maintained as best they could the liaison between the Spanish revolutionaries and the French left. It was a stormy liaison, given the mutual accusations from both sides. Labor union leaders quarreled constantly with one another, split apart, and even betrayed one another, thereby fostering the impression of incredible disunity. Naturally, the right-wing press took advantage of this, declaring that the anarchists were terrorizing the workers, charges that subsequently provoked Falangist attacks on the strikers. In short, given the confusion, Jonathan decided to stay in Paris for a few weeks until he had a clearer sense of things. Brown acted as go-between, for Varlet, anxious to avoid publicity, insisted upon remaining anonymous. During these two months in Paris, our friend wrote his second series of articles on the state of the Western world, entitled "At the Floodgates," analyzing in particular the procrastination of America, England, and France in acknowledging the war, even though Germany and Italy had already chosen sides. "For fear of becoming embroiled in the conflict," Varlet wrote, "the West is setting the stage for a worldwide conflagration."

While Jonathan wrote his articles, he was under continuous surveillance by Russian and German agents. Obviously, neither Russia nor Germany was anxious for Chesterfield to exercise his influence in ways which might prove a bit too contrary to their intentions. Today, of course, we know that both sides had already arranged for the "disappearance of that undesirable" well before he got to Spain, although we still don't know why the order wasn't given immediately. It didn't take Varlet long to find out what both sides were planning, but he persisted in his desire to go to Barcelona via one of the trains ferrying volunteer contingents across the border to various staging areas. Brown has provided us with a fair bit of information about Jonathan's Paris sojourn:

Chesterfield did not seem afraid of the menace that accompanied him everywhere like a shadow. He believed that no one would recognize him under cover of the name Varlet, and when he finally understood his error, he seemed to accept his lot with some humor. He had to go to Spain and thus he *would* go, knowing full well how many would take advantage of the war to do him harm.

Withal, it was decided that certain precautions should be taken, as Brown later explained:

Chesterfield checked into the Delambre, a modest hotel in Montparnasse where, under the name of Varlet, he believed he wouldn't be recognized. During the fourth week of our stay in Paris, I noticed we were often followed by three distinct groups of people, who seemed to belong to the Comintern, the Secret Service, and the Abwehr. When Chesterfield realized what was going on, he burst into laughter. Everywhere we went, we were accompanied by this little knot of followers. One day, as we strolled, purely recreationally, through an old section of Paris called the Marais, we entered a tiny Jewish restaurant on the Rue des Rosiers. Our friends followed right after us, and settled themselves at neighboring tables. Chesterfield called to them and invited them to join us for lunch, but they pretended not to hear. Instead, they went about their meal with vacant looks, each just a few yards from the other; when we'd finished eating, we all left, one after the other, and ambled over to see the Place des Vosges.

The next day, having discovered a restaurant on the Boulevard Saint-Michel with an emergency exit near the restrooms, we decided to lose our friends. We would go in for lunch and in the middle of our meal, Chesterfield would get up casually and go off to the restrooms while I continued eating. Then he would slip out via the back alley, jump into a cab, and go to the Barbès-Rochechouart quarter, where he would rent a room in a small hotel he knew there. Afterward, he'd grow a beard, change his name, rent a car, and drive to Orléans, whence he'd take a train for Toulouse, arriving on the ninth of November at the home of one of our correspondents, a Venetian named Trentin. During this time, I would return to London and then leave directly for Spain. We'd meet up with each other around the twentieth of November at the Continental Hotel in Barcelona.

The plan was successful. Our friends were completely fooled, particularly since Chesterfield left his jacket on the back of his chair and, despite the pouring rain, fled in his shirtsleeves. He took a room for two weeks in the Pacific Hotel on the Rue de la Goutte d'Or, using the name Cyril Charmer, while, wearing a fake beard, he waited for his own chin to sprout. The hotelkeeper, a sentimental horse-faced woman of about thirty, practically threw herself into Chesterfield's arms the moment he walked up to the reception desk, a fact which greatly simplified the question of lodgings. Her name was Alberte and she knew everything there was to know about the Paris underworld, which made it easy for Chesterfield to procure a passport and visa for Spain.

As planned, Chesterfield drove to Orléans, for we were certain the various secret services would be watching the railway stations. He arrived in Toulouse on the eighth of November and went directly to Trentin's, where the arrangements for his departure had already been made. Many trains passed through Toulouse-Matabiau, trains from Paris, Lyon, and Marseille, filled with volunteers of every nationality, all resolved to lend the Republicans a hand. There were rich young men as well as peasants, intellectuals and workers, idealists and failures, Catholics and atheists—a whole world lured by the scent of adventure and heroism. Chesterfield scarcely shared their wild and naïve enthusiasm, but it interested him as a positive phenomenon, a contribution to the balance of power necessary for peace.

Since early November, the Nationalists, who had risen up against the Republic on the eighteenth of July, had been closing in on Madrid. It was in this atmosphere of high tension that Chesterfield, alias Charmer, left Toulouse on November 14 in a train full of Czechoslovakian volunteers who sang hymns and drank vodka all night long, with their fists upraised.

After waiting for hours in the Perpignan railway station, and then in Cerbère—the frontier had been officially closed since July 26—the train arrived in Barcelona on the morning of November 16. Trentin had given Charmer a letter of introduction to John McNair, a socialist who ran the Independent Liberal party headquarters in the Catalan capital. This party was connected to POUM, the Partido Obrero de Unificación Marxista, which was fighting the Falangist rebels alongside the more Communist-oriented labor unions.

We remained in Barcelona for several days, then joined the anarchist troops of the Twenty-ninth Division in the trenches on the Aragon front at Alcubierre. The weather was freezing, the men as badly dressed as they were armed and organized. In fact, it seemed the rats were a more aggressive enemy than the Nationalists, from

whom we didn't hear a single shot during our brief stay. On the
other hand, when we got to Monte Oscuro in the Saragossa hills,
where a substantial English detachment was stationed, we were
shocked to see how relentlessly the Fascists harassed the troops
with their exceptionally accurate machine-gun fire. Just about all
the Republicans could offer in return were some old carbines, which
they fired with the careful casualness of people shooting at clay
pigeons at a fair.

We celebrated a rather austere Christmas in Barcelona, after which
Chesterfield decided to go to Málaga and, under his assumed name,
get in touch with Juan Montes de Mola, who'd been a personal
friend of Franco's and who might, therefore, be able to give us
some precious information on the general. I tried to dissuade him
from making the trip because Montes wasn't completely trust-
worthy; in addition, the Nationalists had just taken Seville, which
meant that Málaga could fall to them at any moment. But he was
obstinate, arguing that an interview with one of Franco's intimates
might shed some light on his intentions. I let myself be persuaded,
and we left in a military truck for Valencia where we stayed three
days, then took the train for Almería, and a car to Málaga. We
arrived on the eighteenth of January, in the midst of glorious sun-
shine. How far away the war seemed!

Juan Montes invited us to his sumptuous villa in the Real, overlooking the sea. He was a short, jovial fellow who hastened to assure us that he had no interest whatsoever in politics but that he'd
be delighted to help two English journalists describe General Fran-
cisco Franco Bahamonde, whom he'd had the honor of knowing
since 1923, when he was in Morocco. Thus we learned that the
general was an excellent bridge player, that he adored paella va-
lenciana, and that while he was commander of the Foreign Legion
he'd learned Arabic so that one day he might deal directly with
Abd-el-Krim. Anxious to prolong the interview, Chesterfield asked
about Franco's religious beliefs.

"A practicing Catholic," Montes affirmed. "Ever since the Moor-
ish invasion, the Church has been our fortress. All Spaniards are
Catholic. If they aren't, it means they've betrayed Spain, or are
planning to betray it. You English cannot possibly understand how
much religion in Spain is a matter of blood."

"But then how could Franco have hired on Moroccan troops for the reconquest of Spain?" Chesterfield asked. "Isn't that too a form of treason?"

"Listen," Montes replied, excitedly, "the general took what he could get. The Popular Front had booted him out and relegated him to the Canary Islands. But the army was still loyal to him, particularly the southern garrisons. As far as he's concerned, Moroccans are Spanish through and through. In fact, they're proving it right this minute. There's only one combat here—Catholics and Royalists and army against Republican trash. Do you know they've actually disinterred our kings and queens and laid their bodies out in front of the Epedralbes Monastery for everyone to see?" He was positively purple with indignation, and poured us all an absinthe.

After we left Montes, we went back to our hotel, the Almería, where Chesterfield wrote an article entitled "Moors and Catholics" which we intended to take to the post office that evening. Then, after a stroll down the narrow streets and along the port, we entered a small restaurant, anxious to try the local cuisine. We'd just walked in when three men rushed up to us, knocking over tables and chairs on the way, and upsetting a bottle that smashed on the tiles. We thought they were robbers, but they demanded to see our passports, gave them a cursory glance, and then dragged us off to the rear of the restaurant. Chesterfield struggled for the door, but one of the men flung him against the wall and, shouting incomprehensible threats, shook a revolver in his face. The two others handcuffed us and dragged us into a back room, occupied only by an old woman and a very pale child, both paralyzed with fear. From there, we were led across a vegetable garden, down a narrow street, through a low doorway into a very dark building, and down numerous corridors until we reached a dimly lit sort of cell where we were finally left alone.

We were locked into that cell for two weeks—it seemed an eternity—without our having any idea why. We were given food and drink but our jailer remained deaf and dumb to all our questions. We were, of course, unaware that the Falangists were closing in on Málaga and that the Republicans thought we were spies and had imprisoned us to be on the safe side. After all, hadn't we just paid a visit to one of Franco's close personal friends? The local censors had read the article Chesterfield had dropped at the post office and deemed it antigovernment. And that's how Chesterfield, or rather

Cyril Charmer, was imprisoned by the Republicans and turned over to the Falangists when the rebel army took the city on the eighth of February.

We did not find out that Málaga had fallen until an officer and two soldiers appeared one day instead of our warden. The officer made a few jokes about our situation, sat down familiarly beside us, pulled our passports from his pocket, and casually leafed through them.

"Gentlemen," he said in English, "the anarchists think you are spies in the pay of Germany or Italy. Quite ridiculous, no? The fact is, however, that we still don't know exactly who you are, although we do know the anarchists are wrong. Both you, Mr. Charmer, and you, Mr. Brown, write for the *Daily Herald*, which is not terribly well disposed toward us. Aside from the anarchists, who are after all only animals, everyone knows the *Daily Herald* is a den of Communists, traitors of all sorts actually, whose aim is to turn Europe over to the Bolsheviks. Mr. Charmer's article, which the anarchists were good enough to leave behind, the one called 'Moors and Catholics,' is quite simply a mass of irrelevancies designed to deceive the British public opinion. Therefore, I'm sure you can understand why we must keep you here until we have fuller information. . . ."

We demanded to be allowed to contact our embassy, but the officer only smiled ambiguously and left.

During this time, the English press had peppered the public with headlines like CHESTERFIELD VANISHED! All sorts of amazing hypotheses were bandied about, but in fact no one had heard from the writer since he'd left Barcelona, on a date that coincided exactly with his last dispatch to the *Daily Herald*. The paper immediately contacted the embassy in Madrid but, given the circumstances, could learn nothing. Not until February 20, when the Málaga police realized that behind the name of Charmer lurked the famous Chesterfield, did we learn what had actually happened. Richard Brown described this discovery as follows:

As soon as the Falangists in Granada realized who Charmer really was, they informed their superiors. They'd caught themselves a fabulous treasure, too fabulous in fact. Everyone knew of the writer's international reputation; his works had been translated into

Spanish three years before. On the other hand, Chesterfield had been the first to claim that Luftwaffe pilots were giving "technical advice" to the Falangists, a fact Franco could scarcely forgive.

We were transferred to another prison in the city that held everyone awaiting sentencing by the Fascists. From our cell, we heard the firing squad executing partisans, spies, unionists, Communists, and other opponents of the regime Franco dreamed of establishing, and this at all hours of the day and night. Chesterfield awaited death calmly; he had no doubts that the chance to muzzle him definitively was just too good to pass up. From time to time, someone came to interrogate him; when he was returned to the cell, he told me they'd asked him questions like "Who are you working for?" and "What foreign power sent you to Spain?" and "What makes you think Germany and Italy are supplying us with arms?" and "Just what gives you the right to think that the German Nazi party is anti-Semitic?" The triteness and hypocrisy of the questions dismayed him more than they alarmed him. He was, in fact, quite certain that his destiny was being decided not in Málaga but in Franco's headquarters; he was also certain that the future Caudillo took orders from the Germans, who couldn't fail to condemn him to death.

But Jonathan was wrong. Franco had no desire to provoke the ire of Great Britain or America by making Chesterfield a martyr. What he wanted was to find some way to make a fool of him in order to weaken his influence. Thus, on the fifth of March, the Nazi paper *The Falange* began to publish Chesterfield's "sworn statements" acknowledging his "errors." This scandalous tactic was reinforced by the publication *in extenso*—with sardonic commentary—of these statements in the German, Italian, and Portuguese press, as well as the two extremist London papers. On the other hand, articles in the British, American, French, and Scandinavian papers proved that no one believed for a moment in the writer's change of heart. Even *Pravda* denounced Franco's lies, although the official newspaper of the Soviet Union did not exactly disdain those very same procedures.

The articles in the Falangist press ran something like this:

The celebrated writer Gilbert K. Chesterfield, author of *Beelzebub* and *The Monkey King*, well known for his anti-Germanism, signatory of numerous papers denouncing so-called anti-Semitic "conspiracies," decided to tour the Spanish front for the London paper, the socialist *Daily Herald*. After having directed his most distinguished attention to the government coalition of socialists and Communists in Barcelona, the verbose novelist traveled to Málaga where he intended to make contact with Nationalist authorities, who, as everyone knows, liberated this symbolic city on February 8 from the socio-anarchist yoke. Our military correspondent in Málaga, Lieutenant Colonel Juan Montes de Mola, had the privilege of witnessing the English writer's disenchanted observations, whose errors he freely confesses in the following interview.

Question: Why did you come to Málaga?

Answer: Because I wished to make contact with the Nationalist army led by General Franco Bahamonde. During my sojourn in Spain, I've been able to see firsthand that the internal workings of the socio-Communist coalition are really run by the anarchists. From my perspective in London, I was swayed by a sort of romanticism that led me to support certain forces which I believed were progressive. Once in Barcelona, however, and at the front, I found that the reality was quite different. There we saw an amalgam of political ideologues and confused soldiers manipulated by foreign powers, the Bolsheviks in particular. I might add that the Soviet strategy is clearly to take advantage of this socialist pseudorevolution to wreak havoc throughout Europe.

Question: From your present perspective, how would you describe the role of General Franco Bahamonde?

Answer: General Franco is clearly a rampart against those who are determined to annihilate essential Western values such as country, religion, and family, a rampart similar to Hitler in Germany, Mussolini in Italy, and Salazar in Portugal. Spain is a Catholic nation founded on the chivalric values of the Holy Roman Empire. These are notions which Protestant England can scarcely understand or appreciate, but which are nonetheless fundamental. The instability created by the anarcho-Marxist coalition in the very heart of a Europe which has always been attached to these values can only create terror and devastation. The security of the Spanish nation is at stake, and through it, all of Europe.

Question: You once claimed that the Nationalist army, led by General Franco Bahamonde, received military aid from Germany and Italy. What do you think about that today?

Answer: My information was incorrect. It's only natural, given the worldwide subversive activities of pro-Marxists and misinformed intellectuals, that the national forces of defense regroup, but it would be untrue to claim that Spain has received any armaments at all from either Germany or Italy. Any aid from these countries has been in the form of pharmaceutical products, canned goods, and clothes for the care, feeding, and clothing of a population that the socio-Communist coalition is systematically reducing to penury.

Question: You were one of the signers of certain petitions aiming to undermine, if possible, the Third Reich, petitions which purported to expose the racist policies of Chancellor Adolf Hitler. Do you still believe in the existence of such policies?

Answer: Shaken by internal revolution—strikes, anarchy, and ideological conflict—Germany fell into chaos. Economic analysis has shown that all successive monetary and intellectual devaluations have been the products of the ongoing treachery of foreign powers—on the one hand, Marxists controlled by Moscow, and on the other, Jews and related groups. This is why Chancellor Hitler's first task was to combat this treachery and to prevent these subversive forces from continuing their lethal work. Hitler is, therefore, not anti-Semitic in principle, but it is a fact that the imperialism of the Jews, and others like them, has long been directed against the German nation.

Question: Certain dubious tabloids have claimed that your son was kidnapped for political reasons. Can you clarify this?

Answer: My son was kidnapped by the American branch of the Mafia, and anyone who argues otherwise is mistaken.

The interview concluded with the following comment: "Thus are the lies mouthed by the Marxist intelligentsia of Spain, and of other countries, placed in their proper perspective." Three additional, and similar, "confessions" followed, on March 7, 9, and 12. During this time, Jonathan and Richard Brown were confined to their cell, and knew nothing of this lamentable publicity. According to Brown:

Executions by firing squad alternated with training sessions in the use of weapons. We heard both distinctly from our cell. Chesterfield talked about his childhood; about an aristocrat who'd taken him in and whom he called "my lord"; about his wife, Sarah, whom he'd left at Kells and whom he loved dearly; about his son, Yehudi, who'd been kidnapped by Nazi strongmen. He still did not know if he was alive or dead. This thought tormented him and he regretted not having fought hard enough against those responsible for the kidnapping. The feeling of his own impotence, and that of the world in general, in the face of both Nazism and Bolshevism, was even stronger than his remorse, however. He also spoke of his mother, who was Jewish, and his father, an important politician, and of Cyril Charmer, his friend and secretary, whose name he had assumed before entering Spain. He also asked me many questions about myself, my life, my relationship with Felicia Johnson. He spoke calmly and gravely, with no show of nervousness, as if his despondency were merely a passing fatigue, but I knew that in that Málaga prison, he had reached the depths of despair. He felt he hadn't used his celebrity sufficiently in the service of what he called "the active Utopia of the spirit."

One morning, at five o'clock, an officer woke us up and told us to get ready for our execution. It must have been around the tenth of March. "Do you believe in God?" the officer asked. "Would you like to see a priest?" He looked to be about thirty and seemed upset, almost intimidated. There were two armed guards with him. We stood up; it was scarcely a time for flowery phrases. All I said was "How is it that the king has done nothing to free us?" Chesterfield shrugged. "No one knows we're here. Franco's taken care not to publicize his prize." We got dressed, except for our shoes, which had been taken away on our first day. The officer handcuffed our hands behind our backs, and we walked out into the corridor. I've no idea what Chesterfield's thoughts were at that moment; as for my own, I couldn't possibly describe them.

Dawn was breaking as we crossed a courtyard; there was a strong acrid odor I couldn't identify. A priest in a white soutane, Dominican probably, came toward us, a corpulent fellow, completely bald, with a kindly face. His eyes sought ours, and in broken English he said, "May the peace of God be with you!" Or some cliché like that. My legs were so weak I could scarcely stand, and I was trembling with cold and certainly with fear. Chesterfield stopped for an instant, said, "May God forgive me," and then continued walking.

The silence was so profound I thought I'd suddenly gone deaf. They backed us up against a wall; there was a line of soldiers opposite us. "How odd!" Chesterfield said, turning to me. I didn't ask him what he meant, for I was incapable of uttering a word. I would have liked to scream some moving appeal, but my mind was paralyzed, blank. An officer barked something in Spanish; the soldiers raised their rifles. Another order rang out and they took aim. It was like a dream, and yet we were going to die. The image of Goya's man in a white shirt came to me, but it was too late to think anymore. What good had my life been? That was my final instant of lucidity before the officer shouted, *"Fuego!"* The word snapped through the courtyard like the crack of a whip. The soldiers pulled their triggers—click! The guns weren't loaded! The whole thing had been an act. They took us back to our cells. "Dogs!" Chesterfield said, and spat on the ground next to the officer's boots.

This scene heralded the imminent liberation of the two prisoners. Frustrated by the release order, the prison officers had decided to enact their execution, since they couldn't actually do it. On the ninth of March, King George VI had sent General Franco a letter demanding Chesterfield's immediate liberation, accompanied by a thinly disguised threat in case anything unfortunate were to happen to the writer. On the same day, Pope Pius XI, alerted by the prime minister, Stanley Baldwin, and by public rumor, had requested the "supreme commander of the Spanish Nationalist forces, our beloved son," to pardon Chesterfield. Finally, on March 17, as petitions circulated just about everywhere demanding that Franco release him, Jonathan and his companion left Málaga under the aegis of the Red Cross and, in accordance with international convention, were turned over to the French police, who moved them to Vernet-les-Bains in the Pyrénées-Orientales, a town famous for its hot springs, which were said to cure sore throats and rheumatism. The Hôtel des Pyrénées was now a clearinghouse where people in "irregular political situations" were allowed to stay until their respective consulates could receive them and arrange their passage to their native countries.

Not until his arrival in Vernet did Jonathan learn of the false declarations the Falange had printed in his name. He immediately wrote a retraction that the French authorities were good enough to distribute to the major newspapers. The British ambassador to France traveled from Paris to Vernet to greet the writer and offer the good wishes of the

British people. He also gave him a telegram from the Honorable Harold Spencer that contained only two words: CARRY ON! On March 28, Chesterfield and Richard Brown took a boat for Dover, where they were given a jubilant welcome. Thousands of people had gathered to watch their hero's arrival, although no one was quite able to define just what sort of heroism they were applauding! Brown's eyewitness reports, which he'd sent to several different papers while still in Vernet, had caused quite a sensation; the simulated execution stirred up more consciousnesses than the most moving speeches, for the British sense of fair play had been profoundly violated by that macabre comedy. The sales of *The Man Without a Face*, which Goldman had published in September of 1936, picked up again instantly, which made Peter Warner rue the day he'd broken Varlet's contract. And after so much agonizing uncertainty, I, too, was finally able to breathe freely.

A week later, I went to see Jonathan Absalom Varlet at Kells, which was now guarded by an impressive police force. Apparently, the prime minister feared that Fascists of every ilk might try to assassinate Chesterfield, as they'd recently attempted to do on the person of Harry Pollitt, the general secretary of the Communist party. When I finally got through to the entryway, Jonathan greeted me with great feeling. He was considerably thinner, and it seemed to me his eyes had lost that keenness which had been a not negligible ingredient of his charm. We shook hands, and entered the main drawing room.

"It was grotesque," he said. "Just as they were about to shoot us, or so we believed, the last words that came to me were 'How odd!' But I'm certain I was really thinking, *How grotesque!* All those men and women and children dying in the name of values that are even more tragic because they're so grotesque. Franco dreams only of returning Spain to feudalism, which is grotesque enough in itself. The anarchists want direct rule by the people, without God or master, which is also grotesque. The socialists are controlled by the Communists who are duped by Stalin, which is even more grotesque. Who or what are they fighting for in Spain? For freedom? But what kind of freedom? That of the landless peasant or of the omnipotent landowner? That of the oppressed worker or of the bureaucrat in his sedan? None of them knows the price of freedom; they're all prisoners of values that have been inculcated in them. Worn-out threadbare values. The whole thing's become an exercise in formalism. Even the words *God* and *man* have no meaning. It's not God they've killed; it's language! Modern man is tragic because he's lost his language! His speech is no longer anything but a hollow victory over devalued objects. The accumulation of meanings is a sign of the loss of meaning. And yet, Cyril, despite the absurdity of it all, despite those rifles they kept teasing me with, I knew that the grotesque itself had a meaning. Those guns had the power to annihilate me, but not to make me lose my mind. Cain kills Abel and, in so doing, believes he's changed him into an object. But he hasn't. It's Abel who acquires meaning and Cain who becomes absurd! Do you remember what my lord told me in Venice in front of the church of San Moisè—the death that petrifies and the death that invigorates! That's exactly what this is all about!"

Sarah sat curled up in an enormous cathedral chair, looking even more minuscule in this grand piece of ancient furniture. The nurse had propped her up with cushions and as she sat there, her dark hair barely flecked with gray and pulled back so tightly one could see the pale scalp beneath, she looked like a slightly delirious little girl with a fever. She murmured softly in German, her voice surprisingly clear.

"She didn't even notice my absence," Jonathan said. "She has conversations with invisible people and doesn't eat anything. She's like a lamp whose oil has been completely consumed and is burning only its wick. The shadows are gathering about her."

We went into the library.

"This—this library—is what I dreamed of in prison. I remembered every book; I remembered exactly where it was, the binding, the frontispiece, the drawings, and even certain passages which struck me when I was an adolescent. I've read a lot since that time, you know, but these books are still the most familiar. And yet, what are they? Treatises on alchemy and the Cabala, each more abstruse than the next. It was Jacob Boehme I thought about in my cell, the same Boehme behind your Jacob Stern, the Boehme my lord so often quoted in his letters. And do you know why?"

He studied me with intensity.

"Because 'virginity is precious but it must give birth, for if it doesn't, it is like a sterile country.' That's from Silesius. That's the message Boehme gave the Western world, but our philosophy paid it no mind. Purity's only purpose is creation. But we, citizens of this tormented century, we've lost all desire for this elemental purity without which there can be no creation, and thus no meaning! We've lost ourselves in a mass of beliefs, and thus we've lost our faith. We've all become mechanics and so understand nothing anymore but methods. We invent, but we no longer create. The prostitute of Babylon has proffered her cup of insanity and we've drunk it!"

I couldn't help smiling, he was so exalted.

"And do you think people are ready to hear this sort of language? Whatever could anyone understand today of Boehme and Silesius? I rather think your talk of virginity will make people laugh . . . and as for procreation, isn't the world preparing to bring forth some hideous monster?"

"I suppose," he sighed. "What's essential has become trivial, point-less, laughable. What do they mean, those words *pure* and *impure*, in a world that knows only a mixture of the two? When I was in Bardcelona, I used to see this left-wing militant every once in a while. A radical leftist, actually. A Belgian by the name of Winaert. Flemish. All he could talk about was purity, political purity of course. He was a Stalinist. No matter what came from Moscow, he accepted it—trials, purges, defa-mations, assassinations. And all of it in the name of his famous purity. He was a man of dogma, a real little Savonarola in a way—none of which prevented him from sleeping with boys in the *barrio chino* and doing a lot of black-market racketeering in cigarettes!"

As he stood there, beside the bookshelves that hid the circular stair-case, I suddenly noticed how unkempt he looked, he who ordinarily paid great attention to his appearance. He raised his arm in a vague gesture.

"When all is said and done, I'm nothing but a mass of vanities. I thought I had a destiny, or rather that I was a destiny, and by what right? You, Cyril my friend, at least you had the modesty to hide behind someone else who could play the puppet/monkey in your stead. What am I saying, modesty? Intelligence, rather. You'll leave a whole body of work behind you. Elsbeth, little Jacob Stern, your man without a face— now those are characters! I'm not even one of them."

"You mustn't believe that," I said sincerely. "You are most certainly one of my characters, and the most accomplished one since here you are—alive, complicated, changeable, mysterious, simple! Isn't it the dream of every artist to see his statue come to life, or his hero walk off the page? You're the expression of my doubt, something like a stumbling that allowed me to climb over an unsuspected obstacle. It's all a bit of a game, you know. . . ."

He smiled, amused by the thought.

"We're twins, aren't we?" he asked suddenly.

Later, after Sarah had been put to bed, we listened to recordings, as
if the entire Spanish episode had never happened, as if we were listening
to Sibelius for the first time. And yet Jonathan's peregrinations through
the Spanish Civil War had marked him with a stamp I knew was both
painful and indelible. He talked to me about Simon Partner, who was
making gold out of straw in New York, presiding over the sales of dolls
and the toys that went with them like a king over his court. Yet this was
nothing but the tentacles of an octopus without a soul, a mechanism to
lure the innumerable buyers who no longer bought Souen and Elsbeth
and the cities and the cars and the miniature wardrobes for their children's amusement, but to appease their mania for collecting. Matthew
Tennyson's film *The Right to Love* had been so successful that there was
talk of filming *Jacob Stern*. In short, business had never been better, or
as Varlet put it, Mercury, the god of businessmen and thieves, smiled
more benevolently upon us than Hermes, the god of the spirit. It's true
that thanks to the prodigious success of Chesterfield's novels, and the
various royalties they engendered, my personal fortune continued to grow;
I say this without either excessive modesty or boastfulness, for I was not
at all proud of this money, part of which I'd already begun donating to
charities.

At the end of April 1937, Peter Warner asked me to come see him
at his office. I replied that I was unable to do so, so he traveled to
Ruthford.

"Come, come," he said jovially, "we're not exactly at war, now
are we?"

We were standing on the front lawn, for I refused to invite him in.

"Your political opinions are diametrically opposed to Chesterfield's.
And to mine. Moreover, your anti-Semitism displeases us."

"Such childishness!" he replied, with a forced laugh. "It's true I helped
Margaret research Varlet's origins, and my god, we never suspected his
mother was Jewish! After that, the press got hold of it. That's the price
of success, you know."

"What exactly can I do for you, Mr. Warner?"

He stood on his tiptoes, which only made him seem smaller.

"Our friend Chesterfield, in a passing rage I'd imagine, broke his contract with us. He had every right, of course. We only had a four-book
contract. But we were just at the dawn of his success. After all, we were
the ones who paid for the advertising and publicity. . . ."

"I didn't break the contract, Mr. Warner. Chesterfield did. There's nothing I can do for you, particularly since had I been in his shoes, I should have done the same thing."

"That's what happens when you pay attention to politics. I always regretted Margaret's joining up with that chap Mosley, you know. I found out what part she unwittingly played in your divorce. She's the one who introduced you to that Russian . . . that Charlienko. I can promise you she's seen her mistake."

Once upon a time, I'd had a certain admiration for this man, and now he turned my stomach. Just a few years ago, I didn't dare cross the threshold of his publishing house, and now I was booting him off my property. He climbed back into his car with dignity, ordered his chauffeur to drive on, and so left me. I'd just dismissed *my* own editor! Nonetheless, the monsters from one's past do not vanish like smoke; they grab hold of your skirts without your even noticing and suddenly they leap out at you, grinning horribly. Thus did the specter of Margaret reappear exactly one month after her father's. It had been raining for two weeks and the grounds at Ruthford were slowly turning into a large pond. In this sort of weather, Douglas suffered from rheumatism and walked with a stoop, but she arrived one morning at the door to my study with the Chinese curtains, where I was just beginning to gather material for a new novel, and announced that a car had drawn up outside the gate. Apparently, a woman was asking for me.

"You know . . . that woman who . . ."

I already know whom she meant and was just about to ask Douglas to send her on her way when, having crossed the drawing room and the dining room on her own initiative, Miss Warner entered the study.

"I had to see you, Cyril. . . ." Her hair was soaking wet and the water that dripped from her white raincoat was rapidly forming a puddle on the carpet. She looked rather crazy. Douglas considered this unusual spectacle with horror.

"If ever you had any feelings for me, Cyril . . ."

I invited her to take off her coat, which she did mechanically. Douglas grabbed it and disappeared.

"Cyril, I beg of you, with all my heart, please, please listen to me. . . ."

I asked her to sit down, but she remained standing in her little black poor woman's dress; had she been standing outside a church, one would surely have given her tuppence.

"You must believe me, Cyril! First, I beg you to forgive me. What I did to you was shameful. I wanted to hurt you because I couldn't take revenge on Jonathan, but I swear it wasn't you I meant to hurt, and then things . . . You must believe I'm telling you the truth, Cyril. . . . Things just got out of hand."

"Mary wasn't the right woman for me. I trust she's happy with Charlienko, at least?"

"Charlienko? You mean you don't know? Really? But Cyril, he committed suicide! He's dead. At least two months ago . . ."

"I'm happy for Mary," I replied simply. "How did he do it?"

"I loved him too, you know," Margaret replied, dropping into an armchair. "Not the same way as Jonathan, of course, but there was such unhappiness, such distress, in him. . . . His aggressiveness was simply the reverse side of his confusion. He was a lost soul. We all are, aren't we? But he was more lost than anyone and Mary, as foolish as she was, poor soul, she was touched by that sort of sacrament of suffering which anointed him in the name of a vocation made the more sublime by his desperation."

"A nice turn of phrase, but I wasn't aware that the devil had his own sacraments!"

"It wasn't possible for you to understand someone like Leonid, Cyril. He was at the opposite pole from your comfortableness and your success. One night, he climbed onto the window sill of your Green Park flat with a loaded pistol; Mary was right there, pregnant, watching him. And he . . . you know that frightful game called Russian roulette? Well, that's how it happened. Except it wasn't a game. There was a bullet in each chamber. . . ."

"And Mary?"

"She had a little boy. She's the last one we should pity. You made her a tidy settlement, didn't you?"

Curiously, I was pleased to learn that Mary had had a boy and that I was, in some way, supporting her. The feeling took hold of me suddenly and to my great surprise, for the child had been sired by a man I scorned and born by a woman who was for me merely a shadow.

The aim of Margaret's unannounced visit was not, however, to bring me up to date on my former wife and her pregnancy. She wiped her face with the back of her hand, thus completing the ruination of her makeup; never had I seen her like this, as if she'd just crawled away from a catastrophe.

"I made a terrible mistake, Cyril. It wasn't until I heard about Jonathan's experience in Málaga that I finally understood who he really was. I thought he was an arriviste, self-obsessed, ready to sacrifice whatever he needed to get what he wanted. I felt as if his charm was a vicious weapon that he used to get his way. And then, all of a sudden, I realized he was sincere. How can I explain it? I loved him and I hated him, but my hatred was steeped in a love I couldn't get rid of. Doubtless I shouldn't say these things to you, but you're the only one I can talk to anymore. How can I manage this remorse by myself? If he'd been killed, it would have been my fault, wouldn't it?"

"Let's not exaggerate. Your hatred of the Jews is, of course, quite astonishing; it's also possible that your hatred is a function of your love for Jonathan. . . . That would certainly befit your complexity of style. But from there to think that you're responsible for his being imprisoned in Spain is quite ridiculous!"

She looked at me with a mixture of surprise and fear.

"But you don't know . . ." she stammered. "I must tell you. . . . It was I who suggested to Mosley that he have Jonathan arrested."

"What?" I was stunned. She looked as if she were drowning; her face was pale, her hair glued to her temples.

"Mosley was in contact with Montes . . . Lieutenant Colonel Juan Montes de Mola," she said, lowering her eyes. "He set the trap. It was all a trick, his giving Chesterfield unpublished information about Franco. He was playing a double game, Montes, with both the Republicans and the Falangists. He had them arrested, Jonathan and that other reporter, accused them of spying, knowing that the Falangists were about to take Málaga." She paused, raising her head in that old gesture of defiance. "I wanted him to die! Right then, that's what I wanted!" She burst into tears. "At least I wanted him to suffer the way I'd suffered," she sobbed. "He left me for Sarah, a nobody, a child . . . He was happy over there, in New York, his arms full of prizes. And I was the one who'd made it possible. Without me, my father never would have published *Beelzebub*."

I sprang to my feet, seized her violently by the collar of her dress, forcing her to stand up.

"And the kidnapping? Tell me! Yehudi's kidnapping . . ."

Her eyes filled with terror.

"No! No!" she murmured. "Not that! I swear it! Not that!"

She kept crying, her shoulders shaken by hoarse sobs of a nauseating vulgarity. Collapsed on the floor between the armchair and my desk, the woman disgusted me. Overcome with rage, I pulled her to her feet and slapped her as hard as I could. She clutched at my jacket; her death's-head face took on a look of ecstasy. Her lips trembled.

"Oh, yes, yes!" she cried.

I threw her from me. So that was what she wanted!

I went to the door and called Douglas, who scurried up; she'd heard the to-do and was obviously frightened. Dear old Ruthford had never witnessed a scene quite like this!

"Miss Warner has been taken ill," I said, pretending to a calm I didn't feel. "Do please help her up, get her dressed, and see her to the door." Then I went up to my room. The rain beat upon the windowpanes, and the smell of mildew seemed to have invaded the house—and the world as well, I suspect. Ruthford seemed to be sinking into a swamp filled with decomposing vegetation that gave off a putrid perfume. I could not get to sleep.

On the fifth of May, Guernica y Luno, the sacred city of the Basque country, was bombarded by the Condor Legion, which Germany had ordered into the service of the Nationalists.

THE END OF 1937 WAS BOTH MARVELOUS
and sad. In the same month of October, the Nobel Prize for Literature
was awarded to Gilbert K. Chesterfield, and our dear Sarah passed away.
We had known for some time that the writer's work in Kampala, as well
as in Spain, had prompted the academicians to reevaluate his file; what
we did not know was that His Majesty George VI had instructed the
British ambassador to make certain that the Nobel Peace Prize, which
was to go to Lord Chelwood that year, would not diminish Chesterfield's
chances in any way. I later learned that Harold Spencer had had a great
deal to do with the king's intervention; in fact, Spencer's influence had
been decisive, all in all an impressive way for Jonathan's father to atone
for the abandonment of his son!

The news reached me while I was studying the prehistoric remains of
Dun Aengus on the Aran Islands. This sere and powerful semicircle
overhanging a black cliff, swept by glacial winds that set the stones
moaning, had long intrigued me; I had decided to tour this part of Ireland to cleanse my spirit tainted by certain previous events—Margaret
Warner's confession in particular—which had opened before me an abyss
I simply could not endure. Had she really been involved in Yehudi's
kidnapping, even if only by virtue of her suggestion to Mosley? I refused

to believe it, but the fact that she'd been instrumental in Jonathan's internment, and thus in his narrow brush with death, forced me to look once more upon the terrifying void, and so I'd fled to the consolations of Inishmaan and Inishmore.

I'd arrived in Kilronan morose and uneasy, as if the world were indeed about to succumb to the dualism of the perverse and hypocritical law that divided it into two opposing, and yet fundamentally similar, camps—fascism and communism. They were like the two faces of a material Janus, a true Moloch ready to annihilate the human race, if necessary, to comply with its criminal and wrong-headed rigor. I imagined the Nazis and the Stalinists weaving a double ring around the world, rings manipulated by obscure forces that would eventually propel the free nations into the chaos of war if they tried to resist their morbid attraction. The great open spaces of Inishmore, with their singular marriage of water, air, and stone, had quieted my imagination. Only lichens now withstood the encroachments of the desert where men had once built a city, a monument to their determination to endure. In defiance of our civilization's confusion, its chaos of paper and ghosts, this stone semicircle facing the infinite seemed the bearer of a vital and urgent message.

A few days earlier, on the isle of Inishmaan, I knelt to meditate on the tomb of a man and woman who had lain there side by side, naked and serene, for perhaps fifteen thousand years, in a tomb tradition had dubbed "the bed of Dermott and Grania." No, they were not the dusty vestiges of a confused and shadowy world, but the guardians of the dawn of humanity, witnesses to the durability of a fructifying love in the face of death. As I mused upon this, the events I'd just experienced, charged as they were with somber presages, were restored to their proper, and rather insignificant, places. And now, suddenly, a little Irish boy with clogs was bringing me a very strange piece of news indeed, one that made no sense in this vast and solitary land. The telegram, signed VARLET, read as follows: CHESTERFIELD NOBEL PRIZE LITERATURE STOP RENDEZVOUS KELLS AND CONGRATULATIONS. At the time, it struck me as a trivial sort of joke. Who *was* Chesterfield really? Did he even exist? As I returned to the inn, escorted only by the cries of gulls, I wondered, in the face of the world's madness, whether art was perhaps still a sort of Dun Aengus.

And so once again I returned to Kells. Sarah had ceased to eat; the sheet that covered her was shapeless, as if the body beneath it had vanished. Her face was like a child's; she no longer spoke, and her breathing was so shallow that had it not been for the intensity with which she gazed upon her invisible world, I should have thought her dead. What did she see? Yehudi, probably. Jonathan said she looked more and more like their son, as if she were undergoing some sort of return to a communal origin. In her bedroom, decorated now with autumn leaves, a sort of transmutation was taking place, the young woman moving backward toward the womb that had once carried her. Candles had been lit all around the bed, as is customary in Scotland when a woman is about to die or give birth, for here death is merely another form of childbirth.

"I'm going to refuse the prize," Jonathan said. "It ought to have gone to you."

"But you mustn't!" I cried. "Without your hospital and your campaign against racism and your experience in Spain, Chesterfield would never have been chosen! Anyway, if it hadn't been for you, no more than a handful of people would ever have read my work. You must go to Stockholm and take advantage of the opportunity to deliver yet another warning to the Western world."

He moved to Sarah's bedside where she lay sleeping; for an instant the candles flickered.

"I'm just so tired. . . . I don't think any career has been more rapid and illustrious than ours, Cyril. Your Chesterfield is getting the Nobel at thirty-one, having taken giant steps through every stage of celebrity. You and I have amassed a fortune envied by even the wealthiest industrialists. Your work is appreciated throughout the world—except for Germany, where they burn it, which is only an additional honor. What more can we ask for? And yet what a waste! Here you are, obsessed with writing your books and choosing investments; and here am I, dancing to the tunes of publicity, commerce, and politics—and neither of us has really lived. Yehudi was taken from us. Sarah's going to die. Is that what life is all about?"

I laid a friendly hand on his shoulder.

"Yes. What more do we have the right to ask for? We may be like wisps of straw swept along by torrents, but our gaze remains even after our eyes have closed. The gaze of the human being on the world—the *regard*, Jonathan—is the only thing that's not absurd, were the world a hundred times more insane. It's a mixture of sadness and revolt, fear and courage, lucidity and madness, but it's the only regard in the universe that refuses to accept its death. It knows that the earth will grow colder again, that the stars will fall and the sun explode. It knows that nothing lasts, and yet it affirms the existence of another time, another earth, other stars, and another sun—elsewhere and eternal. It's this regard, this innocent and miraculous gaze, that brings order to the chaos of the world, that cultivates and impregnates it and compels it to give birth to the spirit, to the rare firebird that shivers with cold in the dungeon where our contemporaries disdain it. Without this look, man becomes a slave to death and our world is doomed."

Perhaps it was the solemn sumptuousness of those high walls, or the proximity of a dying Sarah, ringed by the pale glimmer of candlelight. Or was it rather the fever I'd caught in the icy winds of Dun Aengus, or my confusion at the announcement of our literary award? Withal, when I left Jonathan for the guest room at the far end of a hallway guarded by ancient armor, I staggered like a drunkard. My body was burning, perspiration coursed abundantly down my limbs; then, suddenly, my teeth were chattering and I was freezing. Leaving all the lights on, I slid fully clothed into bed and pulled the covers up to my chin. The walls of the room were paneled in oak and decorated with coats of arms, heraldic emblems that seemed to come alive all around me, whirling in a sort of saraband that forced my eyes shut. I lay there a long time, chilled to the bone or shaken by waves of heat that in a few seconds raised my temperature to boiling.

"Hello there!" caroled a voice beside me. "Could it be that our good Mr. Charmer is about to leave us?"

My head snapped around. An exceedingly tall individual dressed in white emerged form the shadows. I recognized him immediately. He seated himself familiarly in the armchair opposite the bed; his face was gentle, as if smoothed by the passage of time and kindness. Although I wasn't frightened, I was nonetheless incapable of speech. He was exactly as I'd imagined him.

"My dear Mr. Charmer," he began, "or rather, if you will permit me, my dear Cyril—for we've known each other a long time, haven't we? My dear Cyril, then, I believe the time has come to have a little chat."

He spoke with a certain nobility, like an aristocrat, and seemed not at all uncomfortable with the oddness of the situation, an oddness that, I must confess, seemed quite curious to me at the time, interesting even, but not really all that strange.

"Things people call mysterious or enigmatic or farcical or baroque, you have written about quite easily in your books. You knew not only that a monkey is capable of speech, but that it can also ascend into the heavens and do battle with dragons. For you, there is no frontier between the visible and the invisible, no chasm between the real and the imaginable. You were not very suited to ordinary life; it might even be said you were afraid of life, that you preferred conversing with a 'beyond' that you drew from the collective memory by the action of your pen on a sheet of paper. And that, my dear Cyril, is why I've chosen you."

Suddenly I was infused with a lovely calm. The room had disappeared and as he spoke, alone before me in his armchair, it felt as if the impalpable veils in the labyrinth of my mind were being swept aside, and the whole lit by an unfamiliar glow.

"You cannot know how many people you've interested. The most diverse characters really . . . even a female spirit, the Alicia who dominated your adolescent dreams and filled you with blasphemies. You were a true masochist, I must say. But enough. You wrote very little for her, actually—because I came along, pushed her aside, and took her place. And it was better that way, wasn't it? Instead of vulgar little chirpings from that ignorant child, you had the right to my full concerto, and because you seemed intrigued by suffering women—in memory of your mother, yes?—I gave you Elsbeth. The sublime Elsbeth . . . ah yes, for at that time you needed the sublime, did you not, my good friend? She was a joint project really, yours and mine. And most successful, if I do say so myself. Rather like a cello partita in which we can all hear the sounds of a soul in despair . . . What delights for a distinguished onanist! A woman who dreams of giving herself to God, but God rejects her! That long awaiting, as if the entire universe were in suspense, nice bit of eroticism there . . . In short, my son, I've spoiled you."

He fell silent. I lay paralyzed beneath my covers, unable to take my eyes from him.

"But alas! Three times alas! You may have been sufficiently talented to capture and transcribe the various niceties of my tastes but you had absolutely no talent for making them heard. Thus I placed upon your path my spiritual son, a marvelous young man, freshly unmolded from my laboratory, whose task was to obviate your lack of appetite. As masterful as you were in the art of listening to me, you were absolutely nil in the commerce of the world. Too timid. Rather cowardly. And very lazy. So I gave you Varlet, to circulate in your stead the tales I dictated to you, of which the first was *Beelzebub,* the second *Jacob Stern,* the third *The Monkey King*, and the last *The Man Without a Face*. I daresay they made you a very honest reputation, did they not? You may judge for yourself; after all, you're at the pinnacle of your fame!"

He spoke with a slight German accent, inserting uncommon words into the labyrinth of a language both convoluted and precise.

"It is crucial, my dear Cyril, that you understand the purpose of this literature which poured out of you like blood from a sectioned artery— forgive me the analogy but I do so like brutal imagery. For of course you aren't pretentious enough to imagine that all those pages filled with all that elegant writing came from your personal verbosity, now are you? The power I exercised so subtly on your pia mater robbed you of the freedom to add your own olio to the themes I'd chosen for you. My plan was too urgent to allow for the psychological rubbish of a century hungry for narcissistic twaddle! You see, it was a question of revealing that mankind had at last achieved its own demise. Oh yes, my young friend . . . The end of time! The end of the world! Through your works, I announced the end of humanity!"

At any other time, this delirium would have made me smile, but now I simply lay there, a prisoner of my bedclothes and fully aware that the madness that had overcome me derived from my own fever. Yet I was unable to rid myself of the gentleman in white who suddenly stood up, approached my bedside, and laid a hand on my forehead.

"Heavens, look how frightened you are! Why, your whole carcass is trembling! Butterflies are whirling inside your head! And—pretentious fool that you are—you think I'm only a phantasm! That's really quite comic, you know, but I think you would do better to listen to me very carefully. Just who is he, this Jonathan Absalom Varlet? The son of an aristocrat who abandoned him in the forest? A spirit who materialized out of thin air? A crepuscular goblin? Nay, good sir. Our ragamuffin is a prince of the Third Power, whose mission is to guard the doors to hell. Ah, yes! Hell has doors, and these doors have guards. Varlet is a sort of sophisticated concierge, if you like. . . ."

He laughed coarsely, in marked contrast to his former elegance. "I commanded him," he continued, walking away from me now, "I commanded him to inform this futile ridiculous world that I, its master, intended at any moment to flip the switch that would set certain mechanisms into motion, mechanisms that would cause everything to collapse. You were my writer and he my salesman, both of you heralds of my good news—the Apocalypse! Do you remember Baruch: 'And then I heard the angel say to the angels who held the torches, "Strike then, and raze the ramparts to their foundations!" And the angels did as he commanded. And when they had demolished the corners of the ramparts, there came a voice from inside the temple which said, "Enter, enemies. Enter, you who hate. The One who has guarded the temple has fled. God has fled the world! God has abandoned His temple! And now I am alone, I the jury, I the mighty prophet, I who announce catastrophes and the triumph of the void!"

He'd returned to his armchair and appeared to me now in the classic guise of the Beast itself—the hairy hide, the dragon's head, the goat horns, like some cast-off carnival costume smelling faintly of the dyer's basin.

"But the moment this Varlet came to ground, what do you suppose happened to him? He who by his acidic sooty nature was doomed to love no one but himself, as befits the beautiful brothers of the Order of Cloven Hooves, he the icy seducer, the snake that charms, he who was made of treachery and rage, who was incapable of feelings other than deceit and hatred, this Varlet . . . he expressed sympathy for these very individuals whom I had condemned! He began to flirt with the diseased, to engage his heart, to exercise his power in a way that went completely contrary to my orders! He betrayed me! Did he not begin by loving that young boy, your servant Ruthford? I forbade it and instead sent him, for his personal use, that little creature from the depths of the swamp, that fake-marble blonde, the same one you almost fell in love with, O Cyril! But no. He allowed himself to be contaminated by some sort of purity bacteria, and so became besotted with the little Jewess. And there's worse! Redoubling his revolt against me, he went off to build a hospital, as if that pathetic effort could make the smallest dent in my leprosy! But that was only a metaphor for the real war he'd resolved to wage against my armies. He knew my plan, that pretentious sot! For—why should I hide it from you?—all those chaste and mystical Germans, those mad mystical Russians, all those men laying the groundwork for the end of the world—they are all dead men! Yes, yes—dead men I concealed behind the mask of life, but nonetheless dead, completely dead, and yet ready to throw themselves into battle against the living!"

A horrible chill seized me once again. What sort of fever was this that could plunge me into such a perverse nightmare? I wanted to cry out, to call for help, but no sound escaped my lips. And over there, at the foot of the bed, the Abyss smiled at me.

"Quite a surprise, isn't it? For a little shopkeeper like you to suddenly find out just what's going on behind the scenes? You, the Pumpermaker, alias Charmer, reduced to the level of scribe. But you were well paid! The hotel! The houses in Cannon Street! I daresay I don't owe you tuppence. But Varlet, that useless traitor, that sterile acrobat, does he really believe his noble voice is powerful enough to stop my monumental plan? No one will listen to him. It's too late. No one believes in anything except what I've fed them, bit by bit. And so from dementia to outright insanity, and under the rarest of pretexts—that of intelligence—your whole stupid race will go gently to its death. It will annihilate itself of its own accord, and thus will I have my revenge against the creation of the Other, that creation He so desired to be perfect! That sumptuous display of fireworks to the defunct glory of God—no Varlet can prevent it! No Varlet . . ."

His voice echoed in my ears like the blare of trumpets. Terrified, I managed to pull myself out of bed and drag myself, like a sleepwalker, to the bedroom door. And then I fainted.

For eight days, I lay in a state of exhaustion that the doctor attributed to a bad case of the grippe. I knew, however, that the delirium of that night came from something rather more serious than a few streptococci! I said nothing about it to Jonathan, for he already had enough worries without my adding my own phantoms to them. Sarah's condition had reached a kind of stasis, for there comes a moment when the body has nothing left to offer in exchange for life. She lay there suspended between two worlds, her eyes wide open, as if she were simply waiting patiently for something or someone before she departed. This distressing spectacle occupied all my friend's attention; he spent hours at her bedside, either wiping her forehead or holding her hand, as if he were accompanying her on the first stage of her journey.

During this time, the press, both international and British, began trumpeting the name of Chesterfield, for the Nobel had made him front-page copy once again. The strictest orders had been given forbidding anyone to come near Kells; even telephone service had been disconnected. During these final moments of Sarah's life, Jonathan wanted nothing to distract him from the silent and reverent performance of his duty, which he executed with the tenderness and piety of the faithful.

"Tenderness is what keeps the world turning round," he said to me one morning, soon after I'd emerged from my fever. "Or sympathy, if you prefer. It's the sympathy of things between themselves that balances cosmic forces, moves the stars and the tides, maintains the heartbeat of the embryo, and sets the energy in the rocks to vibrating. The word *love* is so tarnished, so hackneyed, but the more modest *sympathy* and *tenderness* have kept their virginity. In tenderness there is modesty and intimacy, whereas love involves more strident weapons. And such explosions! Such boasting and illusion! While tenderness endures, and ages without wrinkles."

I pointed out how far we'd come from the lightning he used to talk about—Paul on his way to Damascus, or Actaeon on the edge of the forest, suddenly coming upon the pale nudity of Diana.

"The angel does appear suddenly," he said. "No one knows where he comes from, or how he got in. But afterward, one needs so much patience and tenderness to keep him!"

Our "Jewish angel" left us on November 5. No amount of patience or tenderness could have prevented her ineluctable departure, which we'd dreaded for so long but which, when it came at last, took us quite by surprise. We'd settled ourselves into the waiting mode, and when it ended we found ourselves helpless, unable to decide what to do with ourselves, as if, with Sarah gone, we no longer had any role to play in a theater whose curtain had been rung down. Jonathan said nothing. He shed no tears but remained with the body, which, according to Jewish custom, was removed from the bed and laid out on the floor. Pale, his hair atangle, and with the beginnings of a beard that he was to let grow but that at the moment gave him a rather fierce look, he seemed absent, reduced to a state of ultimate abandonment, utterly alone and with no recourse other than himself. With Sarah's demise, his Yehudi had vanished a second time.

"She was keeping him here," he said to me a few days later. "In that other world, his world, she met with him, she talked with him. Through her voice, I heard Yehudi."

It was decided that Sarah would be buried under the great oak tree next to Dorothy Temple; Yehudi's stuffed bear, which she had clutched to her in her final moments, was to be buried with her. On the sixth of November, the Edinburgh rabbi came to say Kaddish, and on the seventh, we accompanied our friend to her final resting place. There were eight of us—Jonathan and I, the nurse and the rabbi, Cockenzie, and three men sent by the funeral home in Musselburgh. Despite the fact that it was November, the day was glorious. On the tombstone, Jonathan had had engraved: "Sarah Chesterfield-Goethman, wife of Jonathan, mother of Yehudi."

After the service, Jonathan and I returned alone to the castle and instinctively sought refuge in the library. A long time passed before my friend broke the silence he'd maintained for three days, and when he did he spoke tonelessly, his voice muffled by sadness. Phrases came from him like the music from a mechanical organ turned by a blind organ-grinder. Why was he hopping from one such disparate memory to another? What secret connection held these curious evocations together? "When Richard Brown and I traveled south from Barcelona to Valencia in an army truck, there was a Frenchman with us, a boy of about twenty-two. I don't remember his name. He wasn't very tall or very handsome but there was something about him that separated him from the other volunteers. I couldn't figure it out at the time and Richard, who was as struck by it as I, couldn't either. When we stopped briefly to eat some canned rations at the side of the road, the boy told us why he'd volunteered. He'd lost his sister, his twin sister, whom he'd loved. He'd felt about her the way one feels about a lover, although he swore he'd never touched her. And she'd loved him too. And then one night her heart stopped beating. Just like that, for no apparent reason. Grief-stricken, he'd left the family home and joined the International Brigade. As we climbed back into the truck, Richard and I both understood why the young man's face had so touched us. It was because he wore his sister's gaze."

Jonathan leaned back in the armchair and smiled wistfully.

"Do you remember the Titian painting we saw in the Accademia in Venice, the one called *Tobias and the Angel*? The angel is holding Tobias's hand and pointing to the horizon. The look that passes between them suggests the complicity that's just been established, between them and between the invisible and the visible worlds. They're walking side by side, one leading the other. Isn't that the perfect image of the alliance between two worlds that, as far as most people are concerned, never even touch each other? Who still believes in the reality of the divine? Who would dare to think, without blushing in embarrassment, that God or his messenger sometimes speaks to us? If he were a modern painter, Titian would be quite alone. Since there's a dog at the bottom of the painting, Tobias had probably gone out to take his favorite animal for a walk. . . . Absurd, isn't it? But that's the way it is. We've lost our sense of the invisible. Believe me, Cyril, when its angels leave, a civilization begins to die."

Later, as night fell behind the windowpanes and the wind rose suddenly, Varlet spoke again.

"Will we have spent our life contemplating life? Tracing the outlines of our own existences? We vacillate between the tyranny of the self and the certitude that we're only an imperceptible link in the human chain, and we assume that imperative and derisory contradiction with a mixture of modesty and pride which continuously brings us back to the original enigma—we who, empty-handed, aspire to the absolute. Except that as you know, my good friend, nothing is closer to absolutely everything than absolutely nothing—which the Christians understood so well, given the odious death of the Messiah as a slave, whipped, tortured, and abandoned. That isn't at all the kind of cosmic masochism Nietzsche thought; it's the proof that God is minuscule, so minuscule He slips through the openings in every net, so minuscule we cannot see Him, for He crouches in the most minute particle of our very selves. The infinite grandeur of God lies in His infinite smallness, for He resides infinitely in both detail and ensemble. He is always in the interior of the most interior, for He is the center of everything. To give a name to God is in a way to want to catch hold of Him; His name is unpronounceable by our lips and inaudible to our ears, imperceptible as it is in the most abysmal abysses of silence, so that to try to draw nearer to His presence is to commit oneself to the path of absence. One must go to the very end of that absence, and thus die, in order to be reborn into His palpable presence. That's what my lord was trying to teach me at the church of San Moisè. And I didn't understand. I saw God as an immensity beyond the immensity of the universe, but God lies within creation itself, in its most secret center, in its most hidden fibers, in its least accessible energy. To understand that, one must turn oneself inside out, like a glove."

There was another memory, a scene from a film that he'd seen in New York and that went by the rather prosaic title of *Spring Love*. The story itself hadn't interested him, but he remembered when the heroine—a blonde with bangs, the way women wore their hair in the early 1930s—was wandering through a railway station, wearing a raincoat with the collar turned up and carrying a small suitcase. It seemed to be bitterly cold, for steam came from her lips as she paced back and forth, jostled by a motley and anonymous crowd. Who was this woman? Jonathan no longer remembered. But he remembered the way she looked, the perfect image of a lost soul, an ephemeral flitting here and there, unsure of what she sought.

"She was like a white butterfly burning her wings in the shadows," he said, suddenly agitated. He stood up, and began walking about the room.

"I was just leaving the dinner in Berlin. There was some sort of demonstration outside, in the square. Young people waving posters. When I got to the car, Sarah rushed up to me and took hold of my arm. She was wearing a shawl with long fringes. She spoke to me in English. She said she was the daughter of Goethman, the musician. You can't imagine how frightened she was! How lost she was right then! I pushed her into the car. The men who were with me, policemen obviously, started pounding on the car. Sarah was huddled against me. It was then I knew that I too . . . that I too was Jewish. That I was orphaned, exiled, and proud of it! That I was one of the chosen!"

He stopped pacing and returned to his armchair. Outside, a shutter banged furiously against the wall.

"Chosen . . . and thereby responsible," he murmured. "Was I free? No freer than anyone else, I suppose, but certainly less. By plucking me from anonymity, my lord had stamped me with his trust. I had to be worthy of it. I was bound to what he'd made of me, but I didn't really know who I was. I imagined myself the son of a prince, as so many children do, but unlike other children, I wasn't wrong to feel myself among the chosen. It fed my pride, and also my veracity. At that moment, God was immense and I was his son. Except that like Cain, I was well established. When I learned that through my mother, I was Jewish, the whole world turned upside down. God became minuscule and, like Job, I lost my belief in order to assume the faith, that faithfulness even in doubt. I began to walk; like Abel, I never stopped walking. For if I were to stop, if I were to become immoble, I would be lost. In my exile, Jerusalem—the Jerusalem of stone, of consolation—had become inaccessible. But inside me, there came another Jerusalem, impalpable, improbable, and yet present beyond the world of forms. The God of nomads has no other temple but the hearts of men."

I had no idea what he was leading up to, even if I did see how these parables applied to his own life. A man without a name, he'd set out to find his roots, and when he'd found them, he saw how alien they were to the world with which he'd learned to traffic. So he felt like an intruder, like a reject, a man celebrated through a pseudonym and who was, thus, a mystifier. He'd sought a reality that would change individual into person, and when it was revealed to him, it had accused him of creating illusions. All that was left to him was to commit himself to the struggle against the devil, against the deliberate desire to use diabolical means for subversive ends. Thus Jonathan's intellectual combat against Nazism, fascism, communism—against all forms of tyranny. For him, Hitler was the very incarnation of evil because he was the caricature of Cain, Cain pushed to extremes, the image of the cancerous proliferation of an idea of society outside all civilizing concepts, the unnatural union of barbarism and order. At that level, the exile, the ostracized, became the chosen one, capable of stopping the crime—on the condition that he offer himself in sacrifice. It was this idea of necessary sacrifice Rabbi Ivanovich had spoken of when Yehudi was kidnapped, an idea I could not accept. Only with horror could I imagine a world in which one half underwent a holocaust in order to purify the other, the blood of victims washing clean the hands of their own assassins!

"I don't know what you're really thinking, Jonathan," I interrupted, "but could it be that you accept, as a fatality, the sort of empathetic bond that some absurd god has ordained between executioners and their victims?"

He looked at me, his eyes suddenly filled with tears.

"Don't you understand my distress, my friend? Haven't I made a most solemn appeal to reason? Haven't I repeated that appeal over and over in all the ways I believed would move and persuade? Famous people joined their voice to mine, and the result? Three times more concentration camps in Germany last year alone, which didn't keep any country from sending its athletes to the Olympics in Berlin. The Rome-Berlin axis has become a reality, while German troops have entered the Rhineland—none of which has stopped the signing of the Anglo-German Naval Treaty. We support usurpation. Out of our own weakness, we support crime. Because of us, the Beast has grown fat! Tomorrow, an armed and helmeted and booted Hitler will annex Austria, just as he's promised— for he *has* promised! And then it will be Czechoslovakia's turn and then— why not—Poland! Do you realize what it means, Pan-Germanism? It's the shadow of the octopus over the entire world, mesmerizing minds, lulling them to sleep before it corrupts them! What more can I do to warn governments and newspapers and public opinion? Everyone laughed at me, and now that they've begun to feel afraid, they want scapegoats. Well, Hitler has his Jews! Listen, Cyril, I'd love to admit that all values are equally absurd, that even the concept of value is absurd, but there's a higher order than this hodgepodge, an order synonymous with the feeling of tragedy. Neither of us understands why Abel is crucial to his assassin's purification, but it's an indisputable fact that you need innocent victims to purge the city corrupted by dictatorship. Those are our martyrs; they are witnesses to human frailty and to the tenderness of an intimate God confronted with the chaos of dogma and the grandiloquence of false gods. And that's where the tragedy lies—for institutionalized absurdity is fiercer and more powerful than grace. Yet it's grace that loves us and that we love, for it's grace alone that makes us men."

Jonathan asked me to stay for a few days before he had to go to Stockholm to receive the Nobel, on the twenty-sixth of November. I moved into a study on the second floor, overlooking the ocean, and it was there, despite a slight fever and a persistent cough, that I began to take notes on certain memories that later helped me in the writing of this book. As I worked, Varlet wrote the speech he planned to give in Sweden, consulting me from time to time on both content and style. It was our first literary collaboration—and our last. For he was, in effect, writing his testament. Did he have a premonition of things to come? He rose and went to sleep early; he spoke little and ate even less. Morning and evening, he meditated for a few moments on the tombs of his mother and wife. The rest of the time, he read and wrote. All the world's turbulence might smash against the castle walls, but dear old Crispie was a dragon, an expert at frightening away the curious. In fact, the police kept a discreet and efficient watch all around the castle, where dozens of reporters were camped, waiting for some sort of news, although I couldn't imagine what. Sarah's death had stirred the public, and once again Chesterfield's stature had emerged from this ordeal grander than ever. It seemed that the fires of glory were being fed by all sorts of combustible substances, further enhancing the writer's reputation, a reputation that at that time he didn't give a fig for.

The Swedish ambassador arrived on November 12, accompanied by the British minister Harold Jones, whom the prime minister had appointed to work with his Swedish colleague on the details of the trip. After congratulating the writer, both men handed him, first, a letter from the king of Sweden, and second, a message from His Majesty George VI. Then the voyage and the sojourn were explained, followed by prescriptions for the ceremony; Varlet smiled, amused for a moment by all the various dispositions. We'd come a long way indeed from the hungry and loquacious young man who'd held his first press conference in the main amphitheater of the University of London seven years ago!

When the minister and the ambassador had left, Jonathan read both letters. The one from Sweden was generous to excess, written with that amicable and measured courtesy monarchs use with men they admire. There was no mention of anything political, which we attributed to diplomatic finesse. The note from George VI, on the other hand, abandoned all protocol and insisted on the importance of the Nobel Prize for world peace. The tone was urgent, and the message advised Chesterfield to stress, in his speech, the perilous international situation, "for a writer can say what a diplomat can't." In a way, he was giving Jonathan carte blanche, which touched him deeply. He reworked his speech to make it more forceful, while maintaining enough distance to ensure that his solemn warning would not be dismissed as some sort of personal reckoning of accounts.

I would have liked to accompany Jonathan to Stockholm; after all, wasn't the reward also mine? I confess to being quite proud of this distinction; alas, however, my health had deteriorated, and it seemed that a rest cure in a sanitorium was immediately advised if we were to constrain the bacilli of Dr. Koch to retreat from my right lung. I begged the doctor to allow me to make the voyage to Sweden, but in vain, and so on the morning of November 16, I left Kells and arrived that same evening, on intravenous perfusion, at the Murray Lyon Clinic in Edinburgh.

The press spared no details in covering the festivities that surrounded the awarding of the Nobel to Chesterfield. The British saw it chiefly as an opportunity to crow about both their literature and their humanitarianism, for in heaping praise upon their hero, they glorified themselves. A man's fame is his admirers' mirror. I shall not review the details of the event, which, like everyone else, I read in the press the following day. But I shall reproduce the testimony of Richard Brown, Varlet's hapless companion in Spain, whom he'd asked to accompany him since I myself could not.

Gilbert K. Chesterfield was lodged at the British Embassy, not far from the Royal Palace and a stone's throw from the Riddarholmshyrka, the Church of the Knights. I was authorized to help him move into the suite of honor, a vast room decorated with such pomposity, in the center of which rose a canopied bed of such dazzlingly solemn ugliness that it appeared to have been engendered by the marriage of a merry-go-round and a scaffold. Everything was gilded, including the ceiling in the shape of a galley ship with columns representing turbaned black slaves. Poor Chesterfield could not help himself from asking, with dread, if that was indeed where he was supposed to sleep.

"Of course," the cultural ataché replied haughtily. "That is Princess Amalia's bed."

"And just who was Princess Amalia?" the writer asked.

"The one who brought Goethe to Weimar," the attaché replied with a condescending smile.

"Ah, I see," said Chesterfield. "But she wasn't actually a princess. She was only a duchess. The duchess of Saxe-Weimar-Eisenach. And later, the regent. Isn't that right?"

The attaché blushed.

"Well," Chesterfield continued, "princess or no, I simply can't see myself sleeping in that catafalque. Isn't there a small hotel somewhere in all of Stockholm which would suit me better than this horror?"

"But . . . but protocol . . . His Excellency, the ambassador . . ."

"All right, all right," said Chesterfield. "Don't bother. I'll sleep in the chair."

The diplomat bowed stiffly and fled, doubtless to seek advice and counsel. Chesterfield took advantage of his departure to show me a letter. "When we were in Málaga," he said, "I often talked to you about my lord. I've brought one of his letters with me, a letter he wrote to Marcello Edoardo Pizzi on May 20, 1921. Pizzi was one of his Venetian friends, who later became an advisor to the pope." And what did the letter say? "So here is our cenacle, enlarged by the presence of Gustaf Rydberg from Stockholm. I went to see him last week; he's a scholarly man of the most perfect probity. At the moment, he is working on Saint Cyprian's *Testimonia ad Quirinum*, the Würzburg version, which, as you know, comes from the monastery of Saint Kylian and dates from the first third of the nineteenth century. It contains certain interpolations from Baruch, three I believe. In short, Rydberg has much to offer us, inasmuch as he's not yet thirty!" "And so," Chesterfield continued, "if Rydberg was thirty in 1921, he must be forty-six today, and ought to remember my lord perfectly. I wrote to him via the embassy and he answered me! He wants to see me! I'm supposed to ring him as soon as I arrive." He seemed very happy.

The meeting with Rydberg was arranged for the following Friday, two days from then, since the official program, which unfortunately did not exactly measure up to the quality foreseen by the organizers, left the writer no free time until that day. Extremist groups had resolved to wreak havoc with the pretty ceremonial prescriptions, and they succeeded rather well. On Wednesday, after a short luncheon of salmon and herring at the embassy, Chesterfield was received by His Majesty Gustaf V and several representatives from the academy, all of whom were most enthusiastic about his arrival. Nonetheless, the limousine transporting him to the royal palace was stopped by a parade of demonstrators waving posters and flags bearing slogans in large red letters, slogans such as CHESTERFIELD = BOLSHEVIK, STOP THE COMMUNIST, and other expressions of the same ilk. There were perhaps a hundred young people, all chanting, in Swedish and English, while the writer sat in the rear of the limousine and had no idea what attitude to assume, given the fact that none of this had any relation whatsoever to reality. In the end, he deduced that the students were being manipulated by the Fascists and that he was accused of being a Communist only because of his fight against Nazism—a bit farfetched, that!

Mounted police cleared the street so the car could get to the palace, but when the reception was over it proved impossible to leave by the same route. The square had become a veritable battlefield between ever-increasing numbers of demonstrators and the police, who finally had to use tear gas. A few people were wounded. Chesterfield left with a hefty escort by the rear entrance, and managed to arrive at the Royal Library, where an impatiently awaited press conference was to take place. There again, a good thirty Fascists were on the lookout, and the moment he appeared, they began throwing stones. He was hurried inside where the reporters stood and applauded him energetically, wishing thus to show their sympathy for him at a most disagreeable moment. The government representative, a tall, spare, and rather waxlike character, immediately began to speak, "in apology for this welcome so utterly remote from the fervent admiration each Swedish citizen feels, in the depths of his heart, for the prestigious writer and benefactor of humanity, Gilbert K. Chesterfield."

The press conference focused, of course, on the international threat posed by certain political doctrines. Chesterfield insisted on the fact that many well-known writers and artists had been forced to leave Germany and that others, less famous, had been imprisoned without trial. He raised the question of the fate of the Jewish people, stressing their innocence and showing that the facts pointed to a systematic genocide based on the most aberrant racial discrimination. He added that even Christians had become suspect in the eyes of these "ideologues of violence" for whom Christ's message signified only weakness and renunciation. The mercilessness of his exposé left his listeners stunned, for they were far from suspecting the Third Reich of such exactions. The questions that followed were directed principally at explicating the writer's assertions, to which he responded with figures, testimonials, and eyewitness accounts. A palpable shiver ran through the room.

Withal, a German reporter rose to his feet and claimed, in a shrill and irate voice, that Chesterfield was delirious and a provocateur, that the Third Reich had never deported anyone and was committed only to restoring order in a country which the Communists, the socialists, the Marxists, and various agitators in the pay of foreigners had driven to the brink of ruin. According to him—and his thesis was common to many—Germany had been betrayed by a liberal left secretly controlled by the Communists who, through strikes and pay rises, had ravaged the economy in order to restructure it by collectivist diktats. Hitler was simply the incarnation of this reorganization. He had restored confidence in German industry, which the socialists had taxed to the edge of bankruptcy. In short, everything—the defeat of 1918, the monetary debacle of 1923, the economic crisis of 1929—could be explained by the treacherous "backstabbing" which had sapped the national energy and provoked the moral and economic ruination of Germany.

Chesterfield let the reporter carry on, and when he'd finished, queried, "You write for the weekly *Völkischer Beobachter*, don't you?" "Naturally," the journalist replied, "and it's an honor to do so." "You can't write for any other newspaper because the *Völkischer Beobachter* is the only significant publication left in Germany. You are the mouthpiece for Nazi propaganda and that's why your rulers have permitted you to come to Stockholm. No other German publication had the liberty to do so. Allow me to ask what has become of the *Berliner Morgenpost,* the *Vossische Zeitung,* and the *Frankfurter Zeitung*? Three hundred papers have been outlawed since 1933 and woe to those who don't follow the party line! When any power holds democratic newspapers responsible for its failures, it's a sure sign that democracy is dying. And when a government punishes these same papers for telling the truth, that is dictatorship!'"

The press conference ended in chaos; a handful of demonstrators had managed to sneak into the hall and begun to throw garbage. Once again, Chesterfield was forced to leave by a rear door and to return to the British Embassy via side streets. The reception had become a scandal, so much so that that very evening, the Swedish radio stations broadcast an appeal to the general public, reminding extremists of the need for dignity. Chesterfield was stunned by the propagation of Nazi ideas throughout Europe, and especially the underhanded organization that allowed them to be expressed. Even Ambassador Christopher Lodge, who had been in Stockholm for three years, was surprised at the sudden amplitude of events, concluding only that it must have been a plot concocted by the Germans themselves in an effort to diminish the significance of Chesterfield's award.

The writer was moved to the ambassador's son's room, where he spent the greater part of the night modifying his acceptance speech. The next morning, he received a delegation of luminaries from the Swedish literary community, namely Söderberg, Bo Bergman, Nordström, and Wägner, as well as the musician Lars-Erik Larsson and the chemist Svedberg. They spent some very cordial moments together, which allayed Chesterfield's anxiety about the afternoon reception. The police had closed off all the streets used by the limousines of the various laureates to get to the Royal Academy; they also barred the public from the square around the handsome baroque edifice. Tensions ran high in the Staden quarter, especially around the Church of St. Gertrude where a bookstore that featured Chesterfield's works in its windows had been broken into and looted. A fire had barely been averted; anti-Semitic slogans and Jewish stars intertwined with the Soviet hammer and sickle were later found on the walls.

While the ceremony itself unfolded in impressive splendor, about thirty men succeeded in entering the theater located behind the

Parliament Building, where they climbed up to the roof and began hurling tiles down on the police outside. When they were finally taken into custody, at five o'clock, three of them proved to be German citizens. The others were either Swedish students belonging to the League for Viking Renewal or unemployed workers paid to join the action. A few days later, the prime minister, P. A. Hansson, addressed the Parliament on the subject of the "subversive role" played by a foreign power in this unpleasant affair, which "seriously tainted a day consecrated to peace." The king sent a messenger to Chesterfield with apologies from the Swedish people, to which the writer responded by praising the perfect courtesy of his hosts. And there the situation remained.

B<small>EFORE I PURSUE RICHARD BROWN'S</small>
testimony, I feel the need to catch my breath. At the start of my tale,
did I not claim to want to clarify things? To want to bring some order
to these seemingly disparate events? This book is an attempt to trace
the dazzling career of Jonathan Absalom Varlet, and in so doing my
own, but I find myself now, with his speech to the Royal Academy, at
the point of no return. I'm still not certain at what moment the situation
became irreversible; sometimes I think it was the instant we met at the
ramshackle hotel in Glendurgan. After this encounter, events seemed to
come together in such a way that absolutely nothing could have altered
their tragic course. I can say, without romanticism, that Varlet's singular charm—the charm evidenced in the grace of his speech and gestures,
the charm that guaranteed him such sensational success—was none other
than the charm of the Angel of Death reflected in his own face.

Arabian storytellers claim that no one can resist the beauty of the
Angel—or rather, the Archangel—of Death. People give themselves to
him as they would to a lover, for is he not a hermaphrodite, and thus,
does not everyone succumb to the ambiguity of his splendor? Jonathan's
quite particular destiny was not unlike that of a knight in a chess game—
his straightforwardness, his uprightness, lay in the staggered move.

Doubtless, it was that aspect of him that so fascinated me, as if the constant discrepancy between his actions and reality endowed him, whom circumstances had condemned to anonymity, with a certain superiority. Marked by abandonment, exile, and absence, he saw better than the rest the death forces that lay coiled in the machinery of National Socialism. His sensibility rendered him hyperaware of the slightest hint of violence. At the present moment, his will had reasserted itself; with all his might, he had risen up in opposition and thus become a sort of lightning rod for everything he considered adverse.

What can I add, except to reproduce the speech Gilbert K. Chesterfield gave the afternoon of November 26, 1937, to the Swedish Academy? At that moment, I lay in my bed, a radio beside me, at the Murray Lyon Clinic, surrounded by patients and nurses who had gathered in my room to listen. King Gustaf V had just given Jonathan his award; the English announcer described his walk to the microphones on the dais, there was a silence, and then my friend's voice, vibrant with emotion, filled the room.

"Your Majesty, Excellencies, distinguished academicians, ladies and gentlemen . . . You must forgive a wounded man for speaking to you with wounded words, for putting aside literary effects so that he may focus on the essentials of a speech all the stronger, I believe, for having been stripped of artifice. We have reached a time when the language of peace can no longer be tossed before us like the streamers thrown by those on dry land to those who have embarked, weaving thereby a bond between pier and ship. Today, the ship has left the harbor and faces the open sea. It is no longer of peace we must speak, but of war.

"Have we asked ourselves yet when war actually begins? Is it the moment the first man falls, mortally wounded? Or is it that other moment when diplomats retire? Or when treaties have been violated? Does not the cause of future divorce lie precisely in these very treaties, as if one contrives not to sign a peace treaty without first planting the seed of the next conflict? Our memory is filled with human quarrels that have no basis except alibis, all the thousands of alibis the world has created. Nothing justifies the rupture of that difficult equilibrium we call peace, but everything conspires to do so.

"And where are we today? The world is dying, but perhaps it has been dying slowly since the seventeenth century when we began to lose *the* meaning, and to replace it with a *multiplicity* of meanings. At that moment, we lost control of our existence, and from then on our existence has found itself incapable of becoming a destiny. We found the notion of God too convenient, and so we pronounced it useless and replaced it with the twin notions of space and time, or geography and history. And there we stood, encyclopedia in one hand, revolution in the other. We fell into the kingdom of quantity, a realm that knows no laws other than tyranny and subversion. As industry grew, this tyranny and this subversion divided the ateliers, the factories, the press, and the governments, thus ensuring their permanent confrontation, their continuous and essentially absurd warfare, which is the true political motor of our modern world.

"In this way did economics supersede philosophy. But what sort of economics was it, when every one of us knows that, like Moloch's furnace, our nations feed on wars in order not to be devastated by internal crisis? To be sure, these wars are not always bloody wars, physical wars, but wars of paper or gold or raw materials or speculation or goods, for the frontiers of the world have become porous, and are open to all sorts of conflagrations. The destiny of one is now linked to the destiny of others, a fact we have the temerity to deny! Unemployment in the United States has had repercussions in Great Britain and in Germany. And who today can promise us that the policies in Berlin will not, like a boomerang, fly back upon Washington? For all of Europe to burst into flames, only a single spark is needed. Neither Russia nor America will be safe from the fire, for once our economic equilibrium is destroyed, we will be forced to restore it by trying to outbid one another. This is precisely where racial considerations come into play, as if simply to be Roman or German confers the privilege of order, even though that order may have no other foundation than a lack of respect for the other. In this dying world, power triumphs over all; it has no consideration for the weak, the innocent, or the abandoned, although they are the very ferment of the spirit. Without Abel, Cain is doomed. Shall I stand before you now and raise my voice in a hymn to frailty, when everywhere we look we see ever-growing numbers of outcasts? Yet it seems to me that this is both the time and the place. Alfred Nobel wished his foundation to be a haven of discoveries and examples which would save mankind from doom. And yet the most shameful calamity we experience today is that of physical and moral suffering, researched and arranged by those who live off this misery and, in a way, by virtue of it. A vast part of the earth is used to nourish the other part. The rapid economic expansion of the industrialized nations is founded, to a great extent, on the impoverishment of those who have neither the culture nor the money nor the arms to capitalize on the goods others wrest from them. How much longer can this go on? The day will come when the outraged dignity of these people will be transformed into revolt.

"Thus, whether in the West where the overweening greed of a few will provoke a rupture with the many, or in Africa or Asia where we manipulate the contradictions because we cannot cooperate with our fellowmen, our civilization is imperiled. We have wanted to be missionaries, for we were convinced of the benefits we could bestow upon the world. But because economic and racial imperatives have, alas, won out over all others, we find ourselves impotent in the very face of these benefits we could bestow upon the world. We no longer know how to control the mechanism we wished to impose upon others. And so the most dangerous sort of anarchy grows under the aegis of order, grows so compellingly that we cannot imagine what justification the Western world will find when it is no longer anything but an intellectual and moral ruin. Let no one deceive himself! Our pragmatism will permit us to pursue our scientific research to ever more remarkable heights, but the idea of progress which we have always associated with science is now tarnished by the destructive uses to which it has been put. More money is spent on weapons than on food for those who are dying of hunger.

"I shall stop here, and I shall beg you to forgive me. This cry, this lamentation, has poured from my lips like blood from an open wound. But is caution in order when urgency supersedes that prudence? A man cries out in pain; he takes advantage of the opportunity he's offered. In this tragic theater, his only role is to incarnate human distress by affirming that in it resides the very best part of man himself. But who shall hear that call when the contest among the superpowers has begun, when the bursting of bombs and the groans of innocent victims are already mingled in our devastated minds? Let the governments listen! And let the governments decide! At present, they are the only ones who can force the retreat of Death and all his blackmail!"

The silence that followed was so long I thought my radio had gone dead. Then, all of a sudden, the applause began. It was interminable. I lay on my bed, transfixed with emotion. This was no longer the academic speech we'd written at Kells. I wondered what people would think of it, paradoxically so brutal and yet so allusive? Was it not rather naïve to demand that governments suspend their policies in the name of a Utopia whose bases I might understand but which they could not possibly discern? What could a Stalin or a Hitler hear in that lamentation, which he would deem poetic and insignificant at best? A Roosevelt might perhaps be moved for a moment or two by the tone of voice and by the evocation of human suffering, but he too would return to his weighty files. As for Mussolini on his platform, or Britain's prime minister, or the president of France, trapped as they were in internal strife, what could they possibly get out of all this? I was certain Jonathan was fully aware of the gratuitousness of his act, but I was also certain he had wanted to make this act a sort of provocation. Goya's man in the white shirt confronting the firing squad came back to me, his gesture of refusal, a refusal of the ineluctable, what Varlet once called "heroism in the face of the absurd," an odd sort of madness really, and surely something rather more than sainthood.

In fact, outside England, the speech went virtually unnoticed. The press praised it vaguely, preferring to limit itself to descriptions of the ceremonies and a more or less romanticized biography of the writer. As for the weekly *Völkischer Beobachter,* its headline read NOBEL OPERETTA; the article itself, in an attempt to belittle his work and thus destroy its influence, portrayed Chesterfield as a crackpot.

Has the Nobel become a theater for British vaudeville? Yes or no, proud Albion has swept the better part of this odd awards ceremony for conscientious students: Chelwood (the Peace Prize), Thomson (Physics), Haworth (Chemistry). As for Literature, it was bestowed, after various negotiations, on Mr. Chesterfield, whose novels have scarcely less significance than his so-called philosophical ramblings. This is the same young man who once fled Germany in his underwear after he was discovered in the voluptuous company of a minor, a Jewish minor no less, and who has treated us from time to time to his whinings about the decadence of the Western world, the same decadence to which his own works have so amply contributed. Are the Swedish academicians so fond of operetta, especially when it's spiced up by a little sauce from the Torah and served in a chamberpot?

The time has come, however, to return to Richard Brown's testimony.

* * *

ᴵ The next day, Gilbert K. Chesterfield was to meet with Gustaf
Rydberg in his home on Lake Malar not far from city hall. He
asked if I would accompany him, and I did so. A car came to fetch
us at the embassy after lunch and, escorted by four policemen on
motorcycles, drove us to the home of Lord Ambergris's, or rather
the earl of Sheffield's, former correspondent. The writer was deeply
moved by the thought of meeting someone who could speak to the
memory of his benefactor, and despite his various worries, he was
quite gay during the drive. Rydberg lived in one of those large gray
houses built around 1880 and redolent with the bourgeois opulence
of maritime merchants, which seemed strange for a scholar who
specialized in research on the Apocalypse that could scarcely be
considered lucrative! We rang the bell on a gigantic wrought-iron
door that would not have disfigured the Church of the Knights, and
were met by Gustaf Rydberg himself.

A handsome balding man in his fifties with rosy cheeks and a
straightforward look, he immediately recognized Chesterfield and
bowed with a quite military courtesy. He had donned a frock coat
for the occasion, and looked rather like those surgeons one sees in
paintings of the Flemish school.

"It is a great honor for this house to welcome you," he declared.
"Truly a great honor."

He motioned us into a hallway whose walls were covered with
paintings by the old masters.

"You have a marvelous collection," Chesterfield remarked.

"Oh," Rydberg exclaimed, as if embarrassed, "these are only
Swedish artists. Minor paintings my father bought more out of national pride than personal taste. Although this portrait by Pilo is
not so bad. Nor even this Lafrensen, which looks so like a Lorrain.
This miniature is by Per Adolf Hall. And this is a Lundberg pas-
tel." He showed us two more of Hilleström's still lifes, and then
ushered us into the drawing room, where we came to a standstill,
mouths agape.

The walls were covered from floor to ceiling, in the style of the
seventeenth century, with a formidable collection of Venetian masterpieces. The unique arrangement of these paintings only added
to the surprise of finding, in a private home in Stockholm, a Veneziano Paolo, a Gentile da Fabriano, two Jacopo Bellinis, a *Ma-*

donna and Child by Privateli, a Tintoretto, two Titians, and a host
of others of like quality—Canaletto's *Grand Canal*, Guardi's
Piazza San Marco, and a full assembly of angels attributed to
Tiepolo!

"My god!" said Chesterfield. "How strange it all is. . . . Doesn't
this Tintoretto derive from *Christ Walking on the Water* and *Mary
the Egyptian* at the Scuola dil San Rocco in Venice? Christ is
standing with his back to us at the left of the painting, but instead
of the lake stretching out before him, it's the tall trees from *Mary
the Egyptian*. . . ."

"Very good!" exclaimed Rydberg. "You have a prodigious eye,
and a prodigious memory, Mr. Chesterfield! And what about this
Giorgione?"

The writer studied the canvas closely; it depicted the Holy Family, with Mary holding the baby and Joseph leaning toward him.

"It's just like the Benson *Madonna*! Except that here, the Virgin
is on the left and Joseph on the right. It's the same painting, just
reversed! What *is* this?"

Rydberg smiled and begged us to be seated.

"I shan't keep it a secret any longer," our host replied. "All of
these Venetian paintings were done a mere forty years ago, and by
the same artist. My father was the celebrated forger Erik Lagerlöf,
whose dexterity so fascinated the specialists and deceived a goodly
number of amateurs. His trial ruined several dealers. This house
and its contents were all he left behind him. The clever man had
had the foresight to offer it as a formal gift to my mother, from
whom he had separated. I have lived on these ill-gotten gains since
the good woman departed some twenty years ago."

"Lagerlöf . . ." Chesterfield murmured. "Yes, a most ingenius
forger, in fact. And you are his son. . . ."

"I wanted you to know," Rydberg replied, blushing. "Especially
since I took my mother's name when I was very young. You see,
for me my father was always an object of undeclared admiration.
A crook, to be sure, but with such talent and such finesse! But
you must forgive me. You did not come here to talk of my
father. . . ."

"Dear Mr. Rydberg," Chesterfield hastened to intervene, "I'm
very grateful that you consented to see me. My friend, Mr. Brown,
is a loyal companion; we may speak freely in front of him. If I took

the liberty of asking to see you, it was only out of loyalty to my benefactor, Lord Ambergris. According to one of his letters, you once knew him." He removed the letter from his inside breast pocket and handed it to our host, who read it carefully, handed it back, and after a moment's reflection, asked, "But why, if I may be so bold, would Lord Ambergris interest you, Mr. Chesterfield? You say he was your benefactor?"

The writer explained how the earl of Sheffield had taken him in and educated him.

"I did not know that the great novelist Chesterfield was an orphan who'd been adopted by the founder of the Cenacle of the Apocalypse!" said Rydberg. "Fate is very strange indeed, is it not!"

He asked if we minded if he smoked, then chose a pipe from his box and, as he filled it with a honey-scented tobacco, continued, "I met Lord Ambergris in 1921. Right here, in this house. He sat there, in that armchair, dressed in white. Simple, imposing, and sumptuous all at once. The very image of English aristocracy. He'd read a small treatise I'd written on a text of Saint Cyprian's, in which I'd found three of Baruch's interpolations from the Apocalypse. Given his passion for that sort of research, Ambergris wrote to me and I replied. He insisted on coming here to meet me, which was a great honor."

He paused to light his pipe.

"I saw him perhaps ten times after that. I was young and enthusiastic. The man had a great deal of charm. His culture was prodigious. In short, I heeded the summons he issued from time to time which gathered together the members of the cenacle—the Pizzis, the Grundals, the Joliots, and several others, all in all about thirty scholars specializing in the origins of Christianity. In the beginning, we were interested in the passage from Judaism to Paulism as depicted in the literature of the Apocalypse. We met in London, Venice, Strasbourg, and Berlin. And then, little by little, the focus of our interest shifted until soon it was no longer a question of the concentrated study of ancient manuscripts, but the search for a viable spirituality for our age. Lord Ambergris felt that apocalyptic philosophy could provide the seed and the ferment for a new religiosity, a Second Coming of Christ at the end of time, which would reconcile Christians, Jews, and Moslems. 'The Christ returned,' he used to say, 'the Anointed of God, the heart of Zion, the Lamb at

the center of a Celestial Jerusalem.' Pizzi, the Catholic, was the
most ardent supporter of these ideas, but I confess I myself wasn't
quite certain of their meaning. I was a scientist, not a philosopher.
And most suspicious of anything esoteric."

"Have you kept any documents?" Chesterfield asked, clearly excited. "Any letters? This idea of a Second Coming seems as if it
might contain a wealth of lore for an age like ours where there's so
much fragmentation, where religions are lost in historicism and an
obsessive kind of preoccupation with misery."

"Perhaps. I couldn't say. Frankly, I'm rather suspicious."

"Why is that?"

"I don't know quite how to explain it," Rydberg said uncomfortably, puffing on his pipe. "I know how you stand vis-à-vis certain contemporary political ideas. I heard your speech. In short,
you must understand why I mistrust this sort of enterprise, and
why I can assure you that had Lord Ambergris suspected the after-
effects of his cenacle, he would have retracted his statements, but
he died before he saw the painful developments. The spring at the
source is responsible neither to the river nor the sea."

Chesterfield asked Rydberg to elaborate.

"First you must realize that Lord Ambergris's generous idea attracted people we did not know well. They did not belong to the
ranks of scientists and researchers from which your benefactor had
always drawn his inspiration. Among those people were two Germans and a Turk. They were in partnership with one another, but
none of us knew it. Lord Ambergris chose them because the first
two were students of Islam and the third was a Moslem. They also
knew Hinduism, and the combination of all these disciplines created a certain theology of Armageddon, certain aspects of which
might prove in accordance with the apocalyptic view. When your
benefactor passed away, these men conspired to take his place as
our leader. There was a schism, and some of the members of the
cenacle left us to follow them. This new group called themselves
the Society of Thule."

Chesterfield stood up.

"Do you mean the group behind the Nazi ideology?"

"The very same. One of the Germans was Otto Shlegel, the theo-
retician of Aryanism and racial purity, to which Hitler is heir. The
Turk was a disciple of Sobotendorf, the founder of a mixed sect of

Hinduism and Islam which advocated the alliance of all Indo-Europeans, from the Nordic countries to Asia. You will, I think, understand why I was so reticent. . . ."

"Of course!" Chesterfield exclaimed. "But how could the idea of Christ's Second Coming end up with Thule and racism?"

"Such are the perils of cenacles outside the Church," Rydberg replied. "As you move further and further into your research, you inevitably arrive at a heresy. At certain constructions inspired by Satan. I left the cenacle a year after Ambergris's death. And I abandoned my own research. Now I am a drawing teacher. My father bequeathed me some small measure of his talents, you see. . . ."

Chesterfield sat down again and said nothing. The thought that his benefactor had, however unconsciously, sown the seeds of the Society of Thule was a terrible blow.

"In allowing those men to enter his circle," he said at last, "my lord was imprudent." Then he stood up, shook Rydberg's hand, and walked slowly to the door. It was obvious he did not wish to hear anything further. We returned to the embassy, where he shut himself into his room. The next morning, I learned that he'd left Stockholm for Paris around midnight. He'd never mentioned such a plan to me, and I deduced he must have made his decision to leave after our visit with Gustaf Rydberg.

Richard Brown had no idea how disturbed Jonathan had been by Rydberg's revelations; it was not that he blamed the earl of Sheffield for having imprudently allowed the seeds of racism to take root around him, but rather that he suddenly found himself in the presence of a wholly unexpected fact—the purest idea can be used for the most pernicious ends. He felt as if the world had betrayed him, as if it were nothing but an enormous gallery of fake paintings, like Rydberg's collection. When exactly had this betrayal begun? And just what paradigm had it betrayed? Was there a truth somewhere at the source of all these tortuous rivers? And yet it seemed there was no river, no stream, no lake that was not contaminated. Swept along by these vague and treacherous thoughts, the waters of the world emptied themselves into a sea of sulfur. One had to get back to the source, but where was it?

Varlet arrived in Paris on the noon train, changed stations, and took a train for Toulouse, where he went immediately to Trentin, the Venetian refugee who had arranged the departures of the volunteers for Spain and who had helped him once before the previous year. Here follows Trentin's report:

It was the night of November 28, 1937. We'd worked very late, my comrades and I, on the following day's edition of *La Dépêche*. I went to bed about two o'clock. At four-thirty, there was a knock at the door; I looked through the judas and saw a youngish man with a beard. I didn't recognize him and didn't want to open the door, but a hoarse voice introduced the caller as Gilbert K. Chesterfield. This only made me more suspicious, since the press had said he was in Stockholm to receive the Nobel Prize.

"Forgive me," the voice said in heavily accented French, "but you were good enough to take me in last year and to help me cross the border into Spain with the Czechoslovakians."

The detail reassured me, for no one knew of this except the two of us. I opened the door and Chesterfield entered, shivering with cold. He was wearing a raincoat and carrying a small suitcase. I settled him into the kitchen, stoked up the fire, and gave him a glass of grappa, which he drank in one swallow.

"What are you doing here?" I asked him. "I thought you were in Stockholm."

He smiled.

"I'm sorry to disturb you so early," he said in a hollow voice, "but it's so cold outside! The station isn't heated and I've just spent a night and a day and another night in the train."

"But why?"

"Because I couldn't stand the nonsense any longer. The small talk. The discrepancy . . . How can I explain it? My speech was pretty terrible, wasn't it?"

I'd neither heard nor read it.

"I want to go back to Spain."

I sat down beside him.

"Listen," I said to him, "a lot's changed in a year. The Germans and Italians are much more involved. Ever since the *Deutschland* incident, everything's gotten a lot tenser, even though that was clearly only a pretext. The government forces need men, particularly ones that can think. Your presence at command headquarters would raise morale, act as a kind of insurance."

He stretched out his hands to the fire, then rubbed them together, and said, his voice breaking, "I'm afraid I'm going to disappoint you. I'm not going to Spain under the name of Chesterfield. Chesterfield is dead, a defrocked litterateur I'm happy to leave behind. As for insurance and petitions and demonstrations, I no longer believe in any of it. Better yet, I no longer believe in parties or groups or any other gatherings of men who claim to be united in a common cause. I believe only in the individual man—lost, doomed, but unable to resign himself to death. All the rest is pretense."

I attributed his mood to exhaustion; my wife made up a bed for him and he threw himself down on it, fully clothed. He slept until five o'clock that afternoon, took a shower, and shaved off his beard. Then he told me he'd left Stockholm without saying anything to anyone, except the ambassador, in order to throw the reporters off his trail. No one knew he was in Toulouse; he counted on crossing the border into Spain unnoticed. I asked him what name he wanted to use so I could get a passport ready and find him a visa; he said he wanted to go under the name of Cyril N. Pumpermaker. I expressed some surprise at this curious name, but he said he had excellent reasons for using it. I didn't push him. My wife cut his hair quite short, the way he wanted it, and went out to buy him the sports clothes he requested—a jacket lined in lamb's wool, a turtleneck sweater, golf trousers, cap, hiking shoes. In the end, this Pumpermaker bore very little resemblance to the Chesterfield who'd arrived on our doorstep.

He stayed in Toulouse for two weeks, and hardly left the house. Via the radio, we heard that the celebrated winner of the Nobel had embarked on a cruise to the Pole. The British ambassador had obviously followed his instructions to the letter. During his stay with us, he read a Bible he found in my wife's library; he seemed to have no interest in the political works in mine. And then, on December 14, he took a train for Port-Vendres.

As 1937 drew to a close, I received two letters from Jonathan, one from Toulouse, dated the tenth, the other from Barcelona, and dated the twenty-third. The first began:

Dear Cyril,

I've escaped the clutches of the journalistic pack by sneaking out of Stockholm in the middle of the night. Unfortunately, neither that train nor the one to Toulouse was heated! What would our dear Gustaf V have said had he known that his laureate had crossed all of Europe in those conditions, with only one small suitcase in his hand? To put it bluntly, I've "fired" myself. Was it Descartes who wrote, "I am a thing that thinks. But what is a thing that thinks?" Because of our intelligence, we have come round to idiocy, and my lord too. What are those mountains we build out of cards or blocks, like children? Children play and they know they're playing, but we, poor grown-ups, we forget that we're playing, that we have an obligation to play, and that beyond the game there are no stakes. We believe in the seriousness of our undertakings and our systems, but what is a thing that thinks really?

I'll be leaving Toulouse soon and will write from Barcelona. Please tell no one of this trip to Spain. I left Chesterfield in Stockholm, where he was preparing for a cruise with the other laureates. May the tides be favorable. As for you, dear Cyril, how are you? Have those nasty creatures left you yet?

> Warmest regards,
> Jonathan

The letter dated December 23 was the last I received from him.

Dear Cyril,

Here I am once again in Barcelona. The situation isn't good; the day Franco decides to take over, he'll find a fair number of allies among the petite bourgeoisie—the shopkeepers, professional people, and bureaucrats who've been terrorized by the unions. In short, I don't intend to stay in this ailing city very long. But now I must tell you something that will make you laugh—I'm here under the name of Pumpermaker! Chesterfield is indeed well hidden. But let's be straight—I'm leaving soon for the front, and once there, I may never leave it. I sent instructions by registered mail, while I was still in Paris, to my attorney in Musselburgh, Mr. Lennox, whom you know. Would it be too much if I asked you to take care of Kells, where the two women who've been most precious to me lie buried? That is, after all, where my memories are. There, and only there. As for the rest, I have complete confidence in Simon Partner.

Dear Cyril, you've been far more than friend and brother to me.

You gave me a body of work, and now I give it back to you—too famous and imperfectly understood—with hopes that in future, you'll be able to carry on with your writing safe from all the idle clamor. I believed, naïvely, that fame and fortune would allow me to thwart the hideous Beast, but Saint George is long gone. Only the whitest of arms can tame the monster; otherwise we shall have complete chaos. Apparently, and unfortunately, it's to be chaos! We no longer have enough confidence in angels for them to help us, for them to push back the shadows that are lengthening everywhere. A strange civilization—that arrogantly rejects the idea of God but gives itself so easily to the devil!

It's an honor to have known you.

All the best,
Jonathan

A hastily written postscript followed:

I had a moment of weakness and almost of disgust. Everything seemed so futile. But now, even if only for my son, Yehudi, I shall go the limit, humbly, without boastfulness, to my true home. I thank you for understanding my direction.

At first, I didn't understand the postscript; for a moment, I wondered if Jonathan hadn't decided to do away with himself, a thought that kept me awake all night long. At daybreak, however, I realized that what had kept me awake was remorse. I saw I would have to give the old man huddled in his hospital bed a good shaking. I too would have to involve myself in the world, and I too would have to bear witness to that frailty Varlet had evoked in his Stockholm address. After all, what was I doing with all my money—Ruthford, the flats in Cannon Street, the Chester Hotel? Was not my work an alibi for avoiding life? During that sleepless night, an idea that had been ripening surreptitiously suddenly blossomed—I had to leave the clinic. I had to go to Spain. I had to find Jonathan!

The chief of staff lectured me with a thousand warnings, primarily that my health would surely deteriorate as a result of this new folly. But I ignored all his arguments and left Edinburgh for London on December 28, on the eleven o'clock train. Since I'd no idea how to procure a visa for Barcelona, I went to Richard Brown, who lived in a little house in

Blackheath, a suburb southwest of London, not far from the Greenwich Observatory. When I arrived, he was with Felicia; they were planning to marry and seemed the perfect picture of the happy couple. I declined their dinner invitation, explaining that time was of the essence, or so it seemed to me. Richard understood, and told me about the various events in Stockholm not covered by the press, particularly Chesterfield's visit to the forger's son, which Brown thought had occasioned the writer's impromptu departure. He then gave me Trentin's address in Toulouse and John McNair's in Barcelona, and explained that if Jonathan had decided to enlist in the Republican army, he would probably be assigned to the 27th Division where there was a significant contingent of Englishmen. Finally, he told me how to obtain a visa for France, and wrote out a fake assignment for me on *Daily Herald* letterhead.

Following his instructions, I left that night for Dover and, first thing in the morning, presented myself at the main Customs Office where, after the usual harassment and red tape, I managed to get a visa from the French Legation at Folkestone. On the afternoon of the twenty-ninth, I sailed for Le Havre. The crossing could not have been more turbulent; my stomach succumbed at last, and as I leaned over the railing and gave myself over to nausea, I also gave birth to another self. For quite some time already, my judgment of my own behavior had been severe, but now I reproached myself bitterly for having left Jonathan to confront Chesterfield's responsibilities alone. After all, I too was this Chesterfield whom the Nazis had sworn to obliterate; I too was engaged in an insane combat against the Beast—and yet I had spent my days calmly and quietly, a well-fed literatus, while my hero had gone to Spain to get himself killed in my place! I'd used Varlet as princes once used their champions, only I was no prince. My fear of life had blossomed in the realm of the imaginary and now I was being summoned—by reality.

I arrived in Paris exhausted, and took a cab to Austerlitz Station where I caught a train for Toulouse, arriving on the morning of December 30. Unable to find a seat, I'd spent the night in the corridor, huddled up next to the restrooms. Trentin, who remembered Chesterfield's stay well, sent me to a Frenchman named Pilorge, the creator of the fake passports and visas used by Jonathan and Brown. Two days later, on the ninth of January, I crossed the Pyrenees; when I arrived in Barcelona, I went straight to the English socialist John McNair to inquire about a volunteer by the name of Cyril N. Pumpermaker.

Thin and sere, with an angular face, McNair was a man clearly overwhelmed by immediate concerns. He held court in the sacristy of an abandoned church, protected by two soldiers, one of whom was not yet twenty.

"Pumpermaker . . ." he grumbled, looking me up and down like a sergeant inspecting a recruit, "what a ridiculous name! And you? What're you doing here?"

I explained that I wished to join the British contingent, but that first I desired to find my old friend Pumpermaker. He shook his head and sighed wearily.

"Poor Spain! You look to me like one of those English intellectuals who think the civil war's some sort of lawn tennis match! So what's your name?"

I showed him my passport, in the name of Cyril Charmer-Maker. He looked at it and groaned.

"Charmer, for us Brits, the situation is nothing if not ambiguous. This is something you've got to understand. Spaniards are complicated people. Fiery. The way they think tends to clash with our logic. You're going to find yourself in a pretty demented world that claims to be super-lucid. You've got to watch out for everything and everyone!" He leaned toward me. "Moscow's heavily involved," he said, through clenched teeth.

"What does that mean?"

He clapped his hands and ordered the two militiamen outside.

"I won't hold it against you, Charmer, if you don't understand the Stalinist elements we're dealing with here. Nobody does. But I've no desire to go out tomorrow and find your dead body on the Ramblas. There's a counterrevolution in progress, led not by the bourgeoisie but by the Communists themselves. And not just any Communists! What's happened to Andrès Nin? Rhein, Moulin, and Trotsky's secretary, Wolf, have all disappeared. Weren't they all good militants? Everyone who belongs to POUM is suspect, and it won't be long before they're all caught and shot. Kurt Landau's dead. Marcial Mena, the commissar of the Lérida uprising, has been executed. The Russian advisers have been recalled. You've got to see what's going on. Rosenberg's been executed. Antonov, executed. Koltsof, the correspondent from *Pravda* in Madrid, executed. Even Stachevski, the embassy's *éminence grise*, executed! And as for General Goriev, the man who organized the entire defense of Madrid, well, he too, Charmer, he's been executed too. Stalin's got a heavy hand. Frankly, I wonder if McNair's got all his marbles. . . . Listen, Charmer, the revolution's been smothered by the very people who claim to be supporting it. And why? Because communism, Russian style, can't stand anarchy, and Spaniards, when they're not Fascists, are anarchists. They just can't be lukewarm about anything. The socialists were dead wrong to think Spain could become a democracy. You just can't go from the Middle Ages to Owen's Utopia overnight! So, Charmer, you still want to join up? You still anxious to get involved for nothing?"

"I'm not sure what to do," I replied with a shrug, "but can't you help me find Pumpermaker? I know he came here to enlist."

"Stubborn, aren't you? All right, all right. I remember that ridiculous name. Pumpermaker . . ."

He opened a shoebox that had been lying on the floor and rifled through the forms inside. It didn't take long.

"Pumpermaker . . . Training Camp Number Twenty-seven. Radio. Number 724332. You're in luck. He hasn't been assigned to a division yet. Ought to find him at the Lenin Mess at lunchtime."

He wrote out the barracks address for me and I left, persuaded the man was a definite oddball.

Barcelona was far from what I'd imagined; it felt like a fortress under siege. Trucks filled with workers and soldiers came and went in the almost deserted streets. I walked to the barracks, which was located at the opposite end of the city, near the wholesale food markets; there were no trams or taxis. Every once in a while, a distraught man rushed up to me asking if I hadn't something to sell; one wanted to buy my overcoat, another my suitcase. Further along, a motorcycle policeman stopped me and demanded to see my papers; he went through them word by word, and then invited me to accompany him to a brothel. When I resumed my walk without answering, he cursed me roundly; I presumed he was some sort of agent provocateur and that had I accepted his proposition, I should have found myself stripped of suitcase, belongings, money, and especially papers. I was just too British to get by unnoticed; at least twenty people accosted me during my trip to the barracks.

The junior officer guarding the door wore bedroom slippers and had never heard of Jonathan, alias Pumpermaker; he leafed casually through a register but found nothing that sounded right to me. On the other hand, when I told him, in my schoolboy Spanish, that my friend belonged to the British contingent, Training Camp Number 27 to be precise, he seemed to go into a kind of trance, gesticulating and speaking with such passion that his face became positively scarlet and he almost lost his dentures. In the end, he turned me over to a soldier with a rifle who escorted me to a guard post to have my identity verified; I was asked a great many questions in Spanish, which I completely failed to understand. Finally I suppose they decided I was a half-wit and so let me in.

Two Englishmen wrapped in blankets were playing backgammon; when they saw me standing there with my suitcase and my rather too-well-cut overcoat, they let out a whistle. One of them exclaimed, in a quite remarkable cockney accent, "So now they're sending us ministers, eh?"

I introduced myself and asked for Pumpermaker.

"Ah yes, the Jew!" the most portly cried immediately. "And who'd you think he'd be with then, if not the others?"

"What others?" I inquired.

"The other Jews, of course . . . I think we're going to have to set up a separate Jewish Brigade, you know. Quite funny, that, don't you think, guv?"

They both laughed and returned to their game. I coughed politely.

"This brigade, as you call it . . . where might I find it?"

They looked at me and burst out laughing again.

"At the synagogue, guv! But as for tellin' you where to find this synagogue . . ."

I did not pursue the issue but returned to my junior officer in the slippers, who shrugged deliberately when he saw me coming.

"Tourist, right?"

Once again, he seemed not to understand what I was trying to tell him, but quite simply turned his back on me.

Just as I was beginning to feel alarmed, a soldier on a motorcycle roared into the courtyard. He wore an odd uniform composed of various civilian elements—canvas shoes, black trousers, officer's jacket, white shirt, leather cap, red scarf, and sunglasses held on by elastic. He pushed the glasses up on his forehead and gazed at me with exaggerated superiority. Then he turned off his motor, put his feet on the ground, and remained astride the seat.

"Hello!" he said. "English, I presume? Only one of His Majesty's subjects would be strolling about a Spanish barracks as if he were visiting Buckingham Palace! Allow me to introduce myself—Captain Littlewood. How do you do?"

"Charmer here."

"Charmer? I once knew some Charmers, a long time ago. In India. Your family spend any time in India, Mr. Charmer?"

My response disappointed him, and he frowned.

"No matter. Not everyone can be in New Delhi at the same time, righto? One can just imagine the scene—two thousand million people in one little corner of this bloody planet, and no one anywhere else! Do you think the world would tip over?"

Captain Littlewood clearly enjoyed laughter, so I laughed.

"Excellent," he continued. "And what may I ask are you doing in Barcelona? Ah yes, the war. And how do I know that? Let's be frank, Charmer. This is no nice simple war where you know who's who. The goodies on the right, baddies on the left, you know. Here, everything's twisted, corrupt, falling apart—how can I put it? Reminds me of the rubber man at the circus; you think you've got hold of a hand but you've got a foot instead, or an ear. . . . In short, Charmer, let me tell you what I really think, and if the Comintern's sent you, you can take what I tell you right back to your masters. There are so many people in this war and they've got such utterly fantastic ideas about it that frankly no one quite knows where he stands. No one, that is, except the general himself, the Moroccan, the so-called traitor to the Republic, our Señor Franco. He, at any rate, doesn't waste time in perverse subtleties! Believe me, Charmer, as true as it is that I stole this motorcycle, Barcelona will fall in six months."

"I don't understand much about this war," I replied, "and I've no idea what will become of it. I came in this morning from Barcelona in hopes of finding one of my English friends. They told me he'd be here, at Training Camp Twenty-seven."

Captain Littlewood raised his eyebrows.

"And just what is the name of this gentleman, Mr. Charmer?"

The name Pumpermaker amused him, but he'd never heard it before.

"They told me he was certain to be at the synagogue. . . ."

"At the synagogue?" he echoed, astonished. "You must be joking, Charmer. All the churches have been shut down for ages. Wake up, young man, wake up! We're in Republican, socialist Barcelona, not in London or Jerusalem!"

"But I *must* find my friend. I'm afraid something awful's happened to him."

Littlewood burst out laughing.

"Charmer, you've got to be one of the best jokers I've ever heard. What are you, some kind of mother hen looking for one of her chicks? Just between us, what can you possibly imagine your chum Pumperwhatever is doing in a synagogue? In a church, that I'd understand. Some very nice paintings to be stolen in churches. But a synagogue? Well, hop up behind me then! Come along now, into the saddle! I'll have to take you to the officers' headquarters."

After a bit of hesitation, I finally climbed up behind him, clutching my suitcase to my chest, and in this ridiculous posture, we set off. It turned out we were only going to a gray building that stood at the far end of the courtyard. Suddenly, snow began to fall.

"Well now, seems to be snowing!" cried an English voice that appeared to come from a small individual standing on the steps in an English aviator's helmet, his chest covered in medals. Littlewood skidded to a stop a few feet away.

"Brought you a Mr. Charmer, who seems to be looking for a certain Pumpermaker . . ."

"Pumpermaker?" echoed the little man. "What an absurd name! Every time I hear it, my ears spin like a weathercock. Just what is it you want with this Pumpermaker?"

I sat there on the rear seat of the motorcycle unable to speak, my valise clutched to my chest. Never before had I felt quite so stupid.

"Come now," the officer said, puffing out his chest and advancing on me with an air of great self-importance. "Here we have a gentleman straight out of a hatbox strolling about Barcelona looking for some sort of a pump maker and thinking that I, Colonel Southworth, might lend him a hand. . . . I'm fed up with anarchists and assholes and morons! Since you're the one escorting this precious young man on your racy little machine there, take him to the guards and have them lock him up! Off with you both!"

There was no time to utter a word; amid a great deal of chaotic backfiring, we'd already taken off on that diabolical motorcycle.

"You're not actually going to take me to the guards, are you?" I cried into my driver's ear.

He accelerated, then turned to look at me.

"What've you got in that suitcase?"

"But my things . . . my clothes . . ."

"New ones?"

"Of course."

"All right then, you give me the suitcase, I get you out of this. Otherwise, to the guardhouse!"

"You couldn't possibly be an Englishman, Captain Littlewood!"

"Quite right, sir. I'm Irish, and I hate the English, especially when they're interested in synagogues. Well, what's it to be—suitcase or jail?"

It was the suitcase, as well as the overcoat and the wallet. He was good enough to leave me my passport, and—irony of ironies—to drop me at the Sagrada Familia, Gaudi's cathedral, whose polychromatic spire sported, in gigantic letters, the word HOSANNA!

For THREE DAYS AND THREE NIGHTS, I wandered through Barcelona searching for Jonathan. Since I no longer had money or clothes, I sought out McNair, who sent me to the British Consulate where I met a young writer, Philip Hamer, who was standing in as best as he could for the absent consul. Despite his discretion, this admirer of James Joyce was clearly amused by my circumstances, but had nonetheless the good taste to lend me a few pesetas and invite me to share his meals. Thus was I able, despite being stripped of everything I owned, to pursue my quest. It proved, alas, to be in vain. Jonathan had already left the training camp the day before my arrival; the backgammon players' allusions were only stupid jokes designed to have a bit of fun with me.

On the thirteenth of January, however, just as I was beginning to despair, Hamer learned that a certain Askenazy might be able to tell us something about "an Englishman who'd had an accident." He didn't remember his name but knew where he could be found. Askenazy turned out to be a Polish Jew who'd lived in Spain for thirty years in a room behind his junk shop. He seemed an honorable elderly gentleman, frightened by the political situation but still willing to see us because we were British and because he dreamed of someday living in London. After a bit of idle conversation, he told us that a British volunteer had appeared three weeks ago at the small Jewish congregation in Barcelona to which Askenazy belonged. This Englishman was Jewish on his mother's side, but had been raised a Christian. Apparently he'd asked to see a rabbi about instructions in the Torah as he wanted to prepare for the bar mitzvah he'd never had.

Recent events had forced the faithful of all denominations to practice their religions clandestinely; the Englishman met secretly every evening, his military duties permitting, with a Rabbi Benjamin Bernstein who'd once lived in America. The rabbi knew Askenazy well and had confided to him that the Englishman had been wounded during some sort of skirmish and was currently being cared for by one of his cousins in Horta. We abandoned our informant to his glass beads and walked north; it was so cold the snow had stopped falling. I had no coat and had wrapped newspapers around me under my shirt, a precaution that did not, however, prevent my coughing as my shoes leaked prodigiously.

Horta had once been part of the suburbs, but so much graffiti now covered the walls of the houses that the whole area looked like the notebook of a demented schoolboy—*"La mano de las Tribus exterminara al fascismo," "Los jovenes revolucionarios exterminaremos a los vividores politicos," "Abajo politicos y sus representados"*—all ornamented with scatological drawings and containing obvious spelling errors. Rabbi Bernstein's house opened on to a small courtyard filled with rusted scrap iron that the snow had modestly tried to cloak. When we knocked at the door, a shrill voice called to us to go away, for "there's nothing here to sell or buy!" Hamer explained in Spanish who we were and what had brought us; when he mentioned Askenazy, the door opened.

Once inside, we found ourselves in what was obviously an abandoned forge. A folding metal cot stood next to an anvil, the table was a workbench, and the only lighting came from two small paraffin lamps. The old woman in black who'd let us in whispered rather than spoke. Apparently the rabbi had been sick for some time, Hamer translated, and never left his armchair. Which was precisely where we found him—a small stooped man, wrapped in a blanket, with yellowed skin, a beard, and a skullcap on his head. He looked at us intently out of deep-set eyes, then spoke softly, in English.

"You are the gentlemen from the consulate? Yes, very good. Askenazy sent you? Very good. Yes, very good. Please sit down. Our home is humble but it suits me. Very good, yes. And you're looking for that fine young man, Cyril Pumper-Acher. Yes, good, very good. We chose for him other names—Jonathan and Absalom. In honor of David, of course . . ." Here he chuckled. "He is your friend, yes? That is good. A fine young man. Poor. Very poor. He wanted a bar mitzvah. But with the war, here, and his age . . . In short, he received it through the laying-on of hands, as it is written in the Talmud, 'If the covenant cannot be passed through blood, it shall be passed through the spirit.' Yes, very good. And so it was passed through the spirit."

The rabbi continued his monologue in silence; his lips moved but no sound escaped. In the dull light of the lamp, he looked like Rembrandt's old man at prayer, and I understood what must have fascinated Jonathan, for he surely saw that here, through this old rabbi, he could renew his connection to his true origins. This man, a stranger, had given him his two names a second time, the names Dorothy's mother had chosen before pushing him through the turnstile. And I could see that as he stood looking at the forger's Venetian paintings, his fictitious identity would have seemed unbearable. And so he'd fled Stockholm and the "defrocked Chesterfield." At the time, I had not, in fact, understood his postscript, but here, suddenly, it came clear: "But now, even if only for my son, Yehudi, I shall go the limit, humbly, without boastfulness, to my true home." His true home lay in the very name he'd dragged about with him like some absurd nickname for lo these many years.

"He didn't know he was Jewish," Rabbi Bernstein continued. "And then one day he learned his mother was Jewish. Good. Very good. He said to me, 'It was then that my exile made sense.' Can you see that, gentlemen? Let me explain. . . . In the first scene, the heavens are silent. There is no sign, on earth or in us. What is the Law? Second scene: Am I Nothingness or am I God? Neither Nothingness nor God. I am exiled both from Nothingness and from God. It is of my exile that I am made. Very good. Third scene: The multitudes of Nothingness and of God surround me. How shall I communicate with them in this desert, in this profound silence that is the heart of my exile? Fourth scene: I am dead to Nothingness and to God. I am blanketed in silence. And in this primordial poverty, absence is more divine than the kingdom. There is a revelation. The Absolute is revealed in the annihilation of the relative, in the annihilation of idols, of concepts and images. That is the temple destroyed. That is your friend. Good. Very good."

"But where is he?" I asked uneasily.

The old man raised his head and looked at me, as if my question had pulled him from a profound dream.

"Where is he?" he echoed. Then, as if he'd abruptly awakened, "Our son, Jonathan Absalom, has been wounded."

"Is it serious?"

"Please . . ." he replied, bowing his head, "gently . . ." Once again, his lips moved silently, then he spoke. "For the poor man, the world is a hard place. Very good, very good. Because for the poor man, there is no kindgom in this world. You see . . . our son, Jonathan Absalom, is the victim of the world, as the lamb of the wolf. Very good. He is with my cousin Esthela, Esthela of Dublin, of Mathalam . . ." He called out, then, in a strange tongue, Hebrew perhaps. The old woman reappeared and went immediately to his side. They exchanged a few words.

"Follow me, *señores*," she said in Spanish. "We go to Esthela of Dublin. Come . . . come . . ."

We said good-bye to the rabbi and followed her. She'd thrown a shawl around her shoulders and trotted before us through the mud-stained snow with tiny steps, a minuscule shadow in the narrow winding streets. What had happened to Jonathan? We went down a dark alleyway, entered a dilapidated house propped up by a frame of wooden beams, and climbed what was left of a shaky wooden staircase. At the top, we picked our way through piles of rubble to a door on which the old woman knocked in a special way. A youthful voice replied and a dialogue began in that language neither Hamer nor I understood. We heard the scrape of a bolt, the door opened, and a little girl of about ten or twelve, with olive skin and dark hair—quite the Gypsy, actually—motioned us to follow her through the ruins of an ancient apartment where the flowered curtains had been partly torn away and a few of the walls had already collapsed. It was obvious no one had lived here for some time; the revolution had doubtless forced the postponement of its demolition. The hallway ended in a room heated by a brazier, in the middle of which, lying on a straw mattress, his body partly covered in a horse blanket, lay a man—still young, his hair clipped short, with a week-old beard and eyes burning with fever. When he turned toward us, I saw that it was not Jonathan. Or rather, it was no longer Jonathan, the Jonathan I'd known. This was another Jonathan, somehow born inside him. He looked at me in silence.

I knelt beside him; he shook his hand feebly, almost like a baby. I did not understand the gesture. His breathing was labored and perspiration ran in large drops down his temples. I took out my handkerchief and wiped his brow and cheeks. He gazed at me, as if asking himself who this man was who'd appeared so abruptly and who seemed to be taking care of him.

"Jonathan . . ." I murmured. "I've come. . . ."

There was no sign of comprehension in his eyes.

I turned to the old woman.

"What happened to him?"

"The doctor came," she said, so softly that Hamer had to ask her to repeat several words and phrases as he translated. "He will come back. Jonathan was hurt by some people. Bad people. Unbelievers. They are everywhere in Barcelona now. Jonathan came to see the rabbi every night, and the rabbi spoke to him of things divine. Every night he stayed for two hours, sometimes three, listening to the rabbi. And the rabbi was happy because Jonathan asked good questions. 'Very good,' the rabbi said. 'They are good questions.' Every night, Jonathan went back to the barracks, in Pedralbes maybe. . . . One Friday night, it was the Sabbath. Jonathan left after the prayers. He was to come back the next day. But someone scratched at the door around midnight. I thought it was an animal. I didn't get up right away. And then I heard groans. It was our Jonathan. There was blood everywhere . . . on his face . . . on his hands. His shirt . . ."

While the old woman continued her tale, the little girl opened the door to admit a quite slender and beautiful woman of about forty with long black hair tied back in a bun. She swept into the room like a gust of fresh air.

"Who are these people? I told you no one was to come here! You brought them here, didn't you, Raquel?"

This was obviously Esthela "of Mathalam." Hamer introduced us and explained that I was an intimate friend of Jonathan's who had come all the way from England to find him. She looked at Hamer with an air of commiseration and replied with the sort of Mediterranean volubility that leaves one absolutely speechless.

"What is she saying?" I asked.

"She says she doesn't want any trouble from the militia," Hamer replied, finding his tongue again. "She doesn't know who Jonathan is and doesn't want to know. She thinks the rabbi's an old fool and she's furious with him for sending her this stranger."

The woman began again, more shrilly this time.

"She's asking who's going to pay the doctor," Hamer translated. "And who's going to pay her back for the firewood."

He pulled some bills from his pocket and gave them to her; instantly, her face softened. She folded the money, placed it carefully in her coat pocket, and said brusquely in Spanish, "Someone stabbed him. Right there. Next to the heart."

"We've got to get him to a hospital!" I cried. "We can't care for him here!"

Esthela shrugged. It was clear that I had no understanding of local custom.

"She says Jonathan was wounded while in irregular circumstances. A soldier cannot leave his barracks without a special pass, and Jonathan didn't have one. He sneaked out to see the rabbi. They think he's a deserter and that he'll be shot. Without a trial. Just like someone she knew named Hermanos Sanchez, three weeks ago. He brought a great deal of trouble upon his family, even though he's Spanish. So this one's an Englishman, she says. It's certain the militia will think he's a spy, and this woman and her daughter his accomplices!"

I explained that since Jonathan was British, his activities were protected by the consulate, and thus neither Esthela nor her daughter had anything to fear. At that moment, I heard Jonathan slowly pronounce my name. I rushed to his side and he reached out his hand toward me, as if calling for help.

"I'm taking you to the hospital, Jonathan," I whispered. "You've lost some blood. You'll have to have a transfusion. You mustn't worry."

He smiled weakly and, without taking his eyes from me, murmured, "Who remembers the Israelites who remained in Egypt?"

Whatever he meant I'd no idea. I asked Hamer to ring up the American Hospital, assuming there had to be one in Barcelona since they seemed to be everywhere else.

"It's been shut down," the young writer replied. "Here they see Americans as Franco's allies. Objectively speaking. I'll try the French Hospital; I know a surgeon there."

He scribbled a few words in a notebook, tore out the page, and gave it to the little girl with instructions to take it to Catalan Square. When she heard him, Esthela of Dublin began shrieking in protest; the offer of a large bill, however, calmed her instantly. I returned to Jonathan and knelt beside him. Once again, he held out his hand.

"Cyril . . . ?"

"Yes, Jonathan."

He had such difficulty speaking that the veins stood out in his neck.

"I've gone, haven't I?"

I didn't understand, but I took his hand and held it.

"No, Jonathan, you're not leaving us. We're taking you to the hospital."

He shook his head.

"Not that, Cyril, not that!"

"But whyever not?"

"I have al-read-y gone," he whispered, syllable by syllable. Then he closed his eyes, breathed deeply, and grew calm.

Immediately Esthela began to recite a sort of prayer that little by little became a chant. From time to time, the old woman echoed a phrase, as if it were a refrain. Her cracked voice mingling with the shriller tones of her friend formed a rather savage duet that Hamer and I listened to, dazed and prayerful. Doubtless it was a chant to accompany the dying on their final journey. There was a mention of Babylon and of exile far from Jerusalem. It was clear to me that Jonathan was dying, and that in his so doing, an order would be reestablished. What feelings in me inspired this odd conviction I've no idea, but at the time I found it neither sad nor terrible, as if I knew that the events we were living were part of a logic more profound, and in a way truer, than the instinct to survive. Was this in fact the other death Lord Ambergris had described at the church of San Moisè in Venice? Jonathan still gazed at me, observing me perhaps, with the look of someone on the edge of the abyss. Once again, his hand waved; I put my ear to his lips.

"Ye-hu-di," he said distinctly, "is he dead or alive?"

What could I say?

"You will see him soon," I said stupidly, "Yehudi and Sarah, your mother and your lord too."

There was a vaguely ironic spark in his eyes; he said quite clearly, "I am Ye-hu-di," and then he died.

What happened afterward is difficult to say. The two women fell silent and the building seemed to creak like a vessel in a storm. I closed my friend's eyes and turned to Hamer.

"Jonathan Absalom Varlet is dead," I said.

He looked puzzled and was about to ask me to repeat it when the women placed themselves at his head and feet, lifted the body from the straw mattress, and placed it gently on the floor. Then they stepped back, covered their eyes with their right hands, and began to recite the Kaddish. Did I actually hear them? It seemed to me the livid body stretched out before me was my own. Was this what Jonathan and I had come to Spain to find? Then and only then did I understand that we were bound by an umbilical cord that had only now been severed. In a way, we'd lived like twins, sharing a role whose lines we knew only in snatches. Jonathan had chosen between his two lineages—that of Harold Spencer, descendent of the illustrious Marlboroughs, and that of little Dorothy Temple, the Jewish refugee from Eastern Europe. Henceforth, I would be alone with Chesterfield, who seemed suddenly to have no more consistency than a phantom.

When the ambulance arrived a long time afterward, Jonathan was not the only one they took away. Exhausted by the days of searching, I'd reached the end of my strength; my limbs had turned to ice and my chest burned. It was a disarticulated marionette Hamer entrusted to the French Hospital, and a full week was to pass before I awoke.

After a brief stopover in France, I returned to England in early March of 1938 via a special convoy sent to repatriate the wounded who'd fought in the Republican ranks. When I arrived in Dover, I was sent directly to Kent, to the military hospital at Ashford, where I was cared for and, eventually, cured. I owed my life to the stubbornness and competency of the French surgeon in Barcelona, who had very little medicine, but who paid special attention to me. By an odd coincidence, he turned out to be the brother of the Madame Duvalier we'd once known in Paris. It seems she'd divorced her man of letters and later married a colonel who'd taken her to Saigon, where she lived still. In addition, Dr. Lakanal was able to tell me about the cemetery where Jonathan had been buried. Because his death had not been due to natural causes, the local police had launched an investigation and ordered an autopsy, but they found nothing we did not already know. Varlet, alias Pumpermaker, had been attacked by foreign soldiers, Czechoslovakians perhaps, who'd first taunted him, then beaten him up, and finally stabbed him. As far as the police were concerned, the only important fact was that they weren't Spaniards, and expecially not Catalans. Despite a protest from the British Consulate, the file was closed, and this with a certain relief. Jonathan's remains were buried in Montjuich Cemetery, in the communal grave.

As I write these lines today, September 30, 1941, three years have passed since the signing of the Munich Pact sanctioning the abandonment of the Sudetenland to Hitler and embroiling all of Europe in a shameful series of moves and countermoves that, as Jonathan predicted, could lead only to war. Given my fragile health, I was not conscripted; instead I endeavored to write this book, persuaded that by tracing this brilliant and troubled life, I should better understand the one whom I have slowly learned to like and even to respect, even though—as the reader has surely noticed—I have often stopped to wonder about his intentions and to suspect his motives. Yet I must be honest; I don't know if it was Jonathan who changed, or rather the way I perceived him over the course of the years. Doubtless the truth lies somewhere in between, but in writing these memoirs I finally understood my companion's personality, as well as the change that occurred in me. For I fully recognize that this book has transformed me; through this recollection of his life and thoughts, Jonathan has dwelled within me, a more intimate friend dead than alive. What a miracle, this return to oneself! The disparate nature of the life set forth in these pages seems to reveal an order, as if each detail had suddenly found its place in a puzzle whose pieces had previously been strewn about. Thus has my friend's troubling death finally clarified, most luminously, his true destiny.

How not to understand, in fact, that his traumatic quest for identity could be concluded only through divestiture and in a condition of complete deprivation? The seducer was himself seduced by rigor and renunciation, and this at the very moment his glory was assured, a glory, however, that had been fraudulently acquired. He achieved himself in Chesterfield, but Chesterfield was an alien creature, someone who existed only by virtue of my works. Varlet himself had slipped by in a shadow. Later, divided as he was between his aristocratic heritage and his Jewish origins, he opted for "fragility" and, as Rabbi Bernstein insisted, "poverty." His was a poor man's death, in a house slated for demolition, on a bed of straw, and under the wretched pseudonym of Pumpermaker. His life ended in a pauper's grave. But how much richer that lack of privacy seems to me today than all the honors in Stockholm! Besides, after having seduced everyone and having seen the meaninglessness of those victories, didn't Jonathan then try to seduce God himself? He who sought fame and fortune with which to combat the Beast found at last that only by becoming his victim could he deliver his most effective blow. To be sure, this death—infinitesimal among so many others—this death, alas, did nothing to stop the monster's voracity. The entire world is now at war; everything is tumbling down like a house of cards, tumbling right into the hands of Hitler and his allies. Yesterday, Poland and France. Today, Greece, western Russia, and Yugoslavia. In Spain, Franco reigns supreme. As Jonathan saw so clearly, it is not just fascism that hides its hideous muzzle behind the mask, but communism as well. The poisonous inoculations administered by their leaders have contaminated the peoples and compelled them to the violent clash we see today. We are in truth at the floodgates.

Peter Warner, the publisher, died in May of 1940, leaving behind a confession stating he had indeed had Goldman assassinated in order to marry his wife, and then had his wife killed in order to inherit the publishing house. Thus were Margaret's suspicions confirmed and the disequilibrium of Warner's life clarified. A few days before Mosley's arrest, Margaret left England to seek refuge in Venice where, I've just learned, she married the mayor. I've no idea what sort of future she has in mind for Madame Caratini and the house on the Calle del Ca! As for poor Mary, she's opened a small shop opposite Guildhall where she sells occult works and the paraphernalia of clairvoyance. I pay her alimony religiously; it helps her to raise her son decently—Leonid Charlienko's son. From time to time, I drop by to see them when I come to London; that child is the only admirable person left to me from the old days. In a way, his destiny already resembles Jonathan's, and when the time comes I shall be pleased to play Lord Ambergris to him. Kells Castle awaits him, with its library, its secret staircase, and its uncultivated garden where two shadows, of the sort to enchant a child's imagination, lie mysteriously at rest.

Which leaves Chesterfield, Gilbert Keith Chesterfield, born of my adolescent dreams and so oddly incarnated in this chaotic era. The press was told he'd retired to Kampala where, after the Nobel and the polar cruise, he intended to consecrate the rest of his life to the *caritas* of his leprosarium. This book, however, shall put an end to the legend; in a way I shall be killing Varlet a second time, stripping him of everything, including his reputation, for in the eyes of many, he will now seem an imposter. Yet I must remind my reader that if he was the first to assume the role of Chesterfield, he did not do so without my full consent. Thus I confess to being as much an imposter as he. May my readers forgive me, as well as the reporters and the judges we deceived. By these pages, let them understand if not our reasons—ill defined as they may seem— then at least the motives that consumed us and that we obeyed.

"Man is neither Nothingness nor God," Rabbi Bernstein said. But between this Nothingness and this God, he aspires to an identity he achieves but rarely, an identity that can be achieved only by recognizing the ideal identity that he's chosen for himself and that then controls him. Man does not find his identity by looking to others, for others wish him only to be anonymous so that they may glorify him. What, then, is this shadow of identity? From what memory does it arise? If we look closely, we see that this is the person Jonathan so persistently pursued, awkwardly at first, then with increasing subtlety and in direct proportion to his success in losing himself. Quite a paradox, really. As long as he believed he'd found himself, Varlet was lost; only when he truly lost himself, lost everything in fact, did he discover who he really was. May I take the liberty, here, of pointing out how much Jonathan, and also Margaret Warner and Sarah and I myself, were forced to grapple with what I shall call the father's dispossession? Not until the moment of Jonathan's death, stripped bare after so many difficult identifications, was this man, so obsessed by the father, able to assume the identity of his son and thus find peace at last, the *pax profunda* reserved for the righteous.

I do not know how my revelations will be received. The tragic circumstances of these grievous times render certain events, which would once have shocked the public, of secondary importance. What does it matter now whether Chesterfield was Varlet or Charmer, or both, or no one at all! And yet I think our story, which so perfectly embodies the perdition of an entire century, is not completely useless insofar as I have unveiled this perdition. Heroic or commonplace, Jonathan was and remains a witness. In the face of an iniquitous tribunal where the judges themselves have been stood in the criminal dock, where the victims have been pronounced guilty, and where the rabble preside in robes reeking of fresh blood, he testifies to the determination—sometimes naïvely efficacious but always reaching forward—to refuse not only the absurd but its ghastly companion, derision. Is freedom of the spirit, then, a constant concern never to betray even the smallest opportunity for awareness of self and of others? Surely this is so, for we have learned the hard way that freedom and commitment are one and the same. This was the revelation that so struck Jonathan—his road to Damascus, his encounter with Diana in the forest—and that, with the precision of a scalpel, provoked his rebirth, that "vivifying death" of which Lord Ambergris once spoke. He who had been so public a personality accomplished this metamorphosis in secret, and in complete destitution pursued the rigorous labor that ended in his final birth.

And yet, as I end my tale, I, Cyril Charmer, am unclear as to the purpose my life has served. Have my books contributed something, books that only a few people have had the generosity not to confuse with the flattering brouhaha that surrounded them? Have I contributed something in writing these memoirs, in chronicling an era crumbling now in moral bankruptcy and the bursting of bombs? When all is said and done, perhaps I have served only as a *regard*, an eye—cowardly perhaps, and limited, but necessary—so necessary that my precipitous departure for Spain and my feverish quest for Jonathan were, in a way, not mine to choose. I was meant to be there, at that precise moment, so that I might hear the last name my friend uttered, the name of his lost son, the name of a hounded people, the name of all those who from the vast reaches of their exile have remembered the way back. I who never knew how to believe, may, in the commitment to a more honorable future, finally understand the errors of the past as well as the horrors of the present. What does it matter if the world stumbles, if through the darkest shadows it continues its journey to the light? Shall I be able to write about that? We are predestined to happiness, a fact that, despite the overwhelming evidence to the contrary, I still dare to believe. While millions are dying, and shall die—despised and in shame—the only chance we have for survival is to stretch out a hand, in refusal and in affirmation, toward the rifles aimed at us, and to repeat to our last breath, even under torture, that mankind is predestined to happiness.

Is it true, however, that I am always mistaken?